STOLEN
OBSESSION
JO McCALL

Jo McCall

Stolen Obsession: Kavanaugh Crime Series Book 1

Copyright Jo McCall 2023
All Rights Reserved
First Published 2023
No part of this book may be reproduced, stores in a retrieval system or transmitted in any form by any means, without prior authorization in writing of the publisher *Wicked Romance Publication*, nor can it be otherwise circulated in any form of binding or cover other than that which it is published and without a similar condition, including this condition, being imposed on the subsequent purchaser. All characters and places in this publication other than those clearly in the public domain are fictitious, and any resemblance of actual persons, living or dead, is purely coincidental.

**This does not count promos. Just the piracy of this book.

Cover design: Dark Ink Designs
Editing: Beth @VBProofreads
Formatted by: Dark Ink Designs

Synopsis

Cheated on.
Kidnapped.
But hey, at least I have a bottle of Whiskey to keep me warm.

I'd had hit a new low when I found my fiance in bed with her best friend.

And apparently not for the first time.

Life couldn't get any worse.

That was until I suddenly became the captive of a pair of Irish Twins who are set on owning every inch of me.

They commanded me. Owned me. Made me feel things I'd never experienced before.

Secrets would be revealed.

Truths would tear apart everything I have ever known.

Can I spy on the man who rescued and raised me or will I betray the only people who ever made me feel wanted?

Layers of subterfuge slowly begin to unravel and the house of cards has begun to crumble.

Jo McCall

Will the truth set me free or bind me to another cage? The truth may be buried and dead, but secrets have a way of speaking from the grave.

*For all those who wanted a McManus Sandwich.
This ones for you*

*To Norman Reed's and Sean Patrick Flannery for their
beautiful representation of the McManus Twins that inspired
this book and its characters.*

This is as close I'll ever get to that twin sandwich.

*But feel free to show up at my door.
Don't bother knocking.*

Warning

Thee content within this book is DARK and may be triggering to some INCLUDING:
Physical Abuse
Graphic Violence
Dubious Consent
18+ Only
Please read responsibly.

Full list of triggers for this particular book go to jomccallauthor.com

STOLEN OBSESSION

***This is a COMPLETE rewrite of Irish Whiskey Rules. It has a new plot and new characters and extended scenes. Some things may seem similar but it different. Trust me.

MAFIA/ORGANIZED CRIME/MENAGE ROMANCE

BOOK 1. INTERCONNECTED STANDALONE IN THE KAVANAUGH CRIME FAMILY

This book can be read as a complete standalone. However, for better reading it is recommended that you read the Shattered World Series first (Or at least the first two books).

But you don't have to.

I'm not your mom.

You do you.

1

Bailey

The parking lot was dark and wet.

Streetlights shimmered off the side of the brick buildings, casting an eerie glow into the interior of my broken-down Jetta. Tears streamed down my face in torrents as I gulped and sobbed into the steering wheel, an empty bottle of Jameson hanging loosely in my hand.

What the fuck had I done to deserve this?

I'd thought we'd seen eye to eye. Our arrangement hadn't been built on love, but I thought we had an understanding. That maybe, despite our circumstances, we could grow to love one another. Then again, how could a snake love the mouse it strikes at?

Work had been hectic recently, and I knew it had caused a rift between us. Things were heating up on the Ward front, and I was inching closer and closer every day to finding out where my friend had disappeared to. Still, with my busy schedule, I had made time for him when he asked.

If he asked.

Not that he ever did. Now I knew why.

If anything, he should have been grateful for my job and

hours. My career as an investigative journalist had kept us afloat when he'd first started his security company. Everything he had was because I'd spent years working my ass off so that he had the capital to invest in his company without taking on too many business loans. It wouldn't exist without me. All because he hadn't wanted to ask his father for help.

He had wanted to do something on his own.

I snorted at that. Drew hadn't done shit on his own. It had all been done for him—by me. He'd spent five years building up the company with money *I* gave him. He even hired my best friend, Brittany, when she needed a job.

The same best friend I had found in his bed sucking his cock, and apparently not for the first time.

Treacherous bitch.

Three years.

Three years of late nights in the office and weekend consultations. That was how long he'd been sleeping with her behind my back. And who knew how many women had come before her. I'd been nothing but a fool. A completely oblivious fool, because everyone had known but me. My friends' tones when I'd called to ask for a place to stay the night had said it all.

They knew and hadn't told me.

At least I knew where I stood.

No wonder he hadn't wanted me to move in with him full time. How many other women had he found over the years? We'd been engaged since I was sixteen. I knew he'd had women before we made the engagement official. My father had told me it was his right as a man, but I was never given the same courtesy. My father made damn sure that I remained virginal until I was eighteen and Drew could claim it for himself.

I'd been naïve then. Wanting so much to prove to my

father that I was more than just his bastard daughter. I'd looked away when I saw him out with other women, but the moment we became official, it all stopped, and I thought he'd changed.

Fucker had just been getting it closer to home.

We'd made our engagement official five years ago, on my twenty-first birthday. A long engagement so that he could get his company up and running. And then once it settled, we'd get married. I wondered why he waited so long if he was just planning to cheat on me. There was only one reason, really.

All he wanted was my bank account and the backing my father offered.

Our arranged engagement when I was sixteen had come with strings, and I was nothing but the puppet dancing to the whims of the puppeteers. I took fucking shears to those strings today when I'd seen them together. No one was going to be using me anymore.

I was done.

He could marry Brittany for all I cared.

I'd thrown everything I had at his apartment in a bag, ignoring his pleas and protests as I stormed out. Brittany looked smug, sitting on his bed, her naked body proudly on display like she was some prize. She had wanted him, once upon a time, but our families had long decided it would be me he would marry.

He said he'd chosen me. Not her.

Or so he'd led me to believe.

Drew hadn't chosen me at all. He'd chosen my family's name and power. Nothing more.

I was stupid and foolishly naïve.

There was no way in hell I was going home to face my father. He'd send me right back to Drew. The problem was that every hotel in the area was booked.

So much for a place to sort things out.

My plan had been to get my shit together, find a hotel, and regroup. I'd make sure to get every penny back that I gave him for that company. I'd be damned if I let him profit off my hard-earned money.

Not after this.

Now I was sobbing like a baby in my car with only the whiskey to keep me company. The holiday weekend had all the hotels in the area booked. New Year's Eve in Seattle was no joke.

For some, it was practically an Olympic sport.

I'd pulled into the small alley parking lot behind Clover, an up-and-coming Irish club, to sort out my maddening thoughts. It wasn't the best place for me to be, considering who owned it, but I had little choice, and I doubted anyone would be sober enough to recognize me.

When I'd gone to leave and find a hotel out of town, my car refused to start, stuttering like a forty-year-old virgin.

Just my luck.

Calling my father was out of the question. My engagement to Drew was pivotal to the deal he had brokered with Drew's father when I was sixteen. His family, like mine, was full of prominent figureheads in Seattle politics, and our marriage meant more reach for my father.

From the thirty missed calls and forty unread text messages I'd received in the past half an hour from my stepmother, Drew had already informed her of what happened, no doubt spinning everything so that it appeared I was the villain.

Not that Sarah, my stepmother, needed much of an excuse to villainize me. He'd probably complained that I wasn't giving him what he needed because I refused to leave my career to have his babies and become his trophy wife.

Something he hadn't wanted me to be in the first place. It had been his idea to keep my career.

I'd given him everything, and all I got in return was shit.

"Forget this," I mumbled drunkenly as I ripped the keys from the ignition. I wiped away the excess tears with the sleeve of my dress, and after a quick glance in the rearview mirror, I grabbed my purse from the passenger seat and climbed out of my useless car.

Might as well find more alcohol and get even more shit-faced than I already was. It would take at least another bottle of Jameson before I could think about abandoning everything and crawling back home to my father.

Maybe two bottles...or three...

It was beyond luck that I stalled behind a club. If that wasn't a sign, I didn't know what was.

Slamming the door shut, I stumbled behind the alley toward the main road. My heels wobbled slightly on the uneven cobblestone.

Or it could have been because I was tipsy.

Who knew?

The lights in the alley were dimmed and flickering, casting an ominous shadow around me. Fuck, maybe I should have walked around the other way.

A door in the back of the alley swung open violently, raised voices reaching my ears, and I barely managed to stifle a scream before ducking into a small alcove a few feet down. This wasn't the best neighborhood; I knew that. Not that crime was particularly high in the Irish Village, but it wasn't a secret that it was run by the Irish Mafia, who kept things on a tight leash.

"Please..." a nasally man pleaded, his voice echoing against the brick walls of the small alleyway. "I was just hired to do a job. I swear. I didn't know she was with you. The hit said she was a Dashkov. You have to believe me."

"Problem is..." Another voice spoke up, his accent holding an Irish lilt. It was dark, deep, and deadly. There was no mistaking the dangerous edge to his tone, even from here. "We don't."

There was a scuffle and the sound of bone cracking against bone. The nasally man screamed, and then there was nothing but ragged breathing.

"Tell us who sent you," the Irish voice growled. "Was it Dante Romano? Ward? Tell me who the fuck put a hit out on my sister!"

"I don't know," the nasally man whined and sobbed. "The hit was encrypted. Anonymous payer."

"How much?" another voice questioned. It was nearly identical to the first, with the same lilting accent but rougher. Gravelly.

"Three mil."

Someone whistled.

"That's a lot of dough for a wee little woman," the first voice scoffed. "You didn't bother to do any research, huh?"

The man simply whimpered.

"Here's what you're going to do, Jimmy," the rougher voice snarled. "You're going to send a message to your boss." The man's name on the wind had my journalist instincts perking up. Sure, it was a common name, but there were very few men named Jimmy who pulled out hits on people.

"I...I can do that."

Don't do it. Don't do it.

The mantra whispered through my mind like a broken record, my inner caution goddess singing the warning of her people, but the Nancy Drew altar I worshipped wouldn't be subdued. I was a reporter, and this was a front-page scoop.

Stolen Obsession

At least, it would be if I planned on writing about it. Which I wasn't.

Maybe drunk me was bordering on suicidal, pushing aside my logic goddess, who had been waving pom-poms in my face like a red flag.

Still, it couldn't hurt to take a peek. Just a scosche.

I took a deep breath and peered around the corner with ample parts curiosity and fear.

Biting my lip, I swallowed back the gasp that threatened to bubble up my throat and fly free as I took in the scene before me. It was a scene right out of *The Godfather*. Two men towered over another, their looks nearly identical, from their height to the ginger color of their hair to their angular noses and cut jaws.

They didn't sense me spying, their focus completely on the older man they had on his knees before them. I knew I recognized his name. The man begging for his life was Jimmy Burlosconi, a mid-level hitman for the Italian mob. He'd gone to trial a few years back for killing his girlfriend in a jealous rage, but all the witnesses conveniently disappeared, and he got off scot-free.

I had covered his trial.

"Whatever you need me to do, I can do it. Promise."

The man whose face I could see more clearly smirked, his hand tightening on the knife in his meaty grip.

"Only problem is, Jimmy," he sneered, surging forward and burying the knife in the man's throat. Jimmy's scream was cut short as blood bubbled from the knife wound in his neck. His body hit the pavement with a dull thud. "I don't need you alive to tell it."

"Jesus, Seamus," his mirror snorted in disgust. "Couldn't we have at least gotten him in the trunk first or something? Now we have to drag his body down the alley."

The one named Seamus shrugged unapologetically.

"This way, he won't get away, Kier." Seamus smirked at him. "Now help me get his fat ass in the cellar before someone comes out for a drag, aye?"

"Oh aye," the one named Kier huffed. "Let me help you clean up the mess you started. Again."

"You sound like Da." Seamus grinned. "Already getting a stick shoved up your ass over everything."

"Fuck off, Seamus," Kier muttered, elbowing his brother in the ribs. "I'll shove a stick up your—"

Beep. Beep. Beep.

Shit.

Frantically, I struggled to get my purse open as my cell phone let out a shrill ring from within, signaling what was likely going to be my death. *Fuck. Why hadn't I put it on silent?*

Because I hadn't wanted to miss a call from a hotel for an opening.

"Who's down there?" I recognized the voice of the one called Seamus. Maybe if I just... "We know you're hiding in the alcove. Show yourself. Don't make us come after you. It won't be pleasant."

Shit. Shit. Shit.

"Please..." My voice wobbled as I stepped out of the alcove and into the alley. "Don't shoot me."

"Fuck me," Seamus sighed under his breath. His gun was aimed at my chest. "It's a fucking girl."

"Not just a girl," Kier growled. The deep, rough tone of his voice was easily distinguishable from his twin. He eyed me coldly, like he knew me. "She's that fucking reporter Da warned us about last week. The one sniffing around the bombing at the stables."

Damn, he recognized me.

Stolen Obsession

Fuck my life.

Wait. They knew about the bombing at the Ward farm?

Fuck, were they part of the trafficking ring? Was I going to end up trafficked?

Oh, hell no. I'd rather he shot me.

"Look, I'm not investigating anything," I told them, trying and failing to keep the slur from my voice. No such luck. I wasn't quite drunk as a skunk, but I was tipsy-wipsy...or something. "My car broke down in the parking lot back there, and I was just looking for somewhere to drink. I promise."

Kier snorted derisively. "Like we can fucking believe anything you say, lass."

The word *lass* did something funny to my lady parts.

Future Bailey would ponder that later...when she was sober.

If there was a future Bailey.

"Kiernan." Seamus looked over at his brother, his cold expression wavering slightly. "We can't just..."

"You know what we have to do, Seamus." Kiernan snatched the blood-coated knife from his brother's hand before handing him the gun. The barrel was pointed at me the whole time.

Time to go.

Survival instincts were a thing, and mine kicked in the moment the man called Kiernan stepped toward me with the knife his brother had used to kill Jimmy. I was not about to be gutted like a fucking pig in an alley.

I didn't think about the consequences of running, because who the fuck thinks of those right before they were about to be murdered by two overly handsome Irish men?

So not the time brain.

It was a calculated risk, but I doubted they would fire the gun in the alley. It could easily ricochet or set off one of the shot detectors that riddled the neighborhood. I lunged forward, kneeing Seamus in the balls and knocking the gun from his hand before slamming my elbow into his brother's face.

God, that was almost a crime considering how fucking perfect it was with his deep green eyes and panty-melting—

Again, not the time, brain, you fucking hussy.

"Dammit."

One of them cursed, but in my haste to get away, I wasn't sure which. Nor did I care. I bolted toward my car. Hindsight was a bitch since, as I was running, I remembered that it was broken down. My footsteps wobbled, legs shaky thanks to my overly enthusiastic imbibing of old Mr. Jameson, but fuck, I could at least try to lose them among the mass of cars and buildings until I found somewhere safe to hide.

This was the Irish Village, however, and if I wasn't mistaken, those two men were part of the family that ran it. Which meant there wasn't really anywhere safe for me to hide. No one would dare go against them, and I'd be a sitting duck.

Then I'd be a dead duck.

Peking style.

"Fuck," I screamed. My ankle rolled in the heels I was wearing, and I hit the wet pavement hard. Shouldn't have drunk all that whiskey. Panic surged through me as hands grabbed at my hair, pulling me up from the ground.

"Fucking bitch." I recognized Kiernan's rough voice, just a bit edgier than Seamus's, more bitter and controlled. "You broke my goddamn nose."

"It's an improvement." That was a bald-faced lie. "I'll do more than that if you don't let me go," I snarled and dug my nails as painfully as I could into the hand that held my hair. "Someone help!"

"Shut the hell up." Seamus strolled up behind his brother, his neck and face red, his eyes narrowed in a vicious glare. "Or you're going to end up like Jimmy back there."

His accent had thickened with his anger.

"Go to hell," I screamed at them as I kicked out at the man in front of me.

"Fuck this shit," Kiernan muttered, blood dripping down his face, staining his teeth red. "Just do it, Seamus."

Fresh tears fell from my eyes, but I refused to give up. If they were going to kill me, then I wasn't going down without a struggle. I scratched, kicked, clawed, and screamed as Seamus approached me, a devilish smirk forming on his lush, kissable lips.

What the fuck, Bailey? Now isn't the time to be thinking about how handsome his lips are. He's about to fucking kill you.

"Sorry about this, wildcat," Seamus murmured.

The last thing I saw was the flash of metal straight at my head.

Then there was nothing but the hollow veil of darkness.

2

Seamus

Fucking hell.

"How did it go, son?" my father asked from behind the counter of our family bar. McDonough's. He'd bought the building and named it after my godfather, Seamus McDonough, the man he'd looked up to since he was a child. He had a bar towel thrown over one shoulder, his matching green eyes finding mine while he stacked clean glasses on the shelf below the counter.

It was well past five in the morning and none of us had gotten any sleep. I'd left Kiernan and the fiery reporter to their own devices. Last I checked, she was still knocked out cold in Kiernan's trunk while the cleaners picked up Jimmy's body.

We had ample employees to do cleanup at the bar, but my father always made sure to be part of the grunt work. He'd once told me that if a leader cannot do what he asks of those who follow him, then he is no leader. He's a dictator.

Hard work, he'd said, built character. A genuine leader would never be afraid of getting his hands dirty. It was what his father taught him and what I knew I would one day teach my children.

If only my mother carried the same values.

I watched her out of the corner of my eye as she twiddled away on her cell phone, completely ignoring the surrounding workers, who were cleaning up after the late night.

She rarely worked unless my father threatened to cut off her credit card. I loved my mother, there was no doubt about that, but she'd never been the mother my grandmother had been to my father.

"The cleaners are taking care of the mess at the club," I murmured so we weren't overheard. Most of the workers in the bar were part of our operation or family to them, but it still paid to be cautious. Hopping behind the bar, I grabbed a clean dish rag and proceeded to wipe down the sticky bar top.

"Oh, honey," my mother chastened lightly, her eyes flitting up from the screen of her phone. "You don't need to do that. That's why we have employees."

Employees who were already hard at work and champing at the bit to go home to their families.

"I like the work, Ma," I told her. She huffed a bit before waving her hand dismissively at me, her attention back on her phone. "Seriously?" I muttered beneath my breath.

"Your mother will be your mother." My father sighed, the muscles of his jaw visibly tightening. Unlike mine and Kiernan's, my father's Irish accent wasn't as rough. We'd spent years studying and training in our homeland, learning the family business, before coming back to America. My father never had the opportunity because of the clan wars that had shoved his father off the island. "How is your sister?"

"Dashkov says she's tucked back safely in his penthouse." I kept cleaning. "From what I heard, the two had some pretty strong words on the dance floor before she stormed off."

My father chuckled. "She's got her mother's temper for sure." His smile fell, his eyes becoming haunted, like looking into a fractured mirror. It didn't take a genius to know he was thinking of Katherine McDonough. Ava's mother.

It was still hard to believe that I had an older sister. She wasn't much older than Kiernan and me—just a few months, which meant I could still pull out the "nearly your older brother" card when I needed to.

It wasn't a secret that my mother wasn't my father's first love. Kiernan was dead set on the fact that my father only married our mother out of duty, and I couldn't find a reason to disagree with him. The pair were polar opposites. After Saoirse was born, they'd even stopped sharing a bed. Hell, they barely shared a house any longer now that we were all nearly grown.

We'd rescued Ava nearly three weeks ago from the hands of Christian Ward, the man she'd believed to be her biological brother for years. She was terrified of him. I didn't blame her. The man had a sick, perverted obsession with her that bordered on psychotic.

The surprise on my father's face when Vasily Ivankov darkened our doorstep, alone and unarmed, had been earth shattering.

That one had balls of steel, which was the only reason my father heard him out rather than shooting him and dumping his body in Lake Union.

Another sister.

At first, I'd thought the man was trying to blow steam up our asses, but there was no denying the truth when he pulled out her picture. Fuck. She could have been our triplet. We looked that much alike, with our ginger hair and vibrant green eyes.

Then he told us a story.

Her story. As much as he knew, anyhow.

Where she'd been. How she'd gotten there, and it made my blood boil.

In the Kavanaugh family, we had one saying.

A statute we lived by. *Fola roimh gach ní eile*

Blood before all else.

She'd been Elias Ward's prisoner. Locked away, believing that the family she had didn't care about her.

They beat her.

Used her.

God knows what else Ward did to her before handing her over to Dashkov as a fucking bargaining chip to save his pathetic son's life.

Cac. Fuck.

Elias Ward was lucky he was already dead.

"We do have a slight problem, though." I cleared my throat, setting the towel on the bar as I turned to face my father. "Someone saw us take out Jimmy."

My father paused in his cleaning, looking at me askance.

"Did you take care of them?"

I ducked my gaze away from his, heat blooming up my neck in shame, but I wasn't second-guessing what we did. It had been the right thing.

"No," I admitted, swallowing back the lump in my throat as I prepared myself for his disappointment. "She's...Kiernan's taking her upstairs."

Leaning back against the bar opposite of me, he crossed his arms against his chest, eyebrows raised expectantly.

"It's a woman?" he asked. I bit my lip and nodded. "If you keep her, you know what I expect," my father warned me, his gaze hard and serious.

"Yes, sir."

"You and Kiernan will be responsible for keeping her in line." He turned back to finish putting away the glasses. "She needs to understand this lifestyle and what she's given up in exchange for her life. If she escapes and goes to the cops, it's on your heads."

"I understand."

"Good." My father gave me a curt nod, but I breathed easier when I didn't see any disappointment in his eyes. Simply a warning. "Now bus those remaining tables. Natalie had to leave early. Tell your brother to report to me later when he's finished getting the girl settled in."

And just like that, I'd won.

Sort of.

I smirked at myself at the thought of training her to be the perfect mafia match. My hands on her porcelain skin, pinching, caressing, tweaking. Would she take my punishments with regality, or would she fight me? Fight us? God, I loved a good fight, but there was something sweet about a woman who submitted.

The image of the raven-haired woman on her knees before me had my cock twitching, and suddenly, I wished I were the one upstairs instead of my brother.

He had everything to gain from beginning her trainer.

The reporter, however, would forfeit everything she knew.

3

Bailey

I was going to suffocate.

There were no ifs, ands, or buts about it. Soon, the compact trunk they'd shoved me in would run out of oxygen, and I would die. My screams were muffled by the makeshift gag shoved between my lips and wrapped around my head. The knot was caught in my unruly hair, pulling painfully at small chunks. I banged my bound hands against the inside of the trunk lid, but it was no use.

Jesus. I've been fucking kidnapped.

I was going to be sick.

The trunk reeked of oil and gasoline; the fumes making me lightheaded and adding to the nausea that was growing in the pit of my stomach. Damn, I was regretting drinking all that whiskey. I wasn't sure how long I'd been in here. I'd woken up to the feeling of claustrophobia clawing at my back, the only light permeating the small space coming from the dim glow of the taillights.

Every dip, bump, and rolling stop caused me to whimper. My stomach churned with despair and regret as we inched closer to my demise. Where were they taking me? I'd published enough stories on the police finding bodies of victims who'd crossed the mafia to know it wasn't going to be pleasant.

Cement shoes.

Executions.

Exploding cars.

Those were just a few things I'd come across.

Then there was torture, cigarette burns, iron brands.

Knife wounds so precise in the amount of pain they caused.

Were they planning on killing me? They knew who I was, but only on the surface. No one knew about the connection with my family, and that would be a saving grace. They wouldn't try to use me as ransom to get to my father. That also meant that they had no use for me. A meddlesome reporter.

I thought back to what one twin had said. He'd known about the bombing at the Ward farm. The stables were what the Seattle underground called it. The place where traders hid their cargo from the authorities. Elias Ward's worst kept secret among the criminal enterprise. It was where he stored the flesh he was looking to sell. Like cattle.

It was disgusting.

Were these men somehow involved? The bombings likely hadn't crippled Ward's trade. It was only one location out of who knew how many. Rumors had been flying around for weeks that, since his death, Elias's son, Christian, had taken the reins and was looking to expand. The idiot was promising more flesh to those depraved enough to buy.

I'd been digging into the Ward flesh trade for months. Ever since one of my coworkers went missing on assignment. Not that anyone believed me. According to the paper, she'd put in her resignation and moved down south to be with her parents. Except Lina had been my mentor and a good friend to me. We'd talked not only about her research into the sex trafficking ring but also about her personal life. Except her parents were dead.

In my free time, I went digging for the truth. Despite ample protests. Someone had set it up to look like she had just left, and while everyone else wanted to put on their rose-colored glasses and believe the lie, I wouldn't. I was going to investigate, no matter what.

At least, that had been the plan.

The car came to a sudden stop, the engine cutting out. There was a tightening in my chest as panic surged through me, gripping me soundly, and I struggled to control my rapid breaths when the sound of the driver's door opening and slamming shut reached my ears.

It was the sound of my doom.

My death.

I listened for a moment, but nothing else followed.

Where was the other brother?

Both doors would have opened and closed, right?

Unless they had tasked someone else with getting rid of me.

Footsteps echoed inside the condensed space, my heart hammering away in my chest like a jackhammer as they grew louder before stopping completely. *Oh god.* The click of the trunk unlocking had me nearly losing all the liquor I had consumed. My hands grew sweaty, my fingertips tingling as I panted in fear.

The moment the trunk opened; I was blinded by the sudden brightness. I squinted at the shadow looming above me.

Kiernan.

His ginger hair was tied back in a small bun at the top of his head, revealing a jagged undercut beneath that gave him a fierce edge. His cheekbones sat high on his face and easily accentuated his chiseled jawline and lush, kissable lips.

But it was his eyes that stole the show. A deep emerald that immediately caught you up and swallowed you whole. There was so much pain swirling behind them that it killed me. I wanted to know who'd had put that pain there and take it away.

Shaking my head slightly, I threw those thoughts right where they belonged. In the trash.

This is the man who is about to kill you, idiot.

My vagina didn't seem to care. She was too busy throwing a pussy power party.

"Let's go" was his gruff command. Snatching my bound hands, he easily lifted me from within the confines of the trunk, setting me on my feet before him.

Bad idea.

The world around me spun like a tilt-a-whirl at the county fair, and before I could stop myself, I was heaving all over his expensive-looking shoes.

Served him right.

"*Criost*," he muttered and pulled back my tangled hair from my face with a gentleness that bellied his savage expression before untying the gag between my lips. Once I was done emptying the contents of my stomach, I ran my tongue over my dry lips, trying to rid myself of the bitter taste of whiskey-tinged vomit. "Are you done?"

I nodded my head sheepishly, my anger momentarily forgotten as my stomach churned again and the surrounding space spun. Without another word, he swung me up into his arms. My eyes snapped shut, the action causing my stomach to gurgle and protest. Lucky for him, whatever was left in my stomach remained there.

"Where are you taking me?" Ugh, cotton mouth. I

buried my bound hands in his green button-down, struggling to hold on as he stomped away from the car with me in his arms.

"Quiet," he snapped.

I huffed. "I deserve to know if you're planning on killing me, you know."

He grunted like he didn't think so.

Rude.

Realizing he wasn't going to talk, I let my gaze wander. Maybe if I took in enough detail, I could figure out how to escape before he sprung the guillotine and offed my head.

There were cement pillars everywhere, the ceiling lower than normal. It looked to be an underground parking garage. The fluorescent lights above were so bright they mirrored daylight. Several cars dotted the underground structure, ranging from simple four-door sedans to oversized Mercedes G-wagons that I had no doubt could survive a tank attack.

"Sir."

A man in a pair of tight-fitting black cargo pants and a polo nodded at Kiernan and pressed the arrow for the elevator. *Who the hell was this guy who kidnapped me?* He obviously worked for the Irish Mafia. Was he one of their top lieutenants? He'd have to be higher up in the chain of command for someone to refer to him as sir.

The elevator dinged, the untarnished silver doors sliding open to let us in. Kiernan nodded at the man when he leaned into press another button and then swiped his finger along the sensor.

Great, it was fingerprint controlled. That wasn't going to help me escape unless I planned on hacking someone's finger off, and even then, I wasn't sure shit like that worked outside of James Bond movies.

The panel lit up with the number three.

Where was he taking me? Weren't torture chambers usually in the basement?

The doors opened, revealing a dark, wood paneled corridor. Kiernan strode out of the elevator and into the quiet hallway. There wasn't much I could see from where I was curled up against the mobster's chest, the smell of vomit overpowering the woodsy scent of the man carrying me, but the interior seemed to have a proper order. The carpet beneath his feet stifled his booted steps. There were pictures hanging along one wall that looked well cared for and dust free. It was hard to tell from this distance, but they appeared to be family related.

There weren't any windows, save one at each end of the hallway, but the hallway was lined with several doors. He stalked toward one end of the hall, stopping in front of the last door on the right. He didn't let me go, instead clutching me tighter before reaching for the doorknob and pushing it open.

Kiernan didn't stop at the doorway. He kicked the door shut with his foot and continued to carry me through the apartment-style suite toward a back room. I struggled against him as we approached the bedroom. The movement caused my head to spin and my stomach to churn sourly.

Kiernan didn't loosen his grip, but he didn't set me down in the bedroom either. He bypassed the room altogether and headed straight through another door and into an attached bathroom. His strong arms lowered me until my bare feet met the cold tile floor. My body wavered slightly before gaining its balance.

And the world spun again.

A little less than last time, but it was enough to still give me a headache.

He reached behind me and grabbed a small white bottle. Pulling two pills out, he handed them to me.

Stolen Obsession

"For your headache. The doctor will be in a little later to check you out."

What kind of kidnapper paid attention to their prisoner's headaches and asked for a doctor if they were just going to kill them?

Irish ones, apparently. I stared at the white pills in his hand apprehensively, but the banging construction gnomes in my head were going full speed ahead. I took the pills and swallowed them down with a glass of water he tipped to my lips.

"Where are we?" I asked, my voice hoarse from screaming through the gag.

"Nowhere you need to worry about." He stepped back, grabbing my bound hands in his, and worked the knot out. "I'm going to untie you. If you do anything other than what I say, I will punish you, and trust me, you won't like that."

Punish me?

Who the fuck said shit like that?

"Do you understand?" he growled at me, his fingers digging into the bones of my wrist.

"Yes," I yelped and tried to peel my wrists from his grasp.

"The proper response from now on is *yes, sir*."

Oh, come on. Now he really had to be shitting me. When I didn't respond fast enough, he pinched the skin between my thumb and forefinger until I answered.

"Yes, sir," I choked out. The pain was gone in an instant.

"Good girl."

No. Bad vagina. Bad. That was not something it needed to be responding to.

Kiernan turned away from me, leaning into the shower, and turned on the spray. "Now strip."

Oh, hell no.

"Strip," he commanded again when I remained frozen.

"Excuse me?" I stared at him in disbelief. There was no way in hell I was going to be getting naked in front of this guy. Even if my pussy was throwing a party downtown right now. I'd only been completely bare in front of one person in my entire life and...ugh, fucking Drew.

"Strip, Bailey," he growled as he began methodically removing his own clothes, his emerald eyes never leaving mine. "Or I'll do it for you, and if I have to do it, I'm going to be expecting something for my troubles."

A frisson of awareness tingled through me at the less than subtle sexual threat. *Stupid whiskey.*

"I..." My mouth gaped open like a fish out of water as I tried to conjure up an excuse. "I don't need a shower. I'm good. Promise."

Kiernan snorted.

"You're covered in vomit, Bailey." He stepped forward, crowding my fully clothed body with his naked one. Fuck, he was gorgeous. His chiseled torso was painted in a myriad of colorful tattoos. He was lean but well-muscled, with the body of a fighter. He towered over my petite frame by a few inches, making him look like a giant. "Now, Bailey."

Kiernan said my name again.

Wait...how did he know my name?

"Your driver's license." He smirked down at me. Shit. I hadn't realized I said that aloud.

Slowly, I peeled off my black leggings and tank top. He continued to stare at me, heat sweeping up my neck at the look on his face. He was a predator ready to devour his prey.

"All of it," he said once I was down to my bra and underwear. Swallowing back the unease in my throat, I let out a jagged sigh before reaching behind and unlatching my white cotton bra. Boring, I know, but practical.

When I didn't let it drop to the floor, he wrapped a giant

paw around it and pulled it from my grasp, throwing it aside. He did the same with my panties.

"Get in." He motioned for me to step inside the large glass enclosure. The construction of the shower was beautiful. The main wall was light gray-washed vintage tile with a blue fleur-de-lis symbol painted on each one. The two smaller walls were tiled with a simple glossy blue to match. Dark copper fixtures hung high above, creating an almost rainforest-like effect with the water as it cascaded down in captivating rivulets.

I braced for the cold as I gingerly stepped inside but was immediately pleased at how warm the water was. I gave myself a moment to bask in the heat, allowing the warm water to slide over my cold, tingling skin.

The glass door slid shut, a barely audible click signaling that I was locked inside the shower with no way out. I shut my eyes, not wanting to look at him. I'd been painfully careful to keep eye contact with him, but now, so close together, it was hard to avoid.

I turned my face away, covering my eyes with my hands, letting the warm water wash over me.

Kiernan snorted almost derisively. "What? Never seen a man's cock before, lass?"

"I don't want to see yours," I sneered, the venom in my voice muffled by my hands. "I just want to leave."

"You better get used to it, *mo fraochÚn beag*." He leaned forward, prying my hands away from my eyes and dragging them down between us until they rested on his thick, heavy cock. "You'll be getting very familiar with it soon."

There was no inflection in his voice. He was serious. His free hand wrapped itself in my wet hair, forcing my head down. My gaze shifted with the movement until it rested on his muscled legs, his very thick cock hanging heavily between them.

Oh god, was it pierced?

For fuck's sake.

He forced my hand to run his length, my grip barely fitting around his massive width. I could feel the metal of the balls gliding across my fingers.

My inner hussy was performing her own *Cirque du Soleil* at the thought.

Traitorous bitch.

"Your job is to listen and obey," he groaned out, quickening the pace of my hand on his silky member. "But we'll talk more about that later."

Like hell we would. I shook my head back and forth, tears streaming down my cheeks, but not from him forcing my hand around his length. No. The tears came from the shame that welled up inside me at how turned on my body had become at his touch.

At me touching him.

Fuck, I needed some therapy.

If I ever got out of here, I would be getting it.

Lots of it.

"I just want to go home," I sniffled. The show of vulnerability wasn't completely fake, but it wasn't truthful either. I needed him to trust me. I needed to slowly make him believe I could be broken. If he let his guard down, then I could make my escape. "Please..."

Groaning painfully, Kiernan released his hold on my hand. His grip in my hair tightened, preventing me from retreating.

"This is home now," he whispered in my ear, fingers dancing along my pussy lips before a long, low moan escaped me when they circled my clit. If my face wasn't already red from the heat of the shower, it sure as hell was now. "And you can either be a good little girl who gets rewarded or a bad little girl who gets punished. Understood?"

I nodded, gasping when he increased the speed of his fingers against that little button of pleasure.

"Words, Bailey."

"Yes, sir," I breathed.

"Good girl."

My fucking traitor pussy clenched at those two words.

Hussy.

My hands gripped his shoulders as my legs shook. His fingers rubbed me furiously, causing pleasure to roll through my body like a tidal wave. Just before it crested, he stopped.

He chuckled at the small whimper that left my lips, then brought his fingers to his mouth, tasting me.

"Delicious, my little whore." He pulled me out of the shower's spray, ignoring my attempts to shove him off. I was not his whore. Growling, he spun me around and slammed his palm into my ass.

What in holy hellfire?

"Enough," he growled. "Stand still, or I'll do more than spank your pert ass."

Some of the fight had left me when he'd spanked me like an errant child. I nodded, chastised, hoping that if I played along just a bit longer, I'd be free of this prison. All I had to do was wait.

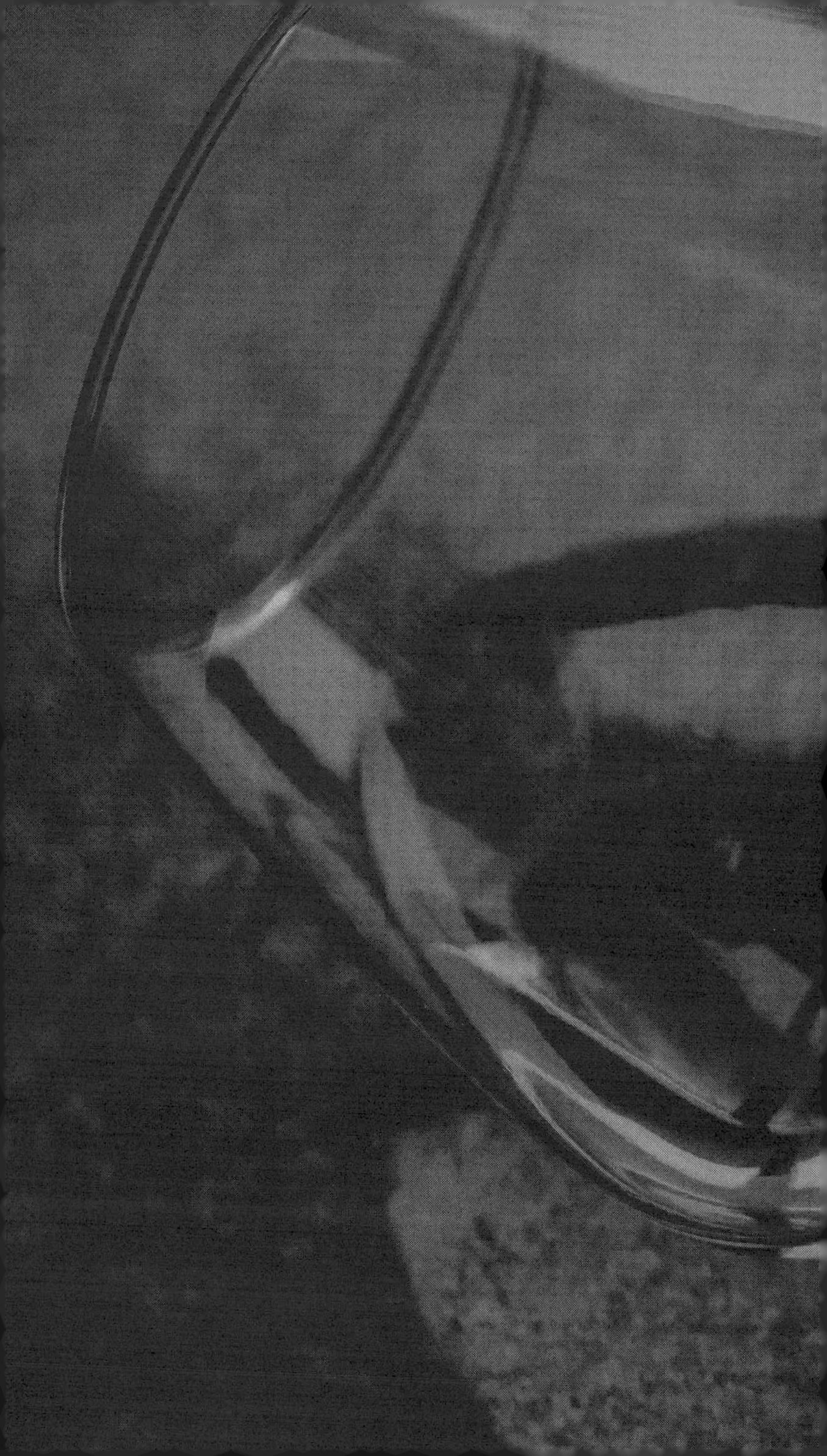

4

Kiernan

Bailey's skin was slippery from the water and soft beneath my touch as I let my hands explore her lush curves. This woman's body was built for sex. She stood several inches shorter than me, the top of her head barely reaching my shoulders.

I reached behind her, noting the slight flinch when I leaned in and grabbed the bottle of shampoo. She would come to learn that, although I would punish her, I would never hurt her or beat her. That wasn't something my family stood for.

Turning the bottle upside down, I emptied some into my palm before massaging the lather into her hair and scalp. She was stiff beneath my ministrations, her arms tight against her chest, muscles clenched. Once I was sure her hair was clean and vomit free, I dipped her head beneath the stream of water until it was completely rinsed and started on the body wash.

"You're so fucking soft," I whispered, once again exploring her body, massaging the soap on to her shoulders and arms. Her breasts were next, and I took my time, gently kneading each one, rubbing my thumbs over her petal-pink nipples until they were standing at attention.

Bailey hadn't said a word, but her breathing picked up, her body subtly shifting as I toyed with her. I let one hand continue working her breasts while I slid the other between her legs.

"Open for me, *mo fraochÚn beag.*"

She resisted at first, clenching her legs together tightly. Sighing, I pinched her inner thigh. A small squeal of surprise fell from her beautiful lips as she tightened her thighs against my intrusion.

"Remember, Bailey," I reminded her as I cupped her sex. She let out a soft moan. I doubted she even realized what she had done. "Good girls get rewarded. So open your legs."

A beat hung in the air between us. The conflict was written across her face, plain as day. This woman may have been one of the city's best reporters, but she hung her emotions out to dry for everyone to see. With a small sigh, she parted her legs willingly.

Licking my lips, I stared down between us. She had a soft triangular patch of hair leading down to the cleft of her pussy, which was neatly shaved. Just how my brother and I liked it. Neither Seamus nor I prescribed to a completely shaved snatch. Made a woman's pussy look like a naked mole rat.

Running my hands over her pussy, I gently cleaned her before caressing them across her lush, pert ass.

God. The things this woman does to me without knowing.

I'd been prepared to do my duty when I saw her in the alleyway. She was a witness. A loose end. We rarely took out women, but a reporter was different. They were sharks in the water and couldn't easily be threatened or bribed.

Then she'd fought back. The second she took a swing at me, I was a goner. My cock had never been harder.

I'd fucked plenty of women, but it was more for release than anything else. I'd never held any type of connection with them, and I rarely saw a woman more than once. I dipped my fingers in the crease of her ass. Bailey tensed before her body relaxed slightly.

"Good girl," I praised her as I slipped a finger into her tight hole. The beautiful girl whimpered but made no attempt to stop me or push me away as I plunged my finger slowly in and out.

Damn, she was tight. She would need to be trained before we could stick our cocks in her ass. It was a tight fit with just one finger.

"Now," I spun her around until her breasts were pressed against the heated tile wall, ass rubbing against my hardened member, "come for me, *a mhuirnín*."

Pressing hard against her cunt, I concentrated on her swollen nub as I ground my rock-hard erection against her luscious cheeks. Soon she was pushing back against me, grinding her pussy onto my fingers, her breaths coming in short, panting gasps as she took her pleasure unabashedly.

Bailey sobbed when I pinched her clit between my fingers, her entire body shuddering as she came. She went limp in my arms. I wasn't far behind, my cum exploding against her ass.

Fuck. She was beautiful when she orgasmed, and she made the cutest fucking sounds. Small whimpers and little mewls.

Like a kitten.

A kitten who needed a collar.

Keeping one arm around her for support, I rinsed us both off before reaching around to shut the water off and grabbing a towel that hung over the shower door. With quick, thorough strokes, I rubbed her down. She didn't protest, her eyes barely open as she struggled to stay awake.

I knew this wouldn't last forever. She was docile now, but

come later, I had no doubt our little kitten would show her claws. A slight tinge of regret streaked across my conscience at having taken her like that so soon. Especially knowing she was partially inebriated, but there was no going back now. Bailey needed to learn she was mine.

And Seamus's.

She belonged to us, whether she liked it or not.

It was the only way we were going to be able to keep her alive.

I tucked Bailey into my bed, drawing the covers over her naked body. There were plenty of clothes—either mine or Seamus's—to dress her in, but having her naked when she first woke would serve as a reminder to her.

She wasn't the one in charge here.

That, and what sane man wouldn't want a woman like her running around his room naked and at his disposal?

Tilting my head, I took a moment to study her, my eyes roaming over her form and taking her in. Touch was a completely different sense from sight. Each sense told me something different about her. My touch told me how soft she was. How pliable. It told me she had scars running down the right side of her flank, the whitish marks barely visible beneath her light caramel skin. The only indication she had any were the raised bumps beneath my fingertips.

What were they from?

How had she gotten them?

Why did I care?

Her voice was gentle when forced into submission, but those fiery moments delivered a delicious edge. She wasn't used to being told what to do. Bailey was no doubt used to being the one in control, but that didn't stop her body from sensing an apex predator. It wanted her to submit to me; it was her mind that was holding her back.

That would soon change.

Her long raven hair spread out over my pillow in stark contrast to the white linen that lay beneath. Quietly, I sat in the wingback chair just a few feet from the bed and tugged her purse into my lap. Some of the men had brought up the belongings she'd had in her car.

She'd been running from something. Or someone.

Bailey hadn't been lying when she'd stated her car had broken down in the parking lot. A quick once over from Patrick, our resident mechanic, had confirmed that. One of her spark plugs had been dirty and split. It was years older than the practically new ones installed around it.

Patrick didn't need to confirm what I'd already guessed.

Someone had wanted her to break down.

But why?

Grabbing my phone, I snapped a quick photo of her driver's license before sending it off to Bridgett, our tech guru and personal hacker. I needed more information on the raven-haired siren. Something other than what I knew about her as a reporter.

A reporter...*Cac.*

I wondered how Father was taking the news that we'd kidnapped one of the city's most popular investigative journalists. Jaysus, he was going to kill us.

Groaning a sigh, I set those thoughts aside as I dug further into her belongings. There wasn't much. A recorder that belonged to the worst side of the nineties. It had a cassette tape and everything. Shit, where had she even gotten this relic? Better yet, why would she use this piece of shit when digital ones were readily available? Not to mention phones.

I'd listen to it later when I wasn't worried about waking her.

Gum. Breath mints. An empty bag of Sour Patch Kids. A few stray pens. Her ID badge. Nothing incriminating and nothing that told me why she'd been at the club.

I couldn't dismiss the idea that she'd been the one to plant the faulty spark plug to cement her story and make us believe she was the victim.

Bingo.

Her cell phone was tucked at the bottom of her purse, beneath all the crap, and it wasn't locked. What the fuck? For a reporter, she was really fucking stupid. Who didn't lock their phone?

She had a slew of missed calls. Jaysus, there were nearly sixty. Most of them from a number labeled *Stepcunt*, while the rest came from one she'd labeled *CHEATER*, in large capital letters with a puke face emoji.

Cute.

Opening her messages, I snuck a peek at some of them. There were a few from the stepcunt asking about where she was and telling her she needed to talk to Drew.

> Stepcunt: You need to come home. Drew said you walked out with all of your things. Where are you planning on going? You two need to figure this out. We can't let your premarital spat ruin your father's plans.

Bailey never answered.

> Stepcunt: Bailey Elizabeth Crowe, I am not kidding. Men cheat. Get over it and get your ass back home before I involve your father in this.

Crowe? That wasn't the last name she'd listed on her driver's license.

Why did that name sound familiar?

Shaking my head, I focused back on the text messages. None of which Bailey had responded to. There was a whole host more of them from her stepmother, mostly dragging on about how she couldn't let this ruin everything her father had worked for and how she'd regret leaving Drew, the one I assumed was labeled *cheater* in her contacts.

Damn, I thought my mother was a frigid bitch. The two of them could be best friends. Both worried about social standings and how things affected the family image, not caring about how the family itself was affected. Not that we had much of an image. It wasn't a secret my father ran the Irish Mafia.

Not even from the police, who we had in our back pockets. Most of them, anyway. There were always the few who thought they could beat the system of corruption we had going. It never worked.

It never would.

We ran this city just as much as Dashkov and Romano, just with less pomp and circumstance.

They called us rats because we kept to the shadows. Hidden from prying eyes. We had more people than most realized we did. More control than they could imagine.

The Wards had the shipping port.

The Romanos had several billion-dollar hotels.

Dashkov had his fancy security corporations.

Businesses like that were easy targets. They were out in the open and everyone knew of them. It made them stand out. It was only a matter of time before someone somewhere got curious. The FBI. IRS. DEA. You name it. There was always some gung-ho newbie agent desperate to prove themselves and willing to go the extra mile.

All it took was one small lead.

One minor mistake.

One very good reporter, like Bailey.

Dammit. We were risking everything by bringing her here. We should have killed her.

But...

My phone vibrated in my pocket. I pulled it out, bringing it to my ear without bothering to look at the number. There was only one person it would be at this hour.

"Tell me you got something for me, Bridg."

The woman on the other end of the line scoffed. "Of course I got something for you. Who do you think I am?" Her playful tone made me smile. "The question is whether you're going to like what I give you."

I groaned internally. This wasn't going to be good. I could feel it.

"Hit me with it."

"There is something off about this girl," Bridg started. "The name on her driver's license is accurate as far as I can tell, but she's not just a fucking reporter."

"What do you mean?" I didn't need more trouble at my doorstep. There was enough shit piled on as it was.

"She's the adopted daughter of Senator Crowe."

Well, shit.

"Jaysus."

Things had just become ten times worse.

Not only was she a reporter, but she was a senator's daughter as well. A senator who had been on our ass for years and who was responsible for a lot of spilled Irish blood.

"What else can you tell me about her?"

Bridgett sighed. "She graduated from high school at

sixteen and college at nineteen. Started her reporting career at the Seattle Times upon graduation, where she was promoted to investigative journalist two years later."

Bridgett snorted. "Yeah, somebody was greasing her career," she interjected before continuing. "Umm...let's see. No other address for her on file except the one on her license, but her car is registered to a Drew Knight, son of—"

"Magnus Knight," I cursed under my breath as I quietly walked out of the bedroom. I didn't want to risk waking Bailey. "Fuck."

"Who's Magnus Knight?" Bridgett asked curiously.

"Chairman of the House Armed Services Committee."

Bridg hummed. "That clears things up a bit," she admitted. "Drew Knight is the CEO and founder of Knightman Security. Private armed forces and security here in Seattle."

"That's not good," I bit out as I made my way toward the elevator.

"Here's the other thing," Bridg edged nervously. "According to every news story, Bailey was adopted at the age of three from Seattle Memorial."

"Okay..." I failed to see where this was going.

"There aren't any records of her adoption in the system."

"So?" I shrugged. "That doesn't mean anything. It could have been a private adoption."

"That's possible," she admitted. "But something just isn't adding up with that."

"Then check into it and get back to me." I hung up the phone without bothering to say goodbye.

Dammit, this day was turning out to be more fucking stressful than I thought it would be. Not only did we have current issues with some of the local MC gangs trying to take our shipments, but now we had Bailey to deal with.

Her father's the goddamn senator. I hadn't seen that

coming. She wasn't a socialite like her sister, who was seen day in and day out in the tabloids, sporting some new designer dress on the runway and out with a new beau every week.

Bailey had been kept in the shadows. Hidden.

So then why was her marriage to Drew so important to her father and Magnus Knight? Bailey didn't even carry the same last name as the senator. Dalia Crowe would have made a better match. I ran a hand through my hair as I stepped off the elevator and into the back hallway of the bar.

Shit was going to hit the fan soon if we didn't figure out what we were going to do with the minx upstairs.

I knew one thing for certain, though.

My father was going to kill me.

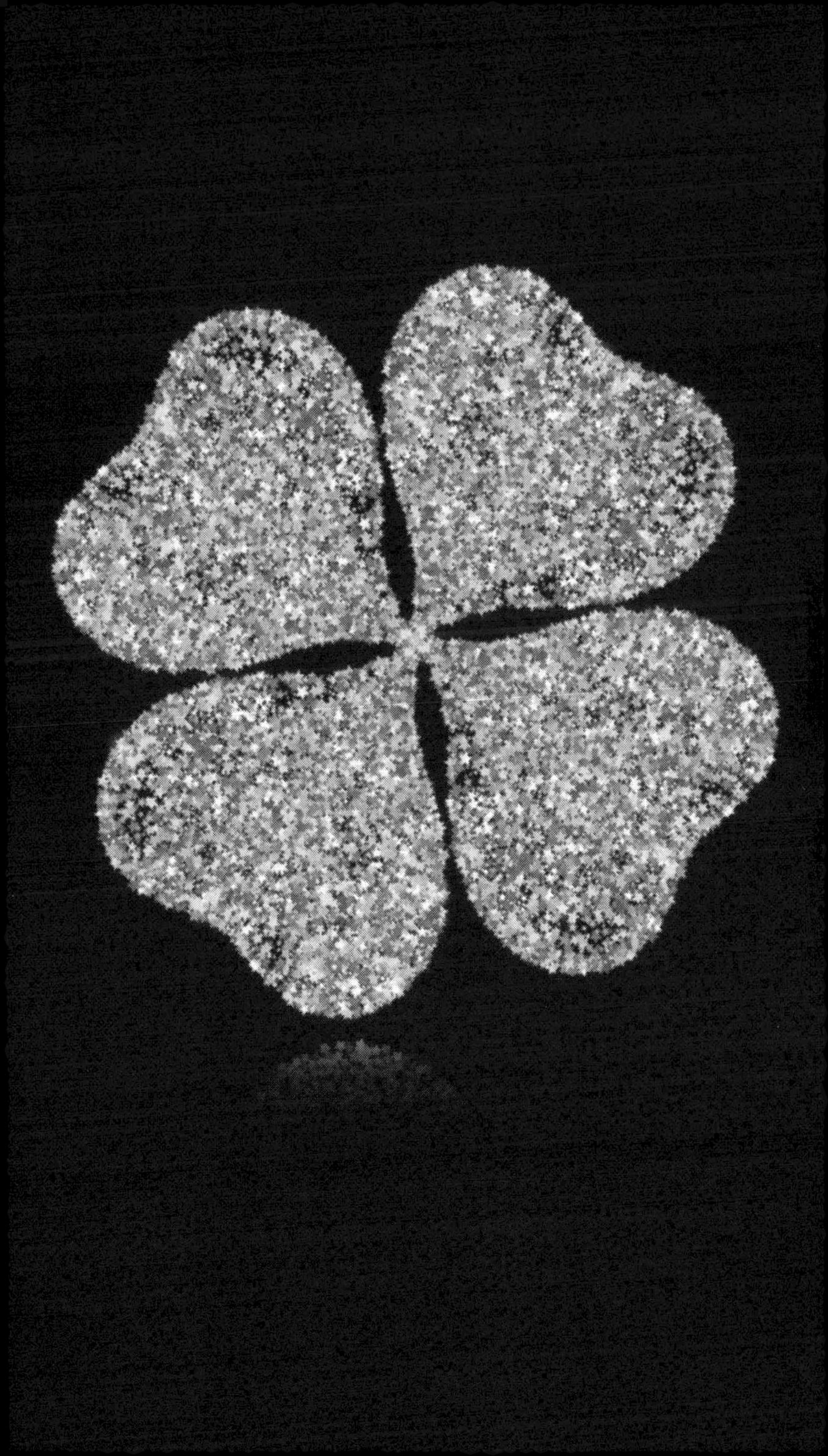

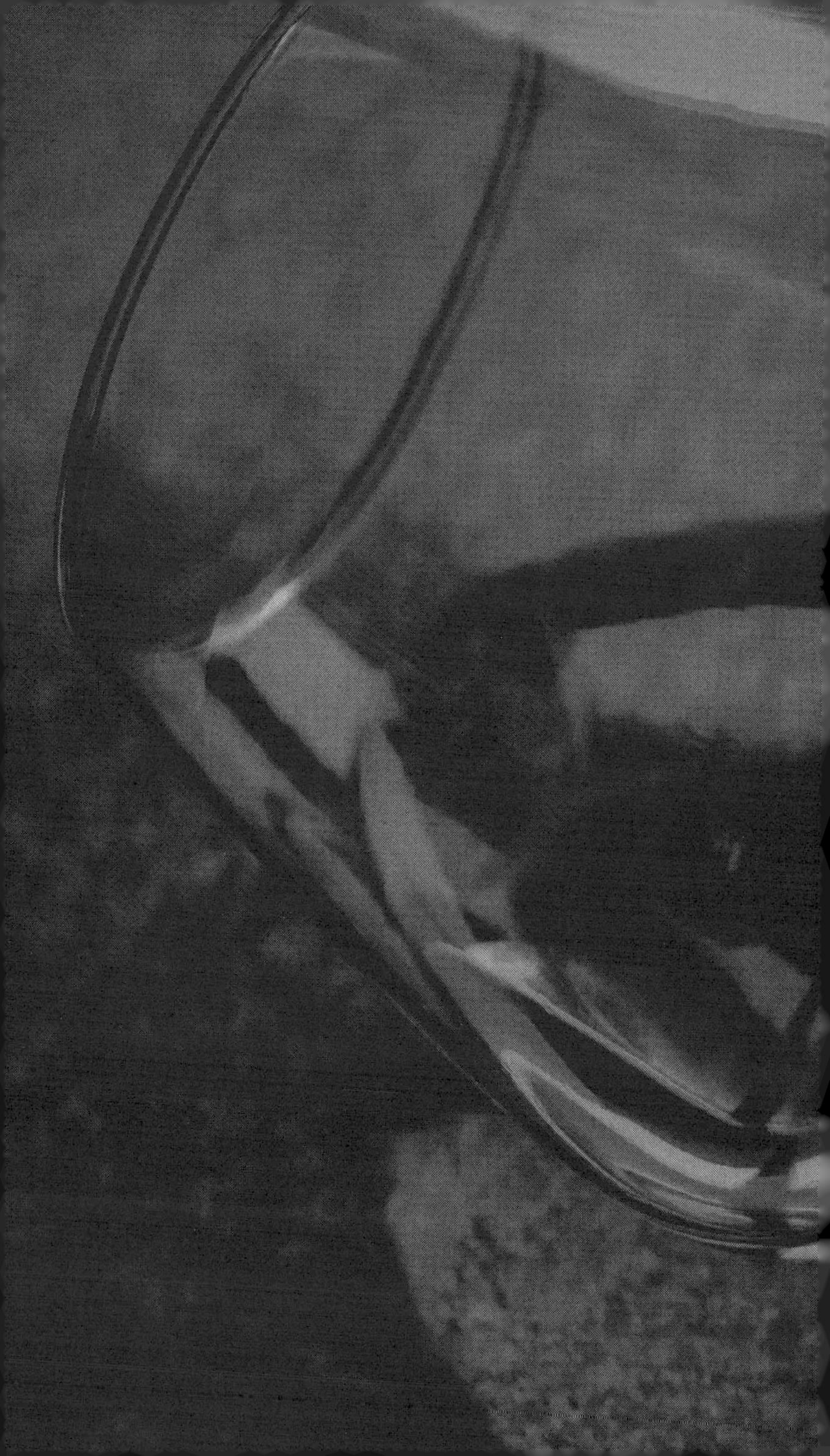

5

Kiernan

"You took your sweet-ass time, Kiernan." Seamus tilted his head back, leaning slightly in his chair as I approached, sensing my heavy footsteps against the worn wooden floor. We'd been trained since we were young to always be on alert. To look. Listen. Feel. Honing the senses that could easily save our lives.

And they had.

"Got a beer for you." He was sitting at one of the small tables near the bar, my father casually sitting across from him. It was still early, nearly seven in the morning. We'd spent the entire evening cleaning up our mess in the alley. We hadn't gotten back to the bar until nearly five. They both had towels draped over one shoulder, their shirts dotted with wetness. They'd been hard at work. Lucky for all of us that the bar was closed tonight. We never opened on Sundays unless it was for family.

One thing our father had instilled in us growing up was the reward of family and hard work. And the understanding that a leader didn't just watch from the sidelines while his people did the work. He got his hands dirty. He dug in.

"If you humble yourself to your people, they will be more apt to follow you when trouble brews. Our community is our family, and we treat family with honor and respect. We don't demand respect like other families might. It is earned, and you must earn it from those who have your back."

"We have a problem," I mumbled, taking the empty seat next to my brother. Seamus and my father frowned, waiting for me to continue. I gulped down half my beer and leaned back in my chair, a ragged sigh escaping me.

Fuck.

"Do leave us in suspense, brother," Seamus drawled dramatically.

I ran a hand down my face, groaning as I thought about how I planned to word the shitshow we'd gotten ourselves into.

"I don't think the girl is lying about being stranded," I started. "Patrick confirmed her car had indeed stalled. But from the looks of it, it was tampered with."

"Tampered with or meant to look like it had been?" my father asked.

"I honestly believe she was just in the wrong place at the wrong time," I told him. "From what I could make out from her text messages, she caught her fiancé cheating on her. Drove somewhere to get away, stalled in our parking lot, and drank her weight in whiskey."

"That the bad news?" Seamus arched his brow.

"Bridg gave me her background details." *Shit*. Father was going to murder us. "Bailey Jameson is the adopted daughter of Senator Richard Crowe."

My father snarled at the senator's name.

It wasn't a secret in the underground that Richard Crowe had a hard-on for trying to send my father to jail. Him and the rest of the mafiosos in the city. He fancied himself a white knight. A Harvey Dent, but he was no better than any of us. In some ways, he was much worse.

The only difference between the criminal empire and him was that he presented himself like a fucking king. Royalty. Untouchable. The dark truth of who was hidden behind the façade of the wealthy businessman. His hands were only clean because he paid others to do his dirty work.

"We need to come up with a plan," my father murmured. "Find out how close she is to her father. What she knows. Maybe we can use her as a bargaining chip."

"You think she knows anything?" Seamus asked. "She may be his daughter, but there is no guarantee she knows anything useful. Hell, we didn't even know he had a second daughter."

Seamus had a point. How the hell had we missed that Crowe had another daughter, or that there had been a union between him and Knight? It didn't feel right.

"She has to know something," I interjected. "From what I gathered, her stepmother is pissed at her for leaving her fiancé. Apparently, their marriage is a large opportunity for him."

"Do we know why?" Father questioned.

"Not the particulars," I admitted with a small shrug. "But we know who. That's the other bad news."

"Just what we need," Seamus muttered, polishing off the rest of his beer.

I took a deep breath. "Her fiancé, Drew Knight, is the son of Magnus Knight."

"Well, shit." Seamus whistled.

"That definitely changes some things," my father mused, stroking his two-day stubble. "One thing is for sure, though." He looked up at me with an amused smirk. "You're going to have to work on your makeup game with that shiner you're sporting. I suggest heavy concealer."

Seamus, the fucker, howled with laughter at my father's dig. I shot him a glare, my hand coming out to smack the back of his head. Little shithead.

"The little siren got in a lucky shot," I growled angrily. "Better than Seamus. She nailed him right in the bollocks. He'll be lucky if anything down there still works."

That shut my twin up.

My father, however, lit up at my statement. He was a cheerful one. That was something I'd always loved about him. He never took life too seriously. Most fathers in his position were known for being stern and controlling. They'd weigh their heirs down with unrealistic expectations. Bars that could never be reached.

Liam Kavanaugh was not that kind of father.

When we were growing up, he'd never set the bar farther than we could reach. When we touched it, he'd move it just a bit farther. His goals for us were never unattainable. He didn't expect us to be perfect, and he never encouraged us to follow directly in his footsteps.

"You'll find your own footsteps," he'd told us when we first learned the truth about the empire we would one day inherit. *"Follow your own paths. Lean on each other, and everything will work itself out."*

His words had yet to fail us.

"We need to come up with a plan." I let out a long sigh. "One that won't have us going to war against the senator."

"Kill her."

The three of us turned to find my mother approaching us from behind the bar. She'd put her cell phone down long enough to listen in on our conversation. Eavesdropping was the only time she managed to lift her eyes away from it.

"We don't kill the innocent, Marianne," Father growled. His patience with her had been thinning since her obvious rebuke of Ava. My half sister's role in our family had become a point of contention between the two of them. "You know this."

Mother snorted derisively. "She is the daughter of one of the dirtiest senators in the country. How innocent do you really think she is?" she asked, eyes narrowed at my father. The tension between them coiled tighter, the air around them thickening. You'd think she'd have been happy to have her best friend's daughter in her life.

But this was my mother.

Selfish.

Shallow.

Out for her own regard.

Ava was a threat to her standing in the family. I'd learned early in life that my mother did nothing that didn't benefit her. She was a viper in the tall grass. A chameleon. And someone who was more than willing to stab you in the back with one of her Louboutins if it meant she'd climb the hierarchy ladder.

I had a bet with Seamus that father had only married her because she had gotten pregnant with us. Another calculated move on her part and "moment of weakness" from what my father had drunkenly mumbled one night. It hadn't stung when he'd said it. I knew he wouldn't trade me or my siblings for the world.

"That may be," Father continued calmly. I could see his green eyes darkening dangerously. "But it still stands. We don't kill women and children. Especially if they aren't any harm to us."

"Any harm?" My mother sneered, her hands coming down on the tabletop roughly as she leaned toward my father,

her face pinched in an ugly scowl. "She witnessed your sons murder someone. She's a reporter. One who could bring this entire family to ruin with just pen and paper."

Mother wasn't wrong. If given the opportunity, Bailey could deliver a large blow to us if she reported on what she'd seen. She'd be the only witness, but her status as an investigative journalist gave her credibility. She could easily sink our organization to its knees if she had both Magnus Knight and her father backing her.

If given the opportunity.

"We're not killing her, Mother." Seamus frowned at her. "Kiernan and I will take care of Bailey our way. It's our mess. We should have cleared the alley before taking care of Jimmy."

"Yes," she hissed, turning her cold eyes on him. "You should have. The two of you are set to be the next leaders of this family. You can't afford mistakes. By not killing her, you are showing how weak you are. How soft you are. I'm disappointed in the two of you. I thought I raised you better. Neither of you ever thinks. You both just—"

"Enough," I roared at her, losing my patience. I watched Seamus pale as she berated him. We might both be hardened men, but that didn't mean our mother belittling us didn't have any effect. Seamus was more sensitive when it came to our mother. He'd always wanted her attention when we were little. He'd do just about anything to garner the one thing she never gave us. He'd simply wanted to talk with her. To have her smile at him. Appreciate him.

She never did. Not unless there was something in it for her.

We might be twins, but I'd seen our mother's duplicitous nature long before my brother. She wasn't worthy of the title. There were those out there who loved their mothers, even when they were cruel and cold. They might have even shed a tear if they died.

I was not one of those people.

Neither was Seamus. Not anymore.

My mother's eyes widened at my outburst. She took a step back from the table, her mouth open in shock.

"You're done here, Mother," I growled. "This doesn't have anything to do with you. Seamus and I are handling the situation as we see fit. We made a mistake, and we will rectify it. Our way. That doesn't mean we are incapable. It makes us human. Sparing her life doesn't make us weak or soft. It makes us men who know where to draw the line."

Her face turned a mottled, angry red, her lips thinning as her shock morphed into a venomous glare. "How dare you—"

"Leave, Marianne," my father glared at her, "before I lose my temper."

My mother didn't need to be told twice. She scurried away from the table without a second glance. There weren't many people she was afraid of. My father was one of the few. And rightly so.

"Now," my father leaned forward, his elbows resting on the table as his gaze traveled between my twin and me, "you made a mistake, and that's all right, sons. Let's discuss how we can rectify it."

Seamus visibly swallowed, his jaw clenching tightly as he struggled to rein in the tumultuous sea of emotions threatening to bubble to the surface.

"I might have an idea."

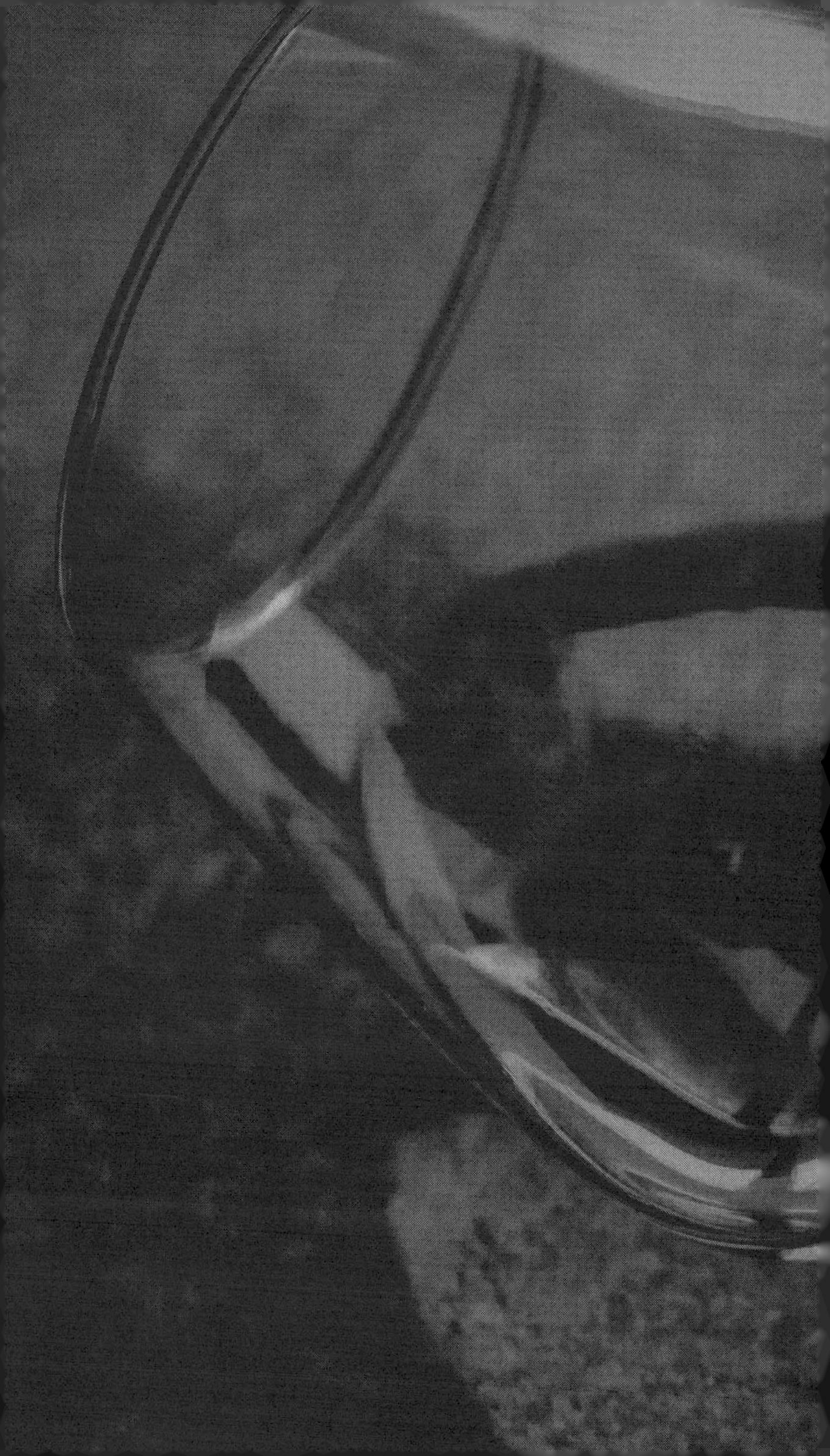

6

Bailey

It was warm.

Too warm.

I was faintly aware of the stifling heat pressed against my back. Hot air caressed the skin of my throat, sending tingles of awareness zipping through me. Something heavy was draped over me, holding me tight. It took a few moments for my groggy brain to process what the hell was going on.

My body was sandwiched between the twins, their body heat surrounding me, creating an inferno.

The more I bordered on wakefulness, the more pressure built behind my eyes, a dull throb spreading through my temples like wildfire. I didn't want to wake. It felt safer to stay trapped in sleep than face the reality that would be smacking me in the face soon.

My inner hussy was primping her hair and putting on her best red lipstick.

My inner bitch, however, was sulking in a corner like a petulant child at how utterly foolish this all was. Jesus, it was like the entire cast of *Inside Out* was rolling through my brain.

Maybe I needed therapy.

There really shouldn't be a *maybe* in that statement.

I needed therapy.

Lots of it.

What exactly happened? My mind struggled to recall how I'd ended up here...in bed...between two men who could double as the MacManus twins.

Minus the red hair.

I remembered breaking down in some shady-ass parking lot, drinking a bottle of whiskey, and then—

Shit. They'd killed Jimmy Burlosconi in that alley. They killed him and...images from the previous night crashed through my mind like a tidal wave.

"Good girls get rewarded."

Heat suffused my cheeks as I thought back on how Kiernan had made me come like Drew never had. I'd nearly passed out, but the sulking child in me planned to blame the booze and not the Irish sex god and his magic hands.

Jesus, what had I done?

You rode his fingers like a debauched whore looking for her next fix, is what you did.

Inner hussy was having a party, her legs split open and ready for more. Miss conservative was narrowing her gaze at me. Guilt churned in my stomach like a bad breakfast burrito.

I wouldn't become my mother.

I couldn't.

Bright side: they hadn't killed me, which was something.

What did that mean for me, though? Maybe I could convince them I had no plans to turn them in, and they would let me go.

Don't be an idiot. My inner cynic was no doubt rolling her eyes like a damn drama queen. They weren't going to just take me at my word.

Stolen Obsession

Fuck.

It wouldn't be long before my father noticed I was missing. If not him, then my wicked stepmother sure as hell would raise the alarm. If only to save her own image. She'd always been cruel to me. I was the product of one of my father's many indiscretions, his illegitimate secret. If anyone were to ask, I was the baby they'd adopted. A poor orphan child in need of a home.

My father, although never cruel, turned a blind eye to the way his wife treated me. All he cared about was her happiness. And Dalia's, my half sister.

My stepmother was all about social standing. Father might not have been the kindest, but sometimes I wondered if he realized how truly poisonous his wife was. Her claws were dug so deep into my father he was practically her puppet. He didn't see what I did.

A manipulative cunt monster.

Or maybe he did and just didn't care.

As the wife of a senator, she had standing. My father was the driving force behind the changes in the city. He was pushing out criminal enterprises to free people from their clutches. It was one of the reasons I became an investigative reporter.

Much to his chagrin.

"We know you're awake, wildcat," Seamus murmured behind me, his lips trailing wet heat up the side of my neck. I suppressed the shiver that threatened to run rampant through my body at his simple touch.

Groaning, I slowly opened my eyes. Kiernan's face was inches from mine, his emerald eyes full of hunger.

"Where am I?" I croaked, my throat dryer than a cotton mill in the heat of summer.

"That doesn't matter," Kiernan rumbled, pushing himself

into a sitting position, his back against the headboard. He leaned over and grabbed a glass of water from the nightstand. "Take these."

Seamus helped me sit up. His brother handed me two white pills. *Déjà vu*. This felt exactly like last night before the shower.

I eyed the pills he dropped into my hands warily, unsure of what they were giving me. Was it a drug to keep me sedated and at their disposal?

"It's just ibuprofen, Bailey." Seamus chuckled at my reticence. "We don't like our woman drugged."

"I'm not your woman," I hissed before dropping the pills in my mouth and gulping down the water Kiernan handed me. Damn, I hadn't realized how thirsty I was.

"Where am I?" I asked again, handing back the empty glass. My gaze drifted around the room, taking in the unfamiliar surroundings. The four-poster king-size bed was the focal point. It stood against the main wall, a nightstand on either side. The only other pieces of furniture in the large space were two wingback chairs settled in front of a tiled fireplace.

Despite the oversized furniture, the room felt open and airy, with billowing cream curtains and light gray walls. It just didn't feel homey or lived in.

"I told you not to worry about that," Kiernan reminded me harshly. "I won't tell you again."

My inner bitch hissed in annoyance at the dominant tone in his voice.

"And I'll happily scream this place down unless you tell me where the fuck I am and why you took me," I threatened. Not that I thought it would do any good.

The screaming part. I had an eerie feeling I was in the heart of the lion's den.

Seamus chuckled darkly.

He dragged me down to lie on my back. "Oh, wildcat," he cooed mockingly, hovering over me, the warmth of his weight surrounding me, making it hard to breathe. "Scream all you want. This room is soundproof. And even if it wasn't, no one is going to save you."

The twins stared down at me, their eyes mirroring one another's with a desperate lust that had me shrinking back into the mattress.

"So what?" I swallowed hard as I struggled to voice what I was terrified of hearing. "You're going to rape me? Keep me as your sex toy?"

"Those don't sound like bad ideas." Kiernan smirked, running a finger along my jaw. "Here's the thing, *mo fraochÚn beag*. We will use you. Pleasure you. Bring you to the brink repeatedly. If you misbehave, we will punish you. If you lie to us, we will punish you. But we will never hurt you."

"Rape *is* hurting me."

Kiernan's smirk deepened. "You'll be begging for us, trust me."

"Don't hold your breath," I sneered, trying to keep the tremor from my voice. If only it was from fear and not because I knew just how good he could make me feel—again. "I won't be begging for anything."

"We'll see."

"You can't keep me forever, you know," I pointed out, trying to pull my mind from the carnal debauchery my inner hussy was currently cheering for.

Traitor.

"People will come looking for me."

Seamus smiled. He didn't look the least bit concerned.

"Don't worry about that," he told me, dragging the covers down my body. I was naked underneath. I'd known this the moment I came to. Kiernan hadn't bothered to dress me after we showered. "Just let us show you how good we can make you feel."

My body was stiff as their hands skimmed along my breasts. Their touch featherlight. I could have told them no. Kiernan had made it clear he wasn't into raping me. He wanted me to beg, but I couldn't get the word out. There was a sick, twisted part of me that wanted to give in to their touch. To fade away into the pleasure they were promising. But the logical side of my brain wasn't letting go of the rope that was barely holding me to my sanity.

"Relax, wildcat," Seamus murmured in my ear before nipping at the lobe. A low moan seeped through my lips unbidden.

"Let it go, Bailey." Kiernan's tone was calm and cool when he gave the command. There were no traces of the brusqueness he'd shown me he was capable of. His hands massaged my breasts, fingers pulling at the nipples until they were stiff and painful. "Let go."

Seamus's sinful lips left a trail of scorching fire down my body, nipping and sucking at the skin, leaving small bites in his wake. He settled himself between my legs, prying my thighs apart. Cool air hit my center as he exposed my wet heat to his ravenous gaze.

"*Go hálainn*," he whispered, voice dripping with need. "Beautiful."

Before I could protest, his mouth latched on to my clit at the same time Kiernan's mouth eclipsed one of my nipples. The sudden contact sent a jolt through me. Straight to my pussy. And from Seamus's muted chuckle, he knew exactly what they'd done to me.

Bastards.

Currents of pleasure washed over me in waves as the

brothers' mouths worked my body like a well-tuned machine. My fists grabbed at the soft sheets beneath me in a vain attempt to ground myself. It was no use. I was lost to their masterful touch.

"That's it, Bailey." Kiernan's voice was deep with lust, and when I looked up, his pupils were blown wide with desire.

A desperate cry left my throat, and I arched my back as Seamus inserted two fingers into my pussy without preamble. He pumped them in and out slowly, curling his fingers at just the right angle, sending my body higher and higher, the coil in my belly winding tighter.

"Now," Kiernan smirked, lowering his head back down to my breast, "scream for us."

He bit down hard on my nipple just as Seamus's teeth grazed my swollen bundle of nerves. The combination, along with my already wound-up state, sent me hurtling over the edge of the abyss, pleasure consuming my body as I writhed beneath them.

My scream echoed through the room.

"So sensitive," I heard Seamus whisper to his brother in awe, his breath coming in short pants.

"So responsive," Kiernan chuckled breathlessly. Opening my eyes, I stared down the length of my body to find Seamus with his hand on his cock, stroking the length of it.

Holy shit.

Whose horse is that?

There was no way that giant hammer was going to fit inside me.

Sure, I'd felt Kiernan's in the shower, but I'd been too whiskey-addled to really take it in.

Now, looking at it in the morning light, I didn't think I'd survive.

"Don't worry, love," Kiernan whispered, drawing my

attention to him. He, too, was stroking his pierced cock rhythmically. His eyes devoured mine. "You haven't earned our cocks yet."

I opened my mouth in rebuttal, but I was cut off by his hand grabbing my face and forcing my lips open. The move was aggressive, but his touch was gentle.

A stark contradiction.

"Be a good girl and take my cum."

Moments later, ropes of hot cum shot out of his cock, landing on my face and in my mouth. I sputtered slightly as the salty essence hit my tongue. I'd never been one to swallow before.

"Take it," Kiernan ordered, his eyes darkening. Every instinct in my body told me to spit it at him. I shouldn't want to swallow it, but I did. It was wrong and messed up, but I took it. Every salty bit of it.

"Good girl." Seamus grinned up at me from where he kneeled between my legs. I'd been so caught up in Kiernan, I hadn't realized he'd come as well.

A knock at the door interrupted my next thought.

"Doctor's here." Kiernan slipped from the bed, tossing a robe at Seamus, and turned to me. "There is a change of clothes in the bathroom. Get yourself cleaned up and come back out here."

Had I just stepped into an alternate reality? One moment, they were making me come and smiling down at me, and now they were both wearing somber faces. Fuck this. Scowling at the sudden dismissal, I rushed from the bed and into the bathroom, making sure to slam the door behind me as hard as I could.

If that was how they wanted to play things, then fine. I hadn't been too far off the mark when I'd asked if they wanted me to be their sex toy. Well, fuck them. Two—three—could play that game. I didn't care if they'd just given me the most blindingly awesome orgasm of my life—it wouldn't be happening again.

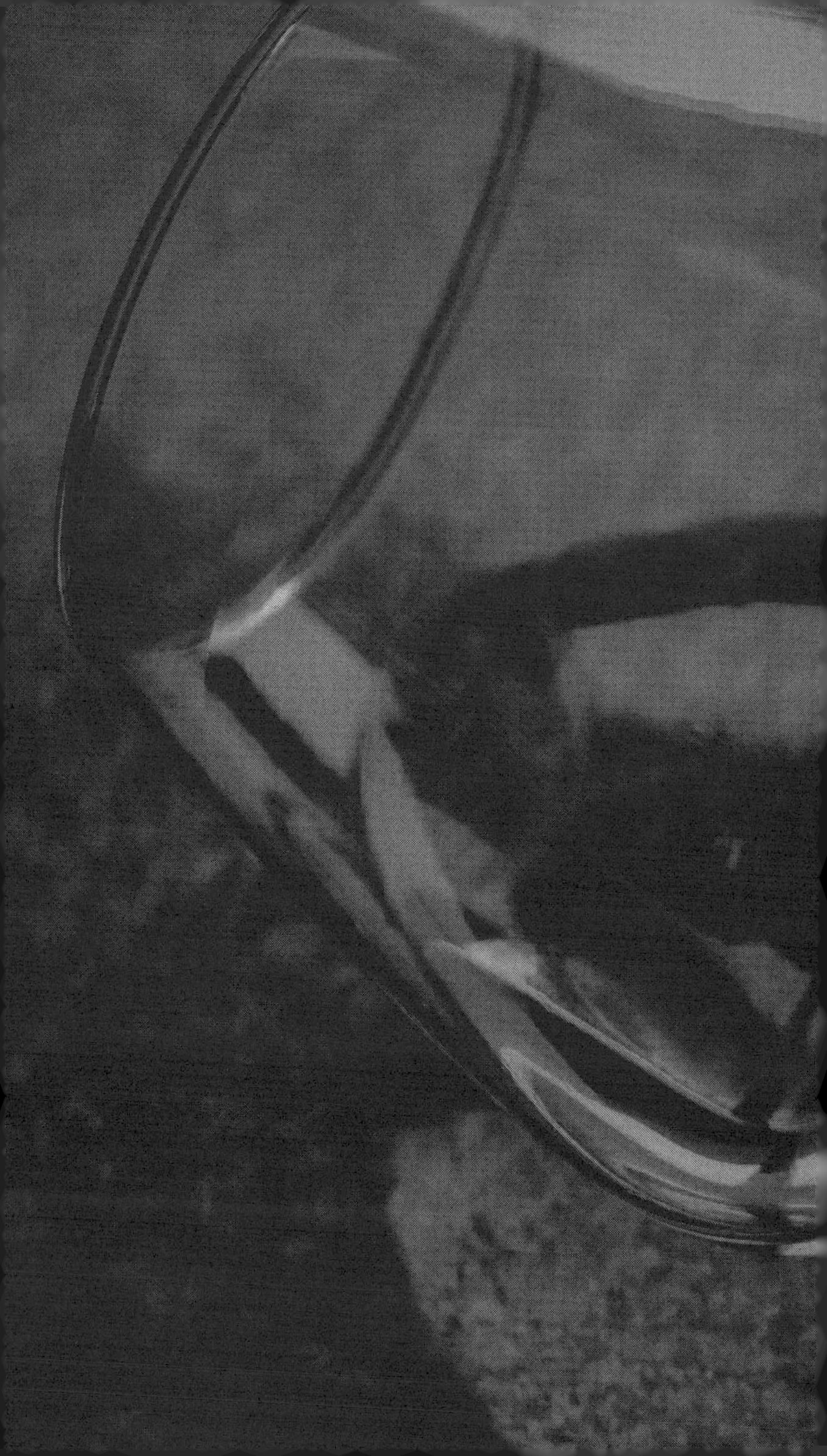

7

Bailey

Seamus and Kiernan had both dressed while the doctor unloaded a large case full of medical supplies she'd brought with her. She was young, with long raven hair and smoky brown eyes. Too young to be a doctor, in my opinion.

"All set here, boys." She gave them a wide, familiar smile as she aligned the last of her instruments. Seamus gave her a boyish smile, and I couldn't understand the sudden squeeze my heart gave at seeing him flirt with her.

Therapy. Therapy. Therapy.

"All right." Kiernan eyed me for a moment before turning his gaze to the pretty doctor. "Just text Nan when you're settin' to be done. She'll come up and take care of the rest."

The doctor nodded. "Will do. Shouldn't take long."

What shouldn't take long?

I shifted my gaze between the three of them, trying to figure out what the hell was going on.

"I don't need a doctor," I told them.

"Yes, you do" was the twins' immediate rebuttal. Together.

"No, I don't," I insisted. "Did it even occur to you to ask me if I wanted to see a doctor?"

"Nope." Seamus shook his head in amusement.

"Not at all," Kiernan followed. "But that's the thing, Bailey." His dark gaze settled on mine. I stiffened at the sudden surge of electricity that shot through my body.

Stupid hussy.

Down, girl.

"We don't need your permission to do anything," he continued. "You're not in your daddy's kingdom anymore, sweetheart. You're in ours."

Smug-ass motherfucking—

"Okay," the doctor drawled as the two men shrugged on suit jackets and left without another word. Apparently, Kiernan had laid down the law, and that was that.

Over my dead body.

I pushed up from the bed, ready to go after them, but a hand on my shoulder stopped me.

"I wouldn't do that if I were you." The doctor raised her eyebrows at me expectantly. "I've got orders to sedate you if I have to, and I really, really don't want to have to do that."

"You know they kidnapped me, right?" I sneered at her. She shrugged nonchalantly, as if this was an everyday occurrence.

"I'm paid to make sure there is nothing wrong with you," she admitted candidly as she pulled a white gown from her bag. "I don't much care beyond that." She held out the gown for me to take. I eyed it warily. "We can either do this the easy way and get it over with nice and quick, or I can call in one of the guards out there and sedate your ass. Mind you, he'll also have to help maneuver you into all sorts of positions that could expose you and—"

"Fuck." I ripped the gown from her hand and stomped toward the bathroom. "I'll fucking do it."

She beamed up at me. "What a good choice."

A few minutes later, I exited the bathroom in the white gown that opened at the front instead of the back. I drew it tightly over my chest, uncomfortable with how vulnerable the small piece of fabric made me.

"Take a seat on the edge of the bed," the doctor instructed with a smile, her voice gentler than it had been with me before. "We'll start with the less invasive stuff first."

Less invasive? What the fuck was she planning on doing to me? She must have sensed my hesitation, because her look grew serious again as I perched myself on the edge of the mattress.

"I'm not here to hurt you, Bailey," she assured me as she wrapped a blood pressure cuff around my upper arm. Not that her assurance meant much. It was said that lions would purr right before they struck their prey. "I'm just making sure that everything is in tip-top shape."

I snorted. "Everything is fine." I winced uncomfortably as the cuff tightened against my arm. "I don't need you to tell me that. I have my own doctor."

"Yes," the woman smirked. "Julia is such a great doctor. She faxed over all of your records for me. Such a sweet woman."

Who the hell were these people?

Shit, I was going to need to find a new doctor.

"Sure." I breathed a sigh of relief when the cuff deflated. "If you like backstabbing doctors who violate privacy laws. Then again, you work for the mob, so..." I let the sentence trail off.

Bitch had the nerve to laugh as if I'd said something funny.

"Well, I can be quite persuasive when I need to be." She removed the cuff from my arm. "Your blood pressure is slightly elevated, but that's not abnormal in your situation."

The side-eye I shot her was worthy of an award. "No? You think?" I mocked sarcastically. "I'm kind of curious how many blood pressures you've taken of women who've been kidnapped by two low-life mobsters to just easily brush that away."

The amused look on her face vanished, a dark scowl forming.

"I know you're not in the best of predicaments right now," she snapped. "But you should feel lucky to be alive. Anyone else, and you'd be nothing more than a pretty face with a bullet in her forehead, lying in a gutter somewhere. You should be grateful that those *mobsters* spared you. I've never seen Kiernan Kavanaugh have that kind of mercy for anyone."

Did she say Kavanaugh?

Even my inner hussy had paused when hearing his surname.

I was an idiot. A fool. A dead, dead duck.

There was no doubt in my drunk little mind that the twins worked for the Kavanaugh family, but I hadn't thought they *were* the Kavanaughs.

"You had no idea, did you?" The doctor chuckled lightly as she placed her stethoscope on my chest. "I honestly expected better from someone who received a Pulitzer Prize for her investigative journalism."

My nose scrunched in distaste. "I was a little preoccupied," I mumbled petulantly. And a little drunk. Shit, I couldn't believe I hadn't put two and two together. Liam Kavanaugh's heirs weren't well known, to be honest. They were hardly ever mentioned in any kind of investigation, and they'd been photographed less than a handful of times in the society pages.

"Can't blame you, though," she shrugged as she moved her stethoscope to my back and asked me to take a deep breath. "Most people aren't aware Liam even has twin heirs. Most of the time, they're only photographed separately."

"For a good reason, no doubt." I couldn't help but comment. The doctor hummed but confirmed nothing as she went through the rest of her examination.

"Any tenderness when I press on the side of your head?" I winced as her hand palpated a particularly sore spot at the back of my head where Seamus had no doubt popped me with the butt of his gun. "I'll take that as a yes. Any double vision?" I shook my head. "Nausea?" Another shake. "Dizziness or anything like that?" Nope and nope. "That's good. Shouldn't need a CT, but if you develop any of those symptoms, let me know and I will order one for you."

"Thanks." Jesus, what the fuck was I thanking her for?

"No problem."

We lulled into a surprisingly comfortable silence as she continued to poke and prod at me like a pincushion. She took a few samples of my blood, performed a chest exam, and then asked me to lie on my back.

Over my dead body.

"I'm drawing the line at a pelvic exam," I sneered, pushing her hand away when she tried to coax me onto my back.

"It's just standard procedure."

Un-fucking-believable.

"So is me breaking your fingers if you try to get anywhere close to down there," I threatened. The doctor huffed.

"I'm not your enemy, Bailey," she huffed. "I'm just trying to do my job."

"Always wanted to be a mob doctor, huh?" I rolled my eyes. "High aspirations you had."

"Actually, yes," she admitted candidly. "I grew up wanting to do exactly this. My entire family has served the Kavanaughs since the clan's inception in Ireland over a hundred years ago."

"Good for you," I muttered. "Still not going to get you in my knickers. My last gyno appointment was three weeks ago, and I haven't had sex since then. You're the one with all my medical files. Take that and shove it up your—"

"Are we having a problem here, Dani?" A feminine voice spoke up from the bedroom doorway. The doctor, whose name I now knew as Dani, turned toward the woman and shook her head.

"Not at all, Nan." She smiled at the woman. "We were just finishing up."

Damn right we were.

"Good." The woman in the doorway eyed me shrewdly. Her cold hazel eyes assessed me as she stepped into the room, a pile of clothes in her hand. Placing the clothes on the bed next to me, she drew herself up, hands on her hips. At full height, she looked to stand about five foot eight. Several inches above my measly five-foot-four frame. She was slender and willowy, with long legs encased in flowing black slacks and a paisley blouse. Her graying brown hair was tucked into a messy bun at the top of her head, accentuating her long neck.

The woman could give my stepmother a run for her money in the intimidation factor. Eyeing me one last time, she turned back toward Dani, and the two started their own lax conversation that I didn't even bother to try to eavesdrop on. I didn't care what the two women had to discuss. What I cared about was figuring out how to get the hell out of here.

I wondered if my father was searching for me at all.

Stolen Obsession

Or even Drew.

Would they have discovered my car in the parking lot? I hadn't answered a single one of my stepmother's texts. She'd sent the guards after me one time for not answering one of her phone calls while I was in a lecture at college.

It had been embarrassing to have them storm into the room during the middle of a lecture and tow me out like an errant child or a criminal of some kind. Some of my classmates had filmed it, and within hours it had spread across campus. Sarah had never done that to my sister.

Dalia, of course, could do no wrong. While my father had kept me in the background of our family my entire life, Dalia had been at the forefront. While I'd worked my ass off in college, she'd walked Parisian runways and posted her vacations on Instagram. Her future had been handed to her on a silver platter, and mine was made with sweat and tears.

A lot of tears.

On the surface, it appeared as if I was one of their shining jewels. They talked me up like I was Queen of the Nile. Once the lights faded, so did the affection, and I was no longer the miracle adoption child but the dirty product of an affair.

It wasn't that I didn't also live in the lap of luxury. Growing up, I wanted for nothing except the one thing I wished for most. Affection. I was given clothes, food, a roof over my head. My father never raised his own hand to me, and I was allowed to pursue my interests.

But I was rarely taken on family vacations unless it was somehow political. There were no hugs or kisses unless it was staged for the cameras. I grew up with what most in the world would kill for. Luxury. But with that came something that no one should have to experience.

Loneliness.

I wondered if that was why I clung to the idea of marrying

Drew so much. At sixteen, most girls would have been mortified by the idea of having to one day marry the boy their family picked for them, but I saw it as a way out of the cold pit of isolation I was surrounded by. My clothes were handpicked by a designer. The food I ate, the classes I took before I stood my ground and applied for journalism school, the friends I was allowed to keep, the events I went to—they were all chosen for me.

Lina had been my first real friend. One that hadn't been hand chosen by my stepmother to spy on me. She never sucked up to me because of who my father was. Lina never knew.

"Into the bathroom with you, love."

"What?" I shook the thoughts from my head, trying to clear the cobwebs I'd gotten lost in. No use reminiscing about what couldn't be changed. The past was the past, and all that mattered was going forward.

"Shower, dear." Her tone wasn't gentle, but it wasn't brusque either. It was more along the lines of pure indifference. That in itself was impressive since I doubted she came across many situations like this one.

My gut churned. Unless she did. How many women had they taken "prisoner" before me?

Why did I care? Shaking off the weird, possessive thoughts, I nodded at Nan, my feet hitting the soft carpet floor of the room as I made to stand up.

"Leave the gown," she ordered.

"But—"

"Leave it," she ordered again, her voice harsher now. "Dani here will need to take it with her to be cleaned. This isn't the place for modesty and weakness. You are prisoner to two of the most powerful Irish men in the country, and you will be put to the test. Swallow your pride and any preconceived notions about what you think you know about mafia families, and you just might survive. Understood?"

Swallowing back the sudden lump of fear welling in my throat, I nodded my head weakly, her words sharper than any blow I'd ever taken.

"Good," she nodded. "Now, into the shower with you and then come on out. I have some clothes for you."

She looked away as I stripped the gown from my body and traveled the brief distance to the bathroom. I hurried through my shower routine, doing more of a whore's wash than anything else. It didn't seem right to keep her waiting, especially since I'd taken a full shower with Kiernan last night.

A sliver of arousal shot through me at the memory of Kiernan's hands soaping my body, and it took everything I had in me not to dip my fingers between my thighs at the thought of him doing it again.

Ugh, there was something wrong with me.

I shouldn't want them.

It was wrong.

They'd killed a man in front of me. Kidnapped me.

My vagina and I should hate them. Little miss hussy, however, wasn't getting the picture. She just continued to wave her pom-poms around like it was the fucking Super Bowl.

Maybe I could get a lobotomy when this was all over.

Sighing in defeat, wondering what the hell was going on with my libido, I shut the water off and grabbed a towel to dry myself off with. I'd never been like this before.

Wanting sex.

No, needing sex.

They had awoken something in me that had been lying dormant. I didn't understand the sudden need to be touched by them. I'd never liked PDA with Drew, mostly because the only time he touched me other than sex was at social functions where we played the joyful couple.

I'd thought we'd been somewhat happy and content. Looking back, I realized how often I failed to see the signs. The red flags. The first time after I'd turned eighteen had been fine. Nothing special. I'd moved some of my things into his condo, but he made it clear he didn't want to live together until after we were married. Our sex life had been active, but for me, undesirable. I did it more out of obligation, and I never initiated it. Drew might have been the one who took my virginity, but Kiernan had been the one to give me my first orgasm. Up until last night, I'd had no idea that sex could be so pleasurable.

Wrapping the towel around me, I stepped back into the bedroom, where Nan still waited. Dani was gone, along with all her stuff.

Good.

The two of us stared at one another for a moment, neither of us speaking. She was the first to break the silence.

"Go on then and get dressed." She ushered me toward the small stack of clothes she'd set on the bed and straightened the room back to what it had been before I arrived. Picking up the first piece of clothing, I realized that they were mine.

"The boys managed to get your suitcase from the car." She smiled warmly as I slipped on the cozy black leggings and blue tunic blouse. "Once things are more settled, I'll have them bring everything up."

No need. I won't be staying that long.

"Thank you..." I wasn't sure what to call her. Nan seemed like a family nickname. Her luminous eyes widened, and her smile grew. She hadn't expected me to thank her. Under the circumstances, I could see why, but having something of my own, even if it was just my clothes, made me feel somewhat normal.

"Siobhan, dear," she informed me as she took the soiled towel from my hands, placing it in the hamper by the door. "But you may call me Nan."

"Thank you, Nan." I smiled at her, more at ease.

"You're welcome, dear." She nodded her head. My stomach growled, my cheeks heating in embarrassment at the loud gurgling echoing in the room. "Lunch is being served. Let's not keep the men waiting."

My smile dropped at her words, my stomach turning queasy. There was no doubt I'd soon be face to face with Liam Kavanaugh, head of the Irish Mafia.

The man who would decide my fate.

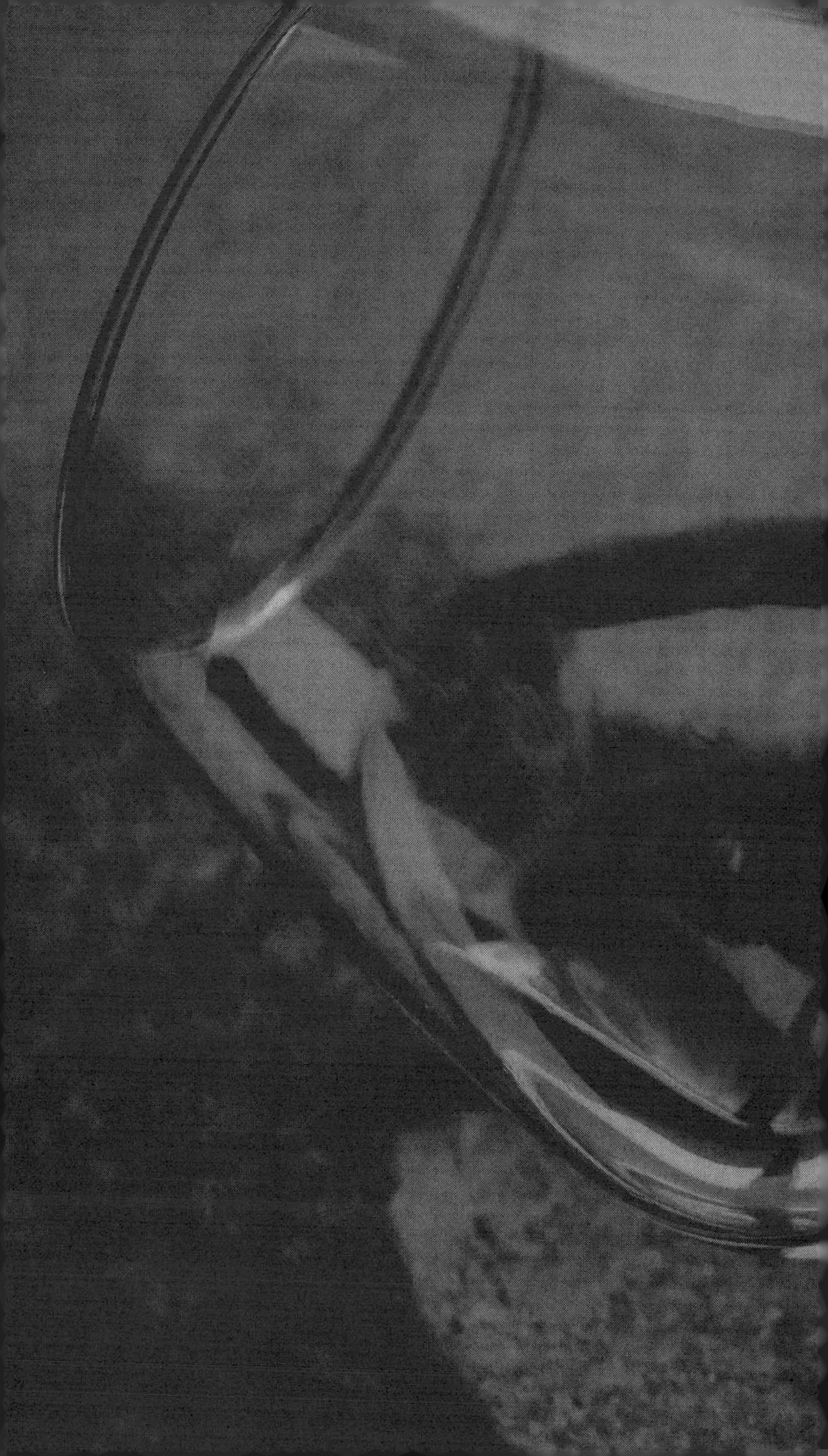

8

Seamus

I could still taste her on my tongue.

That delicious nectar that could sate a thirsting man on the brink of dehydration in the desert. Bailey was perfect, a goddess. I'd spend the rest of my life buried between her thighs if I could get away with it.

"Do you think she'll be of use?" My father sat down at the head of the family table. Sundays were meant for family. If you lived under his roof, you attended lunch and dinner without question. The world had better have ended if it was missed. Not that any of us would. The only person exempt from weekly family time was our mother, and good riddance to that.

Ava had been thrilled about having a weekly family day since she'd never been allowed to linger with the Wards growing up. She'd been isolated most of her life before meeting Dashkov, and even now, I could sense in my sister that there was still the feeling of lingering isolation she was trying to shake.

Unfortunately, her being here also meant that her Russian dick of a husband had to come too.

Just what we needed.

"I doubt she'll be giving us any insider secrets," Kiernan admitted with a shrug. "But we can try to see what we can get out of her. Tell her what we know about him. Make her see that he's not some knight in shining armor."

"What if she already knows and is complicit?" My father raised a good point. We knew little about Bailey. It was possible that she was in on what her adopted father did in the shadows.

"Her career choice in investigative reporting could be so that she can report back to him on what she finds. Make the charges stick? Maybe plant some false leads that lead to arrests? It would be a boon for Crowe to have something like that working on his side."

"I wouldn't think so," I told him honestly. "Out of all the reporters we know, her articles are the least biased."

"You should ask about her father's involvement with Toph Eriksen."

That came out of left field.

"No one asked you, fucker," Kiernan growled, earning a stern look from our father.

"Kiernan," Ava hissed, but the Russian didn't seem perturbed. He was probably used to being insulted.

"Not polite to eavesdrop," Kiernan snarled.

Matthias smirked, taking his seat next to Ava, whose place had become on our father's left side. A place that would have normally been reserved for our mother, but she hardly ever showed up at family dinners, and my father never pressured her about it.

"Your voice carries like a spoiled child begging his mother for candy at the grocery store. Trust me, there was no need to eavesdrop."

Well, shit. Shots fired.

I couldn't help but laugh while my brother glared at the man, his own lips twitching mildly, trying his best not to react.

"Whatever," he mumbled petulantly and took a sip of his beer, his eyes on the elevator.

We'd both been reluctant to leave Bailey with Dani. Our cousin was an amazing doctor, top of her class in med school, but she was a bit rough around the edges. Dani was used to dealing with fuckers in the emergency room at Seattle Memorial, and when she wasn't doing that, she was attending to the wives and girlfriends of our men, and that meant she had to have a certain hardness to her.

Especially since she took after her mother in the looks department. Most of the wives and girlfriends didn't want her anywhere near them because it meant their husbands or boyfriends would see her.

Petty bitches.

Dani was also a mafia princess. Her grandfather was my grandfather's brother. My father's uncle and that meant she was royalty, and that pissed some of the wives off for sure. She didn't have to earn her place or marry into it. Whoever she married would be below her in rank, since we didn't hold women to a lesser standard than men like the *Bratva*.

Most *Bratvas*.

Apparently, Dracula over there had a similar structure when it came to females who served under him. Even allowing them to become enforcers and hold leadership positions. We hadn't gotten that far yet. Women weren't allowed near any type of enforcement positions, but they weren't kept from the day-to-day dealings if that was what they wanted.

"What can you tell me about Eriksen's relationship with the senator?" My father's question dragged me back to the conversation. He quietly ordered a whiskey from one of the kitchen staff we employed on the housing level before turning back to Matthias.

The Russian wrinkled his nose like he'd just caught a whiff of something sour. Dashkov and Eriksen weren't enemies, but like us, prior to Ava, they weren't friends either. Many people had a strong beef against my father in the underground, and Eriksen seemed to be at the top of the list. What none of us could figure out was why. If he was working with the senator, it could spell disaster.

"I've heard about your problems with both of them," Matthias admitted, nodding a thanks to the maid who handed him his drink. "I haven't personally had any dealing with the man, but my little birds tell me he's been seen meeting with several of Richard Crowe's men."

"I thought Crowe wanted the biker gangs and mafiosos out of the city," Ava said. "He and Elias would hold strategy meetings. I thought it was Elias trying to become more political, but since I learned Matthias had him under his thumb, it makes more sense that he was trying to push him out of the city."

"The things you paid attention to astound me, *malyshka*." Matthias held up her hand and kissed the back of it. Kiernan gagged at the show of affection.

"Ouch," he hissed, then glared at our sister. "Did you just kick me like a five-year-old?"

Ava stuck out her tongue at him. "Don't act like one, then."

I couldn't help but laugh at their sibling antics. Even my father was smiling, his eyes darting between the two.

"What I wonder is why the arranged marriage with Knight?" Matthias wondered. "I'd heard rumors of it a few years ago, but not much since. It doesn't seem to have a purpose, especially since Bailey isn't the socialite her sister is.

She doesn't even carry Crowe's last name. Besides a few appearances here and there at social functions, she is practically a ghost. And why wait so long to get married? It would have been more prudent to marry them when she turned eighteen, and she's nearly twenty-six now."

"That does seem odd," Kiernan pointed out. "Knight has a huge amount of political capital, and if he backs Crowe in that election, he's a shoo-in. Maybe that was why they waited. Stage the wedding right before the election. Voters would eat that up."

"Crowe could have run for office years ago," my father said. "Why wait?"

"It is unusual," Matthias said, tilting his head in agreement. "Maybe he is waiting for something."

"Maybe she didn't want to marry him." Ava's face twisted, her nose wrinkling in distaste. If anyone had a reason to hate arranged or forced marriages, it was Ava. Matthias had forced her to marry him when he first took her as collateral against the man she had thought was her father.

Our father had been livid when he'd found out but had come to accept that despite how Matthias had forced Ava to marry him, she was safe with him, and for some odd reason, she seemed to care for the Russian potato.

Questionable taste, in my opinion.

"Bridgett said that Drew Knight has been trying to get out from under his father's thumb," Kiernan added.

"That could have something to do with the delay," Matthias mused. "Maybe he was against the marriage and was trying to figure out a way to get out of whatever contract his father had with Crowe. He would have to do it just right, though. Everyone knows that daddy dearest has had a tight leash on his son's finances."

"Where did he get all the money to finance his startup, then?" Da wondered.

Matthias shrugged. "I'm not sure," he admitted. "When he got into the security game, we looked into every aspect of his business but couldn't place where he had gotten the cash to fund everything. He didn't have any known investors in the first few years. No doubt people would have been too afraid to cross his father. But I do know that there has been an influx in activity the past few weeks with Crowe. Eriksen has been meeting up with Crowe's men, and over the past twenty-four hours, Magnus has been panicking about something."

"Maybe because the arranged marriage he set up is about to come crumbling down," I told him, smirking.

Matthias's forehead creased in confusion. "How would you know that?"

"Because I refuse to marry a cheating pig."

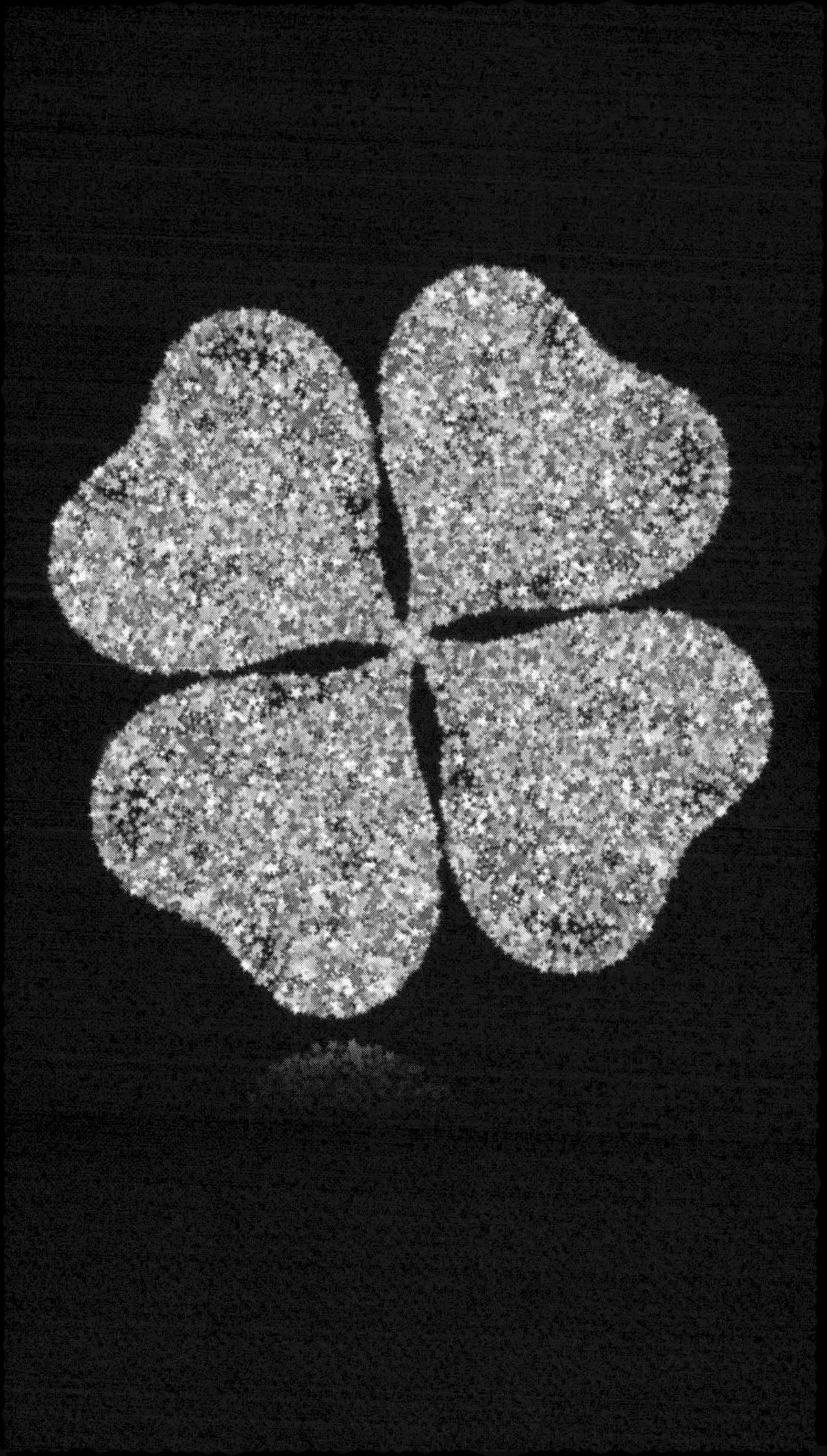

9

Bailey

The building was nothing short of awe-inspiring.

Nan led me down the hallway toward the elevator, filling the silence with idle chatter about the structure. The building was built in the late eighteen hundreds by Kane O'Connell, Seattle's first Irish mob boss. It was continually added on to until the end of the O'Connell mob in the late 1950s. It laid vacant until Nan's husband, Finn Kavanaugh, took claim over it when he moved from Boston in the nineties.

"There are seven floors, plus a parking garage," Nan rambled as we stepped into the elevator. I wondered if she was aware of how much the chatter helped my nerves and racing pulse. "The ground floor is made up mostly of the McDonough's bar. The second floor is the family area. Living room, kitchen, and the likes. The third and fourth floor are the residential suites for the main family. The fourth floor belongs to Liam, and only his print can open it. The final floors house the soldiers without anywhere to go."

"The whole family lives in this one building?"

That was a lot of people all living under the same roof, constantly being underfoot. Liam Kavanaugh had two more sons and a daughter, and I couldn't imagine what it would be like when everyone was home at the same time.

Nan laughed. "Jaysus, no." She smiled at me through the reflective mirror of the doors. "Liam and his wife have a house near Greenlake, and the young'uns reside in Ireland for the time being. The twins have an apartment somewhere. God knows where. The two of them move more often than a plow sowing a field."

"Oh."

Was that all I could say? Nan must have thought my brain was addled. Not that I cared much.

Okay, maybe I did a little.

When the doors to the elevator opened, the scent of freshly brewed coffee and bacon assaulted my senses. My mouth watered, and my stomach rumbled. Shit, I hadn't eaten since lunchtime yesterday.

My gaze took in every detail of the floor, searching and cataloging everything I could. It was an open concept, with windows spanning from floor-to-ceiling across the farthest outside wall that overlooked the main street below. Wooden columns dotted the space that was softly decorated. The walls were red brick, unpainted, left in their natural state. It was homey as much as it was luxurious. Leather sofas in hues of burnt orange sat facing an overly large flat screen that hung on the wall. Bookcases crammed with books littered the space, which smelled of pine and tobacco.

Voices drifted from the dining room as we approached. They weren't bothering to modulate their tone, and it became increasingly clear as we approached who they were talking about.

Me.

"Maybe because the arranged marriage he set up is about to come crumbling down." That was Seamus. He sounded somewhat smug when he said it, his accent dipping slightly. It was one way I could tell him apart from his brother. That and the shiner Kiernan now had was a dead giveaway.

"How would you know that?" That wasn't an Irish accent.

"Because I refuse to marry a cheating pig," I interrupted as I stepped into the massive dining room. My eyes widened slightly, taking it all in. I wasn't sure what I had been expecting, but it wasn't this.

The table was long and sturdy. A rich, handcrafted acacia wood table with a river of blue resin winding through it. Several dishes stuffed with an assortment of foods, from crisp, mouthwatering bacon to a light fruit salad, were spread across its surface. I stopped just inside the doorway. All eyes were immediately on me. Suddenly, I was regretting my sudden outburst.

A sea of emerald stared back at me, plus the stormy eyes of one man everyone knew about, but few barely glimpsed.

Matthias Dashkov.

That was the accent I had heard.

"Thank you for joining us, Miss Jameson." The man at the head of the table pulled my attention. His smile was tight, not quite reaching his eyes. He was older, but his red hair graying slightly along the edges was his only sign of aging.

He looked like a king sitting at the head of the table with his well-trimmed beard, his muscles easily visible beneath the button-down shirt he wore that stretched tightly over his chest. It was a glimpse into the future—a replica of what the twins would one day grow to become.

One word. Yummy.

Yummier, anyway.

They were already mouthwateringly delicious.

Where the fuck do I come up with this shit?

"I wasn't aware it was a choice." I shrugged, feigning

nonchalance. "But thanks for the invite. I'm starving." Kiernan smirked as I made my way toward him. The empty seat between him and the gaping Seamus had obviously been left empty for me.

"Close your mouth, Seamus," I chided playfully as I took a seat. "You are not a codfish."

The woman seated across from him at the table giggled while Dashkov, who sat closely to her right, chuckled lowly. Not every day you see a mafia boss chuckling at a reporter. That was one for the win column.

The man I easily inferred to be Liam Kavanaugh, the head of the Irish mob and the twins' father, smirked in amusement, his green eyes lighting up.

"There is always a choice, Miss Jameson," he told me. "You could have said no and gone hungry."

"Wouldn't be the first time," I muttered under my breath, absently looking down at my bare plate. There weren't many memories of my mother left for my mind to cling to, but the ones that stood out above everything were the days I'd gone hungry. Left without food or care. She'd do that. Leave me without a care in the world while she sought her high in the back of some dealer's car or in a back alley.

Shaking off the depressing thoughts, I smiled up at the feared Irish leader. "Call me Bailey. If your sons are going to hold me captive and feed me, you might as well drop the formalities."

The redheaded woman snorted her drink at my words, which led the burly Russian mafia leader to pat her on the back as she struggled to cough up the fluid that had undoubtedly found its way down the wrong tube.

Oops. Apparently, I had more comedic prowess than I realized.

I stared at the coughing woman for a moment as she struggled to breathe properly again. She could almost be the twins' triplet. Her red hair was wild and untamed, slightly darker in color, the curls falling well past her shoulders. Her green eyes were the same luminous emerald as the rest of the Kavanaughs'. There were faint traces of bruising along her face and scrapes across her knuckles.

This woman was a fighter.

"Tell me who put a hit out on our sister."

This must be the woman Jimmy Burlosconi had been hired to kill. What an idiot. Anyone with half a brain would have stayed far away from the contract no matter how much money was put down. Not only was she obviously involved with the head of the Dashkov *Bratva*, but she was also a Kavanaugh.

"Very well." Liam inclined his head at me. "Then you may call me Liam. Seamus and Kiernan, you obviously already know."

Cue heated cheeks.

"They did kidnap me," I pointed out somewhat jovially to deter attention away from the embarrassment creeping up my neck. *Did they suspect what we did?* Kiernan pinched the bridge of his nose and groaned quietly next to me, his elbow resting on the arm of his chair. If they expected me to be intimidated or frightened, they were in for a surprise. I wasn't some wilting flower or damsel in distress, and I sure as hell wasn't going to be cowed by the amount of power sitting at this table.

I would, however, crawl under the table at the first sign of a sexual innuendo.

Even Superman had his Kryptonite.

"Indeed." The corners of Liam's mouth turned up slightly. At least I amused him. That was better than annoyed or aggravated. "This is my eldest daughter, Avaleigh." He motioned to the woman sitting across from Seamus, who winced at the use of her name.

"Ava is fine." She sighed as she put her hand on the *Bratva* leader's shoulder. "This is my husband, Matthias Dashkov."

Ah, yes. I remember hearing about the Dashkov wedding. Lucille, who had been the journalist covering the extravagant event, had gone on an immediate sabbatical after the wedding turned into a massacre. Elias Ward's daughter Libby had been brutally shot and several others had lost their lives as well. If that wasn't enough of a showstopper, the FBI rolled in during the aftermath and arrested the surly *Bratva* leader for murder.

Those charges were false, of course. Matthias Dashkov had been getting away with murder for years. He wasn't about to let himself be caught on camera killing his rival. They just needed a reason to hold him. I wondered why. I'd been covering the arrest, but since it had led nowhere, the story ended up dead in the water. Even the FBI refused to comment on why they had let him walk out.

I could ask him.

"We're acquainted." Matthias shot me a dark look. Nope, I would not be asking him anything at all. But then again, even if I didn't want to get eaten, that didn't mean I couldn't poke the bear a little.

"I don't believe I've had the pleasure." I tilted my head. Even sitting, I had to angle my chin up slightly to look directly into his eyes. The man was tall.

The Russian smirked dangerously.

"Detective Monty Belgrade told me all about your invested interest in the fire at the shipping port not that long ago," he lazily explained, as if it was somehow common knowledge. "And your interest in the explosion at the Ward stables. Both times, you've tried to muscle your way into the investigation and into interrogating the freed women. He thought that it was something I'd want to be aware of."

Fucking Monty.

Never trust a cop whose name sounded like it came straight out of a bad eighties' television show.

Several weeks ago, there had been a fire at the Port of Seattle where investigators found containers of kidnapped women along with drugs and weapons that had been smuggled in from overseas. Not long after that, the Ward stables, where Lina had been investigating the trafficking ring, also exploded and caught fire. More than a dozen women were rescued then as well. I'd been attempting to get an *interview* with the rescued women since the incidents but had been blocked at several turns.

Someone, no doubt Dashkov, had completely annihilated Elias Ward's shipping containers down at the port. The ones that hadn't been blown to smithereens had been holding the women and illegal contraband from Mexico.

They had to have come from Elias's stables, which meant one of them might have seen Lina. When the stables also blew up, I tried to find Lina, or someone who had seen her. Again, I'd been blocked at every turn for a chance to talk to any of them. I'd even used my father's name.

That had not gone over well.

"Should have known he was dirty," I sneered. "Especially with a name like Monty."

Dashkov chuckled. "He's not as dirty as you think," he told me, nodding his head in thanks to his wife when she handed him his plate. Yum, BLT sandwiches. My favorite. "Monty is actually a very good cop."

"If you say so." I snorted, making a grab for a few slices of bread. Seamus smacked my hand away. "Hey."

The asshat didn't bother to respond. He simply swept my

plate away and grabbed the slices of bread himself to begin layering a sandwich. *My sandwich.* I went to remark about how I could plate my own food and I wasn't some child, but one scathing look from him stopped my complaint dead in its tracks.

Great.

"I do," Matthias continued, amusement written across his face as he watched my frustration mount at having the twins make my food.

My inner feminist was fuming, steam rolling out of her ears and everything.

Were they going to hand feed me too?

But there was that small niggle in my brain, the one that softened at the thought of them caring for me. I'd never had that before. Growing up, I'd learned to do things for myself. Sure, I was taken care of, but I was never held or loved. This small gesture, however misogynistic I thought it was, warmed something inside me. Something dangerous.

"Good for you," I huffed, impatiently waiting to eat. Sue me. I was hungry. If they wanted a docile prisoner, they shouldn't have taken me. "But any cop who's willing to take bribes and squirrel away your misdeed for cash isn't a good cop."

"Says who? You?"

"Everyone?" That didn't come out as confident as I hoped.

"And who is everyone, little one?" Dashkov raised an expectant brow at me. "Your politician father and his friends? Those men and women are just as corrupt as some of my police officers. More so, if you ask me, since they don't need the money. Most of them have less regard for who they are screwing over than Monty does. And believe it or not, he was worried about your safety."

Doubtful.

"He swore an oath to uphold the law."

"So did your father, and those he holds in his grasp like Polly Pockets," he pointed out, taking a bite of his sandwich. My mouth watered. "Monty needed the money to pay for his son's chemotherapy. Something his insurance refused to cover. Now, I'll admit I have some shady cops who do shady shit on my payroll, but Monty is not one of them. Sure, from time to time he might pass along information he finds relevant. Might steer an investigation away from me, but he'll never mistreat innocent people, nor will he plant evidence or put drugs on the street where they don't belong."

That was amusing. I also found it amusing that he was painting my father to be the bad guy. The villain in his story.

"What do you call what you did to Elias Ward, if not evidence planting? Those women were in too clean containers to have been kept there for long. And he may not put drugs on the street himself, but he knows you do. He's still complicit."

Matthias smiled. It was scary. Like a predator smiling at his prey.

"We didn't plant those women or guns. We simply relocated them."

"Elias had another set of storage containers at the port listed under an alias." Ava spoke up before I had the chance to begin my rebuttal. "The women had been held in those containers for nearly a week without any food or water. We knew that if we wanted to take Elias down, we had to move those assets where they could be linked back to him."

"Thought of that plan herself." Seamus smiled proudly at his sister before he leaned over to whisper in my ear. "You can eat now, wildcat."

Thanks for the permission, jackass. My inner bitch bristled. Grabbing the loaded sandwich with two hands, I took a large bite, making a show of shoving it in my mouth, sneering when his eyes danced with amusement at my childish behavior. The table grew silent as everyone ate, too consumed with devouring their lunch to bother with any more conversation or banter.

The food was a culinary masterpiece for being something so simple. The mixture of herbs and spices that had been mixed with the mayonnaise assaulted my senses. The crisp smell of bacon and freshly baked bread made me understand the true meaning of food porn. The potato fries were freshly cut and fried, served with a side of ranch dip.

I couldn't remember a time that I had actually enjoyed eating. Dinner in my house was a formal affair, and my food was often restricted for "image" purposes.

The silence surrounding the table wasn't awkward or stifling, and once everyone had begun to finish up their plates, a low hum of voices began to rise. Nan, who had been sitting quietly next to Dashkov, was currently chatting up the twins' sister in quiet conversation, while the burly Russian sipped his drink, pretending not to listen to the pair.

On either side of me, the twins were shoveling food into their mouths like it was their last meal. My eyes fell on their father. He glanced up from his plate, his gaze flitting to mine before shifting to Ava, who had asked him a question too low for me to hear.

"We need to solidify a plan for the gala." Dashkov spoke up, pushing his plate away. Within moments, the server had cleared it from the table. He leaned back in his chair more comfortably, an ankle resting on his knee.

"We've already gone over the plan." Seamus glared at him. "Several times."

Talk about tension. None of the Kavanaughs seemed

particularly fond of the *Bratva* leader, even though he was married to their kin. I wondered idly what the story was between them. The Irish and Russians had never been allies before, and it had me wondering if Ava was the reason behind the sudden alliance.

I didn't recall Ava's name ever being mentioned in Kavanaughs' family tree, yet he'd introduced her as his daughter.

Dashkov nodded his head. "Yes, but we'll need to alter them now that your twin resembles Mike Tyson with that nose of his."

Ava snorted.

"Can't say he didn't deserve it," I grumbled under my breath. Ava cackled from her chair, hand bracing itself on Matthias's shoulder. The surly Russian also seemed amused. Or his lips were having a minor seizure.

It was anyone's guess.

"Moving on from whether my son deserved his black eye and broken nose," Liam rubbed at his temples and sighed, "Matthias is right. Kiernan won't be able to attend the gala with his broken nose. It should be healed up enough for the auction, but with the gala only being a week away, Seamus will have to go in alone."

"His crooked snout wouldn't be easy to cover," Ava teased. Kiernan lifted his gaze to glare at her. "But a little concealer would cover up his bruising."

"I won't be wearing any of your girly shite."

Down girl.

Damn, he was even hotter when he was mad. The slight deepening of his native accent had my body shivering and my thighs clamping together beneath the table. Who knew I had a thing for accents?

"Actors wear it all the time."

"Do I look like a fucking actor to you?"

"Of course not," Ava admitted. Kiernan shot her a smug smile. "Actors are way better looking than your ugly mug."

His smug smile dropped like a bomb.

Biting my lip, I did my best to hold back the laughter, hoping neither twin would notice with their attention fixed on their sister. Kiernan's large hand squeezed my thigh under the table, telling me he hadn't missed it.

"Enough, you three."

"Three?" Seamus's eyes widened at his father in mock disbelief. "What did I do? I was literally sitting here."

"Reason enough." Liam winked at his son. "Now, let's get down to business."

"To defeat the Huns..." Seamus finished the song. Everyone at the table shook with laughter, including me.

"The lord gave me idiots for sons." Liam shook his head.

"We don't need them both at the gala anymore." Ava spoke up, graciously accepting a cup of coffee from one of the servers.

"Would you like a cup of coffee, Bailey?" Ava asked, her brilliant green eyes finding mine.

"Yes, please," I smiled at her gratefully. The server nodded at me before taking my plate and retreating to the kitchen.

"They make the best coffee here." Ava smiled. "Nan says they get their coffee from a small farm in Guatemala that hand picks the beans to make sure that they roast just right."

"Our sister is a coffee nut."

Ava shrugged. "Just a little. But what I am really into is information. And you, Bailey, have all the information we need. Don't you?" The sweet smile she'd adorned throughout lunch dropped faster than a guillotine. In its place stood the smile of a shark that smelled blood in the water. My blood.

"I don't understand." I glanced from one twin to the other, eyes wide, but they gave nothing away. Their faces were nothing more than stoic masks, unrelenting.

"Why are you so interested in interviewing the women at the port?" Ava tilted her head at me, mug pressed between both of her hands. The look in her eyes was calculating and cold. A far cry from the jovial, carefree woman that had been there just moments ago.

"Who wouldn't want a scoop like that?" A shrug of my shoulder conveyed an innocence I didn't feel. "That was one of the biggest human trafficking busts in years."

Ava huffed mirthlessly, her head shaking slightly as she continued to eye me from across the table.

"I don't believe that."

"Believe what you want." I frowned, no doubt giving away my air of nonchalance.

Tension in the room was strung tight, and I was walking a thin rope above a pool of hungry, hungry sharks that wouldn't hesitate to devour me if I gave them a chance.

"I think you were looking for someone," Matthias spoke up. "A Lina Davenport, if I'm not mistaken."

"Monty has a big fucking mouth," I growled, wincing slightly when Seamus's hand tightened on my thigh in warning.

"Watch your language," he warned. My nose flared as I met his hard stare with one of my own.

"I checked into her." Matthias kept going, as if Seamus hadn't reprimanded me. "No one but you seems to be worried about her being missing."

"Lina and I were working on a sex trafficking story together. She said she'd found a weak link in Elias Ward's organization. Someone who could get her in undetected." I took a deep breath and slowly let it out. "Lina was supposed to check in with me three days later. She never did. When I went to her house, everything was cleared out. It was like she suddenly became a ghost. Tony, my boss, said she'd quit. Planned on moving to Texas to be with her parents."

"And you didn't believe him?"

I scoffed, taking a sip of the hot coffee the server had brought me. "Lina's parents were abusive alcoholics who died in a house fire last year. Kind of hard to move in with their ashes. Lina and I have been friends for years. She wouldn't just up and move without telling me."

"So you thought the girls at the port might have seen her." Dashkov confirmed what he already knew. "Thought maybe they could tell you where they'd seen her last."

I nodded. "Only problem was," I wrinkled my nose, "both the port and the stables Elias had been holding women in were blown to smithereens." I shot a pointed look at Liam. "Thanks for that."

"I'd do it again if it meant rescuing Ava." He looked over at her, eyes glowing with affection. A lump grew in my throat. My father had never once looked at me with even a fraction of the affection that Liam was giving his daughter.

"None of the girls in the *stables* were named Lina," Kiernan told me. "Nearly all of them were Mexican, and the rest Ukrainian. All of them underage as well."

Silence settled over Kiernan's statement. All eyes were focused on me, their gazes soft as they gave me time to process what I'd learned.

Lina was gone.

Lost.

If she hadn't been at the stables, then she'd either been sold or was dead. Either way, I wouldn't be finding her, especially not on my own.

"There might be a chance," Matthias spoke up, his

Russian accent filling the heavy air, but his words lightened the fog that had descended around me.

"No," Kiernan growled. "I know what you're thinking, and absolutely not. We agreed to get information from her, not use her as a tool."

"What?" I asked, brow furrowing. My gaze shifted between the pair.

"She's the perfect spy and our best chance at getting the information we need."

Kiernan's lips twisted into an ugly snarl. "If you think I'm going to risk her like that, you're bloody fucking crazy."

"What?" I repeated, my voice gaining a frantic pitch. Did Matthias know something about Lina? Did he have a way to find her? Maybe he planned on having me become bait and go undercover. I turned to Kiernan. "What is he talking about?"

"Nothing." His jaw clenched and the hand on my thigh gripped tighter.

"She's the perfect—"

"I said no," Kiernan roared, surging to his feet. His chair scraped across the wooden floor loudly.

"Kier." Seamus bit his lip anxiously, his eyes darting between his brother and me. "Maybe we should see what information we can get from her about him and then let her hear the truth."

Kiernan sneered at his brother. "And if he catches her?" he snapped. "Say she believes what we tell her. What then? Even if she does believe the evidence, who is going to protect her if she gets caught?"

Evidence?

Evidence against whom?

Kiernan's rage continued. "I am not going to take the chance he catches her and sells her to some perverted fucking—"

"Enough," Liam barked. His hand came down roughly on the table, shaking the wood. I startled, my body stiffening at his outburst. When my father got that way, it meant a beating. A lesson to keep me in line. He'd never raise his hand to me himself, though. Fernando would be the one to strike at me. His whip, he called him.

"Sit down, son." Kiernan hesitated. "Now."

Growling, he did as commanded, sliding the chair closer to mine so we were nearly on top of one another.

"I don't understand." My gaze darted from one person to the next. "Who are you so worried about?"

"Your father, lass." Liam's jaw ticked. "Richard Crowe."

My father? What did he have to do with any of this?

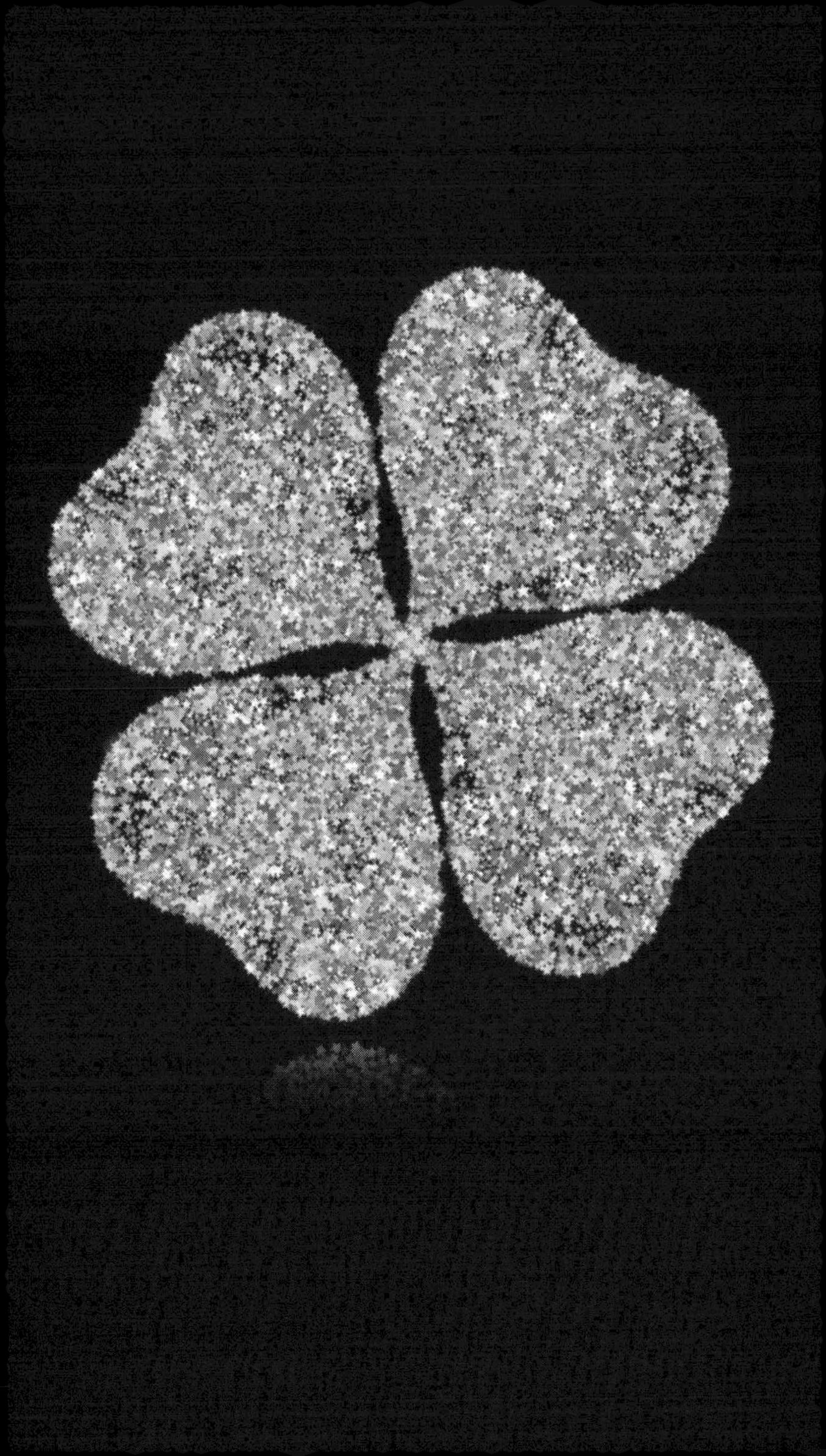

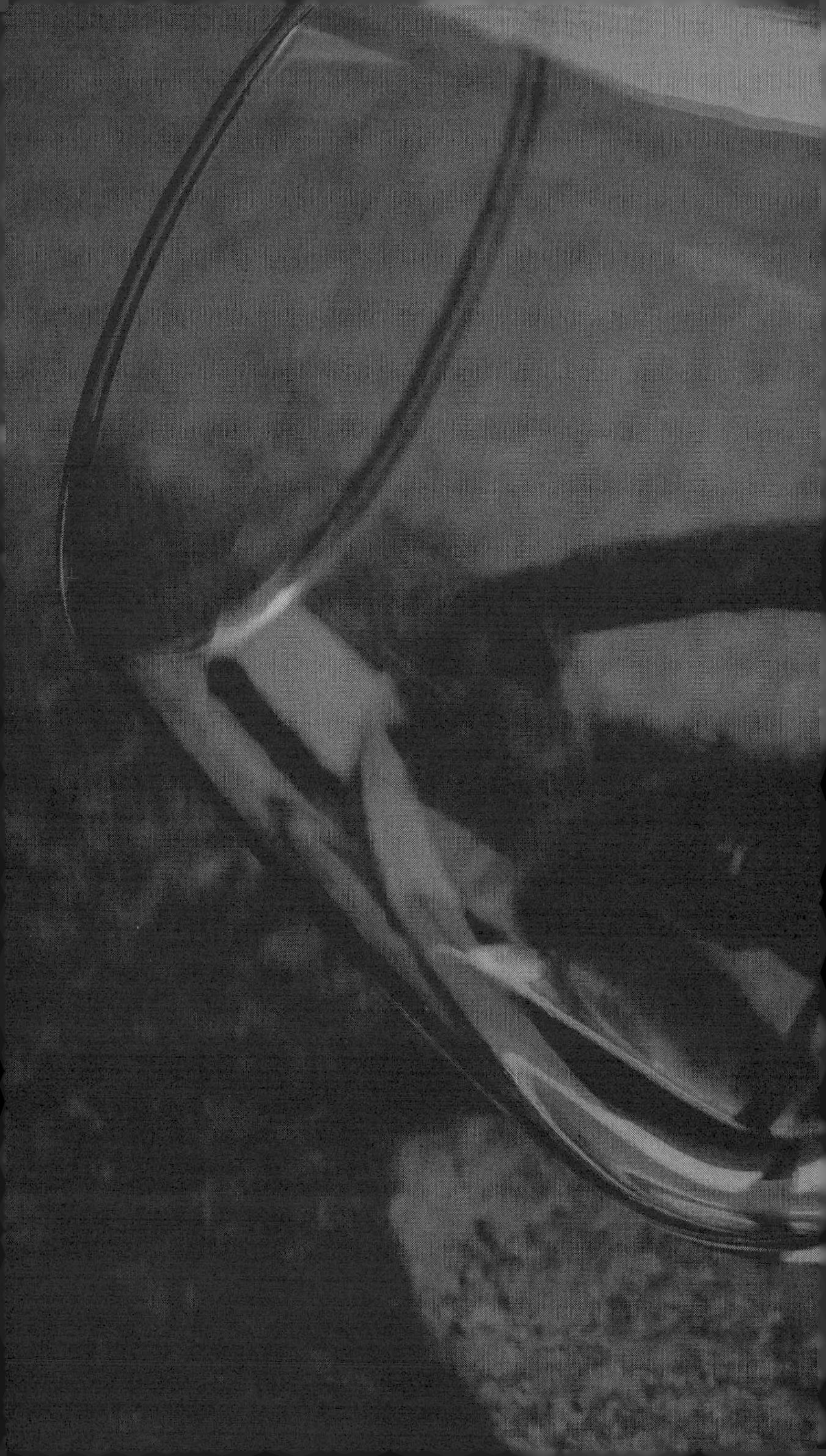

10

Bailey

My father? Why would they be worried about my father hurting me? Sure, he was stern, and I'd had to learn a lesson or two over the years, but he had never raised a hand to me himself. My father was an exacting man. He'd spent years in the Marine Corps before becoming a politician. He required order and discipline.

That didn't mean he would ever hurt me.

"My father is a good man," I assured them earnestly. "He would never hurt me."

It unnerved me to know that they had somehow discovered the link to my father. I was very careful not to use his name in any way outside of our social circles, which I was rarely invited to, anyway. We didn't even share the same last name. When he'd "adopted" me at the age of three, he'd let me keep my mother's surname, telling the media that he didn't want to diminish the memory of my biological family.

I barely remember the media storm that had ensued after I was adopted. My father had told everyone that my stepmother couldn't bear any more children and that she'd always wanted another daughter. They'd said that it had been love at first sight when they saw me.

As if. My cunt of a stepmother barely spent more than a few moments in the same room as me unless it was required. Over time, the media storm around my adoption died down and so did the family fanfare. They shoved me in the background. I'd been put away like fine china. Only to be glimpsed on special occasions before being packed back up again.

"He may never have laid a hand on you," Liam told me, "but he is far from a good man. Trust me on that."

Trust him? The mob boss who killed people and ran drugs and weapons through the city wanted me to trust him?

"You don't know my father."

Liam smiled sadly. "Adoptive father," he reminded me. "And I know more than you think."

"Still my father," I bit out. "And if you're expecting me to give you some inside information, you can forget it."

That was a fine line between truth and a lie.

I knew little about his work or campaigns. He never involved me in his political career like he did my older sister. She was his legitimate daughter, and I was nothing more than his hidden indiscretion.

There was something I was aware of, however. I knew that he and the DA were launching an all-out attack on the criminal underground, and Dashkov and Kavanaugh were at the top of the list. Washington was crawling with mafioso types. You wouldn't know it, mostly because everyone believed the mafia had been nearly eradicated in the 1970s when the RICO act had been passed.

That was a lie.

The American Mafia had simply slid beneath the radar, moving west, taking over old Yakuza and Chinese Triad territories. It was in the late 1980s that the underground had been established, spreading up from California like a cancerous disease, slowly making its way back toward the East Coast.

From what I'd been able to ascertain, the underground was run by one representative from each of the most powerful ruling families, but that was just a rumor.

Now, most mafia families were legitimate business owners. Casinos, hotels, resorts—anything that gave them an opportunity to funnel blood money through. It was genius, really.

If you didn't get caught.

My father had been trying to topple the mafia empire for as long as I could remember. He was constantly cursing and complaining, murmuring about how they were an infestation. I wasn't sure where the animosity came from. Crime wasn't running rampant in Seattle, not like it used to, but nothing would deter my father. He was dead set against every mafia family in the city, even if it meant going against the mayor.

"Not really selling yourself, are you?" Seamus quirked a brow. "You're supposed to be giving us a reason to keep you alive."

My chest tightened and my eyes widened slightly at his statement. Did they really plan on killing me?

"Seamus," Ava scolded.

Playing off my fear, I let out a derisive snort. "It wouldn't matter what I told you, anyway." I sniffed. "I'm well versed in how the mafia works. If you wanted to kill me, it wouldn't matter what reason I gave you to keep me alive; you'd still eliminate me."

"Well versed?" Kiernan asked.

I shot him a smug look. "Did you think I got into investigative reporting by accident?" I snarked. "My father has told me everything about how you mafioso types want to destroy the good he's worked for."

Chuckles of amusement rose up around the table. I didn't see what was so amusing about what I'd said.

"Let me guess." Dashkov eyed me from across the table. "Your father is the one who got you into reporting."

"No," I told him smugly. "He was against it."

"But he was the one who nudged you to work on investigative reporting, wasn't he?" Was it bad manners to punch a smirking mafia boss in the face? "And when you did, he no doubt pushed you into writing your little stories about the mafia. Telling you all the bad things we do and how we're out to get him."

I huffed. "They're not just stories. They're facts."

Kiernan grunted. "Sure, they are." He smirked. "But we'll come back to that later."

Not if I have anything to do with it.

How and why I became an investigative reporter was inconsequential. What did it matter if my father strung me along the path? I was doing good. Helping to shed light on the criminal activity in the city.

My father never pushed me to write about the mafia or the Seattle underground. He tolerated but did not support my career as a reporter. The only reason he had allowed it was because Drew had supported it for his own personal gains.

Marriage and becoming a dutiful housewife were what my father had planned for me.

There were times when my father talked more openly about what the mafia had been doing in the city. I'd chased some of my best leads with the information he'd let slip at the dinner table or at business meetings he'd have in his office.

"Why don't you tell us about your father's deal with Magnus Knight?"

Not gonna happen.

The twins exchanged an unreadable look at my silence.

"Bailey." Kiernan's voice held a darkened edge to it. A warning.

Good girls get rewarded. Bad girls get punished.

Yeah, fuck that shit. I wouldn't be telling them anything related to my father or his business. Not that I knew much, but they didn't need to know that.

"What about your adoption records?" A smile spread across Liam's face at my sudden flinch. Shit. "No one can seem to find anything on your sudden adoption, Bailey. Not even sealed records. I find that rather interesting."

My hand clenched around my mug. "You really shouldn't."

"It just piques my interest that there wouldn't be a single trace of you." He leaned back in his chair, eyes gleaming as his gaze challenged me. "Your birth certificate doesn't list a father, and the woman listed is labeled as a missing person."

"You're a real Jack Taylor," I drawled. "Got it all figured out." My jaw ticked, and my teeth clenched as I struggled not to give anything away. I knew it was too late. I might as well have just screamed that there was something wrong at the top of my lungs. One thing I'd never been good at was deception. My father said I wore my emotions on my sleeve. Too open and naïve, he'd told me.

"Answer the questions, Bailey," Seamus growled next to me, his hand coming to the back of my neck, applying just enough pressure to exert his dominance but not enough to hurt.

"Don't pretend like you know anything about me or my family," I hissed at them. "My father is a good man who's made it his life's mission to see men like you wiped out of business."

"You want to know about your family?" Seamus hissed, tightening his hold on my neck. "Your father is a murderer. A coward who hides behind his social standing and the men he sends to kill those who are in his way. And for what? Prestige? To get into office? He may be a pillar of the community to the people of your fancy country club, but down here, in the real world? He's in bed with some of the city's worst gangs. He's a killer, just like us. The only difference is we do it to survive. Your father does it for his own selfish reasons. So before you laugh at how little we know, remember that you're still the enemy's daughter and show my father some respect. Hear me?"

I nodded as much as I could with the harsh grip he had on the back of my neck.

"Good."

He let go of my neck. His mouth turned down slightly at the edges when I eased away from him, but his face remained hard.

"He's not like that," I whispered, my hand massaging where he'd gripped me. Seamus hadn't gripped me tight enough to bruise, but it still wasn't pleasant. Didn't stop my panties from being soaked through at his sudden display of dominance. My thighs had clenched together beneath the table, and I was glad that no one seemed to notice my body's sudden arousal.

I wondered if I could get that lobotomy now.

Maybe electroshock therapy.

"He is," Kiernan insisted lowly. No. My father was a good man. He had never been my knight in shining armor, but he was still my father.

"I may not know a lot about his political career, but I know one thing for sure. He's not a murderer. And he sure as hell isn't in bed with any gangs. He's been trying to run the gangs and mafia out of the city. That's his whole political stance."

"That is what he sells to the press, Bailey." Kiernan's tone was gentle. "Your family has been involved with the local gangs since long before your father became a senator. Your own grandfather moved and manipulated many of the gangs in the city to do his dirty work."

"No."

"We've had proof of it for a very long time," Seamus told me. "We can show you everything. His deals run deep, Bailey. From embezzlement of charity funds to gunrunning. Even human trafficking and drug distribution."

Human trafficking and drug distribution.

My father would never be involved in any of that. These people were tainting his name, trying to get me to turn against the man who'd taken me in. The man who'd kept me when he could have given me away. Even if I wasn't known as his biological daughter, he had still adopted me. Claimed me.

"Tell us about his deal with Magnus Knight," Kiernan urged. "Help us and we can help you."

I lifted my gaze from where it had been focused on the table to his darkened gaze. He wasn't pleading. Wasn't begging. His eyes were hard, but there was something I didn't recognize behind that stern façade. Something that made my gut churn with butterflies. Something I refused to name.

Fuck this.

Two simple words that I hadn't realized I'd uttered aloud until Ava gasped in surprise and Kiernan's gaze darkened murderously. He reached for me, and in that moment of panic, I did the only thing I could think of.

I hit him with my empty coffee mug and ran.

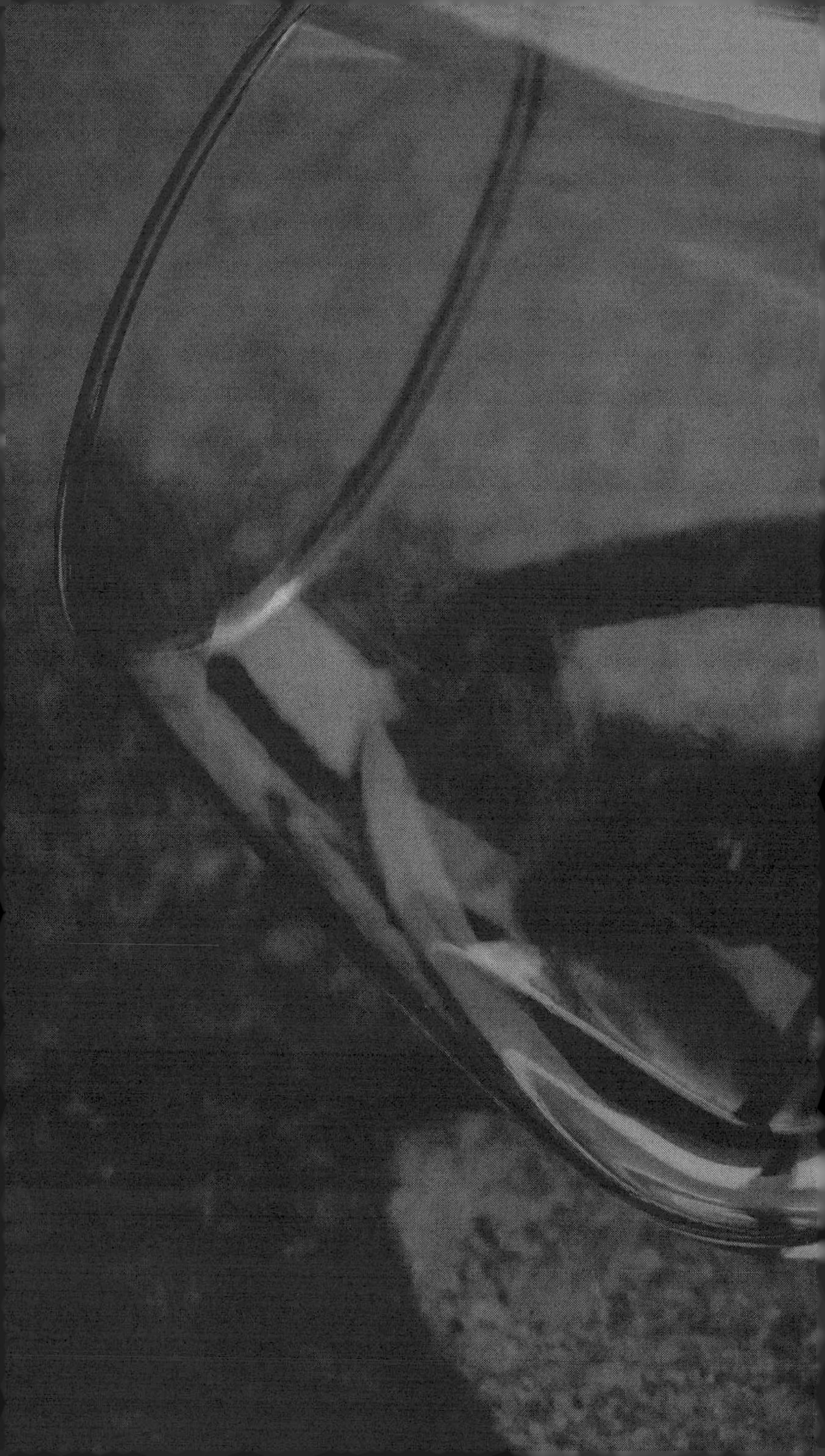

11

Bailey

*S*hit. Shit. Shit.

Kiernan's heavy footsteps echoed ominously against the wooden floor as he stalked after me. His father's voice called after him, a stern warning, but he ignored it as he continued on his mission. I turned, just barely, to glance back at the monster who haunted my footsteps. His emerald eyes were cold, darkness surging through their crystalline depths.

With frenzied hands, I pressed at the button of the elevator, willing it with all my might to open. Maybe if I was lucky, it would let me down to the main floor without needing a fingerprint.

Fuck. Why wasn't it opening?

"*Mo fraochÚn beag.*" His voice was thick with anger, his accent slightly harsher when he uttered the familiar Gaelic words that were still a mystery to me. *He's probably calling me his sex slave or some shit.* Panicked, my eyes bulged as his broad, muscled frame strode toward me with determined steps. Backing away from the elevator, I held my hands up in surrender.

"Wait..." I stammered. "Please. I'm sorry..."

Kiernan's silence frightened me more than if he were to threaten me. He took another long step and then another, closing the distance between us with ease. Before I could think to dart away, he bent down and pressed his shoulder into my stomach, lifting me.

The world turned topsy-turvy, my hair falling around my face like a curtain.

"Put me down," I cried out, my fists pounding on his muscled back. Not that it did any good. The man was built like a linebacker. How many hours did he spend in the gym to get like this? "Ow." His hand came down harshly on the curve of my ass.

Even through the material of my leggings, it burned. Tears blurred my vision, threatening to flow. I wouldn't give him that satisfaction. He didn't get my tears. Not when he was the one acting like a brute.

His hand reached out to press the button of the elevator. It immediately opened with a small chime of a bell.

What the fuck?

He really did have magic fingers.

"Kiernan," I pleaded with him, hoping to soften him toward me. "I'm sorry. I was just upset."

More silence. Blood boiled in my veins at his silent treatment. At least I was attempting an olive branch. My hands continued to beat uselessly against his back as he lugged me out of the elevator. "Let go of me, you asshole," I swore at him, my frustration mounting until it snapped. "You can't do this. Put me down, Kiernan."

"I love it when you say my name, *mo fraochÚn beag*." He chuckled darkly. "But I like it more when you scream it. Why do you think I call you *my little whore?*"

"Fuck you," I sneered. "If you think I'm going to be screaming your name, you're dead fucking wrong."

Stolen Obsession

The man had the nerve to just laugh, as if I had uttered something funny. I couldn't deny, however, that the sound was dark and delicious. It emanated from deep in his chest, the vibrations traveling through my body, causing my thighs to clench together tightly. Kiernan's hand came up to swat my ass again, causing a gasp to fall from my lips as he continued to stride toward our room.

Our room? Why had I said *our*? Jesus, talk about Stockholm syndrome. I'd been a captive for less than a day. Fucking wonderful.

"Oh, sweetheart." Opening the door to the room, he slid us in, mindful of my head, and kicked it shut behind him. "I promise you will be screaming my name. Whether it's in pain or ecstasy is going to be up to you."

"You think your father will just let you beat me?" I snarled. Another chuckle from below me.

"Seamus and I don't beat women, Bailey," he told me, his tone turning serious. "But we do punish them when they misbehave. And my father has the same views on punishment as I do. You won't find any help from him."

Great, an entire family teeming with controlling and dominating men, and somehow, I ended up in the sights of two of them. When we entered the bedroom, he set me on feet and tore at my clothes.

"I am not your sweetheart," I objected as I pushed at his hands. He ignored my futile attempt to stop him, and before I knew it, the man had me completely naked before him.

"Do you remember what I told you when I first brought you up here?" he asked as he unbuttoned his shirt slowly. My eyes followed the trail of his hands as he popped one button after another until the broad expanse of his chest was revealed. Neither he nor Seamus was built as thick as

Dashkov, but they held a lean, agile power that set my panties on fire.

"Um..." I faltered a moment when his hands settled on his belt buckle. My inner hussy was priming herself, but I wasn't about to give it up so easily...again. "Something about being a controlling jackass, if I remember correctly."

He smirked, his eyes darkening and his pupils dilating with uncontrolled hunger. We hadn't fucked yet, but I could feel the tension mounting, and sooner or later, it would snap. The question was, did I want it to?

The clink of his belt buckle sounded in the quiet room, and I licked my lips at the thought of what came next as he slid it through his belt loops. Dread and anticipation coiled in the pit of my stomach.

"Good girls get rewarded," he growled, pushing me to my knees. The carpet was soft on my skin, and I'd relish the burn it would give me later. "Bad girls get punished."

Looking up at him through my long lashes, I smirked as I removed his hardened member from the confines of his black pants, giving it a few strong strokes. His metal piercings along the shaft felt odd in my hands, but not in a bad way.

If Kiernan thought I would shy away from sex, he was wrong.

Inner hussy was practically melted on the floor, giddy with excitement about what those piercings meant for our pussy. There were seven of them in total. *Fuck me, my luck was finally turning around.* I was a second away from adapting one of her spread-eagle poses and telling him to take me like one of his French girls.

Maybe that was supposed to be paint?

Nah, my saying was definitely better.

"This doesn't seem like much of a punishment," I purred in what I hoped was a seductive manner. I didn't have much experience in that particular area, but I was desperate to take some control of my own. To show him I wasn't one of the weak submissives he was no doubt used to.

"Remind me later that you said that." His hand tangled in my hair, pulling at my scalp, the rush of pain only increasing the desire pooling in my core. The snapping of his belt caused my pussy to clench. The rigid edges bit into my skin as the worn leather wrapped around the back of my neck. Kiernan tugged on it, forcing me to look up at him, my hand still gripping his length. He widened his feet and stepped closer.

"I don't think you'll be feeling the same way when you're choking on my cock, begging me for air, *mo fraochÚn beag.*"

"Wait—" Before I could utter another word, he thrust into my mouth. I gagged and choked as he shoved his hardened steel rod in as far as he could before sliding out again, only to repeat the process several more times.

Tears stung the backs of my eyes. My nails dug into the backs of his thighs as he pistoned his hips again and again, each time hitting the back of my throat. It was a calculated move. He'd told me he'd choke me, and that was exactly what he was doing.

And I was loving every minute of it.

Wetness slicked my thighs as desire pooled in my stomach. Fuck, this was wrong. I'd researched breath play once for an article I'd done on a BDSM club that had opened several years ago. The research had made it seem as scary as it did erotic. My interest had been piqued, but Drew had never been anything but plain old vanilla with me, and the thought of broaching the subject with him had turned my stomach.

Spit dribbled down my chin. My lungs burned and my jaw ached. He'd only been leaving me breathless for a few seconds at a time, but as his thrusts grew more erratic, he slowed. The leather edges of the belt dug into the delicate flesh of my neck, the pain chasing on the heels of my pleasure at watching the powerful man towering above me be brought to heel with my mouth on his cock. He used the belt to push in deeper, my nose nearly touching his stomach. Tears streamed down my reddened cheeks as he kept his cock buried deep in my throat for several moments until I was pushing at his thighs, desperate for air.

"Look at me, *mo fraochÚn beag*," he growled, removing himself from my mouth. I lifted my eyes to him, unable to disobey the deep, masculine command. What I saw left me more breathless than I already was. Kiernan's pupils were blown wide, the black pits swallowing up the green of his irises like a black hole. Fervent hunger and molten desire bored down on me, casting off him in waves, causing my stomach to churn with unease, while at the same time, my heart was exploding.

No one had ever looked at me that way before.

Like they wanted me.

Needed me.

Couldn't live without me.

"Good girl." I flushed at the praise. He turned his head and spoke over his left shoulder. "Think she learned her lesson, brother?"

Seamus chuckled from the doorway.

"Only one way to find out." He sauntered into the room with the grace of a panther, licking his lips as he took in my state of disarray. No doubt my lips were swollen and red, cheeks flushed, and hair mussed. "Stand up, wildcat." I took his offered hand, letting him pull me to my feet.

In one swift movement, Seamus lifted me from my feet and tossed me onto the bed. A grin stretched across his face as he pulled his shirt over his head. My teeth bit into my lower lip, eyes widening as I took in his chiseled features. The twins were nearly perfect mirror images of one another, but that didn't dull the chest squeezing sensation I felt each time one of them undressed.

It was like looking at an original Rembrandt in all its glory and finding that he had painted another in its exact image with hints of deviation to it. From a distance, they looked the same. Up close was where one could see the differences. The subtle shift in brush strokes, the slight deviation of colors that could only be seen if you knew what you were looking for.

Seamus and Kiernan Kavanaugh were two original Rembrandts, painted one right after the other. Similar, yet different. I could see the subtle nuances that each man had, and it took my breath away. They were both solid muscle, but Seamus was slightly broader than his brother, whose lean body was meant for speed and agility. Tattoos littered their bodies, the ink a mix of Celtic knots and imagery that was unique to their own person.

Their personalities varied as well.

I'd noticed this at lunch. Seamus seemed to be more light-hearted and relaxed. He worked in shades of gray, twisting the rules without snapping them. Kiernan was black and white, constantly assessing for threats. For him, the rules were less of a guideline and more finite. They were two sides of the same coin, and even now, as my heart beat a staccato rhythm of fear and anticipation, I relished every minute of them.

Damn. I sounded like some insta-love heroine from those romance books Lina constantly threw at me.

The clink of a belt buckle thrust me from my thoughts. The leather swished through the belt loops of Seamus's pants, causing my thighs to clench. With a small smirk, he threw the belt to the side, his pants following, along with his shirt, and then he was standing before me, naked in all his erect glory.

He palmed his cock with his hand, giving himself a long, rough stroke.

All my thoughts disappeared, and there was nothing left but the hot flow of desire surging through me. The twins glanced at each other, another silent conversation between them, before Kiernan divested himself fully of his own clothes and strode toward the bed. Seamus sat down on the edge, slowly easing himself back.

Kiernan's hand grabbed at my ankle, pulling me until I was bent over the edge of the bed, my ass high in the air. Licking his lips, Seamus adjusted himself so that his legs were on either side of me. He fisted my hair, shifting until his hot length was in line with my mouth.

"Here's how this is going to work, wildcat," Seamus purred dangerously. "We're going to ask you some questions. If you answer honestly, we'll reward you." His eyes shifted to his brother, whose warm body had briefly left mine to rummage around in a drawer to my right. It was only moments before I could feel him behind me again, a slight buzzing echoing his footsteps.

A gasp fell from my parted lips as the tip of the vibrator pressed against my already swollen clit. A wanton moan slipped through me at the feel of the vibrations lighting up my core, the sensation sweeping through my body, lighting my neurons on fire. My skin erupted in goose bumps and my nipples pebbled.

"Understand, Bailey?" Kiernan growled from behind me.

Not trusting my voice, I simply nodded.

It sounded easy enough.

If he kept that vibrator on my pleasure button, I'd tell them every nuclear launch code I had...which was none, but it was the sentiment that counted.

Right?

"Good." A small whimper surged through me when the vibration came to a sudden stop. Seamus's fingers gripped my jaw firmly, but with a gentle touch, redirected my gaze to him. "Now, tell us your name, lass."

I snorted. "You already know my name."

Seamus's gaze slid from mine to his brother, something unspoken shifting between the two of them before something swished through the air. I cried out as a line of hot fire lit up my ass. Seamus gripped my hair tightly in his hand. Taking advantage of my wide-open mouth, he thrust his cock inside, burying himself in the back of my throat without preamble. I gagged, spittle forming at the edge of my mouth as he controlled the movement of my head up and down his long shaft without giving me a reprieve.

Another line of hot fire had me screaming around Seamus's cock, the vibrations of my cry making him groan in ecstasy.

Then it stopped.

Seamus lifted my head off his cock, leaving me panting for air, my chest heaving and arousal dripping down my thighs.

Fucked-up seemed like such a tame word to describe my reaction to their brutal yet somehow intimate treatment of my body.

"Ready to play, lass?"

"Christ," I clenched my teeth against the ache that had developed not only in my ass but also my cunt. "It's Bailey Jameson, for fuck's sake."

"Good girl," Kiernan cooed, his hand coming down to rub at the ache in my ass, kneading the abused flesh. God, would I be bruised from his belt? "See how easy that was?" He leaned down to whisper in my ear. "You lie; you get punished. You tell the truth; we'll reward you."

"Where's my reward, then?" I snarked. Seamus laughed.

"He stopped spanking you, didn't he, wildcat?"

I'm so glad he found it amusing.

"Why isn't your last name the same as the Crowes'?" Seamus jumped right into the next question.

"Because they didn't want to dishonor where I came from." I shrugged nonchalantly. It wasn't a complete lie, although not changing my name didn't have anything to do with disrespect and everything to do with the fact that they didn't want anyone putting two and two together. If the media got hold that Richard Crowe had a child as a result of an affair, when he'd built his entire political campaign off family values, he'd be done for.

The twins seemed to accept this answer, but there was something in Seamus's gaze that I couldn't identify. Wariness, maybe? He didn't seem to fully believe my lie, but if he had reservations, he kept them to himself.

"Tell us what you were doing in the parking lot."

Not this again.

"My car broke down."

"And it just happened to be outside our club?"

Our club.

I'd forgotten Clover was theirs. In hindsight, I should have realized who they were long before the good doctor mentioned their last name.

"Coincidence."

Kiernan's hand came down on my sore backside. A warning.

"Answer the question fully, lass."

I sneered. "Only if you answer mine."

Seamus smirked as he looked over me at his brother.

"And why would we do that?" Seamus's gaze slid back to me. The height difference between us, with me leaning over the bed between his legs, made it so that I had to crane my neck to stare up at him.

"Because you want me to answer your questions." *Duh*.

Kiernan smirked. "You're going to answer our questions regardless."

"Meh." My mouth twisted. "Probably not. You two are the ones who need my cooperation, not the other way around."

Seamus snorted. "Or we could kill you."

"You would have done so already if that were true" was my rapid-fire response.

Another look shared between them.

"All right," Seamus inclined. "But we're going to sweeten the pot."

"Umm..." I bit my lower lip almost demurely, my eyes lowering to the bedsheet visible between Seamus's thighs. God, I was going to regret this. "Sure."

"You get five questions." Kiernan spoke up from behind me. He trailed his fingers along my rib cage to the underside of my right breast. The shiver of desire chased away my reluctance.

"What's the catch?" I eyed Seamus dubiously. He laughed.

"Smart girl," he praised. I hated the way my body preened.

Great, my inner hussy had a praise kink I wasn't aware of. Drew had never complimented me on much of anything, let alone during sex. He was a pump and done kind of douchebag.

"Well, I want your pretty mouth wrapped around my cock." Seamus smirked.

"And mine wants a sweet taste of that cunt."

My eyes widened at their crude admissions.

"At the same time?"

The twins nodded.

"I only get to ask five questions, but you two get to spit roast me?" I shook my head. "Yeah, that's not fair. I want ten questions." I countered.

"You think you make the rules here, baby girl?" Kiernan growled in my ear. His fingers pinched my nipple. My back bowed at the sudden pain, ass pressing against his hardened length. A small gasp burst from me as I grew undoubtedly wetter.

"Eight questions."

"Six," he countered. "Take it or leave it."

He twisted my nipple harder. I bowed my head against Seamus's thigh, groaning.

"Deal."

I moaned when his fingers released my nipple and soothed the ache.

"Good girl."

What the hell had I gotten myself into?

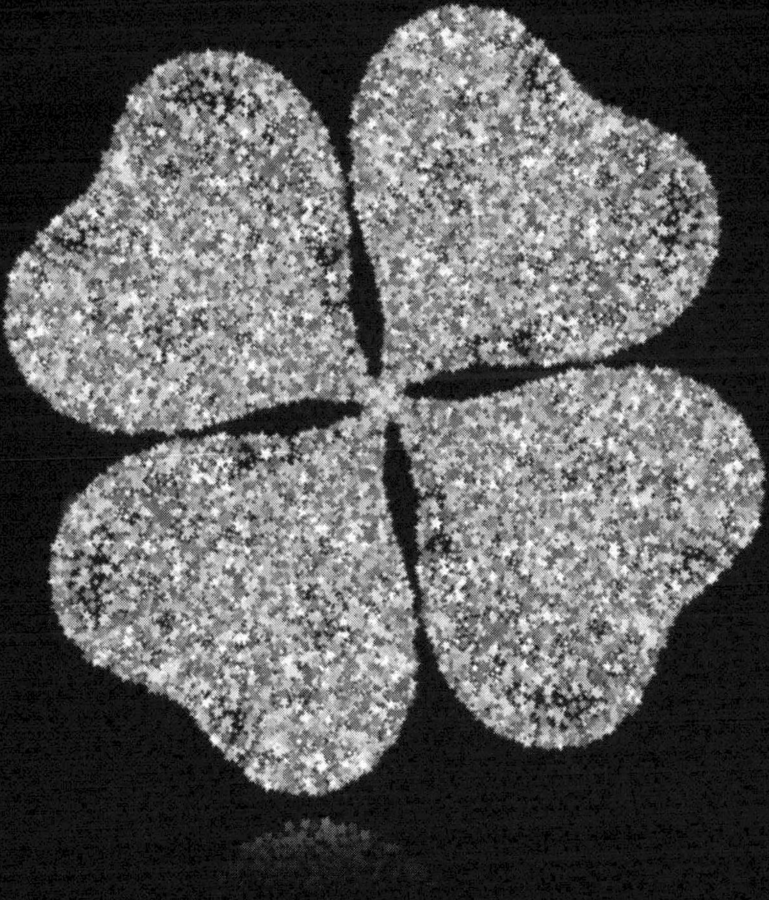

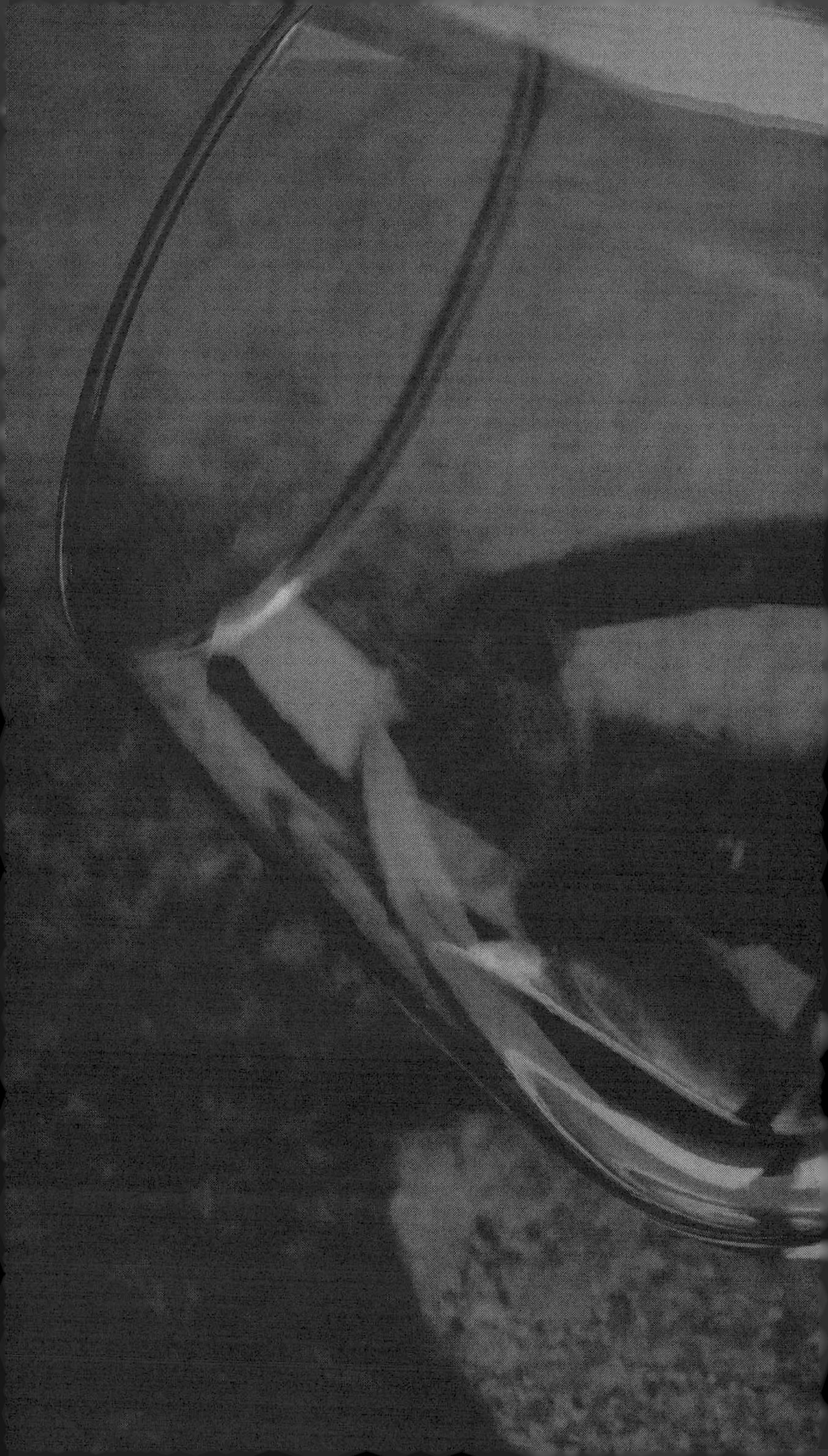

12

Seamus

Bailey was gorgeous.

I'd spent time with some beautiful women, each one desirable in her own way, but there was something about the raven-haired wildcat in front of me that had me wanting to lose control. I could take her right now. Her mouth was inches from my throbbing cock, desire dripping from her pussy like an offering to a deity. I slid my hand along her side, noting the subtle tremor of her body at my touch, until I was caressing her ass. The heat from her punished skin had my hardened length jumping with excitement.

I wanted nothing more than to fuck her mouth again while my brother kneeled behind her, licking and sucking at her sweet button until she was screaming my name around my cock, her eyes begging us for release.

Soon.

Soon we would claim her as ours.

She'd scream our names, and everyone would know who she belonged to.

"Go on, wildcat," I urged. "Ask your question."

Her crystalline blue eyes held buckets of uncertainty as

she stared at me, her throat bobbing nervously. Her darling pink tongue came out to lick her chapped lips before she took a deep breath, the action causing her breasts to sway beneath her.

God, I wanted to suckle those petal-pink nipples until she writhed with pleasure beneath me.

"Are you going to kill me?"

It was the question I suspected she'd ask first, despite her bold statement that we needed her. Couldn't blame her for wanting assurances. She knew what being held by the mafia meant. We should have killed her in the alley, but if there was one thing that set us apart from other families, it was that we didn't kill women and children. Not unless it was well deserved. I'd only ever known my father to order a hit on a woman once in his entire time as head of the family.

And she wasn't innocent like Bailey.

She'd been a killer herself. A manipulator. There was no regretting that decision.

"No," I answered her honestly. We didn't have plans to kill her. Use her? Yes. Trade her back to her father? Maybe, but not if we had our way.

"Then what do you—"

"Sorry, babe." I wagged my finger at her. "Our turn."

The small huff she gave was adorable.

"What can you tell me about your father's business with Magnus Knight?"

"Seriously?" Bailey scoffed a laugh as she rolled her eyes. I could see my brother's belt hand twitch with the need to punish her for the disrespect. But he let it go. This time. "I don't know anything about my father's business. He's a senator. He does politics. If that's why you're keeping me, you're shit out of luck."

"We already told you why we're keeping you," Kiernan

reminded her. Despite his reservations at the dinner table about using her to spy on her father, we both knew it was the only way to get what we needed.

"Not going to happen."

Ignoring her last comment, I fisted her hair tightly, forcing her to stare up at me.

"You know something," I pressed. "So, if you don't want to be punished, tell us what you know."

Bailey shook her head. "Do you honestly believe that I'm going to betray my father that way?" she asked incredulously. "No way. My father gave me everything. I wouldn't be here if he hadn't rescued me. If I betray him, he'll ruin me."

Cocking my head to one side, I studied her, taking in the swell of her chest as a wave of anxiety settled over her. Bailey's hands trembled slightly where she had them braced against my thighs, but her face had settled into a mask of indifference. My little wildcat was trying to hide her fear.

"We won't let that happen, *Mo Stoirín*," Kiernan assured her. His hands came up to rub at her shaking shoulders, easing the goose bumps that had settled over her fair skin. "We won't let anything happen to you, lass. You belong to us."

I doubted that would ease her fear, but the minx surprised me when her body relaxed back into her submissive position, her breaths evening out.

"I don't know much," she admitted, her voice drifting to a low whisper. "Just what I've overheard and what Drew has told me."

Bailey shook her head, denial and fear trembling through her again. She was afraid, and I didn't think it was us she feared in this moment, but the man who raised her. But why? What reason did she have to fear her father? He was a scumbag, there was no doubt about that, but would he harm his own daughter?

"If I tell you," she looked at Kiernan over her shoulder, meeting his gaze before turning to me, "you can't use anything I say. They'll know it was me."

Kiernan and I exchanged a look.

"All right." We nodded.

"And...you can't tell anyone what I'm about to tell you. If you do, you'll be signing my death certificate. Don't let them take me." The look on her face told me she was serious. Whatever secret she held about her father was bad enough that she feared for her own life.

Don't let them take me.

Those weren't random words she'd thrown out. The look in her azure eyes spoke volumes. She'd meant to say those words. Bailey hadn't said *my father* or *him*. She specifically said *them*. If it wasn't her father she was afraid of, then who?

"We won't." I cringed internally at Kiernan's promise. I was supposed to be the impulsive one, not him. It wasn't a lie. Technically. We wouldn't let anyone *take* her. We had planned to use her as a bargaining chip, and part of that was making sure there would be no retaliation against her.

Bailey breathed deeply, her lower lip trembling as she exhaled. Her mask of indifference fell back into place, the political mask she had worn her entire life. The one that showed no weakness. I didn't like that mask.

"What did you want to know?"

"There aren't any adoption records on you." I leaned back on my elbows. My cock was still rock hard beneath her, but that wasn't going away anytime soon. Not until those pretty lips were wrapped around it, and even then, I doubted it would be satiated. Pushing back my primal need to claim the vixen on her stomach in front of me, I focused on the task at hand.

Getting answers and her cooperation.

Bailey shrugged, but I could see the frisson of anxiety running through her. "Can't adopt a blood daughter."

Kiernan eyed me.

"Elaborate, Bailey." Not that much elaboration was needed. If she was about to confirm what we thought she was, this was our smoking gun.

The minx rolled her eyes. "Richard Crowe is my biological father. He had a one-night stand when he was younger, and boom. Me."

"Who was she?"

"Don't know. Don't care."

"You never met your biological mother? Or tried to find out more about her?"

"I lived with her until I was three or four. I can't remember. She was a no-good junkie who left me in a room filled with needles on the floor and used condoms in the corners." Bailey's jaw clenched tightly. "I don't care about who she was. She lived like a junkie and died like a junkie. That's all I need to know."

Fair point.

"Still doesn't explain the secrecy, lass."

"Do I have to spell it out for you?" Her tone became exasperated. She didn't like dredging this up. There was a deep-rooted pain she was holding on to. One she didn't want to confront. Too bad. "My father was the DA. Do you know what a scandal like that would have done to his career path? So, when he learned of me, he told the media they adopted me after seeing me in the hospital during one of Sarah's fertility treatments. They'd told everyone they were struggling to conceive after my sister was born. Made a big heartbreak, boo-hoo about it, and the media lapped it up like the good little dogs they are."

"Is that why you became a journalist?" Kiernan asked. "So you wouldn't become a simpering fool like them?"

"No." She sniffed haughtily, her little nose in the air in stiff indignation. "I wanted to be a fiction author, but my father wouldn't hear of it. Journalism was the next best thing."

"How did you become involved with your fiancé?"

"Ex-fiancé," she growled before sighing. "Drew and his father came to mine. I was sixteen. Magnus wanted an alliance. He knew of my father's political aspiration, and he wanted a seat at the table."

"Why did your father offer up an arranged marriage?" I wondered. There were several ways to go about political alliances these days in the political world. Not just marriage. It wasn't mutually beneficial in my opinion. What did Richard gain from selling his daughter? And why her and not her socialite sister?

Bailey shook her head. "It was Magnus's idea," she contradicted. "He wanted the political alliance, and marriage was the option he thought best. I wasn't his first choice, but Sarah, my stepmother, refused. Plus, Sarah had lined up a match of her own for Dalia with the son of the current DA."

"What did your father gain from an alliance with Magnus?"

"Power," Bailey said simply. She made it seem as if it was the only obvious answer. "My father may be a senator, but Magnus had far greater reach and sway in DC, and with his current political track, he's looking at campaigning for president during the next election."

"President?"

Fuck. So that was why the old man had been campaigning so hard to clean up the city. Taking down the Seattle underground and the mafia families who ran it would place him so far ahead of his opponents they wouldn't stand a chance.

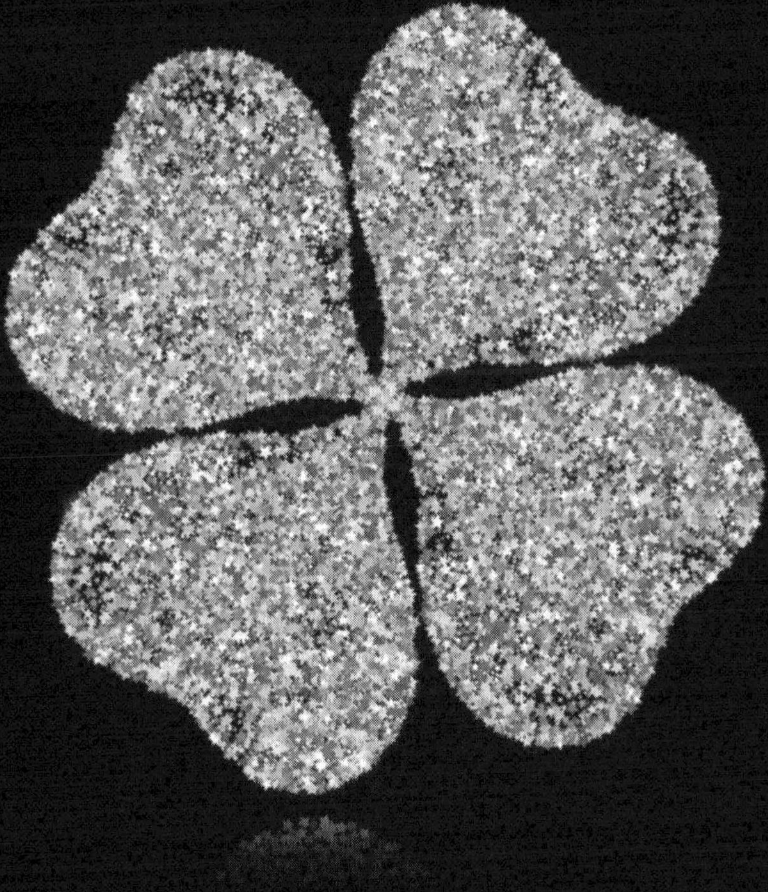

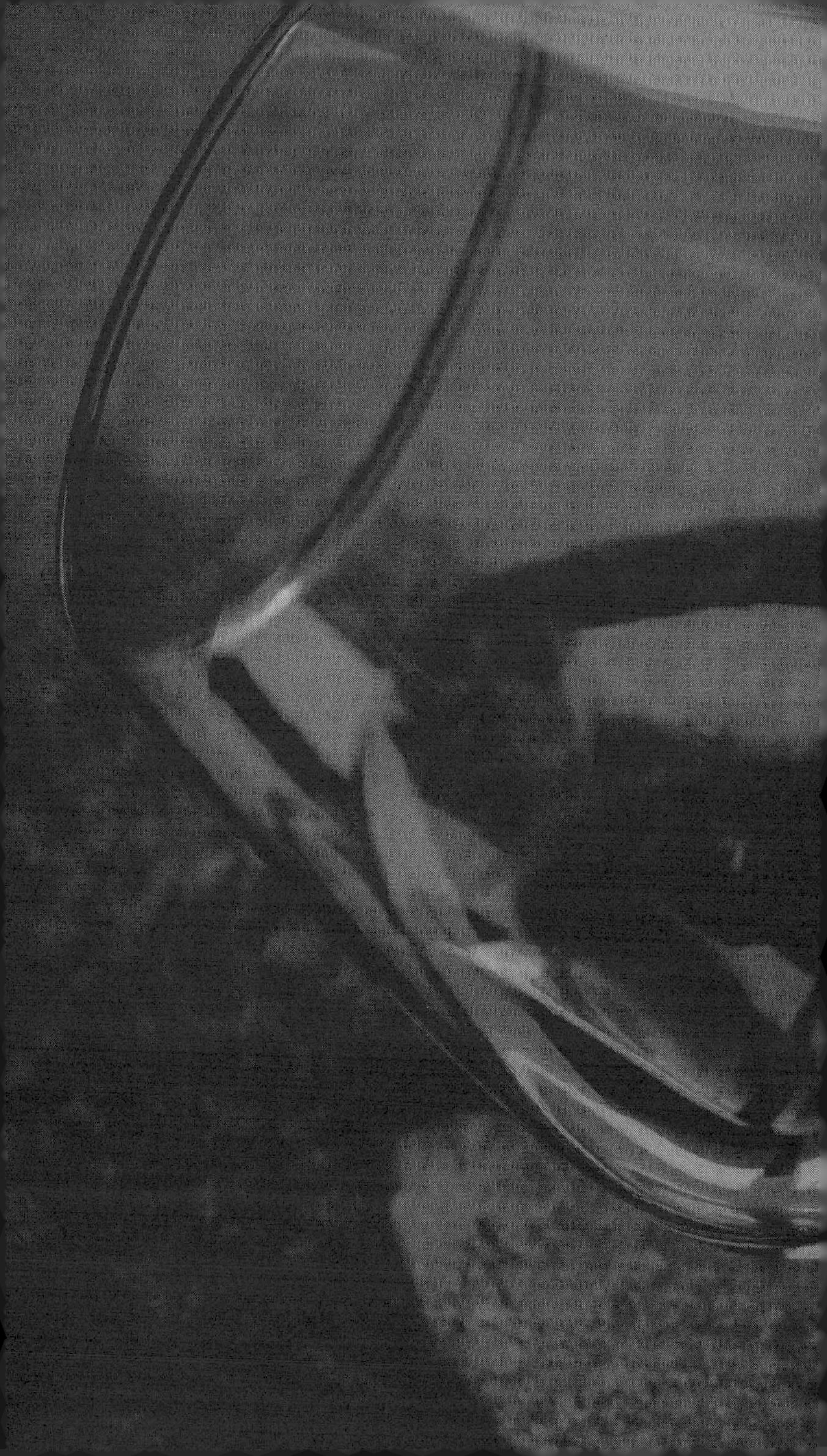

13

Bailey

Seamus was staring at me like I had lost my marbles.

My father's bid for president shouldn't have surprised them. He was an ambitious man.

"That's pretty ambitious for a man with skeletons in his closet," Seamus sneered.

"My father isn't who you say he is," I argued. "He may not be winning any father of the year awards, but he isn't a bad man."

Kiernan scoffed. "Your father makes mine look like a saint."

"Fuck you," I spat, pushing back against him with enough force that he stumbled back. Taking the moment of surprise, I lashed out at Kiernan with my fist aimed at his stupidly handsome face. I wasn't going to let him talk about my father that way. He'd saved my life the day he found me. If it wasn't for him, I would have died in that rat-infested hell hole. Or worse.

Seamus's strong arms wrapped around my waist from behind, holding me tight to his chest. But I wasn't going to let that stop me. I pummeled my fists against Kiernan's chest. The man was unmoved by my violent outburst. Seamus grunted as one of my flailing limbs knocked him in the side of the head. "Let me go!" Tears streamed down my face as I scratched and clawed, kicked and screamed.

The dam had been broken. The fresh hell of the last twenty-four hours catching up to me faster than a tidal wave against a tugboat. At the moment, I didn't care about the consequences or what it meant that I had struck the heirs to the Irish throne. I just wanted to go. Even if I had nowhere to go.

I dug my nails into Kiernan's flesh, earning a threatening growl as he took both of my wrists in one of his large hands.

"Enough," Kiernan roared. Ignoring his command, I kicked and screamed, twisting my body as far as I could out of Seamus's hold. Another silent exchange between the twins I didn't understand, and suddenly I was thrust into Kiernan's arms. His large arms encircled my body, entrapping my arms, effectively keeping them still.

He took three steps toward the bed before pivoting and sitting down on the edge. Kiernan stretched me over his lap as I twisted my body against him, but it was no use. I didn't have anywhere near the strength necessary to fight him off.

I wasn't even sure if I wanted to.

My vagina sure didn't want to.

"Get off me," I howled, my feet scissoring and my hands slapping at his leg. A whistle pierced the air and then a burning sting. I stilled, the sudden flash of pain short-circuiting my brain. The eroticism of the spanking he'd given me before vanished. This wasn't a kink punishment. It was a real one. "You can't—"

Another line of fire lit up my backside. I squealed at the sudden impact, my feet desperate to find purchase on the soft carpet to make a no doubt vain attempt to push off his lap. All I'd successfully managed was to rub my aching pussy against his thigh, which, judging from their chuckles, they'd both noticed.

I dug my nails into the skin of his calf, a hiss whistling through my chapped lips when he delivered another stinging blow. Then another.

"This is enough, Bailey," he punctuated each word with another sting of his belt. "You will cease this tantrum." He wasn't playing games. It stung like fucking hell, tears streaming down my cheeks like little rivers. Then suddenly, it was gone, leaving a fiery ache on my ass and a wetness between my thighs. I took a deep breath, my body shaking and trembling as his hand rubbed soothing circles on my buttocks. The motion was soothing, but the moment I felt his rock-hard erection on my belly, I panicked.

"You're getting off on this," I accused, rocking my body a bit in protest. It only caused him to harden more. "Is that what gets your engine revving? Beating women?"

Kiernan chuckled, but it was cold and mirthless.

"I don't beat women, Bailey." He ran his fingers along the seam of my ass before dipping into my wetness. "Neither Seamus nor I will ever raise a hand to you in anger. But that doesn't mean we won't discipline you or that we won't enjoy doing it."

I scoffed. *Okay.*

"Discipline?" I asked in disbelief. "I'm not a fucking child."

A finger curled beneath my chin, forcing my head up. Seamus's green eyes met mine, a smile forming on his lips. A lion watching his prey.

"Even big girls get spanked when they're bad," he whispered seductively. "Do as we say, and that won't be a problem."

What fucking looney-bin dimension had I woken up in?

Do as they say?

What the fuck? Did they honestly think I would just become their docile sex slave? They had another thing coming if they believed I would go along with this shit.

"Look at the cogs turning in her head, brother." Seamus smirked. "I wonder how many ways she's already planning to kill us." Kiernan laughed. *Fuck*. Why did that laugh send the butterflies in my stomach fluttering?

"Now." I found myself suddenly sitting up, Kiernan's chest pressed tightly against my back. My legs were splayed open in front of me, his feet hooked around my ankles to keep my legs from closing. My hands shoved at his thighs, but it was useless, and I knew that if I kept pushing, they might tie me up, and then I'd be really stuck.

Huffing, I settled back against his chest, my muscles coiled and stiff as the pair continued to stare at me.

Intense.

That was the only way to describe the twins. From their strong jaws, shaded with stubble, to their emerald eyes that lit up with gold flakes when they stared at me hungrily. Their ginger hair hung loosely to their shoulders in gentle waves, hiding the side fade that was only visible when it was pulled back.

I didn't need to see Kiernan's body to know it would perfectly match his twin's. I could feel him beneath me, naked and hard as granite. I eyed Seamus. His body was carved from stone with his chiseled muscle and hard lines, and I felt myself subconsciously lick my lips as my gaze dipped down to where the V of his hips perfectly accentuated the hard mass of his cock.

Would my pussy ever stop pulsing at the sight of his hardened length studded with piercings? I'd heard of the Jacob's ladder piercing before, but now that I'd seen it. Felt it in my

Stolen Obsession

mouth and beneath my hand, I wondered what it would feel like as my pussy clenched around it as the twins drove into me.

"Still wanting more, wildcat?" Seamus winked at me, palming his dick. Shit. His dirty talk had my inner hussy performing backflips and cartwheels in her birthday suit.

Fucking traitor. She did know they kidnapped me and spanked me like a child, right?

"I..." There were no words for the turmoil that churned my stomach. How could I want them? It was wrong to want your kidnappers, right?

Did I have Stockholm syndrome already?

"Now that we're done with the temper tantrum." Kiernan shifted below me slightly, his cock rubbing against my lower back, causing me to arch into it.

Seamus chuckled. "She's ready, all right."

I froze.

"We aren't done with our questions, Seamus," Kiernan reminded him. "She needs to earn our cocks first. Like a good girl. That was the deal."

I tried to tilt my head back to see Kiernan's face, but Seamus grabbed my chin, forcing me to keep his gaze.

"You wanna do that, baby?" Seamus nearly cooed. "Wanna be a good girl and earn a reward?"

Swallowing back the lump of anxiety growing, I nodded.

"I still have questions," I whispered, my mouth suddenly drier than the Sahara Desert.

"We'll answer your questions," he assured me seductively. "And if you answer ours honestly, we'll give you that reward before taking ours."

A gentleman did always put a lady first, and I had two of them.

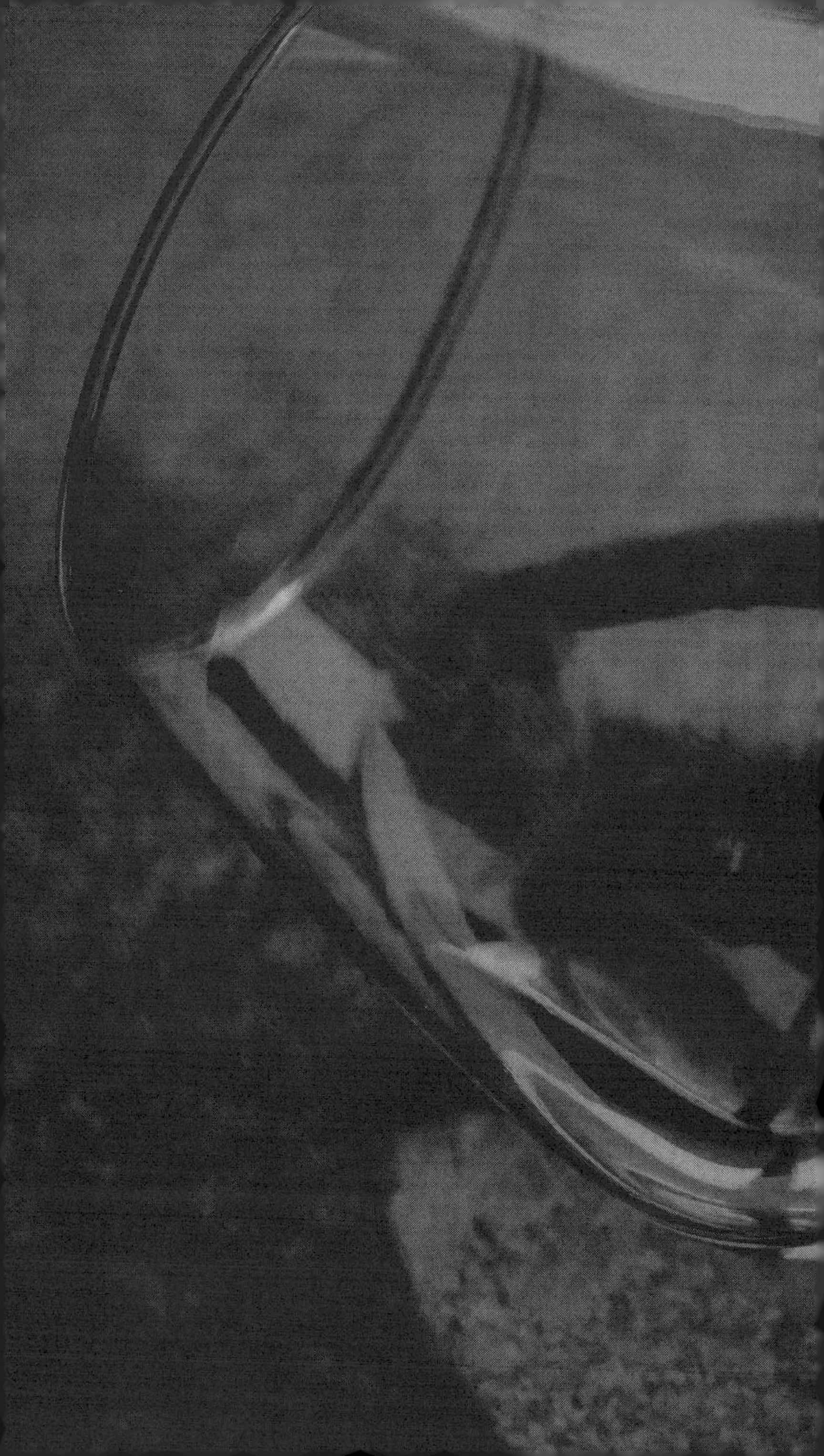

14

Bailey

"Go on, then," Kiernan murmured before kissing the side of my neck. "Ask your question."

The small action shouldn't have affected me the way it did, but a frisson of awareness spread through my body like a live wire. I'd never felt anything like it before. Drew was the only man I'd ever been with. Not that I had much choice. We'd been promised to one another since I was sixteen. I'd never been allowed to date or go out to the movies with my friends growing up. There were no parties or keggers. Even at college, I simply went from one prison to the next. Drew was more lenient when it came to my comings and goings, even going as far as to let me study and practice journalism.

Now I knew why.

I loved being a reporter. It was the one thing that was truly mine. Drew had wanted to branch out from under his father's thumb. He wanted to earn his keep, and I accepted that. I respected that. He'd only ever treated me with love and kindness. Never forcing me to do something I wasn't comfortable with.

When it came to sex, Drew was more vanilla than an ice

cream cone. I'd thought he'd come to love me and that we could have a sliver of bliss together, despite our arranged marriage.

How wrong I'd been.

So very wrong.

The excitement these two men managed to elicit from my body was nothing like I'd ever felt. The orgasm they had given me this morning was far beyond anything Drew had ever managed to do. Drew rarely did foreplay and even on the rare occasions he did, the way these men played me like a well-tuned guitar made what Drew did amateur hour. The Irish god had plucked at my strings until I was singing how he wanted me to.

"Well?"

Heat crept up my neck as I pulled myself from my thoughts of this morning. Seamus stared down at me with a knowing smile on his lips. Shaking it off, I took a long breath.

"What can you tell me about the explosion at the Ward stables?"

Please don't be involved.
Please don't be involved.

"What do you mean?" Seamus asked.

"In the alley, you said your father warned you that I was looking into it," I told him. "Why did he feel the need to warn you?"

Kiernan huffed a laugh. "Why should we tell you?"

"You said I had six questions," I reminded him petulantly.

"True," he mused. "I never said we had to answer them."

"Are you fucking kidding me?" I growled as I pushed back against his chest to get free. "I'm not going to be doing anything unless you—what the hell?" I squealed. Like actually squealed when Kiernan's hand came down to smack my mound. My vaginal walls contracted as the sharp sting radiated through me.

When had my hussy side decided to join a whorehouse?

"Did you just—" He didn't give me a chance to finish the sentence before his hand came down again. I hissed, my back arching against his chest as a wave of pain-tinged pleasure washed over me. My thighs clenched automatically, but Kiernan's legs had mine locked with his.

I was open.

Vulnerable.

Exposed.

And I'd never been wetter.

"She liked that, brother," Seamus purred, his eyes darkening, taking in the sight of my aroused pussy. "Give her a reward." Kiernan sighed dramatically.

"I can't tell you everything," Kiernan began with a long sigh. "It isn't my story to tell. Ava, our sister you met downstairs, was taken by Christian Ward just as she left her wedding. He'd been holding her at the stables. We rescued her and the women there before blowing it to smithereens."

"Good riddance," Seamus snarled.

"And you're sure there weren't any women there named Lina?"

The twins shook their heads.

"Most of them were foreign and barely spoke English."

"Oh..."

That didn't set me at ease. If Lina hadn't been in the stables, that meant she could have been sold or killed.

Jesus.

"I think we're done for now." Kiernan's tone brooked no argument.

"Wait, but—"

"You still get the rest of your questions," he assured me,

his nose following a trail on the side of my neck. "But right now, we all need a break."

"Yes, sir," I murmured so low I doubted they could hear me.

"Good girl." Apparently, he had, and my cheeks heated at the praise.

Seamus kneeled in front of me on the bed, and I was overcome with the sudden desire to feel his mouth pressed up against my clit again. For his tongue to dance along my pussy while his brother sucked and licked at my breasts.

Smirking at the obvious desire spread across my face like a wanted ad, Seamus dipped his head between my thighs, his hot breath cascading over my heated core before he dipped his tongue into the entrance of my sex.

I threw my head back against Kiernan's shoulder as I moaned. Kiernan's mouth came down harshly on mine, his tongue conquering and plundering, taking no prisoners, while his brother tasted my pussy. Seamus's licks were slow and sensual as I soared higher and higher.

"Fuck," I whimpered into Kiernan's mouth as Seamus pulled away from my core. "She's sweeter than fucking honey."

"No need to tell me, brother." Kiernan smirked, finally letting me up for air. They exchanged another silent look I couldn't decipher. "Time for you to pay up, *mo fraochÚn beag*."

What? What about my reward?

Seamus chuckled.

Shit, I'd said that out loud.

"You'll get your reward, wildcat," he snickered. "Don't worry."

There wasn't a chance for me to protest before I found myself on all fours, facing Kiernan. He was massaging his hardened length, and my eyes widened at the sight of his thick, pierced cock. Precum was already leaking out the tip, and when I looked up at him, he smirked.

How had I not noticed how large and imposing it was while he was coming all over my face?

Oh, right. I was in orgasmic bliss.

"Open your mouth, *mo fraochÚn beag*."

I wanted to hate him for calling me his little whore. I really did. My body had other plans. Instead of revulsion, my stomach clenched in anticipation. Fucking traitor.

Licking my lips, I took Kiernan's cock in my mouth. I looked up at him through hooded eyes. His eyes were closed, his head thrown back in ecstasy as I ran my tongue along the underside of his shaft. He groaned when I swallowed him to the back of my throat, his cock twitching with pleasure.

"*Cac*," he swore, bringing his hand up to tangle in my hair. He pressed against my head, guiding me over his length, setting a slow, steady pace. "Harder, baby. Suck harder. Show me what a naughty little whore you are for me."

My pussy was drenched at his words, no doubt seeping onto the bedsheets below, ruining the satiny material. He tasted like sin and chocolate, and I wanted nothing more than to make him come undone in my mouth.

Drew had never come in my mouth before. He'd pull out and shove it in my vagina for a few quick thrusts before spilling his seed. I knew what he was trying to do, and I'd made sure to have a plan in place as soon as I'd realized it.

Nexplanon was a beautiful thing.

I'd managed to hold off our wedding for several years. It hadn't been too hard to convince Drew to set the plans aside for a few years while he put his business together. The man had been so absorbed in starting it that he hadn't even bothered to fight me on it. Didn't stop him from trying to get me pregnant, though. Up until last night, I thought we had shared something special. An understanding. A kind of kinship. We had both been shoved into a marriage neither of us wanted.

Sure, the sex wasn't great, but he'd supported me through journalism school, and in return, I'd taken care of the expenses while he built his company. He listened when I talked. Took me out on dates.

But it was nothing like this.

Every nerve in my body was surging with electricity. My body was on fire, a wanton slave to their desires so strong that it silenced the blaring alarms in my brain.

I gasped as the soft heat of Seamus's mouth descended on my pussy again, this time from behind, allowing Kiernan's cock to slip farther down my throat.

"Jaysus, Bailey," he moaned, forcing my head down until his cock was bumping against the back of my throat. I gagged, my back arching as I tried not to heave. He pulled out, and I sucked in a jagged breath before he shoved back inside me just as deep.

"Mmm," I moaned, rocking back when Seamus inserted two fingers into my sopping cunt. Kiernan groaned heavily as my moan vibrated against him. The two of them were in perfect sync as they wrung me with pleasure.

As Kiernan's thrusts became more frantic and forceful, so did Seamus's. He fucked my pussy with his fingers like it was his job, one hand on my clit, sending me higher and higher. I'd never been fucked like this. Never known this kind of bliss.

"Shit." Kiernan threw his head back, his thrusts coming more sporadically, his pleasure climbing. I smirked around his cock, relishing in the power I held over him in this moment. I'd never felt anything like it.

I hollowed out my cheeks, sucking harder as I ran my tongue along the bottom of his pierced shaft, careful to keep my teeth from catching on the silver balls. When I got to the tip, I let my top teeth graze slightly over the head.

That was all it took.

He shoved my mouth to the base of his cock, his balls on my chin, and came with a roar. I barely even tasted his cum, he was buried so deep, but it didn't matter to me. I'd done that. I'd made him come apart like an animal.

Gently, he released me, his large, calloused hand running soothingly down my hair before wiping at the tears on my cheeks.

"*Go Hálainn*," he breathed, gazing tenderly down at me.

Those two words sent me crashing over the edge.

Seamus sucking on my clit might have helped.

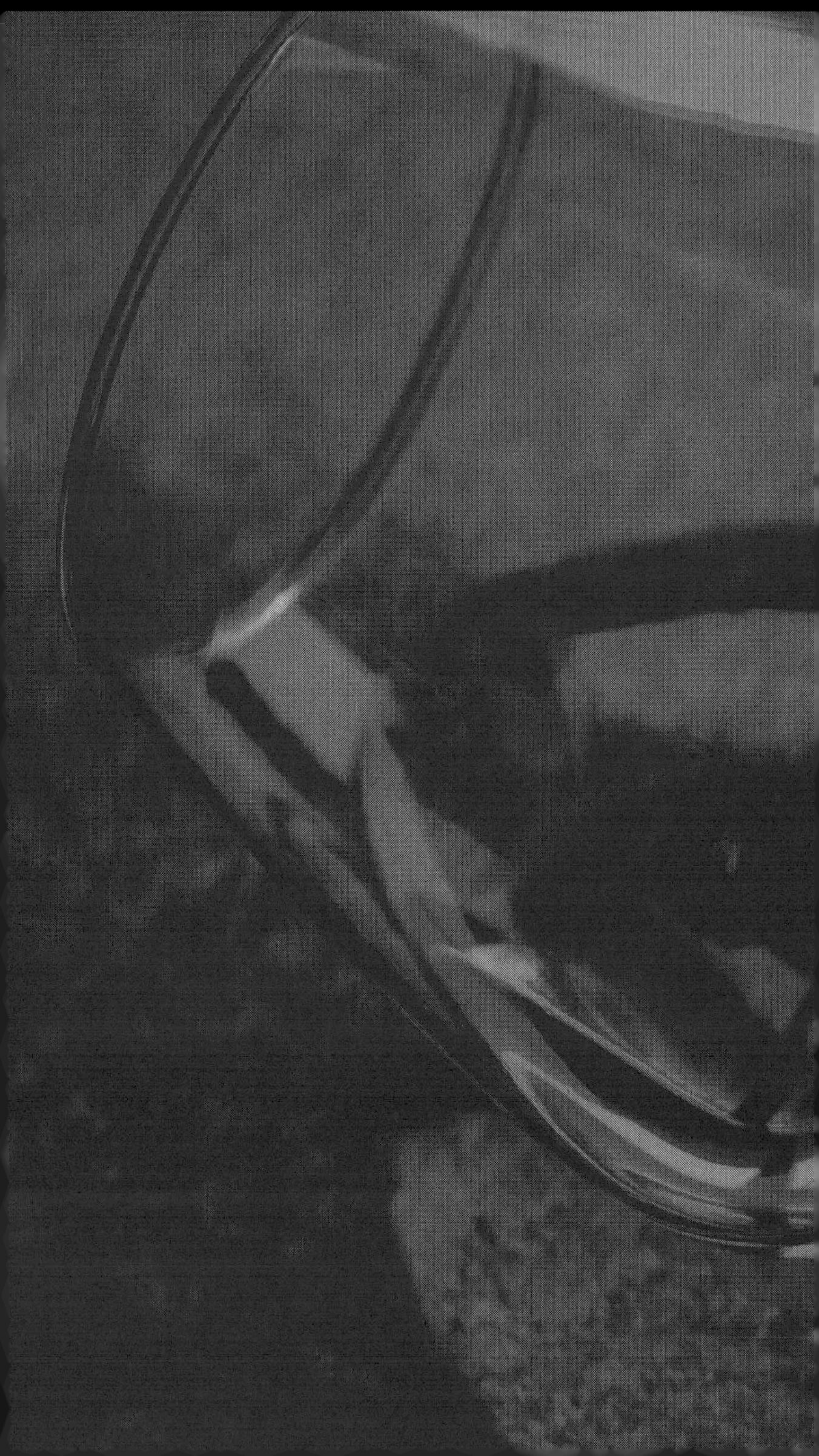

15

Bailey

By the time we came up for air, the dinner bell had been rung.

Like, literally, a dinner bell. One that clanged and everything.

After a quick shower, which ended with another mind-blowing orgasm, we got dressed and headed toward the elevator. I followed the twins, silently contemplating what the fuck I was planning on doing. I didn't want to spy on my father for them, but if the only way to gain their trust was to pretend that I believed them, so be it.

Then why was there a ball of dread in the pit of my stomach?

Something wasn't adding up. These men believed my father was the bad guy here. They didn't try to dissuade me when I told them they were the criminals, but there was no way in hell my father could be complicit or responsible for the crimes they alluded to him committing.

Murder?

Organizing hits?

There wasn't a black mark anywhere on my father's

record. Not even a speeding ticket. Whoever was feeding them this information was wrong.

They had to be.

"I take it everything is settled now." Liam addressed the twins as we took our seats at the table while the servers set down plates of steaming vegetables, pot roast, and potatoes. Damn, a girl could get used to food like this.

"We made sure everything was well understood." Kiernan smirked as he eyed me. I could feel the heat rising in my cheeks at the not-so-subtle innuendo.

"Good." Their father crooked his head at one of the servers, who began immediately plating the food and passing it out. His eyes turned toward me. "We don't need any more unrest in the house than there already is."

Fucking fuckity fucker.

Who the hell did he think he was chastising me like that?

He was lucky he was the head of the Irish mafia, or else I'd give him a piece of my mind.

Hell, the only reason I wasn't was because my ass was still sore from earlier.

"Have you given any thought to what I said?" Dashkov asked me from across the table. "The gala would be an easy place to trade the information we are looking for, and from there, we could come up with a strategy for the next auction."

"What auction?" I asked curiously.

"The one we believe your friend Lina to be at," Matthias told me. "Where she will be sold."

"I already told you she isn't doing it," Kiernan growled next to me.

"It is our best chance," Dashkov prodded dangerously. "If we don't act now, we will lose the edge. We need that information to take down Ward and the rest of them. If we don't act soon, that opportunity will be lost."

"Fuck the opportunity," Kiernan hissed. "Do you honestly think that Crowe won't sniff out a rat? He didn't get where he is today by being stupid. He knows how to read people, and Bailey is shit at hiding her thoughts."

I let out a weak protest, but he ignored it.

"She'll be a sitting duck."

"He'll be blind to her," Matthias assured him. "She's his daughter." There was something in the way he said *daughter* that felt off. As if he didn't believe it. I wondered if he'd been filled in already about me not being adopted.

"It isn't just him she's worried about," Seamus piped up. "If any of the men backing him get wind of her spying, they'll find a way to get rid of her to keep everything shut down. He's making a bid for president this year. Do you honestly think that the men pushing his career to the top will let her live if they find her spying on him? She'll be a loose end."

"She already is," Matthias growled. "She's been digging into her friend's disappearance. Do you honestly believe that has gone unnoticed? This could give her an opportunity to help find her with us watching her back."

"Wait," I interrupted. "What does—"

"Enough," Liam roared from the head of the table, his fist banging on the worn wood. "This is something for Bailey to decide, not all of you. She's the one taking the risk."

All eyes were on me.

Fuck my life. This wasn't what I needed right now.

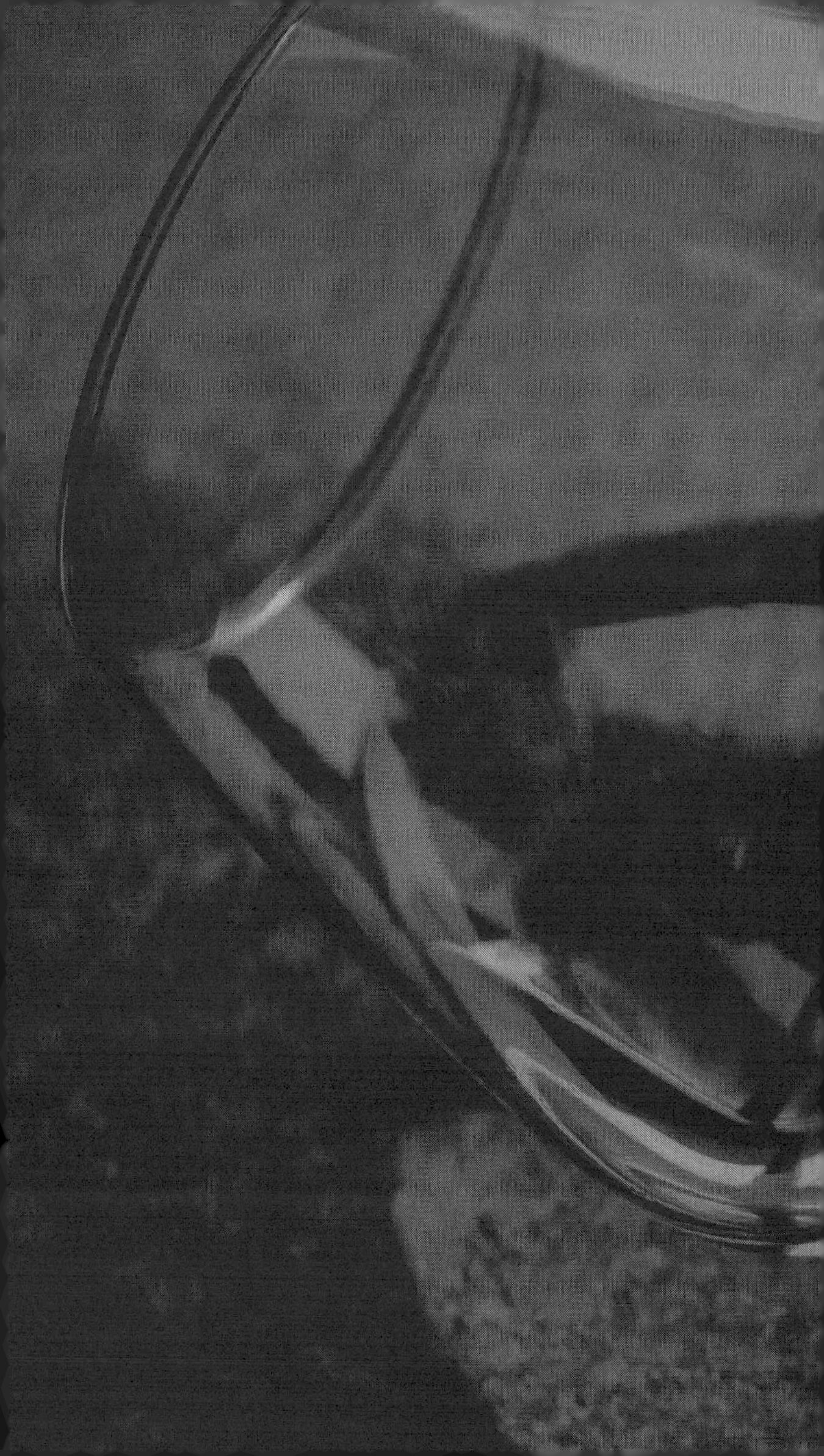

16

Kiernan

I was fuming.

The blood in my veins edged closer to its boiling point the more the conversation kept on. I couldn't believe my father was on board with subjecting Bailey to the sick depravity of her father and his men. Even my own fucking brother had hopped on the train to fucking looney town.

Who the hell did Dashkov think he was bringing something like that up in front of her? Spying on her own kin? There were so many ways that could go wrong. He knew Bailey was desperate to find her friend, and he was using it to his advantage. I may not have known the raven-haired vixen for long, but there was one thing I knew for sure. Bailey was selfless when it came to those she called friends because she had so few.

"I'm not even sure what it is you think I could do," Bailey admitted, her blue eyes sweeping around the table. She was holding her coffee cup in both hands, close to her chest, letting the warmth of the liquid comfort her as she tried to process what everyone was saying. "I'm not going to spy on my father for you. He isn't the man you think he is."

"Maybe we should give her the evidence we brought," Ava whispered to her husband. "The ones my brothers asked for."

A derisive snort escaped me, my scowl turning dark at her words. "Why not?" I fluttered my hand toward her. "Get it all out."

"Kiernan," my father hissed. "Show your sister some respect."

His words were sharp and had the intended effect. Softening my tone, I murmured an apology. Ava gave me a soft smile before turning her gaze to Bailey, who sat back in her chair, awkwardly watching us all interact.

I knew I'd said that we would show her the evidence we had against her father. Bailey had said that if it were true, if we could prove it, she would side with us and tell us what she could. But that was different from putting her in harm's way. If we told her the truth and then sent her back to her father, it would be harder for her to keep up the charade of innocence and naivety she had lived with for so long.

Crowe was smart.

Ava reached down and dug around in her bag, drawing out a large manilla folder. She handed it across the table. Bailey took it from her with shaky hands. She didn't make a move to open it, just held it, her eyes on the bold print lettering that spelled out her father's name.

"Before you dig into that," Ava bit her lip, "there are some things you should know."

Bailey raised a suspicious brow at my sister. She wasn't buying any of it, but once Ava told her story, she might be more open to the idea that her father wasn't who he said he was.

"Where to start..." Ava pondered for a moment. "Your

father and Elias Ward have been friends since before college. They were part of the same fraternity."

"I don't understand." Bailey looked around the table, confused. "What does Elias Ward have to do with any of this?"

Ava pondered what to say next. Hers was a long and complicated story that brought up wounds that still hadn't healed. They were too fresh. But my sister was strong. She took a deep breath and launched into her story, her hand tight on Matthias's as she recounted her life with Elias Ward.

Bailey listened with rapt fascination as my sister recounted growing up within the Ward household. She was eleven when her mother was murdered in a botched home invasion. The assailant hadn't known she'd been hiding in a small space her mother had designated for emergencies. When the police arrived sometime later, they had found her, and social services shipped her off to live with who she'd been led to believe was her biological father.

Elias Ward.

Ava divulged her past openly, unshed tears crowding her eyes as she recounted how she had been treated growing up in that godforsaken household. The mental and physical abuse. Her obsessive, perverted brother. Father's hands were clamped so tightly around his cutlery, I thought they might bend beneath his hands.

There were a few things we knew about her time with Elias, but most of what we'd been told had been watered down or skipped altogether. We'd all been waiting patiently for a time when Ava would tell us on her own.

Part of me wished she hadn't.

If I ever saw Christian Ward again, I'd kill him with my bare hands, only to bring him back and do it again.

Fuck that.

I'd bring him to the brink of death, only to heal him and do it over again. Time after time. Slice after slice. He'd spend years being tortured by me and my family the exact same way he had tortured my sister.

"Wait." Bailey smiled behind her coffee cup. She set down the envelope in favor of the new mug of steaming coffee she'd been brought. Her plate of food had been set aside, uneaten. I'd have to make sure she ate before we left the table. "You ran away and the only thing you changed was your last name, which had been your last name prior to it being changed to Ward, and no one found you for an entire year?"

Ava smirked mischievously. "Yep."

"You had Elias and your husband searching for you, and none of them found you?" Both Bailey and Ava were cracking up laughing. Even my father was chuckling silently from his seat, the anger that had been rolling off him earlier dissipating slowly. He was looking at Ava with so much love and affection it was stifling.

Not that he didn't show his love for us, but there was a twinkle in his eye when he thought of Ava and a softness to him when he dealt with her. He wasn't much different with our sister Saoirse before she'd left for Ireland.

In a fit of rage.

But that was a story for another day.

"Let's be fair here." The Russian rolled his eyes, less amused than the rest of us. "No one thought you would make it out of the state. Let alone nearly halfway across the country."

"But I did."

"I can't believe no one found you when all you did was shorten your first name." Bailey was still cracking up over that tidbit of information. "Why didn't you come up with something different? Like Vivica Storm or something?"

Ava scrunched her nose in distaste. "Vivica Storm?" She snickered. "That sounds like a stripper name or someone who writes dirty erotica."

"I think all erotica can be considered dirty," Bailey pointed out.

"Not the point."

Bailey just shrugged her shoulders like she didn't care one way or the other. "Just saying."

"She's got a point, Ava," Seamus piped up. "It was kind of like you weren't even trying."

Our sister's mouth fell open in a dramatic gasp. "Well, excuse me, Mr. High and Mighty, but I didn't exactly know any better. It wasn't like I could watch television or anything, and the only books I was allowed to read had to be either from the school or smuggled in by Libby and Kenzi."

"Anyway," she added. "James Bond doesn't change his name everywhere he goes."

Seamus and I groaned. We should never have introduced her to those films.

"That's fiction," I reminded her, a small smile flitting at the edges of my mouth.

Ava shrugged. "All that matters is that it worked."

Bailey began cackling again, and Matthias sighed before saying, "Move this along, Red. Otherwise, we'll be here all night long, and I have plans for you later."

A flush crept up her neck. "Right. So back to the story…"

Ava went back to regaling Bailey with how Matthias had taken her from Elias. Who'd, of course, insisted she spy for him. She never did, much to my surprise. Or maybe she simply didn't have the opportunity. Then continued on about how Dashkov forced her to marry him.

I was waiting for my father to jump across the table and strangle the poor sod. He didn't. Much to my utter dismay.

His jaw was still clenched, his teeth grinding together, but he didn't make a move.

Damn.

Her voice was choked with sadness and regret as she remembered Libby, the one she called sister. The one she would always call sister. The poor lass had been shot in the head by a sniper during a trap they had tried setting for Elias.

"So that's how you ended up at the stables," Bailey reiterated after Ava explained that her getaway car had been hijacked and then plowed off the road. My sister nodded, biting into a small bit of cake Nan had brought out.

"Christian kept me there for nearly two weeks before Liam and the twins rescued me." Ava's smile glowed. "Then they blew it all up. That was my favorite part." She laughed lightly.

"What does any of this have to do with my father?" Bailey questioned.

Ava set her fork down on the porcelain plate and stared across the table at Bailey, her emerald eyes lit with determination, but I could see the sorrow lining the edges. She didn't want to reveal to Bailey the secrets she held. Ava may have been quiet and submissive in her time with Elias, but she listened and learned. He paraded her around like a prize to his meetings, believing he would always control her.

He was wrong, and now she used those secrets to crumble his empire and those associated with him.

"Because your father is the reason Elias and his associates have had such success with trafficking in Seattle," Ava told her, face calm, emotionless. "He's the one who started it."

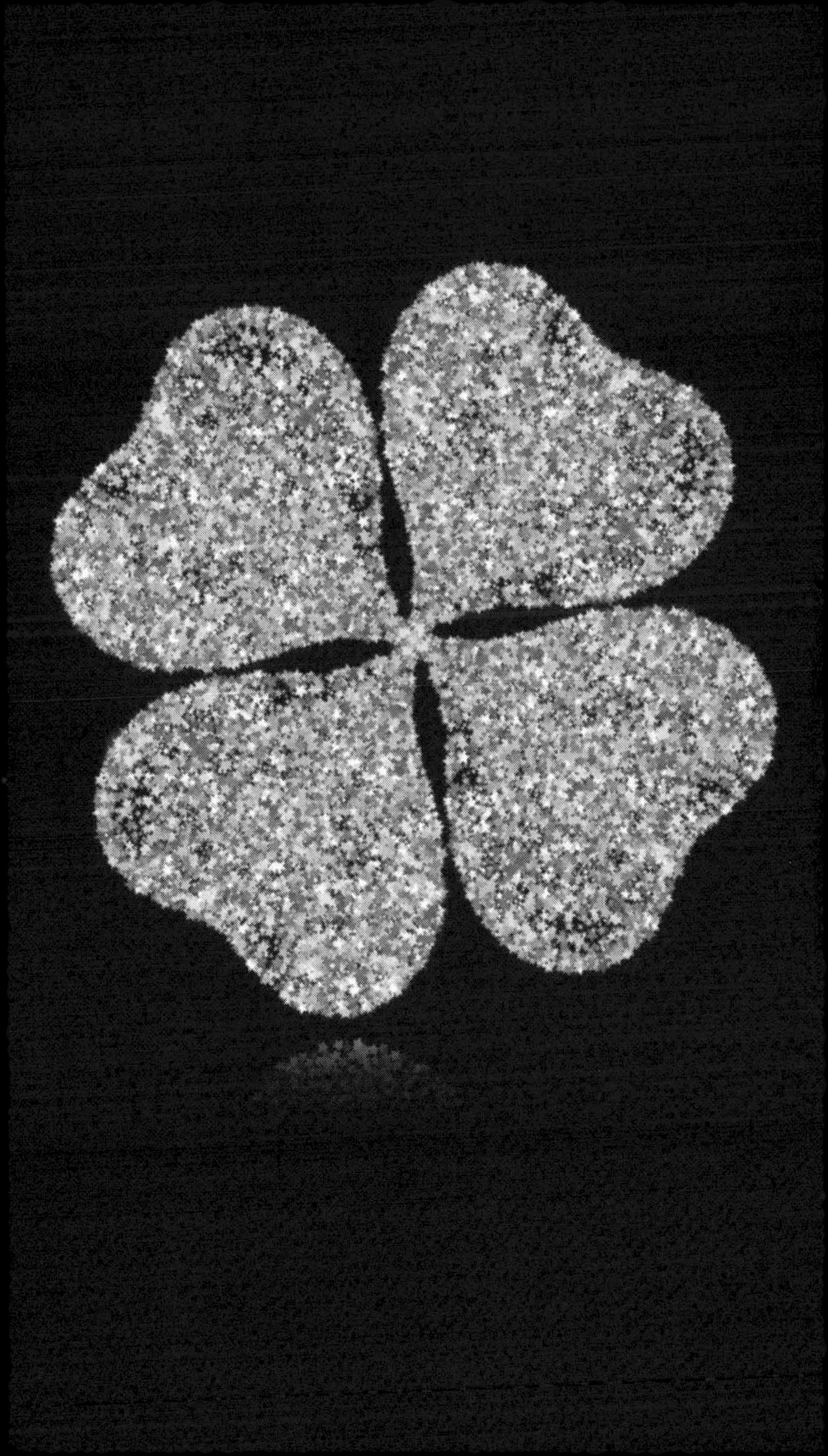

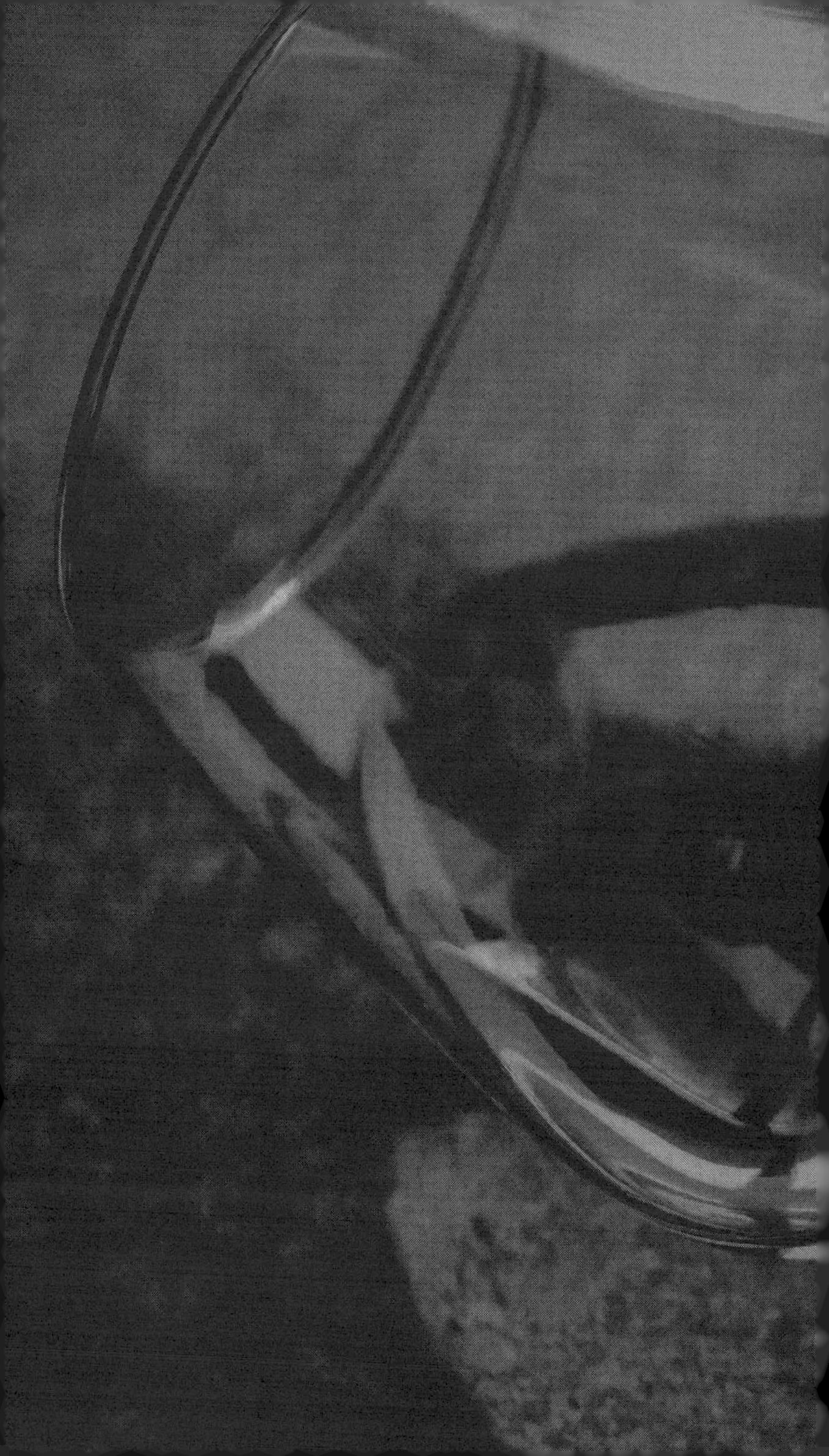

17

Bailey

Her words hung heavy in the air around me.
Choking me.
Suffocating me.
Suddenly, it felt hard to breathe as denial and panic surged through me. This couldn't be right.

"He's the one who started it."

I stared down at the file I had disregarded on the table in favor of my coffee. It sat there, taunting me, but I couldn't bring myself to open it. The table had grown quiet. My father was in no way a saint, but what these people, these *criminals*, were accusing him of made him out to be a monster.

A trafficker.

The very men he had sought to put away were the men who surrounded me. My father was nothing like these men. He couldn't be.

"Open the file, Bailey." Liam Kavanaugh's voice brooked no argument. Gingerly, I set my coffee down on the table and slid the file toward me. With shaking fingers, I opened the folder, the blatant truth staring back at me.

A smoking gun.

Still, this couldn't be what they thought it was.

Dashkov wasn't pulling punches when he put this file on my father together. The first paper that rested on the top of the stack was a photo of my father at the Ward stables they had blown up a few weeks ago on Mercer Island. He wasn't just admiring the horses.

"For fuck's sake," Seamus growled, grabbing the photo from the top, only for it to be replaced by a worse one. A strangled cry escaped me at the sight of the photo. "Dammit, Dashkov." He grabbed the file and sorted through the photos, pulling out the ones that clearly showed my father nailing underage girls in various positions. My stomach turned, bilious and sour, bile creeping up my throat. I barely held it back.

"Was that really necessary?" Liam raised an eyebrow at the Russian. Dashkov shrugged. "No use in sugar dusting."

"Coating," Liam corrected, receiving a sneer from his son-in-law. Glaring at the Russian, Seamus placed the folder in front of me, sans photos. Steeling myself, I pulled up the mental walls I had learned to erect, pushing forward with a dissociated interest.

It's just another story you're writing.

None of the documents made any sense to me. There were shell corporations on top of shell corporations mixed in with a few subsidiaries I didn't recognize. I wasn't sure what they wanted from me. My father didn't involve me in his business.

"This might as well be Greek," I admitted as I scanned through the documents. Fuck, there were so many. "I don't understand what you want me to do. You have those"—I swallowed back the bile in my throat—"photos. Why don't you just turn them in?"

Matthias scoffed. "If I wanted him to go down for fucking

underage girls, I would," he sneered. "But those charges wouldn't hold, and we both know it. He's got every judge in his corner. He'd be out on bail before the ink was dry on his arrest warrant."

"I still don't understand what you expect me to do," I bit out. "If you think for one second that my father involves me in anything other than to be the billboard for his campaign, you're wrong."

"I don't need him to tell you anything," he smirked. "I need you to access his safe where he stores his little black books. He's got blackmail on almost every politician in the state and some of the local gangs."

I snorted. Very unladylike, but who cared.

"Sure," I drawled sarcastically. "Let me just go and grab my safe-breaking kit from my little Mini Cooper, and Jason Statham and I will get right on that."

Blank faces all around.

Shit. What a wasted line. That was such a good movie.

"We have someone who can take care of that."

"Better be a damn good person," I muttered. "It's an electronic safe. Passkey protected on a local network that can't be hacked from an outside source. It would require a direct line using a verified ID card."

"Taken care of." The son of a bitch sounded so matter-of-fact it made me want to strangle him. Problem was, I wouldn't be able to get both of my hands around his meaty Russian neck. Did the man have body fat to speak of?

"Oh, well, if you say so." Kiernan's hand tightened on my leg when I rolled my eyes. One look from him told me he didn't appreciate eye rolling. Even if he wasn't on the receiving end. Which meant he wouldn't appreciate me sticking my tongue out at him. So I refrained. Barely.

Imagined it in my head instead.

"What about the auction?" Ava asked, nervously chewing on her lower lip.

"What about it?" Seamus repeated. "We won't be able to do much with it. The only way you can be a part of it is if you enter as a bidder."

"So we enter one of you as a bidder," Matthias stated simply. "You have something to bid. Or at least, under the pretense, you do."

"No," Kiernan growled. "Spying on her father is one thing. I will not subject her to that."

"To what?" I questioned.

"Nothing," Kiernan snarled.

"It must be something if you're all riled up about it," I pointed out.

"It's a flesh auction," Seamus muttered darkly.

Oh.

OH.

"Umm…you want to put me up for sale?"

My question was met by two emphatic *no*s, a hesitant *kind of*, and a very Russian-sounding *yes*.

Well, that answered everything perfectly.

"It could benefit her, too," Ava pointed out. Kiernan glared at his sister.

"For someone who abhors the skin trade, you sure as hell are pushing her into it."

"That's not what I—"

"What you meant?" Kiernan snarled. "What happens if we can't get her out of there or they drug her? Huh? Did you think of the ramifications of that?"

Ava looked away, somewhat chastened, but it didn't stop her from whispering, "It might help her find her friend. That's all."

"Putting her up for bid would also guarantee a spot for you," their father put in. "She is of worth."

Of worth?

"Every woman has worth," I pointed out.

"Yes," Liam agreed. "But you are the daughter of an esteemed senator. That holds power. People would pay a lot of money to own something so precious to their rival."

Yeah, I was precious all right.

As precious as fucking coal in a stocking at Christmas.

But if it meant finding Lina…

"I'll do it."

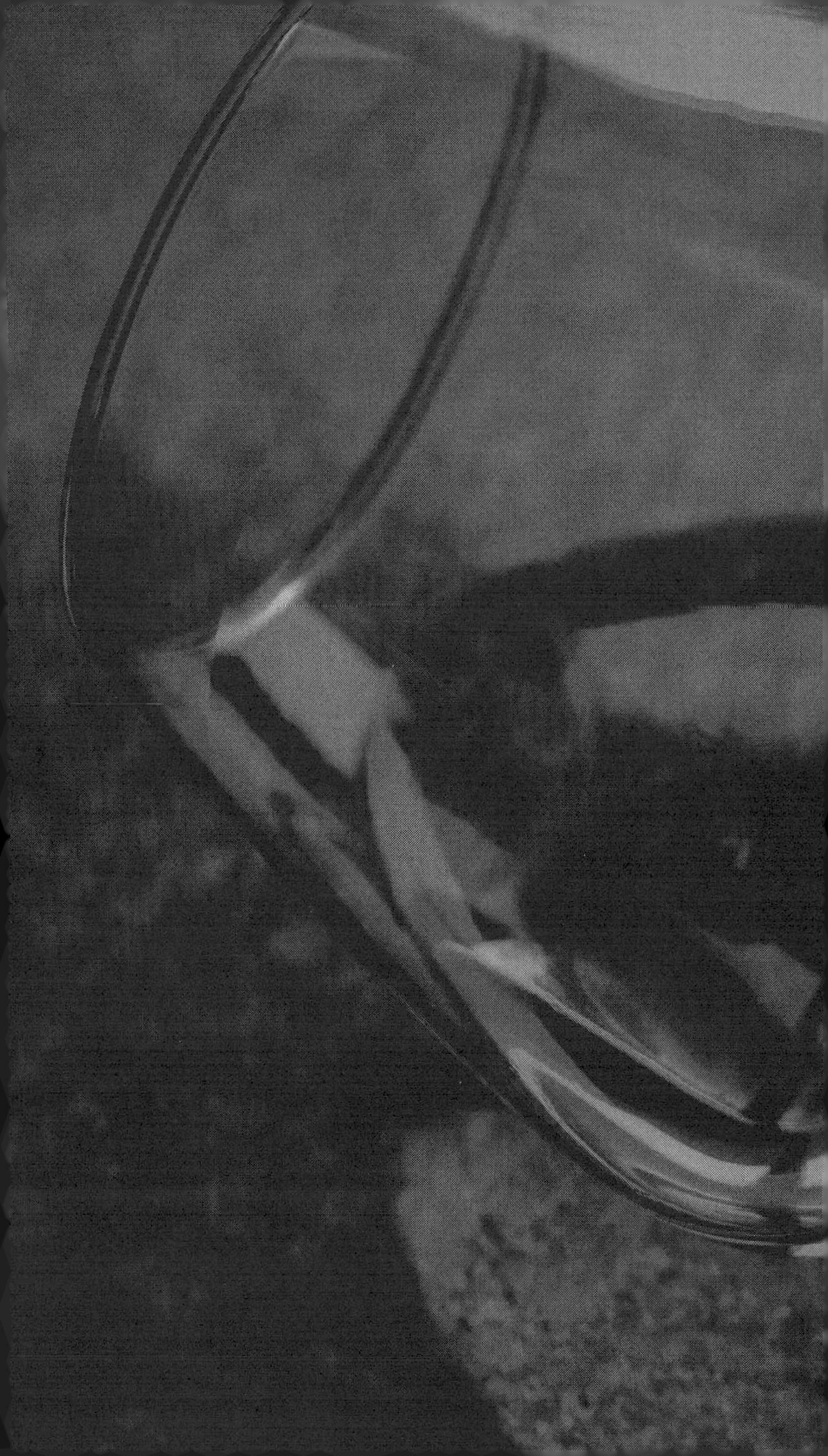

18

Seamus

She was grumbling, but it was kind of cute. Her little nose was scrunched up, making her look like a kitten. My breath caught in my throat at the sight of her when she first walked into the room.

Bailey held her coffee tightly in both hands, clutching the warmth to her chest. It wasn't freezing in the basement of the bar, but it wasn't exactly Hawaii either. Her raven hair was bundled at the top of her head in a messy bun, errant strays framing her heart-shaped face, blue eyes piercing me

through her obvious irritation.

My cock was already hardening, my mind barraging me with images of what I had planned on doing to her the night before. Instead, we'd tucked her into bed and headed downstairs to make a new plan. One involving Bailey.

I'd much rather have spit roasted her.

It wasn't a secret that Kiernan and I had been through many women. Owning our first club at twenty-one, plus our devilish good looks, had us in no shortage of available cunts, but Bailey was different. Special.

And completely forbidden.

Maybe that was part of the appeal.

Our father hadn't pushed us when it came to our plans for the blue-eyed vixen, but there was no mistaking the frustration behind his features whenever she was mentioned. Even at breakfast this morning, the air was thick with his restrained tension as he watched her smile and talk with Nan.

We were short on time.

If we kept Bailey for much longer, we would miss our chance to use her as a spy. The gala was less than a week away. Time was limited, and Bailey's family would soon begin to get suspicious about her absence.

But letting her go was a risk.

She was our biggest weapon against Crowe, and even though she appeared to be on board with our plan on the surface, Bailey was holding back. There was still a part of her that didn't believe that her father was capable of the things we had accused him of.

Even with the proof provided to her.

"Nice vision board you've got," Bailey teased. She was standing in front of the large movable whiteboard, staring up at the plan we'd put together so far regarding the gala. Having Bailey with us changed some of the aspects of it, but it wasn't anything we couldn't handle. The biggest problem was ensuring she stayed on target.

"It's a war board," I grumbled. "Not a vision board."

Bailey smirked. *Brat.* "If you say so."

"I do." Strolling toward her, I added a small blue pin to the board where Kiernan had attached his bid token, signifying that his item had been accepted. The pin represented Bailey. "Now, the purpose of the gala is for Ava to help identify Elias's top players. Her identifying the men Elias allowed into his home on business should narrow down the potential list of people who were supporting him prior to his death.

This will also be where we can exchange the information on your father without being suspicious."

"And you believe that person is helping support her brother now?" she asked hesitantly.

I nodded. "That's our theory," I confirmed. "Whoever was bankrolling Elias no doubt became fed up with his incompetence when it came to Dashkov. Especially after he took down the port."

"I thought Elias had Ava locked away?" Her face scrunched in confusion as she continued to study the board. "How would she know who Elias met with?"

Bailey had only bits and pieces of Ava's story from the time Ava ran away initially. She had no insight into the life my sister led before she was caught and brought back to Seattle. It made sense that she was puzzled about how someone who had essentially been a prisoner in her own home would have insider knowledge.

Might as well start at the beginning.

"I'm going to give you the abridged version. Otherwise, we could be here for years." I pulled out a chair and motioned for her to sit. Like a good girl, she did. "Okay, Ava's mother and our father were childhood sweethearts who grew up in Boston. Katherine, her mother, was the daughter of Seamus McDonough, billionaire shipping tycoon and head of the Irish mob. When my grandfather expanded to Seattle, they followed him, deciding to attend college at the University of Washington.

"They were in love. Yada. Yada. One weekend, while my father was away on business, Katherine went missing. My father searched everywhere for her. Never gave up. A few months later, she showed up on his doorstep without an explanation, and then two weeks later, she was gone."

"Kidnapped again?" Bailey asked, a horrified expression pasted across her pale face. I shrugged my shoulder.

"Who knows," I admitted. "Ava says she was caught by Elias and dragged back to him. Father says she left a note stating she couldn't be with him. That she no longer loved him. So he drowned his sorrow in my mother."

Bailey smiled. "And that's how you were born."

I chuckled. "Exactly." My expression sobered as I thought about everything Ava had told me about her mother. "According to Ava, Katherine found out she was pregnant and managed to escape again with some inside help. No one knows who. When Ava was eleven, someone broke into their house to rob them and ended up killing her mother. And the rest you kind of know. Somehow, Elias managed to bribe the police and social welfare and had Ava declared as his daughter. Except he never told anyone about her."

"So what does that have to do with how much information she knows?"

Right, I'd kind of forgotten to mention that.

I paused, thinking over how to explain the situation without dragging on forever.

"My sister said that someone paid Elias to kidnap and sell Katherine at an auction," I began. "Except, somewhere between kidnapping and selling her, Elias became obsessed with her. Now, this was before he took over the flesh trade from the Polish. He ended up buying her. So when he took Ava after her mother died, he used to parade her around his associates. Ava is very good at going unnoticed. Over the years, she heard enough to level him. Learned enough to set his world on fire. We just have to put it all into action."

Bailey set her coffee mug down on the wooden table and stood facing the whiteboard as she took in everything I'd just slammed her with.

"You think that my father is in league with men like Elias?" I didn't miss the sneer in her voice at her accusation.

Sighing, I leaned forward, knees on my elbows, and looked her directly in the eyes.

"You've seen the proof, Bailey," I whispered. "You're the one who is refusing to accept the truth of it."

"If you're right," I could see how much pain saying those words caused her, "then he will be at the auction that takes place a few days after the gala."

Slowly, I nodded.

"Then why do you need me to spy?"

"Because a man with his secrets would never keep them somewhere other people had easy access to. He'd keep them safe and close to home and somewhere that not even a raid would find. Your father worked right alongside Elias, up till his death, which means he could know who was supporting him."

"And what if he doesn't know?" she asked. "What if he is innocent?"

"Baby girl." I brought my hand up to cup her cheek. Her blue eyes dimmed, sadness filling them. "He isn't."

Her eyes closed, and she nuzzled her cheek into my hand, relishing in its warmth like a kitten.

"There is a removable wall in his safe," she whispered so low that I barely heard her confession. "It is so solidly built that no one knows it's false. He keeps a laptop there, I believe."

Brow furrowed, I stared down at her. "How do you know about it?"

She smiled coyly at me. "Your sister isn't the only one who often goes unnoticed. I don't believe that my father is capable of the things you say he is," she admitted. "But I am aware that he isn't a saint. I know he's blackmailed his opponents and has under the table dealings, but he would never do the things you're accusing him of."

"Bailey," I sighed.

She held up her hand to silence me. "No. I'll help you get the laptop, but only to show you that you're wrong about him."

Letting out a deep breath, I nodded my head, unwilling to push her any further. Bailey would come to the realization herself about the kind of man her father was. If we kept shoving everything at her, it would more likely blind her to the truth even more.

"Only problem with the laptop would be that it is most likely encrypted," I pointed out, running a hand down my face and groaning. "Bridgett would need to create a decryption key, and with the gala less than a week away…"

"We don't need a decryption key." Bailey turned her full attention to me. "I have one."

"You have one?" I asked, dumbfounded. That was surprising.

She shrugged nonchalantly. "Yeah. It's in my purse. Looks like a tube of lipstick, except it's empty. Inside is a small USB drive. I've had it for a few years now. Lina had this hacker kid she used from time to time make me one in case I ever ran into a jam."

Now that was surprising.

"And what were you using this little device for, *a stóre*?" I teased her.

"My porn collection," she deadpanned. I nearly choked at her response. Her blue eyes twinkled and then the minx winked at me before laughing. Jesus, her laugh was like listening to an angel. Pure and innocent. I wanted to hear her laugh more.

I wanted to be the reason she laughed.

The reason she was happy.

I wanted to be there when she cried.

Hold her when she was sad.

If only we could keep her.

But I couldn't begin to fathom how a relationship like ours would work. Our father had named my brother and me both as heirs. We'd rule the next generation of our family together, something that had never been done before. In taking this position, it meant we'd have to give up not only a marriage that revolved round love, but also our proclivities for sharing.

That had never been an issue before.

Even though we shared, we'd never fallen for the same woman.

Until Bailey.

There was something about our blue-eyed captive that set our souls on fire. Our blood boiled in our veins whenever she touched us. I mean, Jesus, the woman had me harder than a rock with just a simple glance. It was something neither of us had experienced before.

And it couldn't last.

We were the heirs to one of the most powerful families in the Pacific Northwest, and nothing we deemed to be good could last.

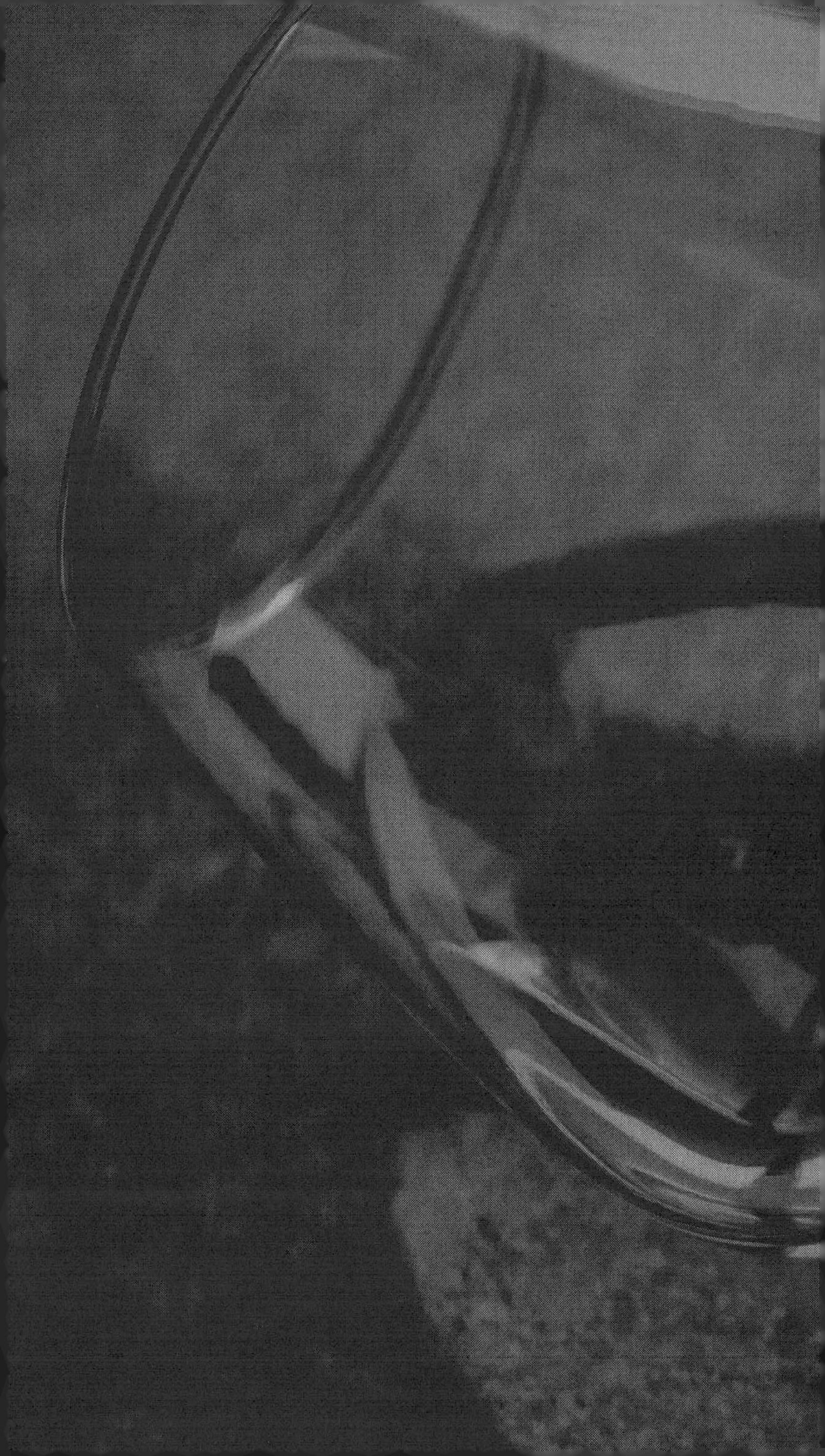

19

Bailey

Seamus had grown quiet as I studied the board in front of me. His jaw clenched and his hands tightened into fists, the thoughts in his mind no doubt taking a dark turn. I wanted to touch him. Comfort him, but the reality of the situation was that I didn't know if that was all right.

Because I didn't know him.

I didn't know either of them.

And yet, I wanted to. Despite the obvious Stockholm syndrome I was sporting. *Fuck.* All those years of dissing *Twilight*, and here I was pulling a Bella Swan. I did have a better excuse than her, though. Two, actually. Two wicked, wicked tongues.

I wasn't ever telling them that, though.

"So what's the plan?" I tilted my head to get a better look at him. "I'm assuming there's a reason you woke me up at the butt crack of dawn."

It wasn't that we hadn't gotten any sleep. Because we had. Too much, in my opinion. This would have been way more worth it if they would have spit roasted me like they promised. Instead, I was tucked into bed like a child and told to sleep.

Which I had.

Like the dead.

Still disappointing.

Seamus didn't say anything for a few moments, his eyes still on the board, but soon he was shaking his head, the melancholy disappearing from his face as if it had never been there.

"The plan," he smiled broadly, the carefree man returning, "is simple. Ava is going to be attending the gala with Leon, one of Matthias's enforcers."

"Why isn't she attending with him?"

His mouth twitched into a scowl. "Because the two of them still have some issues to work out, apparently," he sneered. "No one outside of the family and his men knows they're married. Not even my mother."

"Oh."

A twinge of sadness nipped at my soul for his sister. Much like me, she'd grown up believing her family didn't love or value her above what she could offer them. I was fifteen when it became abundantly clear that, to my father, the only usefulness I held was a marriage alliance and providing my husband with an heir.

It was at that age that I'd been forced to endure my first examination to make sure I was fertile and able to carry children. Because, according to Sarah, a woman was only as good as her womb. I nearly shoved the doctor's forceps into her neck. Instead, I snapped back.

"Guess you're pretty useless then, right?" I spoke. *"Since all you birthed was a girl, and now you're as barren as the Sahara?"*

That earned me three days locked in my room with no food and barely any water.

Good times.

There was one difference between us, though. Ava had found a family that cared for her. That wanted her. While I was still nothing more than a tool to be used until my uselessness became inevitable.

"Ava's job is to mingle and point out the people she's seen with Elias," he continued. "Your job is to slip us the information from the computer."

Wonderful.

"The gala serves two purposes," he informed me. "The first is to bring the most powerful and corrupt people together under one roof for what appears to be a good cause. The second is, during that time, those who are entering goods into the auction will have a chance to drum up interest with bidders and sellers."

Well, that sounded positively wretched.

"How will Kiernan know who the other sellers are?" I wondered.

Seamus pointed to a small blue lapel pin on the board with a black dahlia in the center.

"This identifies sellers, and this one," he pointed to another pin that was red with a blue rose, "identifies bidders. If they're wearing both pins, they are entered as both."

"How are we going to get me to the auction?" I asked. "Once I go back home, I'm going to be watched like a hawk."

Seamus smirked.

"We're going to kidnap you," he paused. "Again."

I snorted. "Good luck with that."

"We have a plan," he admitted with a shrug. "It's a bit of a wibbly-wobbly plan, but there are a lot of variables we can't account for. The one thing we can account for, however, is having an exit plan in place in case things go south."

"We'll all be wearing wireless communication devices that can't be tracked." With a hand on my lower back, Seamus steered me toward a small table in the corner. He picked up a small earpiece and showed it to me. "They can't be tracked or traced or detected. They work off the vibrations in your jaw. All you have to do is speak, and we'll hear you. We're going to sew this into the clothes we send you home in to ensure we have open communication with you."

"Cool." Now that was some James Bond technology right there.

"If for any reason you find that things are going south with your father, your code word is whiskey." He smirked at me. "Thought you might like that."

I wrinkled my nose in distaste.

Whiskey and I weren't friends any longer.

Tequila was going to be my new best friend. It didn't get me kidnapped.

"Okay." I nodded. "Code word whiskey. Don't get caught. Now what?"

Seamus's smirk darkened.

"Now we get sweaty."

Sweaty?

Wait, what?

Seamus's kind of sweaty was no fucking fun.

The bastard had been grinning from ear to ear like he was about to get lucky, and if he got lucky, I got lucky. With multiple orgasms.

Instead, he led me to a room full of mats and proceeded to tell me to take off my shoes and socks. I counted my blessing he didn't have a hidden foot fetish no one knew about. Seamus led me to the middle of the mats where he outlined some basic defensive tactics, playing offense to my defense.

I was trying really hard to concentrate on what he was saying and not on the fact that his hands were roaming all over my body. God's honest truth. Except—it was easier said than done when every time he touched me, I swear I felt a sizzle on my skin.

This was hell. I was in hell. This was a special brand of torture just for me. I knew it. Seamus knew how to move his body—I was aptly aware of that—and I couldn't help but admire his brute strength coupled with what I assumed was flawless technique.

I was by no means an expert on self-defense.

Or a real man's physique.

Drew's body could be described in one word: limp.

That maybe wasn't the best word choice, but compared to Seamus and Kiernan, he was nothing more than a limp-dick unicorn. He wrapped his arms around me in a bear hug from behind, and I bit the inside of my cheek, drawing blood as I tried not to think about all his *other* moves. The ones I'd orgasmed to all night long.

Seamus moved one hand to my throat, hooking it under my chin. We were both sweating pretty good by this point, and I was acutely aware of how his sweaty, muscular body pressed up against mine. And it was naked.

Somewhere in the lesson, his shirt had magically disappeared, and I prayed to whatever god was listening that it never came back.

Maybe if I prayed hard enough, his pants would magically dissolve too.

My inner hussy was panting with her tongue hanging out,

begging me to jump his bones right here and now and just put her out of her misery. Jeez, two days with these men, and I was becoming a sex-crazed maniac. I ignored her rampage, instead focusing on Seamus outlining how I was going to break the chokehold he currently had me in.

"Come on, good girl," he purred in my ear, his tongue licking the shell. *And there goes my inner hussy with her pompoms out, buck naked, ass wiggling in the air for more.* "Break this hold, and I might just give you a reward."

Asshole. If I broke this hold, I was going to deck him for getting me all wound up.

Hard.

Every single inch of his delicious frame was firmly pressed into my back, rendering me immobile. My hands were wrapped around his forearms, trying to create space for my airway. Our height difference had me on my tiptoes.

A shiver rushed down my spine as his deep, gravelly voice washed over me. Yep, my inner hussy had passed out from lack of oxygen at this point. I felt the smug bastard smiling at my reaction.

Oh, it was on like Donkey Kong.

I arched my back, pressing my ass into his crotch. Taken off guard for a moment, he didn't see what was coming next. I slammed my heel down onto his foot while simultaneously dropping down to lower my center of gravity. My right elbow rammed into his abs—hard—and I had to suppress a groan of pain. I was convinced it may have hurt me more than it hurt him.

Screw Seamus and his eight-minute abs of steel.

The reaction from him was immediate. He let out an *oomph* as he lifted his right foot, his body hunching over as he struggled to regain his breath. His arms loosened against my neck just enough that I was able to twist and duck, releasing myself from his hold. His mind seemed to be catching up with his body now as he lunged at me with his left hand. I side-stepped his advance, and using his momentum against him, I grabbed his outstretched hand, twisting it over my head as I dropped down to one knee.

Seamus flipped over, landing on his back with a loud slap on the mat. A moment later, I was straddling his hips, grinding my pelvis down onto his erection.

"I want my reward now," I panted, running my hands up his chest. "And it better be in orgasms."

"Fuck," he growled. His hand grabbed the back of my neck, pulling me down to his level, smashing his mouth against mine. This wasn't like the sweet kisses he'd given me last night. No, this was fierce and all-consuming. I ran my fingers through his hair, basking in the softness as I pulled it from the bun at the back of his head.

Irish hippie.

A gasp tore through me as he tore at my tank top. Literally. The fucker split it right down the middle of my back. His hands pushed me to sit up, removing the tattered garment from my body before flipping our positions.

Seamus licked his lips, the sea of emerald in his eyes drowned out by his dilated pupils. He flicked the front clasp of my bra, palming my breasts in his hands. They were warm and calloused, a working man's hand. My feet crawled up his legs, and I used them to push his sweatpants down, revealing his muscular, shapely ass.

Jesus, I could bounce a quarter off that thing.

He tore at my leggings, yanking them off my legs in one swift motion before he was on me again. I wrapped my hand around his massive cock, stroking firmly. Seamus groaned low in his chest, sounding more animal than man as he feasted on my mouth, exploring every inch.

"Jesus on a pancake," I moaned as he surged his hips forward, burying himself to the hilt. He stilled, his hair creating a veil around us as he simply gazed down at me.

There was something in the way he stared at me that caused my core to tighten and my heart to surge painfully. I knew in that moment that I'd fallen for him. My captor. My prison guard. A man I hardly knew.

Maybe it was Stockholm syndrome.

Or maybe I was just rebounding.

I'd never been in love before. Not even with Drew. I'd also never been with any other man besides the twins. What did that say about me that I'd fallen for the first two men to show any interest in me after the only man I'd ever been with cheated?

Was this love?

Or was it something else?

I tightened my legs around his waist, bucking my hips to get him to move, quickly becoming uncomfortable with where my thoughts were taking me. Seamus needed to fuck me —now.

"Seamus," I moaned, rocking my hips, pleading with him to move. I needed him to move. "Please."

The Irish sex god smirked, my begging drawing him out of his soft gaze.

"Ask nicely, wildcat," he whispered heatedly.

I groaned, wishing I could take it back. Fuck...I really wanted orgasms. The Kavanaugh twins had created a monster. An orgasm-loving monster.

"Please, sir," I purred, licking my lips as I ran my hands down his chest, my nails scraping at the skin hard enough to leave little red lines in their wake. Seamus shuddered. "Please fuck me."

"All you had to do was ask."

Then he began to move in earnest. I bucked against him like a woman possessed, meeting each of his brutal thrusts with my own. He sucked one of my nipples into his mouth, one hand coming up underneath my ass, pushing him in even deeper. I whimpered needily against his lips, snaking my hand down between us and teasing my swollen clit. The added stimulation sent me hurtling toward the abyss, my muscles tightening and my core clenching as I screamed his name.

"Fuck, wildcat," he cursed as he pumped into me like a lion taking his bitch in heat, prolonging my orgasm until I was sobbing into the crook of his neck, holding on for dear life. "Jesus, you're a dream."

Stars exploded across my vision as the first orgasm bled into the second, and I was nothing more than a boneless heap beneath him.

"Now that was the type of sweatiness I'd been hoping for," I laughed breathlessly. Seamus chuckled as he rolled us onto our sides, his cock still buried inside me. We remained like that for a while, catching our breath and basking in the afterglow of our fucking. My head rested against his bicep; his arm curled possessively around me. I ran my hand down his pecs, sweeping my fingers along the masterful paintings of his chest.

The rumbling of my stomach broke through the comfortable silence. Seamus must have heard it talking, because he smiled before easing himself out of me.

"Let's get you fed, wildcat." He stood, gently dragging me along with him. When he turned away from me to grab his clothes, I got the perfect view of his round, muscular ass, and my pussy was throbbing all over again.

A sheepish grin formed on my face when he turned and caught me staring, the heat in his eyes returning as he took in my naked state, his cum still dripping down my legs. A part of me wanted to be embarrassed, but I was far from it. If anything, it turned me on even more.

My heart sank in my chest, and my thoughts darkened. Was this just sex to them? None of us had discussed the finer points of what we were. If we were anything at all. I was their captive, after all.

Were they laughing at me while they were alone? Joking about how easy it was to seduce and fuck Crowe's daughter? Was this nothing more than revenge? The joke would be on them if that was the case. My father didn't give a fuck about me, but he would care if I fucked the men he was trying to take down.

"Stop staring at me like that," he teased me with a wink, breaking through my thoughts. Bending down, he passed me my discarded clothes. "I'm more than just a piece of meat, you know."

"Is that so?" I teased him back as I pulled them on, sans tank top. That wasn't going to be an option since he'd torn in right down the middle of my back.

"That's right." He grinned, handing me his T-shirt. "I've got brains up in here, baby." He pointed to his head.

"I'll keep that in mind when I'm making my selection." I winked at him. His face fell comically.

"Selection?" he asked, feigning hurt, hand splayed across his chest as he let out a dramatic gasp. "You think you can choose between the two of us?"

I raised an eyebrow at him. "Who said either of you were in the running?" I joked, heading for the elevator.

"You got someone else in mind, wildcat?" His pace quickened as he made his way toward me. "Someone else who can satisfy your greedy needs?"

Looking over my shoulder, I shot him a smirk. "BOB has always been pretty good in that area."

"Who the hell is Bob?"

I laughed but didn't answer as I broke into a sprint.

"Who the hell is Bob, wildcat?"

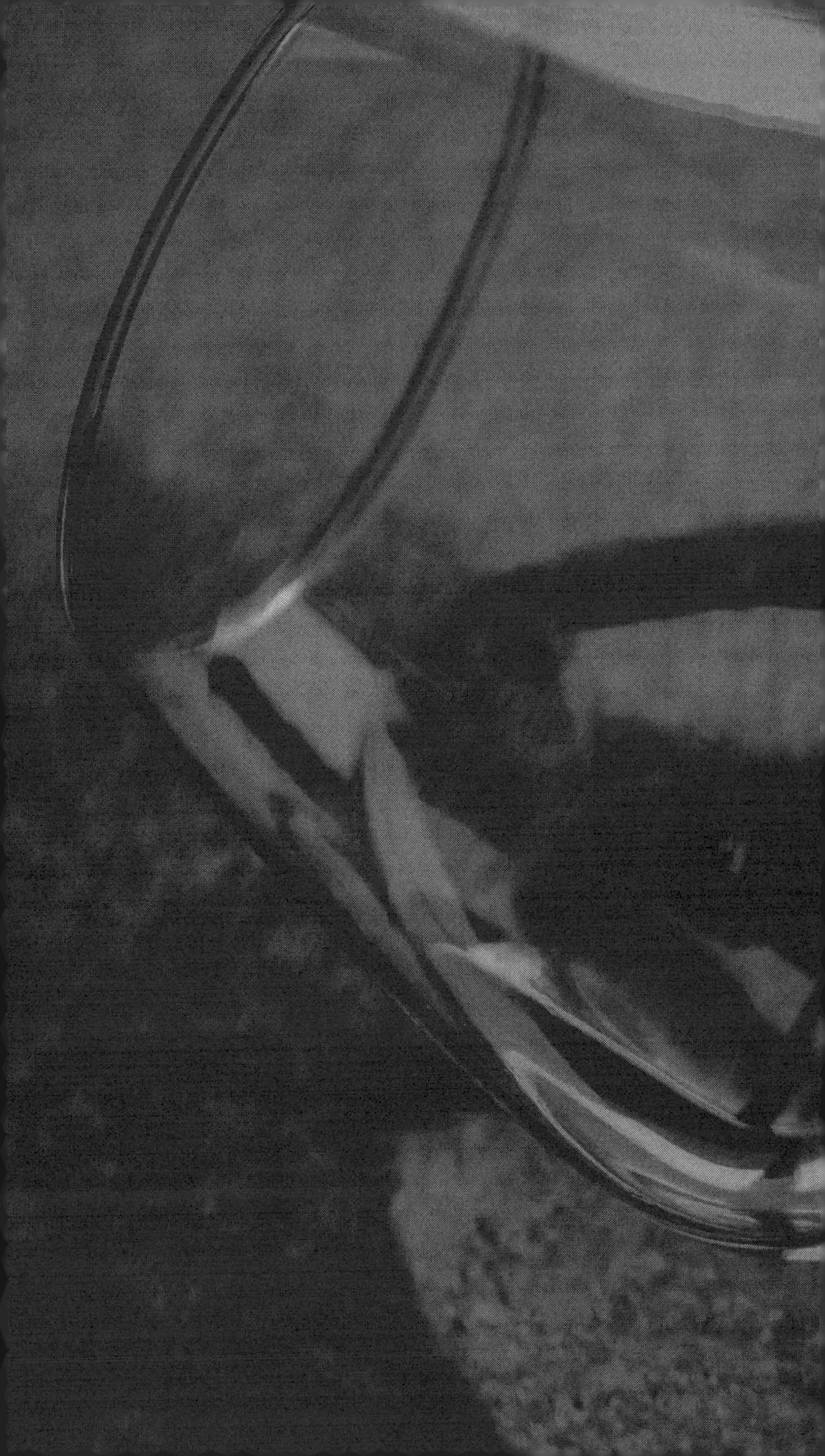

20

Bailey

Traitor and whore.

Those were the two words that were currently rattling around in my brain as Nan held up the dress that had been set aside for me to wear to the auction that was being held just days after the gala.

The word *dress* was a bit of a stretch. It was nothing more than two poorly sewn together pieces of fabric with thin armholes.

"There is no fucking way I am wearing that." I narrowed my eyes at the scrap of fabric. Maybe if I glared at it hard enough, it would burst into flames. "I'm pretty sure my vagina would pull a Paris Hilton."

Ava snorted. The redheaded bombshell was currently sitting on my bed, her legs folded under her, flipping through some trashy magazine she'd brought with her. Next to her sat a pile of clothes she'd washed for me to wear back to my house. My car had magically been fixed, and everything was set for me to make my sudden appearance back home.

"I know it's not the best, lass," Nan said gently. "But it is what's expected of you."

Stupid, stupid idea.

"You couldn't find something with at least a little more length?"

This was what I had signed up for. Being paraded around like Kiernan's whore, which was a lot more fun in the bedroom when he was whispering dirty Irish sayings in my ear and less fun when it required me to be pranced around like a brood mare waiting to be mounted.

"We can't always get what we want, now can we?"

"Sure, I can," I told her. "If I set it on fire." Although that might be hazardous to the environment since it was no doubt made from some toxic material.

"I'll get the matches." Ava winked conspiratorially at me, and I laughed. She was a lot like Seamus, easygoing and quick to laughter, but the glint beneath her emerald eyes told me she could be just as cold and stubborn as Kiernan.

Or her father.

"Might need to find a crater to burn it in," I sighed. "It's probably also considered hazardous waste."

Nan tutted at our banter, scolding us like two small children, but there was no mistaking the laughter behind her eyes.

"For a prisoner, she sure is growing bold." A sharp voice cut through our laughter. Nan's smile faded and her eyes narrowed into slits as she stared down the intruder.

"For someone who says she's not a witch," Ava snarled, "you sure know how to appear out of thin air when you're not wanted. Where's your broomstick? Did you lose it? Or is it just shoved so far up your ass no one can see it?"

Well, holy fucking shit balls on a tortilla.

My vagina just exploded.

Fuck, I wasn't into chicks, but whatever the hell they were putting in the Kavanaugh sibling gene soup was sure as hell stirring my pot.

"I'd remember who the guest is here, Avaleigh," the woman hissed, her red painted lips turned up in a snarl. She was slender, with pin-straight strawberry-blond hair that fell just past her stiff shoulders. Her face was narrow and her porcelain skin was nearly flawless. Muddy brown eyes were framed by long lashes caked in mascara.

She looked familiar, but I couldn't place where I'd seen her.

"You." Nan glared at the woman. "How many times do I have to remind you of that? You, Marianne, are the guest here, and how the twins choose to handle Bailey is their business, not yours."

"My sons once again disappoint me," the bitch, Marianne, muttered. I'd have taken the fireplace irons to her face if I hadn't been so shocked at her being the twins' mother. The woman hadn't been at dinner the other night, and since the twins hadn't bothered to share much about their normal lives —outside of growing up in Ireland—I hadn't known why.

Now I could see exactly why she wasn't invited.

Debbie downer. Bitch on a stick.

How had this woman birthed two amazing men?

Ugh, there's that Stockholm syndrome talking.

Kidnappers, Bailey, they're your kidnappers. Hot fucking kidnappers who managed to light my vagina on fire.

"Did you have something important ta say, Marianne?" Nan's forehead raised and her eyes narrowed at the woman. "Or did you just come here to complain?"

Marianne put on a plastic smile that was so fake even the Russian space station could see it.

"I was hoping to have a word with our little captive here," she gritted, the smile still in place.

Nan snorted. "She's busy."

The twins' mother went to protest, but Nan was having

none of it. "Why don't you do us all a favor, dear, and make yerself scarce? Ye've never been a help before. No reason ta start now."

Ava cracked a laugh as Marianne huffed, turned on her heel, and stomped from the room. *And I thought I had temper tantrum problems.*

"Snake, that one," Nan muttered darkly. "Judas in the flesh."

I really wanted to know, but I didn't.

But I really did.

So I asked.

"What's her deal with you?" I turned to Ava, sneering at the red pumps Nan laid out with the dress. "I'm not wearing those. I'll break my leg."

"Fashion is pain, dear."

"You know what's also painful?" I shot back. "A broken leg."

Nan ignored me and then shuffled out to the room, closing the door as she went. Meanwhile, Ava was smiling brightly at me from the bed.

"She's a hoot, right?"

"Oh yeah," I deadpanned. "I've always wanted a grandmother who would dress me as a hooker."

Ava laughed.

"But really." I shifted myself to the bed, keeping a few feet between us. Seamus had told me that Ava didn't enjoy being crowded. "What's your deal with the Wicked Witch of the West?"

"It's a long story." She sighed. "Marianne and my mother were best friends growing up. When my mom went missing the first time, she didn't file a police report until a week later. Even suppressed evidence of their dorm room being raided."

"Jesus," I muttered.

"When I confronted her about it, she got defensive," Ava murmured sadly. "And every time I try to bring it up to Liam, he shuts me down. Doesn't listen to me. It's like he's completely blind when it comes to Marianne."

Her life was a real-life soap opera. A Korean drama. A mafia romance. There were more moving parts than I could keep track of, and part of me wanted to reach out and hold her. I wanted to assure her. Keep her safe. This sudden flare of protectiveness I'd never felt before took hold of me.

With Dalia, I'd never been allowed to be a true sister. Not that the spoiled brat or her demon mother would let me. Dalia wasn't my sister, and I'd never felt a kinship with her. Not like I do with Ava. She was like a younger sister, even though we were pretty close in age.

"I'm sorry," I whispered, a lone tear tracking down my cheek as I took her in. This amazing woman had been through hell and survived. She'd been beaten down. Used. Abused. And she'd still come out fighting. "I don't know if anyone has said that to you, but I'm sorry for what you had to go through. I'm sorry no one was there to protect you or defend you."

Her emerald eyes found mine, and she silently wept, her shoulders shaking with the force of her quiet sobs. Acting on instinct, I pulled her into me, wrapping her in my arms and soothingly rubbing her back.

I hoped it was soothing. There wasn't exactly a manual for this sort of thing, and I'd always been shit at comforting people. We sat like that for what felt like hours. Two damaged souls taking comfort in one another.

"They like you." Ava shifted, her hand wiping at the tears that had dried on her cheek. "The twins. They really like you."

I snorted in disbelief. "More like they like me in their bed."

Ava sat up, her nose scrunching in distaste as she looked at me. "That was not an image I needed."

"But it's the truth."

"No, it's not," she shook her head.

Running a hand through my disheveled hair, I sighed. "I'm their prisoner, Ava," I reminded her. "They don't talk to me about anything. Don't ask about what I like or don't like. They don't tell me about themselves besides random stories here and there about growing up. Hell, I don't even know their favorite colors or how old they are."

"Are those things really important, though?"

"Uh..." I wasn't sure how to answer that. Of course they were important. Right? How else did you get to know someone? Wasn't that how you learned about the ones you wanted to be with? By knowing that they seemed to both favor a dark maroon that brought out the green in their eyes. The way they vehemently refused to put cream or sugar in their coffee. Seamus seemed to thrive off verbal praise, while Kiernan was more about subtle touches.

They were hard, sometimes exacting in the way they dealt with their men, but they were fair, listening to the complaints of their people. I'd heard them on video calls countless times, checking in with their lieutenants, inquiring about the community. They were caring and passionate.

"You know more about them than you think you do." Ava grinned cheekily. "One of the first things I learned from my asshat of a husband is that words are nothing more than wasted air. Pretty lies wrapped up in decadent packaging. What matters are the actions. Their touches. Their smiles. Your mind pays attention to them, even if you think it doesn't.

They might not ask, but that doesn't mean they aren't paying attention."

Now I was the one crying.

Stupid tear ducts.

Stupid Irish Yoda.

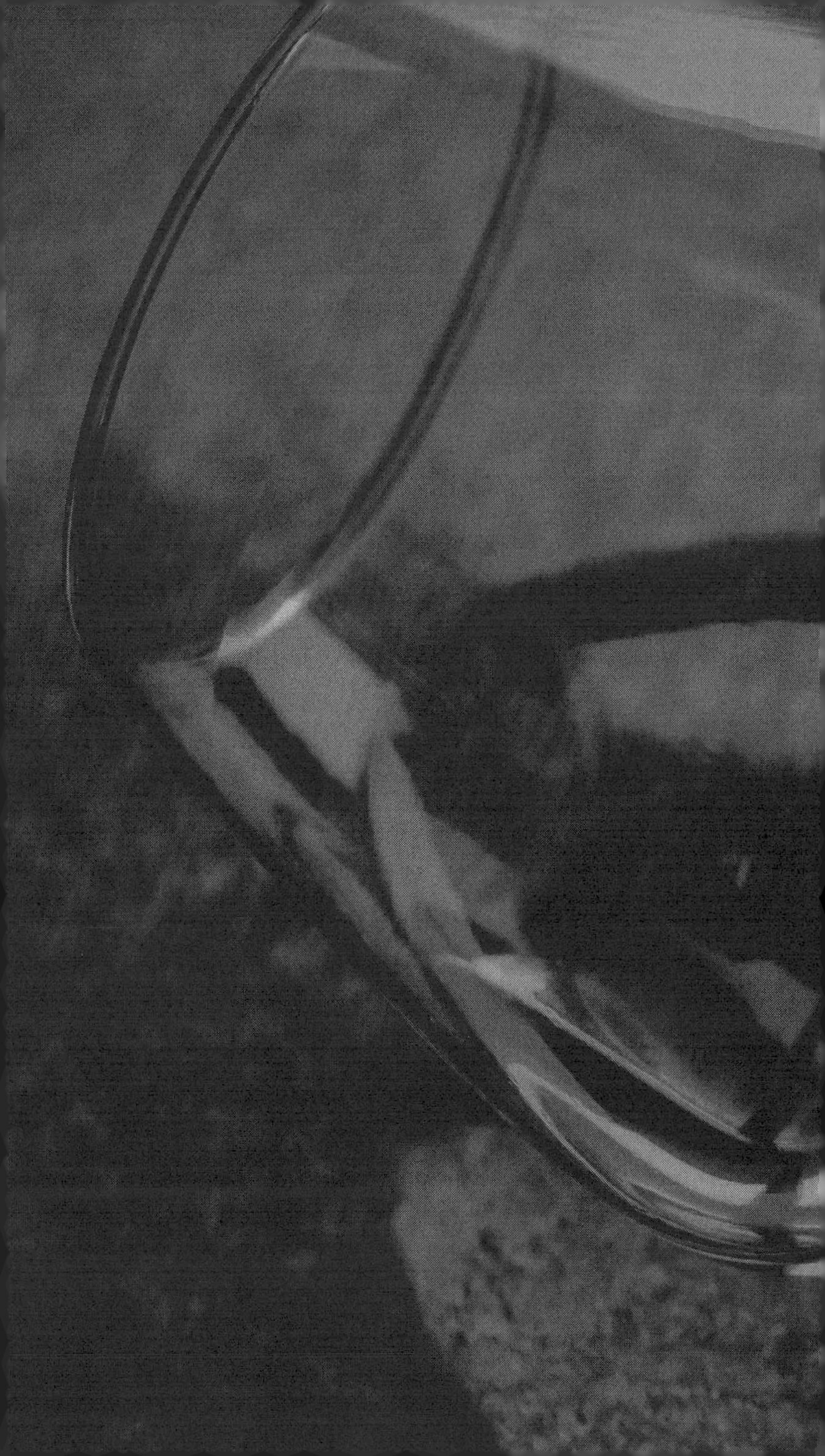

21

Bailey

I stayed in the spare room long after Ava left, curled up on the bed as I stared out the window facing the main street. Tomorrow night was the night, and a pit of unease had begun to grow in my stomach. The twins had been gone all day on business, muttering about taking care of a few loose ends before the gala.

Ava's words stayed with me as I watched the sun sink behind the steel trappings of the city. Was anyone looking for me? Ever since I could remember, I'd been obsessed with working. Making my own way. I'd graduated from high school at sixteen. College by nineteen, and I'd become one of the city's leading reporters by the time I was twenty-two.

The signs were all there. I'd just continually ignored them.

For years, I'd pushed myself, and for what? It never brought me any joy. I did it to get out from under my father and away from Drew. As much as I had wanted the arrangement to work, I'd known in my soul, all along, that it wasn't a right fit. Even if I'd done everything right—married him and been his trophy wife—he still would have wound up in bed with Brittany. Because that was the type of man he was.

The last week had shown me things I'd never have found if Seamus and Kiernan hadn't kidnapped me. They opened my mind to what I'd been missing.

Me.

For so long, I'd done nothing but live in the shadow of my father and stepmother. Shunned and kept away simply for being born. I was a mistake, and I'd let that dictate my life. I may have won my small freedoms, but now, away from the influence of my family, I realized that I hadn't won those. They'd allowed them because they were useful.

Drew was meant to be my escape. Even if he'd been arranged by my father, it was still more freedom than I'd ever had. But, in reality, he'd been another trap set to keep me subdued. The only thing that had saved me was his desperation to get out from under his father.

I'd always been a pawn, and I hated that I never truly noticed that nothing was my decision.

I just wanted to be able to make my own choices.

"There you are, wildcat." I'd been so caught up in my inner musings that I hadn't heard the door to the room open. "What are you still doing in here? Nan said you finished trying on your gala dress hours ago."

Shrugging a shoulder, I continued to stare out the window, not moving. Ava's words were still churning in my mind, and I couldn't seem to let them go. The side of me that still believed in princes and knights, the little girl who dreamed of fairy tales, wanted with all her heart to believe that these two men cared about me.

That I was more to them than just the sum of my last name.

"Hey, now," he whispered. The bed dipped behind me,

and then Seamus was pulling me into his lap. "What's all this?"

"I don't know." I cuddled closer to his warm, broad chest. "Just anxious about going home tomorrow night, I guess." Seamus's arms tightened around my smaller frame, one hand running soothing circles down my back while his other hand came to my cheek.

"We won't let anything happen to you, Bailey." He held my gaze, his emerald eyes holding mine as he conveyed how serious he was. "I promise you that. You're ours, wildcat, and we protect what's ours."

That was the crux of the situation, though, wasn't it?

I wasn't theirs. I could never be theirs, and I opened my mouth to tell him so, but he silenced me with a kiss. Soft, tender, and slow. Like we had all the time in the world.

"You're ours, Bailey," he vowed, edging himself off the bed with me still in his arms. "And we're gonna show you just how much."

I held on to his neck as he carried me out of the spare room and back to the one I'd spent every night in. The bed they pleasured me in, held me in.

"Found her, I see." Kiernan strode out of the bathroom, a towel around his waist.

"Aye," Seamus confirmed cheekily as he set me down on my feet. "Thought she could escape us and hide away."

Kiernan beamed. "And here I thought we could give our good girl a reward."

Fuck me, those two words were like a fucking spell.

"I was too a good girl," I told them obstinately. "I was very good. Ask Nan."

The twins laughed. "I don't think we can trust yer word, lass."

Well, shit.

"Look here, mister," my eyes narrowed playfully at him, "I'll have you know I was on my best behavior. I deserve orgasms."

The twins stared at each other in shocked silence for a moment at my words. I'd been forward with them before, but not when it came to the bedroom. In the bedroom, I was still as demure as I'd started. It wasn't my area of expertise, and the twins were more than happy to take control.

"Oh, did you hear that, brother?" Seamus smirked, the hunger in his eyes sending a shiver of desire to my core. "Our lady wants orgasms."

"Lots of them," I made sure to add.

Kiernan raised a brow at his brother. "Lots of them, indeed, *mo fraochÚn beag.*"

And there goes my inner hussy and her cartwheels.

"Better start stripping if you want those orgasms, wildcat." Seamus winked at me. He dug around in the nightstand by the bed as I all but tore my clothes from my body until I was standing naked before them. Seamus dropped an unmarked bottle on the bed and then proceeded to remove his own clothes. All Kiernan had to do was drop his towel.

All my thoughts disappeared, and there was nothing left but the hot stroke of desire surging through me. The twins glanced at each other, having another silent conversation, before Kiernan moved to one of the wingback chairs, pulling it to the end of the bed. He sat, his legs spread wide, lazily stroking his cock.

"Let's give him a show, wildcat."

I squealed as Seamus pulled me to the end of the bed so my legs were dangling off. Leaning back slightly, I spread my legs, giving him an unobstructed view. I gazed at Kiernan through hooded eyes as I trailed my fingers down my chest, letting them linger on my breasts before inching them down my stomach to my mound.

"Show us how you make yourself come," Kiernan demanded, his chest rising and falling in shallow pants of unobstructed desire. My hand paused, trembling slightly as it hovered over my vagina. I'd never made myself come before, at least not with my hand. Sure, I had a vibrator or two that latched on to my clit like a champ, but I'd never been one for sticking my own fingers inside my pussy.

Why?

Because I wasn't one of those unicorn women who got off on penetration. It was all about the clit rather than the dick.

I should get that printed on a T-shirt.

"What's stopping you, baby?" Seamus whispered in my ear. "Stage fright?"

Swallowing past my anxiety, I shook my head before whispering, "I've never...done this before."

Cue the laughter.

There wasn't a sound.

The twins' faces were twisted in confusion as they stared at me.

"You've never masturbated before, wildcat?" Seamus asked, incredulity tainting his voice.

I shrugged like it was no big deal. "Not with my hand." Coughing, I cleared my throat. "Just with those clit stimulator thingies when Drew didn't get the job done."

Kiernan smirked deviously.

"And how often did Drew not get the job done?"

And cue the dick measuring contest. If there was a contest. There really wasn't. They were lightyears ahead of Drew.

"Um—never."

The twins shared a look before breaking out into a bout of laughter. I honestly didn't see what was so funny about having to provide myself with orgasms, but to each their own.

"I'm so glad my boring sex life amuses you," I grunted. "It's not my fault he never listened or paid attention to what I wanted."

It sure as hell wasn't. I wasn't experienced in bed, but I'd seen pornos, and I'd been vocal with Drew on plenty of occasions about what I wanted. The asshole just never listened. I wasn't a virgin, but the twins had been my first in a lot of things. Like oral. Sure, I'd given my cheating ex-fiancé a blow job or two, but after the second time, he never asked for it again.

Something which I was grateful for.

Kiernan was the first man I'd gone down on and enjoyed.

Heat engulfed my back as Seamus sidled up behind me.

"Boys like him don't know how to pleasure a woman." Seamus took my hand in his, leading it down between my thighs. His other hand seamlessly parted my lips before he pressed two of my fingers against my clit and applied pressure. I jolted at the sensation. I hadn't expected the sensitive bundle of nerves to react so viscerally. "What you need is a man."

Leaning my head back against his shoulder, I closed my eyes and let myself feel. Seamus's hand stayed curled around mine as he led my fingers down the cleft of my pussy to my opening. He curled his own against mine, forcefully dipping them inside my wet channel. The walls of my vagina clamped around my fingers like a wet, heated glove.

I whimpered, my feet sliding along the sheet. My legs shook as he continued to control the depth and speed of my assisted masturbation. Tension coiled inside me; my heart raced like a wild animal trying to escape my chest.

"Look at me, Bailey." My eyes opened on Kiernan's command, my head tilting up to look at him. "Good girl, just like that."

Fuck. My pussy clenched again, and I moaned, my eyes never leaving his.

"Do you wanna come?" he asked. Not trusting my voice, I nodded.

Kiernan shook his head. "I asked you if you wanted to come, Bailey."

"Yes," I whispered breathlessly because I did. I really, really did. Frustrated at Seamus's slowed pace, I curled my fingers, my walls trembling at the feeling before increasing my pace.

"I'm sorry. What was that?" A sly grin crept across Kiernan's lips. "Yes…?"

Clenching my teeth, I took a long breath in through my nose before answering, "Yes, *sir*."

Seamus chuckled at my obstinate use of the title. My pussy didn't mind calling him *sir,* but my mind was still trying to catch up. Plus, I wasn't planning on making my compliance easy for them.

At least, not outside the bedroom. They could believe all they wanted that I was their submissive little toy when it came to sex. Hell, I'd enjoyed their dominance so far, but they had another thing coming if they thought I'd be a little slave beyond that.

"Then make yourself come."

So I did. I came with a small cry, shattering around my fingers, the pulse of my orgasm almost painful if it hadn't been so good. When it finally ebbed, I slumped back in Seamus's hold, a satisfied grin stretched across my face.

"Look at her, brother." Kiernan stood from his chair and sauntered over to where Seamus held me in his arms, his fingers idly playing with my erect nipples. My back arched, pushing my breasts further against his hands as he played me like a guitar. "Already wanting more. Seems one orgasm isn't enough for our girl."

"Don't worry, wildcat," Seamus whispered in my ear, nipping at the lobe. "You want orgasms?"

I nodded my head enthusiastically, no doubt resembling one of those bobbleheads on a dashboard.

"Words, baby."

"Yes, sir." This time, there was no tension in my words when I uttered that phrase. The past week had taught me that it wasn't about them trying to degrade or humiliate. It was just their kink. Even now, I could see how those two words affected Kiernan as he lay out before me, waiting.

"Good girl."

Yep. I could completely understand how words affected them. Because their praise affected me. I crawled up on the mattress, licking my lips at the sight of Kiernan's erect cock. I gave him a slow, smooth stroke, relishing in the feel of his hard, silky shaft beneath my hand. He groaned at the contact, and a heady sensation filled me at how much I affected this man. Not just with my words, but with my touch.

Hands gripped my waist, shifting me until Kiernan's cock was directly in front of my face, and my pussy was hovering over his.

"Wait..." A low moan left my lips at the feel of Kiernan's tongue swiping along my center. *Mother Theresa on a biscuit.* My pussy clenched, and a hot static surge of electricity shot up my body. He dug his hands into my ass, pulling my dripping cunt closer to his mouth. The pain mixed with the pleasure, sending another spike of desire through me.

"Take him in your mouth, *a stóre*," Seamus commanded

huskily. "Get him nice and ready." Without hesitating, I sucked him down like my next breath, refusing to play the coy, naïve woman I'd been before. Kiernan called me *his little whore*, and fuck if I wasn't going to own it.

Because I could. Inside these four walls, there was never any shame for the wanton desire I seemed to possess. They encouraged me to explore and push my boundaries without judging. It might have seemed like they had all the control, but the truth was, I did. I was the one who decided our boundaries and when things needed to stop. And I knew they'd always listen.

I could feel the edge slowly approaching. My pending orgasm hanging on by a thread, and I rolled my hips against Kiernan's face to try to ease myself over. But the Irish asshat wasn't having it.

"Not until we say so, Bailey." Seamus picked me up like a rag doll, holding me to him, his lips meeting mine. The rustling of the bedding told me Kiernan had moved.

"Time for the main event."

Seamus tossed me down on the bed and cocked his head in the direction of his brother, who was now settled back against the headboard.

"Take him for a ride, baby."

Smirking, I crawled up the bed toward Kiernan, my breasts swaying beneath me, ass in the air. Straddling him, I braced my hands on his shoulders as he guided his cock to my entrance. The angle was deeper, and I still had trouble taking either one of them this way.

But I wasn't a quitter.

Bit by bit, I worked him deeper, stimulating my clit as I slipped down his length. Once he was sheathed fully inside me, I took a deep breath and began to move. Using my thighs,

I raised myself up the length of his cock before dropping back down, both of us groaning at the sensation of being so full again. I ground down on him, working my clit against his pelvis, my breasts brushing against his bare chest.

Kiernan's hands were on my hips, helping me to find a rhythm, urging me faster, my pleasure building and building until—

"Fuck you, asshat."

I'd just been about to fly off the edge. A hot smack on my ass jolted me, my rhythm hitching as white-hot fire seared across my ass. I shrieked and clamped down around Kiernan's cock.

"She liked that, brother," Kiernan huffed. "Didn't you, my dirty whore?"

Oh, that sounded so much dirtier in English.

Another hot lash against my ass had me moaning and clinging to Kiernan's neck as Seamus laid down a line of fire. I was sobbing, my senses overwhelmed, as I climbed higher and higher. Kiernan muffled my sobs with his mouth, tasting my tears as I rode him faster than a prized stallion at the Kentucky Derby.

And then it stopped.

A weightlessness settled over me as my orgasm took hold, and I dove over the edge. Kiernan's hand was buried in my hair as he continued to thrust into me from below. His strokes had slowed. They were long and deep, drawing me back to reality slowly. I slumped against his chest, faintly aware of something cold and wet against my ass.

"Now, we both claim you." Seamus nipped my ear while his fingers probed the tight ring of my ass. "Together."

I'd barely come back to myself before he surged forward, burying his dick balls deep in my ass.

"Seamus!" I screamed his name as the air whooshed from

my lungs. My nails bit into Kiernan's shoulder as the force of Seamus entering me triggered another orgasm. Then they began to fuck me, to really fuck me, and with one cock in my pussy and one cock in my ass, I lost myself between them.

"That's right, good girl." Kiernan's words were heated and heavy. "Take us both like the dirty little whore you are."

"Kiernan." His name was a long, throaty moan. Kiernan sucked one of my nipples into his mouth, his thrusts stuttering as he sank closer to his own release. Seamus turned my face to the side, kissing me deeply, his tongue devouring me like it was the last taste he'd ever get. The brothers sucked, kissed, and nipped at me until I gave them one last orgasm, with the two of them right behind me.

I winced as Seamus slowly removed his softening member from my ass. My eyelids were already starting to droop shut as he lifted me off his brother and laid me down beside him. Kiernan caressed my hair gently, speaking in a muted voice as Seamus cleaned me like he had so many nights before.

Sleep was approaching, but I fought it back, blinking rapidly to keep it at bay as thoughts of what was to come flooded my mind. The brothers must have felt the sudden stiffness in my body, because they immediately surrounded me.

What if something happens to them? What if I lose them?

"You will never lose us, wildcat. No matter what, we will always find you," Seamus whispered as he snuggled in behind me, the heat of his body providing a safe, warm cocoon, with Kiernan at my front.

"Sleep, *ár shíorghrá*."

Something in the way he said those words weighed heavily on my tired soul. I didn't know much about the Irish language, but I knew a whispered profession when I heard it.

Something about tonight had changed things for us.

There was no going back from here. This connection, whatever it was between us, wasn't something I could just walk away from. I would always want them. Always need them. Together. Because having just one of them would be like having half of my heart. The other half would simply be dead and broken.

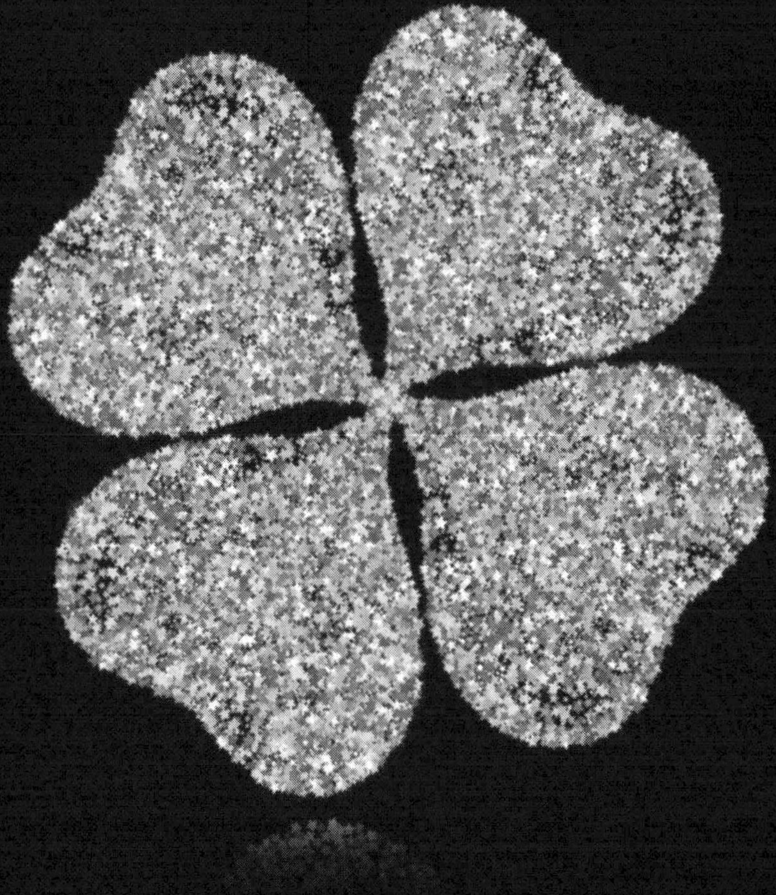

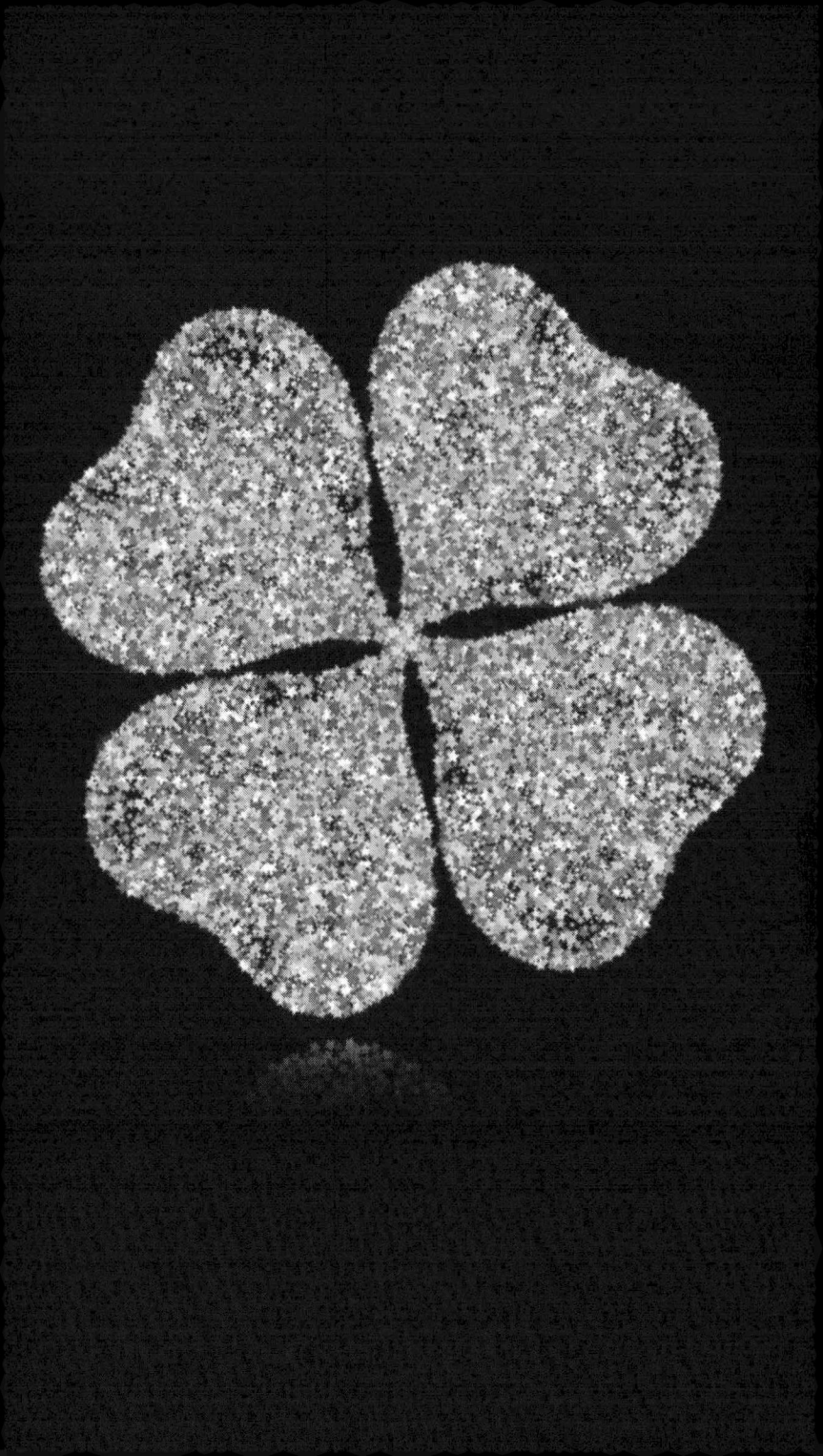

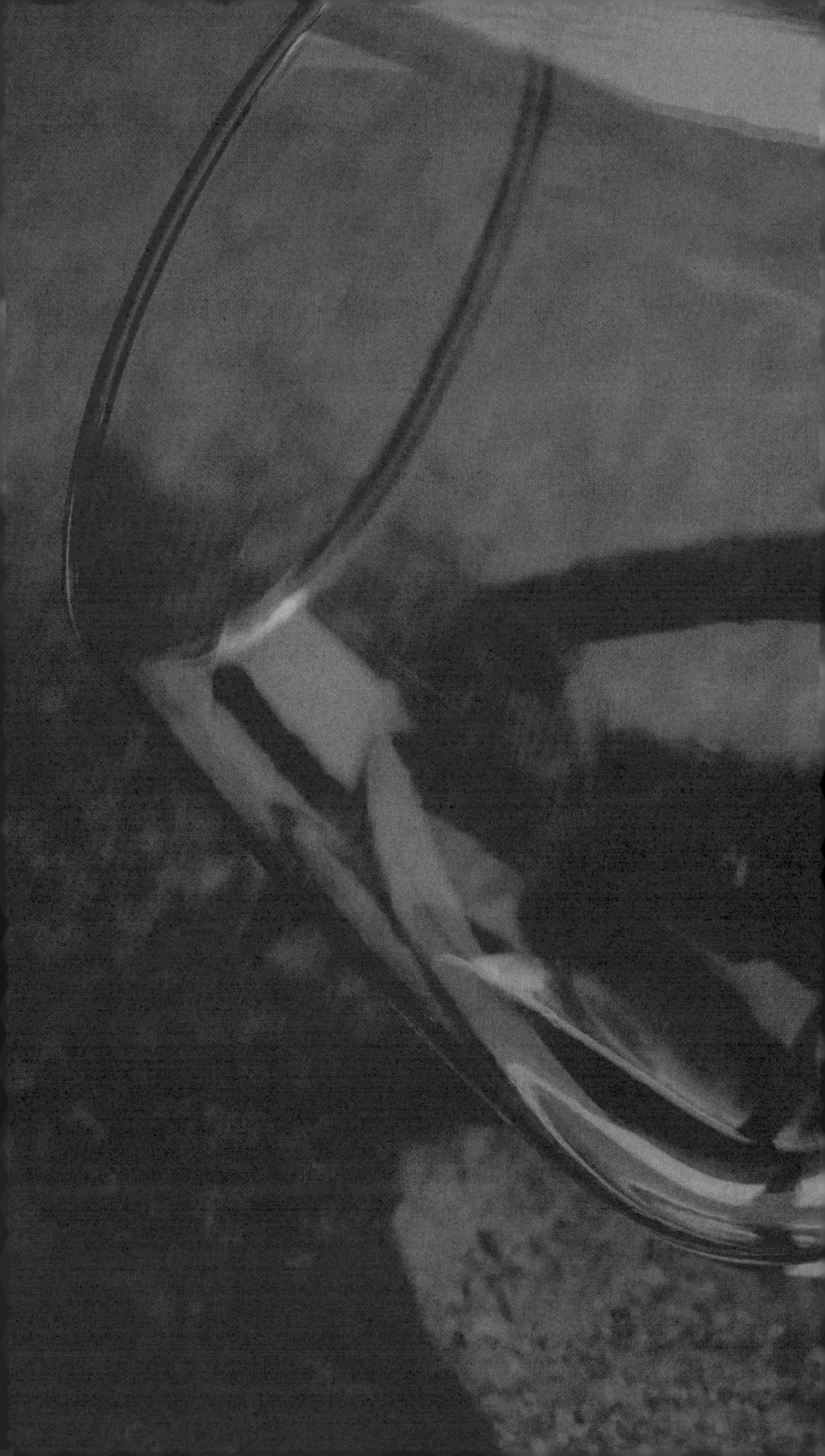

22

Kiernan

I watched as she drove away.

We should have been going after her and forgetting this idea. Forget that we came up with the idea for her to spy on her father and become a thief in her own house. It was too much of a risk. For her and us.

A niggle of doubt rolled up my spine and clenched on to the stem of my brain, holding tight. Anxiety slithered underneath my skin. What if she was lying? We were placing a great deal of trust in her to fulfill her end of the deal without turning on us.

That was where it all hinged. We could make do without the information, but if she turned on us, it could end up being our undoing. She only had four days to get what we needed. We'd spent the last three training her, but that wasn't enough. I'd had men who had spent their entire lives training, and they still ended up with holes riddled through their bodies.

Clenching my jaw, I turned away from the window. It had been better not to say goodbye. Pain pulsed around my heart knowing what would happen in just a few nights. Everything was set. The pieces on the chessboard were all in place. The pawns ready to be sacrificed. This was what we had to do. Crowe was involved in a lot more than just what we had shown Bailey.

We knew he was backing Christian Ward. He was the one who had set up the FBI sting at Matthias and Ava's wedding. He'd arranged for my sister to be taken. There was no way our family could let that stand. He'd made us the enemy for far too long, and it was time to strike back. If Richard Crowe wanted to play with the sharks, we would show him our teeth.

Blood had been spilled in the water.

"She's gone." My brother's cold tone filtered from the back of the room. He'd voiced his dissent about the plan several times, but that wasn't enough to stop the train we'd already set in motion.

"You knew this was the plan, Seamus," I reminded him, my gaze still fixated on where her car had left the parking garage. She'd hesitated at the entrance, as if she wanted to change her mind and turn back. I would have let her, but it was for the best that she kept driving.

"Funny how you're suddenly so on board with something that you vehemently disagreed with just a few days ago."

Sighing, I turned to face my twin. His tired eyes were drawn with sadness and regret and wreathed in dark sleepless circles. I doubt I looked any better. We'd tossed and turned the entire night, taking turns waking Bailey in the middle of the night to take her once again. Sometimes together. Other times separate.

Seamus had the opportunity to build a better rapport with our little captive. While he'd been training her in Krav Maga, I'd been busy plotting and planning. The board she'd seen had barely broken the surface of what we had in store for Crowe.

"It's better this way."

We can't keep her.

Even if I wished we could.

"For who?" Seamus snarled. "Not for her. And sure as hell not for us. I know I'm not the only one who felt that connection, Kier. You did too."

That was the problem.

I had felt an immediate connection with her. The moment she landed that punch, I was a goner. I just hadn't known it yet. That feeling of obsession, though, was dangerous. Bailey Jameson wasn't just any woman; she was a reporter and the daughter of the man who had been spilling the blood of my men for years.

She was Eve in the garden, coaxing us to take a bite of the forbidden fruit.

We couldn't afford to be Adam.

"We need to do what's best for the family," I told him. "She isn't it, Seamus. Keeping her would bring a war we can't afford."

"We're already at war, Kiernan," Seamus roared, his face red with anger. "Crowe is gunning for us, and that isn't going to change."

"Do you think I don't know that?" I roared back, eyes narrowed at my twin. "You think I don't want her? Because I do. More than I have ever wanted anything. But she can't be ours, Seamus. She's a reporter and his daughter. Do you honestly think that she's going to forgive us after what we do to him? Ruining his career, maybe. But we both know we can't stop there."

"You don't know that..."

"Get your head out of your ass, brother," I hissed. "The moment we spill his blood is the moment she stops loving us, and you know it. Just let it the fuck go. We'll use her to get the information we need, and that's the end of it."

"And what about the auction?"

"The gala is where it all ends, Seamus," I told him. "I put another plan together for the auction. We don't need her to gain entry. Father agreed that we use Dani instead. She's not as valuable, but Matthias's man said he would make sure to bid her out."

"You just changed the plan without consulting me?"

If looks could kill, I would be six feet under.

In all our time ruling together as my father's right-hand men, we'd never gone behind each other's backs. We never altered plans without the input of the other. We were born together, and we would rule together.

"I knew you wouldn't be able to let her go."

The fist that flew at my face was expected. There was no point in dodging it. I deserved the punch he threw, and I would take it. Blood filled my mouth, the tangy iron all too familiar. This wasn't my first hit, and it wouldn't be my last.

"Fuck you, Kiernan," my brother growled as he stalked from the room without looking back. Then I was left alone, the pain in my heart growing stronger as each second of silence ticked by.

In that moment, I felt the one thing I had never felt in my entire life.

Alone.

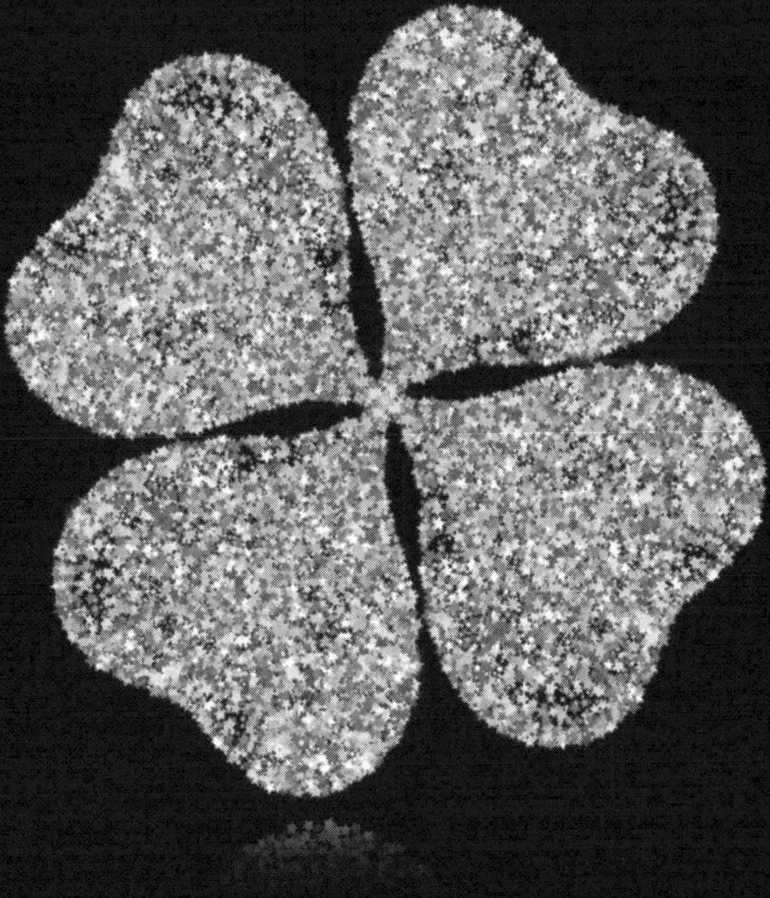

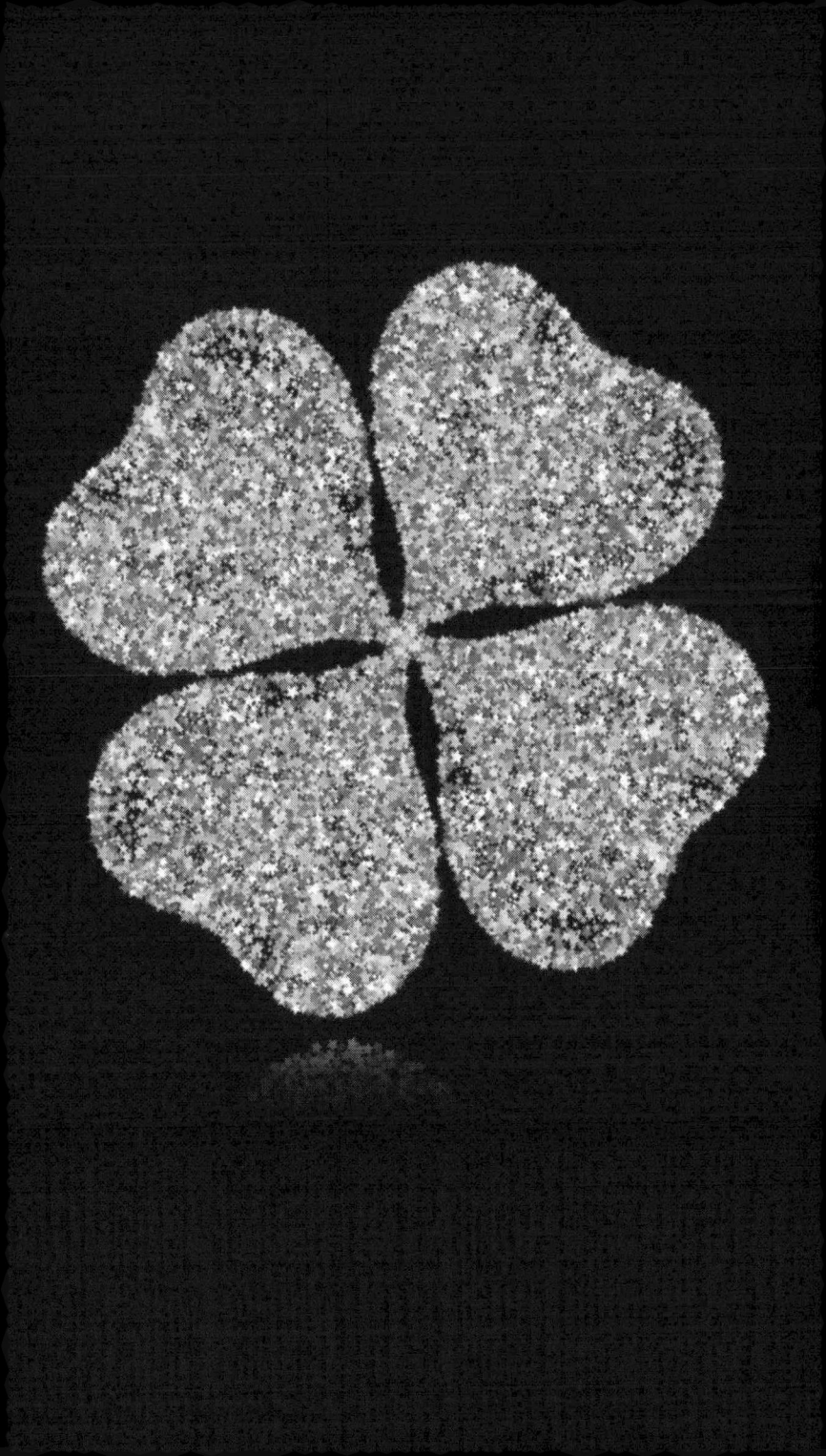

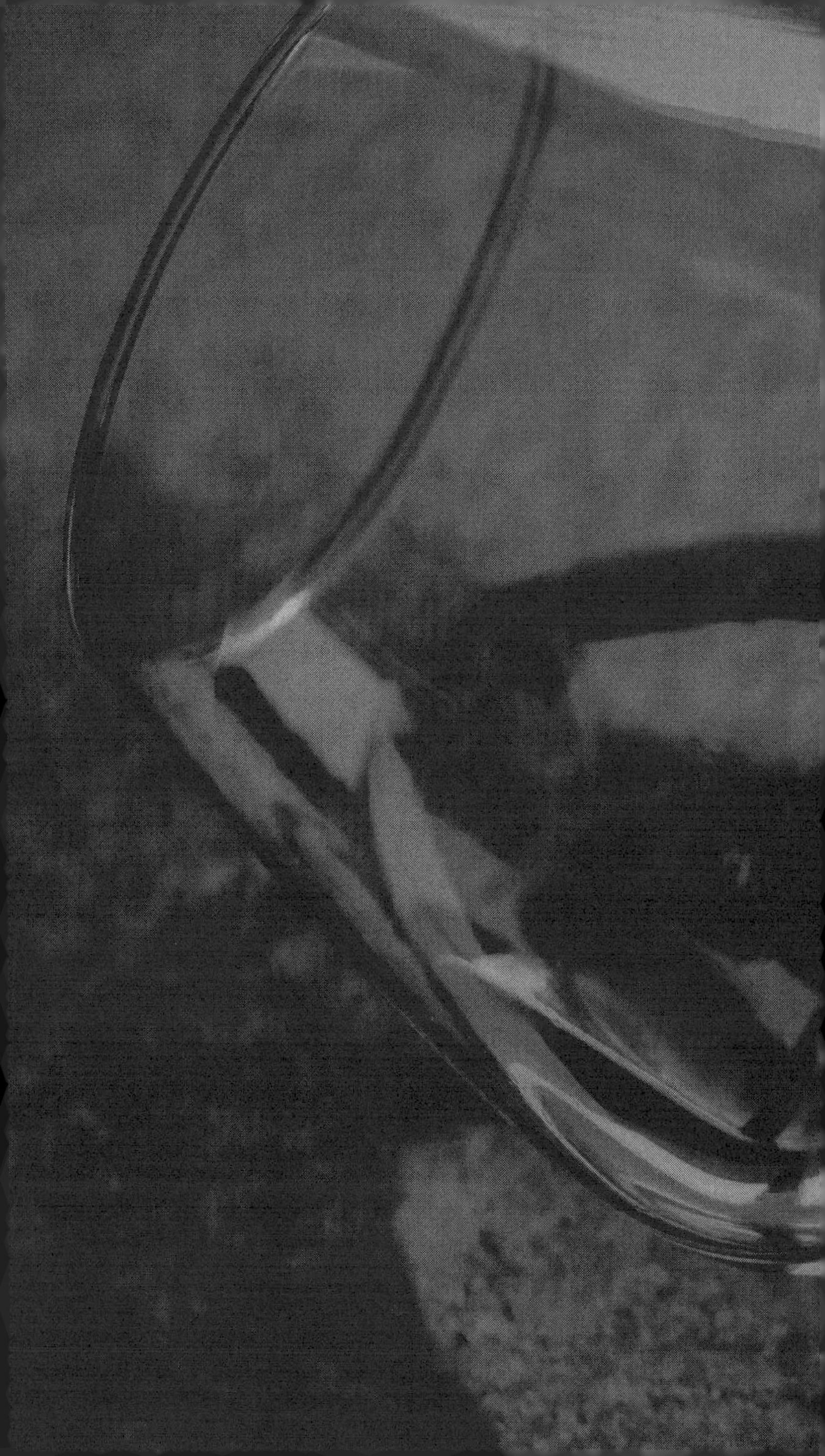

23

Bailey

There it stood.
Home.
There was a sliver of discontent as I pulled my car up to the security shed that stood in front of the gleaming metal gate that led to the place I'd called home since I was three years old. There'd always been an unease that lingered in my core when I drove through those gates. I'd always chalked it up to simple jealousy. Knowing that the moment I stepped inside, I was no longer Bailey Jameson, star reporter, but Bailey Jameson, unwanted daughter and mistake.

Rolling down the window, I showed my face to Grant, the regular daytime security guard my father employed.

"Welcome back, Miss Jameson." Grant tipped his head at me as he pressed a small button on the high-tech panel inside the shed. "I already radioed ahead to let your family know you've arrived. They've been worried." He shot me a disproving look.

"Wipe that look from your face," I sneered at him. Grant had always been cordial to me, but he was my father's lackey. A spy who documented my comings and goings. His brows buried in his hairline, and his eyes went wide at my sudden hostility toward him. It wasn't often that I portrayed much beyond the docile and meek daughter my father had tried to raise me to be.

In this house, everyone wore a mask.

Not bothering to waste any more time, I drove through the open gates. Gravel crunched beneath my tires as I pulled into the opulent circular driveway. I let my car idle in front of the grand steps that led up to the porch, waving off the porter as I pulled my suitcase from the back seat. The story I had planned on telling them ran through my head a dozen times, again and again. My family needed to believe that I had been holed up in a hotel in Portland to heal my broken heart.

Pfft.

Broken, my ass.

My fingers played nervously with the hem of my long sleeve blouse, fiddling with the small communication device they had sewn into the lining. It wouldn't be able to be detected, the frequency too low for my father's anti-listening devices to pick up. Somehow, despite my reticence about my father being some criminal mastermind, having it made me feel safer.

With a long sigh, I stepped inside the house. It felt cold and impersonal compared to the warmth and design of the Kavanaughs' penthouse. The furniture was large and garish. It was also as uncomfortable as hell. There was no family media room, and dinners were rarely taken together unless father had his business associates over.

"You little cunt."

Hindsight is twenty-twenty.

A painful sting radiated across my cheek, catching me off guard. I stumbled, tripping over my suitcase and landing painfully on my ass. Fuck, that hurt.

"Nice to see you too, Sarah," I sneered, holding my hand to my cheek to quell the burn.

"Where the hell have you been?" she snarled. "You think you can just walk out on the deal your father made with the Knights?"

"Well," I picked myself up from the floor, "I'd say that, yes, I could. I'm not marrying someone who has been actively cheating on me."

Sarah crossed her arms against her chest and rolled her eyes. "Oh, grow up, Bailey," she chastised. "Men cheat. It's who they are. You've always known this marriage isn't about love," she spat the last word out with disgust. "It's about forming an alliance. It's about power."

The edges of my mouth twitched in disdain. "If you think I'm going to marry someone who makes me as miserable as my father makes you, think again," I spat at her. "It's over. If you want this alliance so bad, give him Dalia instead."

Sarah stepped toward me with her arm raised as if to hit me again. She stopped at the last moment, her eyes hardening. "Ungrateful little bitch," she sneered. "I told him to get rid of you when we had the chance. Told him you were useless, even as a pawn."

Get rid of me?

Her jaw set as she lifted her chin. "You will marry Drew, Bailey." She took a long, resolved breath. "Or I'll see to it that you end up just like your mother. Slit throat and all." Without another word, she turned on her heel and stalked out of the entry hall.

There wasn't much time to contemplate what she had said before Carson, the family butler, cleared his throat from the entryway to the long hall that led toward my father's office. I turned my head to look at him, taking in his tailored coattails and polished shoes. He stood firmly erect, shoulders pushed back, chest out. The perfect slave in a dynasty of masters wrapped up in an air of civility.

He'd served my father's household since he was seventeen, but in the end, he was nothing more than a cog in the machine. Just like me.

"Your father is requesting you, miss," he informed me, his crisp voice tainted somewhat painfully. Out of everyone in the household, he had been the one to take care of me. My father didn't bother with nannies for me like he had Dalia. Instead, he'd given me away to the household staff. I'd been raised by Mary, the cook, Celia, the maid, and Carson, the butler. It was where I'd gotten my drive to work hard for what I wanted.

Not that anyone would have handed it to me anyway.

I gave him a tight nod and smile as I stepped past him. The man laid a gentle hand on my shoulder, stalling my feet. I looked up at him, the lump of unease growing thick in my throat.

"That boy doesn't deserve you."

A choked chuckle left me at his words. He didn't say anything more. Simply removed his hand and led me toward the one person I feared most.

My own father.

"Are you going to tell me where you've been?" I'd barely stepped through the door before the barrage of questions began. "Do you not understand the repercussions of disappearing? Are you honestly that stupid?"

"Hello to you too, father." I sank into the seat across from his desk. "Yes, I'm fine. Thank you for asking. No, I'm not going to tell you where I've been."

Stolen Obsession

My father growled, his lips twisting into a sneer. Looking at him now, I wondered how much of my mother I resembled, rather than him. Sure, we shared similar qualities, but other than the slope of our nose and the color of our hair, we barely looked anything alike. I'd never seen a picture of my mother. I barely remembered what she looked like, but I didn't recall her having dark hair or blue eyes. My father's were brown. His skin had a darker coloring to it. A stark difference to my pale complexion.

Even our personalities differed.

I wondered if this was why he treated me so differently from Dalia. Not just the fact that I was the product of an affair, his greatest shame, but because he saw nothing of himself in me. All he would see was my mother, the woman he held responsible for nearly ruining his career.

"Don't talk back to me, Bailey," he snarled, his fists clenched tightly on his desk. "You need to apologize to Drew about your behavior immediately."

I gave an unladylike snort.

"That's not happening," I told him firmly. "How about he apologizes to me for screwing Brittany behind my back for the last three years? But even then, you still won't get an apology out of me. I didn't do anything wrong."

"If you satisfied him like a woman is supposed to," my father leaned forward, his dark eyes holding mine, "he wouldn't have to fuck other women." There was a coldness there that I had never seen before. A dark, dangerous glint. My mind flashed back to the images of him mounting underage girls in a dirty cell. His face held the same malevolent look while the girl beneath him cried. I'd wanted to tell myself that those photos were faked. Manipulated. Now, however, as I looked at the man who'd raised me, I was having a hard time living in denial.

Maybe it wasn't just a river in Egypt after all.

"I'm not marrying him," I reiterated. "End of story." Rising from my seat, I went to leave the office, wanting to clean off the disgusting film this conversation had left on my skin.

White-hot pain pulled at my scalp. I cried out as I was wrenched backward. My feet stumbled, but the hand in my hair kept me standing. Another hand wrapped around my throat, squeezing hard enough to cut off precious air.

"You listen to me, you little slut," he hissed, spittle flying. His face was red hot with anger, his eyes bulging as he glared down at me. "You will apologize to him, and you will be marrying him. Otherwise, I will sell you off to the highest bidder. There are men out there who would take great pleasure in breaking you. So you are going to be a good little whore, just like your mother, and do as I say? Understood?"

Air. I needed air.

I nodded my head the best I could, tears streaming down my cheeks as I fought the blackness surrounding me. My father tightened his grip on my throat before letting me go completely. Coughing, my knees buckled beneath me, and I sank to the floor, holding my throat and crying.

"I have given you everything, Bailey," my father reminded me as he looked down at my crumpled form. "None of that was given for free. You will obey me in this, or there will be consequences. Your mother faced hers, and I'll make sure you face yours."

My brow furrowed. What did he mean by that?

"How did my mother die?" I rasped. "Did you kill her?"

He hesitated. It was barely there. Less than a microsecond, but I caught it.

"You know how she died, Bailey," he uttered in disgust. "She overdosed."

"Sarah said her throat was slit."

There. The slight widening of his eyes before he shook his head.

"Sarah is no doubt drunk and rambling. You've caused her a great deal of stress over the past few days." He walked back behind his desk and took his seat. The overlord on his throne. "Now, get out of here before I decide to call Fernando in to give you a real punishment."

Something wasn't right, but the threat of a beating from Fernando was enough to get me to drop the subject and hightail it out of his office like my ass was on fire.

I wasn't going to let it go, though.

Not yet.

I barely resisted slamming the door shut to my room after the talk with my father. The only saving grace was that Drew wasn't there to gloat in my face. That and I had managed to get a good look at the safe as well. While he'd had his hand around my throat, I'd stared over his shoulder, gauging the safe's keypad.

"So finally Rapunzel has returned."

I gave a small gasp, my hand flying to my chest as I spun around toward the unexpected intrusion. Drew sat casually in one of the chairs by my window, his phone resting in his hand. He'd dressed himself up in a black Armani suit and crisp white shirt. He liked to dress in suits because he believed that it gave him more power. Made him seem manlier. Drew had the muscles of a man who spent hours in the gym, but he was a coward who would never use them. One punch, and he'd be crying on the floor, begging for his mommy.

I'd seen it.

"What are you doing here?" I rasped, my voice still hoarse from the swelling. Drew tilted his head before he stood from the chair. Depositing his phone in his pocket, he straightened his jacket before casually strolling toward me. I took an instinctive step back, only to hit the door.

"Where have you been?" His arms caged me in on either side.

"None of your business," I snarled.

He chuckled, the sound mirthless. His eyes were narrowed down at me, face cold.

"You're my fiancée, Bailey," he sneered. "Everything you do is my business."

A growl erupted low in my chest. "I stopped being your fiancée the moment you stuck your dick where it didn't belong," I hissed. "Should have suspected it, though. Honestly, I should have known it was you the moment Brittany described the micropenis she was fucking."

His hand snagged in my hair, wrenching my head back painfully.

"Who have you been fucking, little Rapunzel?" he demanded. "You think I believe for one moment you were out there mourning me cheating on you?"

I shrugged a shoulder, keeping my body in a state of nonchalance. "Why do you care? You have that trailer park trash back at your condo, right? Is she kinda like Fun Dip? Stick your white pasty dick in and pop out covered in chlamydia? Because you sure aren't coming out coated in sugar."

Drew pursed his lips, eyes darkening.

"You're mine," Drew hissed at me. "And when I stop wanting you to be mine, I'm going to make sure the next man your father makes a deal with will fuck your shit up." He smirked. "If there's anything left, that is."

He tipped my head back, his gaze running along my

throat. It was no doubt bruised from my father's steely grip. "Nothing a little makeup won't fix. We need to make sure you're looking your best for the gala." He chuckled to himself like he'd told a joke. Was there something he knew that I didn't?

"Good to know where you stand on domestic violence," I snapped at him.

Another chuckle, this one darker, more dangerous. In all the years I'd been with Drew, he'd never been cruel. I didn't think him capable. Not once had he ever raised his voice to me or given me a reason to think he would. But the look on his face now?

It was deadly.

"I've been too lenient with you, Bai." He dragged me away from the wall. My hands automatically went to the wrist of the hand he still had wrapped tautly in my hair. The pain wasn't erotic. It stung, the roots pulling from my scalp. If he wasn't careful, he'd give me a bald spot. He pushed me into the vanity of the bathroom. I groaned as the marble countertop bit into my back.

Drew reached into the shower, hitting a few of the elaborate buttons that turned the spray on. The bathroom immediately began to fill with steam.

"That is going to change." He turned to face me, his dangerously dark gaze boring into mine. "No more freedom. Little Rapunzel is going to sit up in her tower until she's needed, or she's going to feel what it's like to fall. Understood?"

Swallowing past the lump in my throat, I nodded my head, afraid of what I might say if I spoke.

He smiled smugly. "Good," he stepped back, eyes roaming my body. "Now strip."

"*Strip, Bailey.*"

Kiernan's voice rang in the air, my mind pulling me back to our first encounter. I'd been scared. Petrified. But there had been something in Kiernan's gaze at the time, a softness that told me he would never hurt me. Drew didn't have any softness, and the warm memory of being in the shower with Kiernan washed away.

"What?" My brow furrowed and my mouth fell open, stunned.

"I told you to strip." His voice darkened, his eyes growing colder.

Folding my arms across my chest, I scowled at him. "Fuck you, Drew," I hissed, going to brush by him. He was nothing but a show pony. There was no way in hell he'd actually hurt me.

Oh how wrong I was.

"Don't say I didn't warn you." His eyes widened with delight as he snatched at my blouse, tearing it down the middle. I cried out as buttons went flying, their pings on the marble echoing loudly as my ears rushed with blood.

He'd managed to shove my blouse down my arms, flinging it carelessly to the floor before the shock wore off. "No!" My screams filled the air, and I shoved at his hands that were currently pulling my jeans down my hips.

"That word doesn't exist between us anymore," he snarled as he pulled at my clothes. Fuck, where was that training Seamus had drilled into me the other day? Not that I expected myself to suddenly become *Kill Bill*, but being able to at least shove the bastard off me would be nice.

Where was the extra strength that came with a shot of adrenaline?

Apparently, it didn't exist, and all those videos of people in distress lifting cars were lies.

"You will do everything I ask with a nod and a smile," he

hissed, grabbing my throat and slamming me into the wall next to the walk-in shower. I clawed desperately at his hand. It wasn't as harsh as my father's had been, but the memory of having my air cut off still lingered at the front of my mind. "Or I will make your life a living hell. Understood?"

One sharp nod from me seemed to satisfy him.

Drew ripped the rest of my clothes from my body before yanking me away from the wall and shoving me into the shower stall. A sob ripped from my throat as I hit the tile hard, my knees buckling beneath me.

"Now be a good girl and wash the filth from your body and meet me downstairs for dinner with your family in an hour."

My chest heaved as I struggled to get myself under control.

I sat there, trapped. Shivering. Vulnerable.

How could he do this to me? What had changed?

I didn't know how long I sat there under the spray. Long enough for it to turn cold and my lips to begin to tremble and my teeth to chatter. Drew had left me alone, shaking his head with disgust as he swept from the room.

When I worked up the strength to stand, I quickly soaped myself and rinsed under the icy shower spray before turning it off and grabbing for a towel. It took me less than half an hour to dress and dry my hair. I picked up the clothes from the floor but left the shirt laid out on the counter while I balled up the rest and threw it into the hamper.

My room wasn't a safe place for me. For all I knew, my father or Drew could have bugged it or put up a hidden camera. I doubted either of them would do something like that in the bathroom. Turning on the tap, I dug my nail under the loose seam of my blouse and prayed that the communicator hadn't been damaged.

It still looked intact.

Sighing with relief, I hid it inside an unused cotton ball and placed it behind a container where it wouldn't be seen. I didn't want to risk using it until everyone was in bed. Seamus had told me that my father's security shouldn't have been able to detect it. I assumed since I made it inside the house that it was fine. Still, I would wait until there was little possibility of interruption before reaching out. I wanted to be safe.

Even if I no longer felt it.

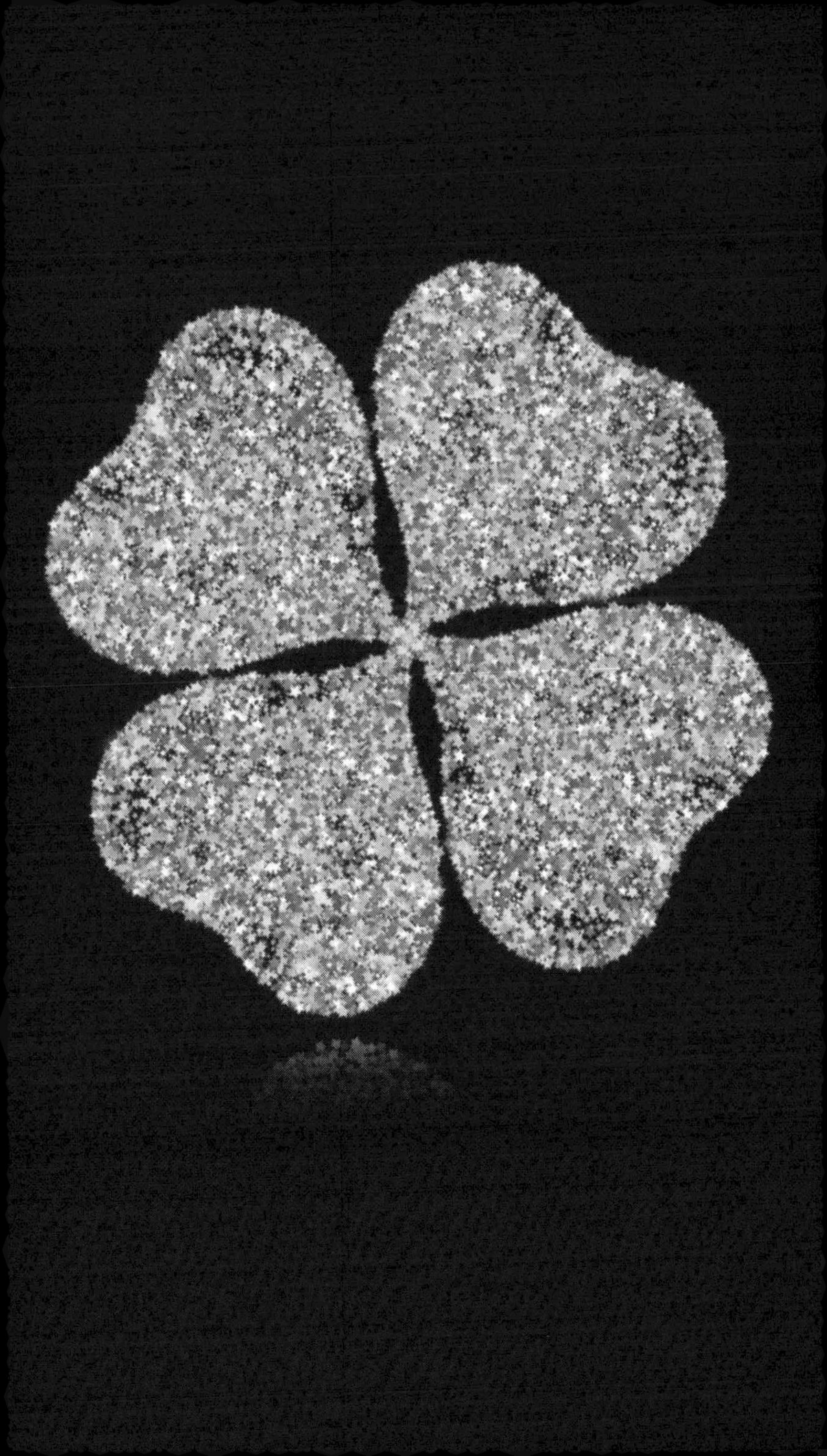

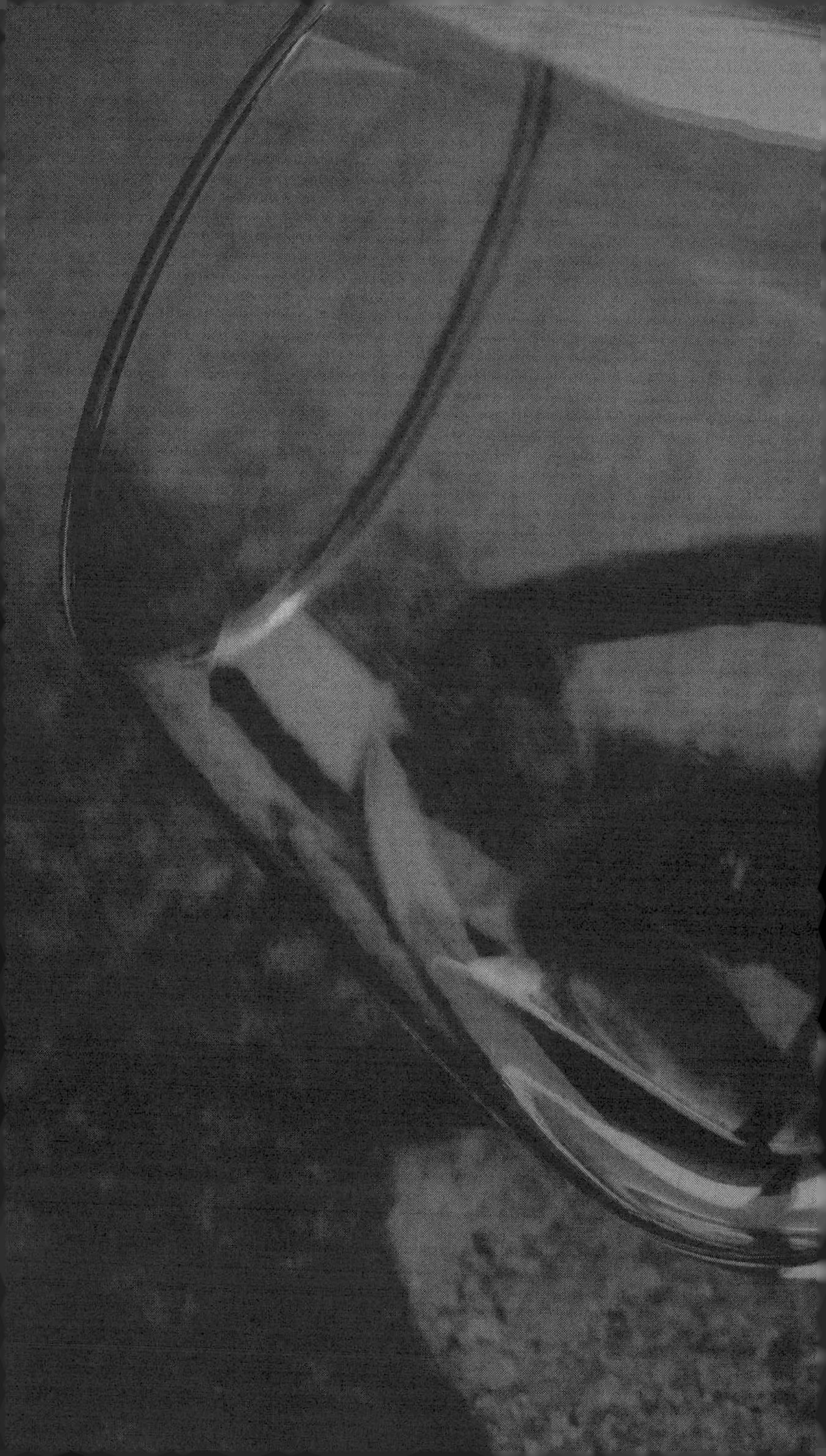

24

Seamus

My fist slammed into the man's face. Again.

He groaned, but there was nothing more he could do when two of my men had his arms pinned behind his back.

"All you have to do is answer the question, and this all stops," I told him. "Or you can keep quiet, and I can get more creative."

The man shook his head, but it wasn't defiance I saw in his eyes. It was resignation.

"I can't tell you what I don't know, man," he whined. "Toph has never been looking to expand. That isn't who he is. We do just fine with what we have, I swear."

He honestly believed that.

There was no deception in his words. No hidden truths behind his eyes. If Toph Eriksen, president of the Iron Horsemen, was expanding, this man didn't know about it.

Or we were missing something.

"Tell me why Eriksen keeps targeting our men."

The man groaned again. "Man, you know I can't tell you that shit. He'll kill me."

I snored. "I'll kill you if you don't tell me so..."

"You honestly think you're scarier than Toph?" The man shook his head. "Shit, I've seen Prez do some fucking nasty shit to those who cross him. I'm not fucking snitching."

"See now, I'm willing to keep it a secret if you are." I winked at him. "No one has to know."

"Fuck you, man." There was no heat behind his words, just simple resignation. "Look, he doesn't tell us much..."

He was stalling. The biker needed a bit of incentive. Removing my knife from its holster, I slid the tip along his throat, hovering it just above his carotid artery.

"Just a nick," I threatened. "That is all it would take. Then I could sit here and watch you bleed out on the pavement. Then I'll plant evidence of you and your pretty little wife snitching to the cops and—"

"Leave my wife out of this!"

"Then tell me what I want to know!" I roared as I dug the tip in further.

"Okay! Okay!" he cried out. "Crowe has Prez's daughter captive. That's why we've been targeting your men. Under Crowe's orders. He's got it bad for you guys. I'm not even sure why."

"Eriksen has a daughter?"

Why hadn't we known that?

"She was taken when she was three years old," the biker rushed. "Crowe provides photos every now and again to keep Prez in line. He's tried to get her out a couple of times, but then he gets photos of her, the girl. Ones where she's beaten or starving. Crowe threatened to sell her at auction if he didn't get his shit straight."

Well, fuck.

This was more complicated than we thought. Maybe

Eriksen didn't have a grudge against us. And if that was the case, we needed something to bring him to our side.

Chucking my chin at my men, I ordered them to release him.

"Not a word about this," I threatened. "Or you'll have more than just a beating to contend with. Understood?"

The man nodded fervently before lumbering down the alley toward the bar. It had been a risk to come this far south, but I needed answers. There'd been another hit on our men. A drive-by. They'd open fired into one of our neighborhoods. Everything that our witnesses had told us made it sound like it had been the Iron Horsemen, but it wasn't adding up.

What the hell were we missing?

I slid into the back of the SUV, signaling to my driver. He pulled away from the curb and eased into traffic. The streets were bustling today, which meant that it would take twice as long to get home.

Normally, I enjoyed the silence of a long drive through the city. Even with stop-and-go traffic, but today, my mind was troubled. Bailey had barely been gone a few hours, and I was already champing at the bit. My body was riddled with anxiety. What if she'd been found out? The device we planted in her clothing was undetectable, but shit happened. It could have become damaged, or it could be that she didn't plan on contacting us at all.

Not that I could blame her with what we had planned.

Bailey wasn't stupid, and if she thought something was off, she'd no doubt bolt.

Fuck.

I'd told my brother we shouldn't go through with it. Sure, our plan to ruin the senator and see him behind bars would ultimately free her from her father's control, but she'd never forgive us.

And I wouldn't blame her.

Fishing my phone out of my pocket, I dialed Bridgett.

"Yeah?"

"I need everything you can find on Toph Eriksen. His marriage, his family—everything. He's got a daughter, and I want to know who the hell she is."

"Well, hello to you too," Bridgett sighed. "I'm doing good. How are you? Oh, I'm fine, thanks."

I pinched the bridge of my nose. "Hello, Bridgett."

She snorted. "Well, that's a start," she sassed. "What can I do for you?"

"I need to you to find everything you can find on Toph Eriksen," I told her. "Apparently, Crowe is holding his daughter captive. I want to know who she is."

"How long has he had her?"

Fuck.

"Since she was three."

"Birthdate?"

"Fuck if I know."

"That's not a lot to go off."

I let out a long breath. A headache was drilling its way through me. "I know this. But it's all I have, Bridg. Find out everything you can about Eriksen. Do a deep dive. We never really did that."

We should have.

"Okay." She groaned. "But I'm not making any promises."

"Deal."

I hung up the phone, dropping it to the seat next to me.

Something was coming.

I could feel it.

My gut was churning, and that was never a good thing, and my gut was never wrong.

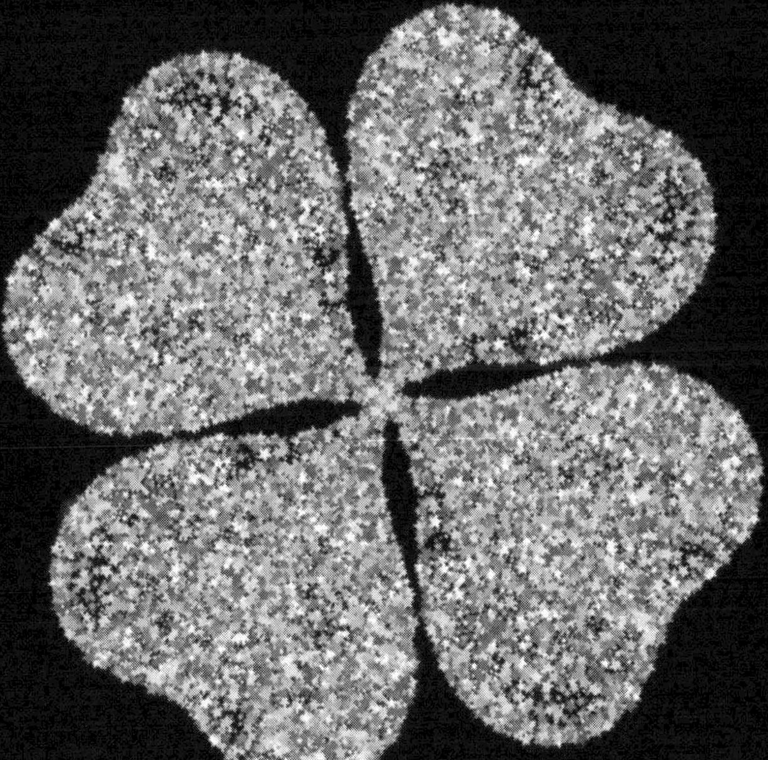

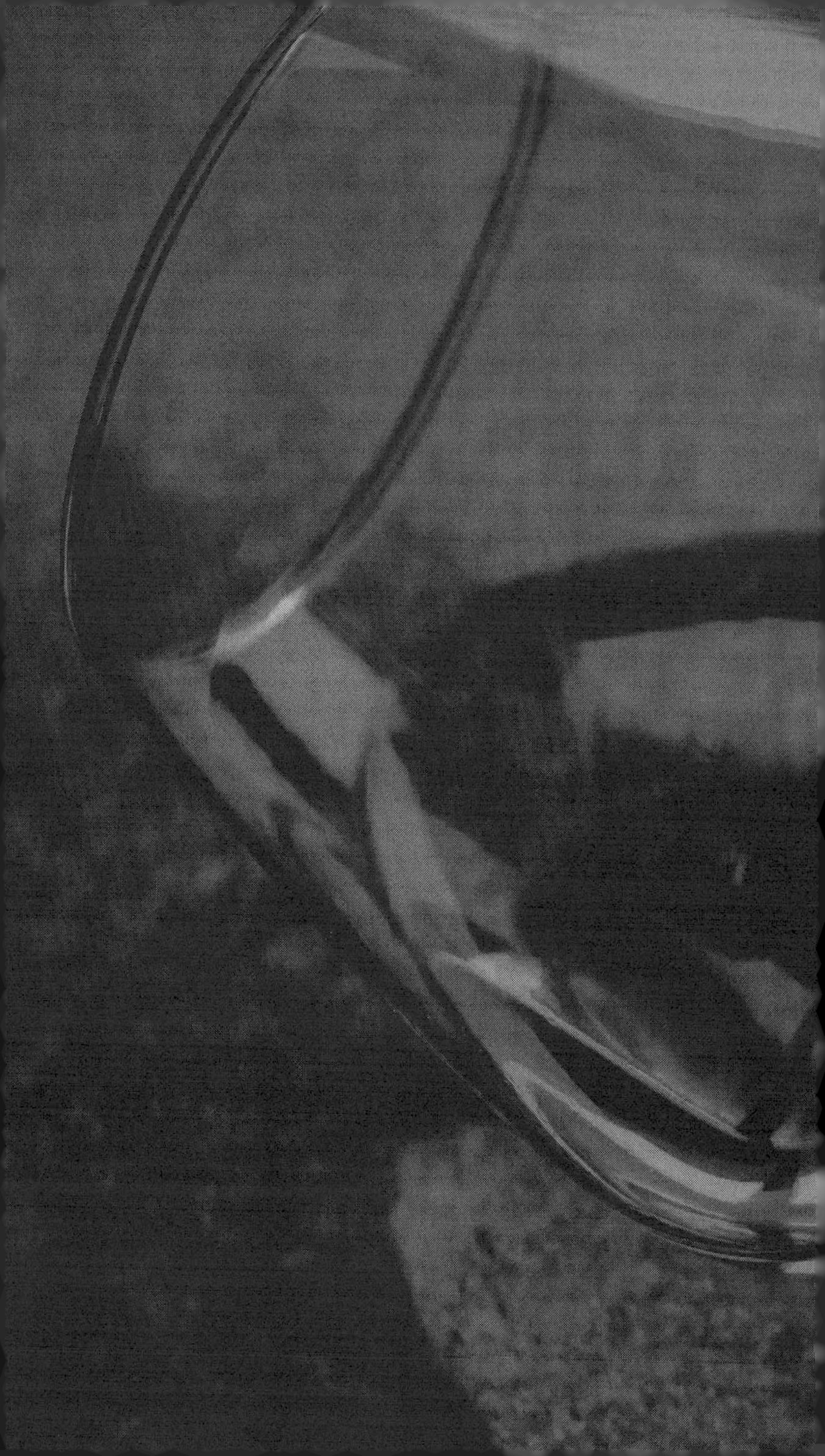

25

Bailey

"The gala is only two days away," Sarah pointed out petulantly. "You can't expect to take her with you. She hasn't been announced, and god knows she doesn't have something appropriate to wear."

I wondered if I could crawl under the table without being missed.

"I've already added her to the list," my father told her firmly. "She deserves a reward for coming to terms with her engagement to Drew, despite his indiscretions. Isn't that right, dear?" His tone was laced with a threat. Arsenic threaded with the lace of civility.

"Yes, father." I lowered my eyes in submission. Fake as it was, he bought it, sending me a large smile.

"Good." He turned back to Sarah. "Everything is settled, dear. Dalia didn't want to attend in the first place, and Drew wants to show off his fiancé officially." Something about the way he'd said *officially* made my skin crawl.

"I've been waiting for this for a while," Drew admitted casually as he cut into his steak. "It has been years in the making. A great buy, if you ask me."

"Indeed," my father agreed as he pushed his finished plate away, waving to the server with an idle hand.

I'd barely touched my food. My tongue was thick in my mouth, heavy with the words I wanted to slash their way. I remained silent, like a good submissive daughter, despite the volcano of emotion erupting inside me.

"Well," Drew pushed away from the table and stood, "As much as I appreciate the hospitality, I have someone I have to get back to." His eyes drew to me, categorizing my reaction to him mentioning that Brittany waited at home for him.

Good. He could fuck her while I figured how the fuck I was going to get into my father's safe.

"Of course." My father stood as well, offering his hand and shaking Drew's. "You're welcome anytime."

Drew smiled thinly at my father, then cast one last glance at me before strolling out of the room.

"May I be excused?" I murmured.

"Yes," my father approved. "Sarah will have some dresses delivered to your room tomorrow for you to try on. Do remember to be on your best behavior."

"Yes, father," I mumbled as I left the table, head lowered. Dinner had been suffocating to the point where all I'd wanted to do was flee. Run and never look back. The more time I spent at that table, the more I'd begun to realize that what I had seen in those documents the twins had given me was true.

If that was real…what stopped those photos of him raping underage girls from being true as well? As a reporter, I'd always been taught to be unbiased. To not form opinions of my own. Reporters were observers. Fact-checkers.

Shit.

Work.

Closing my bedroom door behind me, I dragged out my cell phone and dialed my boss, Lucas.

"Hello?" His voice rang through.

"Lucas, it's Bailey."

"Bailey!" He sounded surprised. As if he'd thought he wouldn't be hearing from me. "How are you?"

"I'm good," I told him. "Look, I just wanted to check in. I know I've been MIA the past few days but..."

"MIA?" he asked. "What do you mean?"

"Umm...well, I haven't checked in. I've been working on—"

"Checked in? Bailey, you put in your resignation last week, kiddo," he told me. "I know I'm getting old and senile, but that usually means you don't have to check in." He chuckled.

"My resignation?"

I'd never submitted my resignation.

"Yeah," he said. "You emailed it to me. Said you needed some time and that you didn't think you'd be back."

"I never—" A voice on his end interrupted me.

"Look, kid," Lucas rushed. "You were a great reporter, but this isn't meant for everyone. Anyway—" Another interruption. "I've got to go. Stay safe."

Then the line went dead.

What the hell had just happened? I tossed the phone on my bed and made my way into the bathroom. Pulling the communication device from its hiding place, I placed it in my ear.

"Hello?" I whispered, wondering if they were even listening. "Seamus? Kiernan?"

Nothing but dead air hung around me for several moments and then...

"Bailey?" It was Liam, the twins' father.

"Liam?" I breathed a sigh of relief. Just hearing his voice set me at ease. Even if I wasn't his favorite person.

"You're safe?" he asked. "You're okay?"

I nodded and then, remembering he couldn't see me, I told him I was.

"I haven't been able to get the information yet," I admitted. Liam chuckled.

"You've only been there a few hours, Bailey. Even I don't have that high of standards."

I let out a breathy laugh, but it was tinged with unease.

"What's wrong?" Concern bled into his voice.

"Everything," I whispered, sliding onto the bathroom floor.

"Have you been hurt?" he demanded.

"No," I assured him. "Not...my father..."

"Ah," he let out a long, worn-out sigh. "I'm assuming you're beginning to see things you might not have before."

"He's always been strict," I admitted. "He'd have his men keep me in line when I stepped out of it, but today—"

"What do his men do, Bailey?" The sudden anger in his tone shocked me. Was he angry on my behalf? He shouldn't be. My father was simply meting out the discipline I'd earned.

"They'd beat me," I told him candidly. "Starve me. Sometimes he would lock me in the cellar for a few days until I repented. It was my fault for not following the rules, but today he said some things and—"

"Let me make one thing clear, Bailey Jameson," Liam growled. "What your father did is never okay, whether you did something wrong or not. Do you understand me?"

"But—" I went to argue.

"No buts," he argued fiercely. "It is never okay to beat an innocent child or woman. Do you understand me?"

I swallowed back the lump of emotion in my throat. "Yes," I whispered.

"Good."

"Where are the twins?" I asked before I dug further into what had already transpired today.

"Seamus went to meet with one of the bikers from the Iron Horsemen, and Kiernan is getting everything set up for the gala."

The gala.

"I managed to convince my father to let me go to the gala," I told him. "Drew apparently wants to show me off since he's never had the chance before."

"That's one less thing we have to worry about."

I agreed.

"I'm hoping to be able to get into my father's office tonight once everyone is asleep."

"That's good," he said. "Just remember not to take any unnecessary risks."

"I won't," I assured him. A pause hung in the air between us. "Umm...can I ask you a favor?"

"Of course." He sounded surprised I'd asked.

"Could you track down a resignation letter for me?" I asked him.

"Whose?"

"Apparently mine," I said. "When I called my boss to check in and apologize for being MIA, he said I had submitted my resignation last week, but I never did."

"You sure?"

"Yes," I assured him. "I was in Oregon last week, working on a cold case that had links back to one of the Capitol Hill murders. Plus, he said it was emailed, and I haven't had access to my company email for over two weeks due to a security error."

"Why would someone submit a resignation on your behalf?" he wondered. "Could it be your father?"

I shrugged. "Maybe, but why wouldn't he just tell me? I'd

argue, but in the end, I'd have no other recourse than to obey him. Otherwise..." He already knew what would happen. I'd told him what my father did when I refused to obey.

"I'm wondering if whoever tampered with your spark plugs is the same person who submitted your resignation."

What?

"My spark plugs?"

Liam groaned. "They didn't tell you, did they?"

"Tell me what?"

"Shit." Another groan. "The reason your car broke down in that parking lot was because one of your spark plugs was faulty."

"That's impossible," I told him, anxiety welling inside me like a hot-air balloon. "I just had my car serviced before I drove to Oregon."

"I'm not sure what to tell you, Bailey," he said. "But someone out there is trying to move you around like a piece on a chessboard. If I were you, I'd watch your back."

There was an eerie truth to Liam's words. I was being manipulated, and I doubted that these two incidents were isolated. Whoever was doing this wanted something from me, but what? What did anyone have to gain from putting in a resignation letter on my behalf? They must have known that sooner or later, I would find out about it.

Unless whoever did it hadn't planned on me never being able to refute the letter.

I thought back to what Liam said about my spark plugs. I'd just gotten them serviced. The man who had worked on my car was an old friend of mine, which likely meant that it wasn't him. Carlos was too good a guy for that.

So somewhere on my journey to Oregon and back last week, someone had switched one out. But when? And why?

Stolen Obsession

If I were you, I'd watch your back.
Liam was right.
No one could be trusted.
Certainly not him.
Not even the twins.

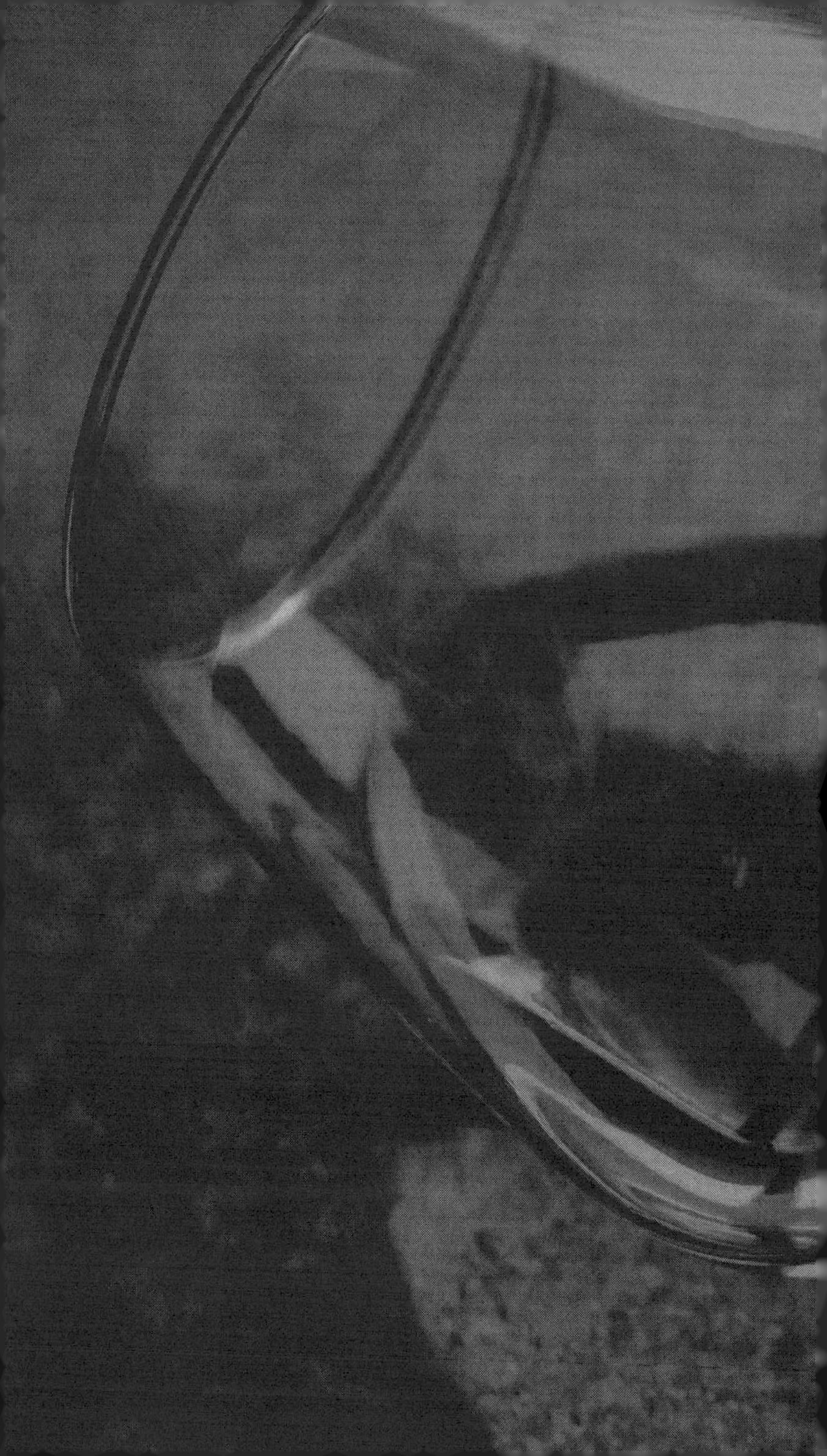

26

Bailey

The house had fallen silent not long after I retired to my room. Most of the staff lived off the property except for Carson, the butler, and the head of the house, Maria. Father had very few guards posted inside the house, but that didn't mean there weren't any at all. There were also the cameras to worry about. None of them were in the same hallway as his office. I realized now that it was no doubt because he didn't want anyone to see who was coming or going.

Or the damage he was inflicting.

My sweaty hand reached out and gripped the door handle, turning it slowly, quietly. The corridor was silent, eerily so in this big house. My feet were bare. The old wood floor often creaked, and I wanted to remain as stealthy as possible.

The pulse of my heartbeat pattered an unrelenting drum beat against my rib cage, threatening to burst through my chest. My breaths came in shallow, quiet rasps. Cold sweat washed down the back of my neck and clung to the collar of my pajama shirt.

I was a wreck. What the hell was I doing pretending to be

some kind of spy? I had no idea in hell what I was doing, but still, I pressed on. Not because of the promise I'd made to the twins, but because *I* needed to know what kind of man my father truly was. Doubt had wiggled itself underneath my skin, causing a persistent itch. My father wasn't who he said he was. He'd never been very caring toward me, but I'd always taken his punishments without complaint, believing I'd deserved them somehow.

What your father did is never okay, whether you did something wrong or not.

Those words still rang in my head. I'd never thought of what my father did as wrong. Simply harsh, but I'd been told my entire life that I was deserving of it. That it was necessary. But the more I thought back on the times my father had ordered my discipline. He had never once told me what I had done wrong.

My silent feet led me to his office.

The place I'd come to fear over the years. His office had never been a safe place in this house. The well-oiled hinges barely made a sound as I inched open the heavy door and crept inside, quietly closing the door behind me. The safe was in plain view. He didn't bother hiding it. There was no need in this house. Not when everyone followed your orders without question. He'd curated a carefully crafted team of devoted sycophants. Men who would do anything for him. Men with both power and means.

There were no buttons on the safe. Instead, it had a scanner for an encrypted barcode that very few people had access to. The problem was recreating the barcode. You couldn't. Although barcodes weren't unhackable, encrypted barcodes were hard to simply copy. The barcode itself contained specialized data that the reader readily interpreted. Without that specific data, the safe wouldn't open.

Unless you were able to short circuit the entire system.

Which I could, thanks to a handy device I managed to sneak in with my luggage. The Kavanaughs' hacker, Bridgett, had rigged up a small device that resembled a button cell battery. I fetched it from the pocket of my pajamas, running my fingers over the soft metal.

Reaching out, I went to attach it to the safe's interface when a pair of loud voices filtered into the room from the hallway. Shit. Panic rose inside me as they approached. I needed to find a place to hide. Fuck. My gaze whipped around the room, heart beating rapidly in my chest.

Thump.

Thump.

The door handle rattled as I dove into the coat closet to the right.

"You should have kept your mouth shut, Sarah," my father hissed as he stepped into the room. "She isn't as stupid as you think she is. Did you honestly think she wouldn't catch what you said?"

Sarah snorted mirthlessly. "Please." Her voice was full of derision. "She's more gullible than her mother and look how that ended."

"Killing Elizabeth was a mistake, and you know it," he hissed. "Your petty jealousy almost ruined everything for me. If Elias hadn't been able to have Ford cover it up, you'd be in jail."

A sudden longing skated through me at the mention of Elizabeth's name.

Who was she?

Why did her name sound familiar?

"Lin was the one who started it," Sarah practically whined. "You know that. She's the one who changed her identity and inserted herself into everything. Which is your fault.

If you hadn't spilled your fucking guts about Elizabeth and Toph Eriksen, she'd never have become fixated."

My father grumbled something under his breath.

"You still need to be more careful," he warned. "If Bailey finds out the truth before Kenna comes to train her, it could be a problem. It's bad enough she's here now. Barret was supposed to track her after she left the body shop and snatch her up for holding at Wonders. We aren't going to get that chance now. Knight isn't happy about that. He wanted her to be trained before his son's upcoming nuptials."

"We should never have sold her to the Knight boy," Sarah sneered. "She should have gone directly to auction."

"Then we wouldn't have been able to control Eriksen." My father's tone was reprimanding. "We needed her as leverage, but now that has come to an end. Eriksen and the Iron Horsemen will be wiped out just like the Vixens, and we won't have to worry about Bailey any longer."

Sarah released a long sigh.

"All right."

"Good." Feet shuffled outside the door, and I clutched the items in my hand tighter as tears streamed down my face. The sound of the safe opening filled the room. Please don't be taking the laptop. Please don't be taking the laptop.

The safe beeped, the locking mechanism engaging.

"Let's go." My father's voice was tense. "Make sure you dress Bailey in something eye-catching. Don't embarrass me because of your dislike for her."

Sarah made a disgruntled noise but ultimately agreed.

Three steps, and the sound of the door opening and closing. It felt as if I could finally breathe.

What the hell had I just overheard?

Shaking it off, I focused on the task at hand. Getting the information from the safe. I slipped out of the closet, closing it quietly behind me in case anyone was still in the vicinity. Quickly, I placed the small electronic device on the safe's interface and pressed twice to activate it. There was a small hum, then the interface glitched, and then the locking mechanism disengaged.

That was easy.

I turned the knob of the safe and opened the heavy door. The inside of the safe was nearly empty, aside from a few accounting ledgers. I pushed those aside and pushed on the black velvet wall at the back. It tipped downward, revealing exactly what I had come for.

The laptop.

Snatching it up, I placed it on the desk and got to work starting it up and inserting the decryption key. Okay, that was settled. Now to do some digging of my own. I turned back to the safe and peered inside. There was a small stack of manilla envelopes nestled to one side of where the laptop had been.

Pulling them out, I held them in my shaking hands, afraid of what I would see if I opened them. The truth, no matter how freeing it could be, was a deadly weapon. Knowing the truth meant I had an edge, a weapon of my own, but did I want to know the truth that I now suspected? Going my whole life believing in one thing, only to have it ripped from beneath me would be a devastating blow.

Could my soul take it?

With trembling fingers, I peeled back the front of the first manilla envelope. The tears I had been shedding before while huddled in the closet began again in earnest. What I had overheard and begun to suspect was laid bare before me.

There was no escaping reality now that I knew the truth.

Two truths, in fact. And one lie.

A lie they would come to regret.

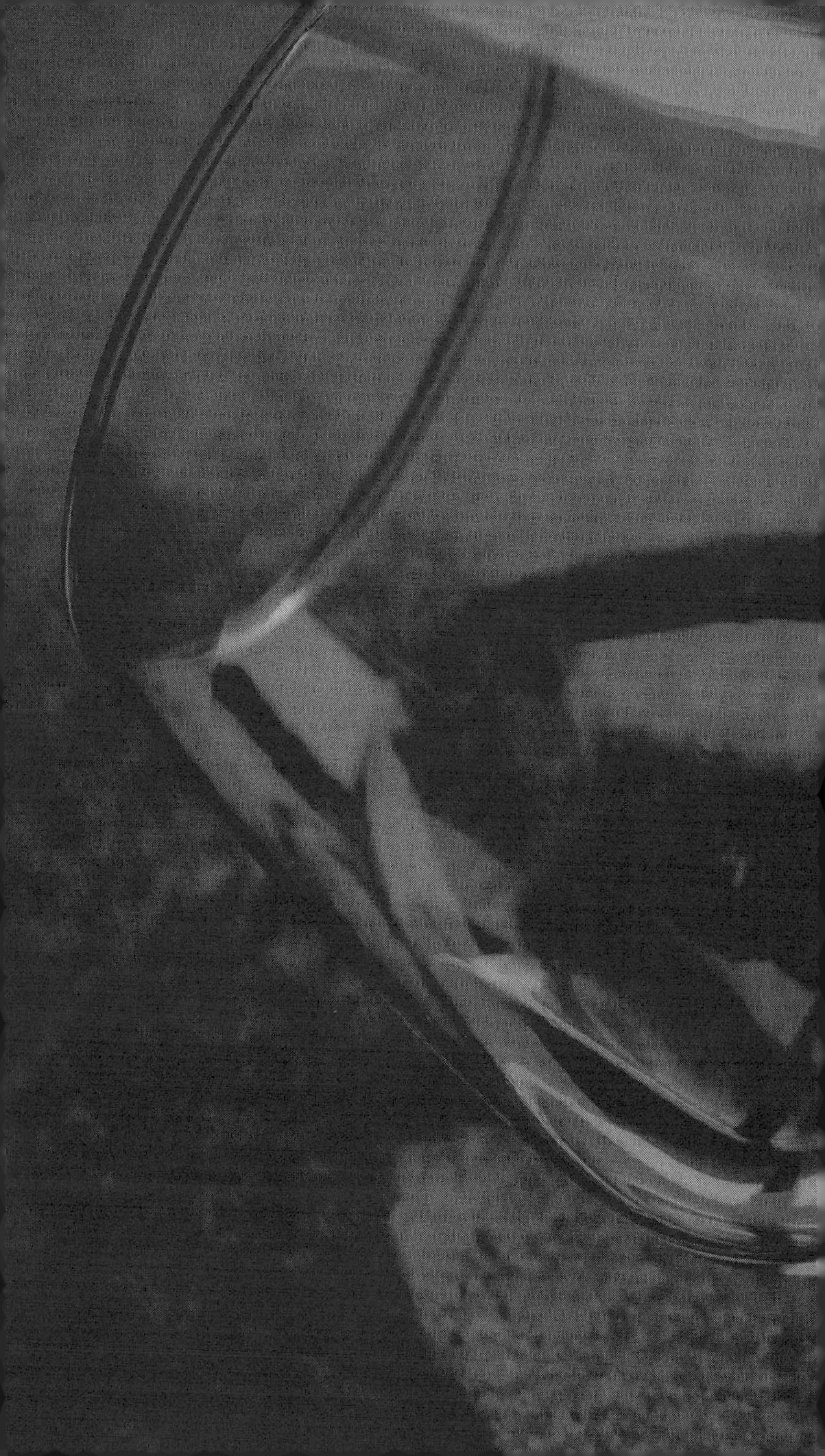

27

Kiernan

I slid out of the back seat of the Escalade, holding my hand out for Dani to take. She easily slid out of the car, her burgundy cowl-neck satin A-line gown gracefully curving around her body. There was a bright smile painted on her face as she posed for the cameras, the paparazzi eating us up. It wasn't often that I was photographed. Not unless I wanted to be.

Most people identified me as Kiernan Kavanaugh, next in line to inherit the Kavanaugh crime family, but to the rest of the world and the paparazzi, I was a business mogul. A billionaire club and restaurant owner who rarely liked to be seen in public.

Reporters lined either side of the red-carpeted entrance to the building, calling out my name as we began our walk toward the ornate double doors that led into the hotel. I never stopped to pose for any of them. I rarely did, and there was no way in hell I was going to put Dani in an awkward position. Instead, I kept my gaze forward, ignoring the flashing lights around us.

"Your tickets, sir." The man at the door smiled at me

before his greedy eyes fell on Dani. My cousin barely batted an eye at his obvious perusal. Good. I'd brought her because she knew how to play the game we needed played. Father had refused to allow Dani to be entered for sale, but he'd agreed to let her accompany me tonight. Her father was a prominent doctor, and she knew many of the people in this social circle well.

"Have a good night." The man's face fell a bit when he realized I was only wearing a bidder pin. I didn't bother to acknowledge him any further as I led Dani into the spacious ballroom. The hotel was grand and historic. The room was cast in dark tones—aged wood with walls painted a dark mauve. A string quartet sat on a recessed stage playing a melancholic tune that set the mood perfectly.

Waitstaff circled the room, carrying silver trays of champagne and hors d'oeuvres to those who allowed themselves to indulge. My gaze searched the room, first finding Ava on one side with one of Matthias's men. The Italian—Leon or something like that. They both held a glass of champagne in their hands, but the moment Ava's eyes landed on Matthias, she downed that sucker faster than a shot of whiskey and reached for another one.

I wasn't going to get into that. Not tonight.

My gaze slid from my sister, searching the room for one last person. I moved us around the room, nodding and smiling at the other guests as if it didn't pain me to be here. A few of them stopped me for some mild conversation, which I reluctantly engaged in until finding some excuse to slip away.

"Where is—" A loud, obnoxious laugh drew my attention toward one side of the room. My gaze caught on her immediately. She stood awkwardly with her hands at her sides, looking forward as the man at her side prattled on with another guest. He had one arm around her shoulder. From the pained look on her face, his grip was no doubt tight. Drew the douchebag.

Bailey looked gorgeous in the deep emerald satin dress she wore. It was a long-sleeved split blouse with a satin pleated skirt that had a deep V-neck and a long leg split. Her raven hair fell in gentle waves, framing her beautiful face. My heart raced inside of my chest at just the simple sight of her.

But I couldn't let that get in the way of what had to be done.

"I've spotted her," I whispered toward Dani to make it look as if we were having a conversation. "Let's get everything moving."

"Got it." Seamus's tone held bitterness and reluctance. He didn't like that we hadn't changed from the original plan. "Her comm is now linked with ours."

I let a moment pass before speaking.

"Bailey," I said into the comm. Bailey's head twitched, no doubt startled to hear my voice in her ear. "Hold out two fingers if you were able to get what we needed."

Her hand tightened into a fist before two fingers descended.

Perfect. Now it was time to put the plan in motion.

"Meet me in the blue room just off the main corridor in ten minutes. We can exchange everything there," I told her. "Two fingers again if you understand me."

Another two fingers.

I smirked. "Such a good girl."

She lowered a finger, and I laughed at seeing her usual fire. The woman had just flipped me the bird. Dani was barely holding her own laughter back. *Brat*.

"Why do you look like you're about to do something you regret?" Dani asked as we made our way around the room again, my ever-watchful gaze still following her around the room.

"Because I am," I admitted truthfully, an unusual weight bearing down on my chest. Dani halted her footsteps, looking up at me with a sad frown on her face.

"You can still change it."

I shook my head.

"No, I really can't."

Luckily, without Seamus looping our comms, Bailey herself couldn't hear us.

I didn't get the chance to respond.

"Finally decided to slum it with the rest of us, Kavanaugh?" My fist clenched at the sound of the man's voice. Fuck. He wasn't even a man. He was just a boy playing at being one. Seamus and I had taken the time to suss out Crowe and Drew. There were a few things that Bridgett had told us that didn't sit right. Parts that didn't add up when it came to Bailey.

Drew's affair with Bailey's best friend was part of that. For years, they'd been meeting at hotels, a time or two in his office, but never at his condo. Bailey had a key and often came and went throughout the week when he was at work. It would have been too risky.

So why the sudden change of venue? Drew must have known the risk of Bailey stopping by.

Then there was the issue with her spark plugs.

The service receipt in her glove box that our mechanic had dug up listed her last repair less than three months ago. That explained why the spark plugs had looked so new. All except one. It had been cracked and dirty, and Bailey wouldn't have known to look for something like that. To her, it was just a case of bad luck.

Drew seemed the likely suspect. According to our sources,

he'd been avidly trying to search her out. Whether it was guilt over the affair or something more sinister had yet to be seen. We'd been sure to cover our tracks when we'd taken Bailey, just in case. Still, despite everything she still hadn't given us up.

Why?

"I'm not quite in the slums just yet, Knight," I sneered at him. "I'd have to sink a whole lot lower to hit your depths."

"You're nothing but a rat, Kavanaugh," he hissed. "A rat thinking he's better than everyone else around him when all he smells like is sewer."

"Just because I don't cover my scent in pot-pourri doesn't mean I'm a rat," I told him. "It means I'm not a snake hiding in the tall grass until easy prey comes along."

"Baby," a reedy voice interrupted before the asshole could rebut. "There you are. The entertainment is going to start soon, and I want to get a good seat."

There was no doubt in my mind that this was Brittany, the woman Drew had been cheating on Bailey with. Everything about her was fake, and I couldn't see the appeal. Her platinum blond hair was an obvious dye job, and her overly large breasts were too big on her stick frame to be real. Her face was wrinkle free and her lips looked almost cartoonish with how plump they were.

"I see your seller token," I smirked, "yet I see no prized mare. Merely a cow parading as one. Tell me, what is the going price for used whores? Is it similar to getting used tires? You measure how loose their tread is?"

Dani snorted beside me, quickly covering it with a cough. The woman's Botoxed lips curled with disdain, making her appear even uglier. Jesus, she looked more like a blow-up doll than a human.

"Who the fuck do you think you are?" Her expression was

one of indignation, as if she couldn't believe I would dare speak to her like that.

"I'm the man who's going to take everything away from your boyfriend here," I sneered. "So I'd get those Botox treatments in while you still can. Not that it will change much about that sour expression of yours. There's only so much surgery can help with."

Then I walked away.

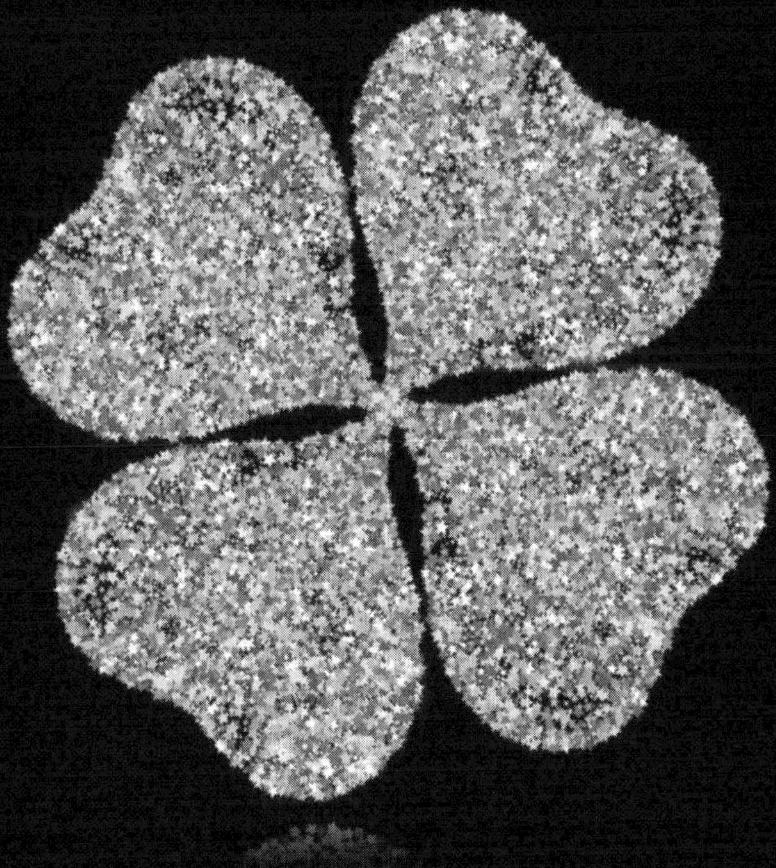

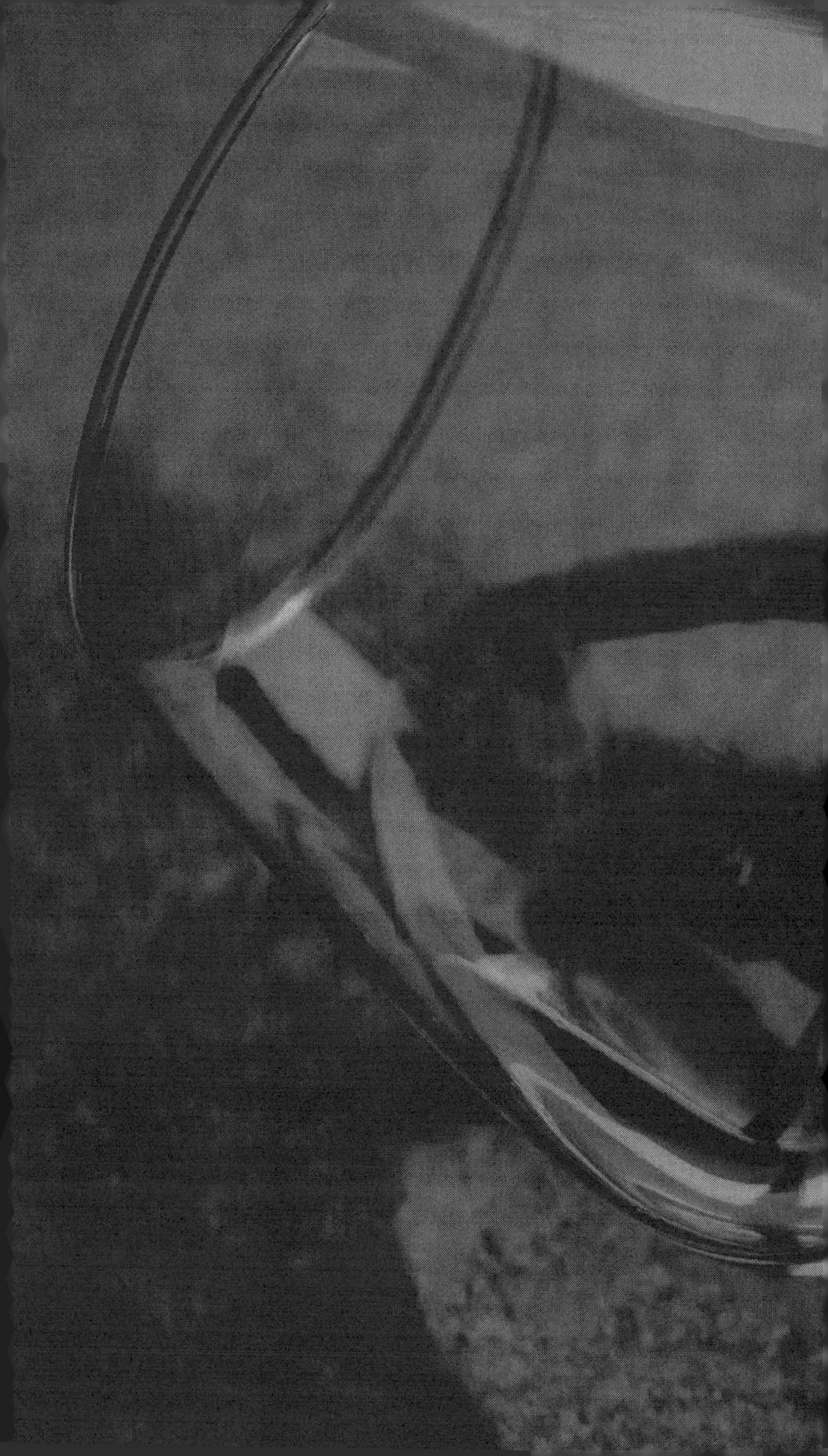

28

Bailey

Ten minutes.

Just ten more minutes.

The drive was hidden inside the small, corseted bra that was currently strangling my chest. I'd barely managed to hide it and get the comm in my ear with everything that had been going on today. From the moment the sun rose, Sarah had an army of hairdressers, waxers, and cosmetologists working on every part of my body until it had been time to finally leave on Drew's right arm.

With Brittany on the left.

My heart had surged when I saw Kiernan entering the gala. Followed by a short plummet when I'd seen Dani on his arm. The two melded together perfectly. Model-like. They belonged on a runway, not in a charity gala with dirty roots.

Something was off.

After our short conversation, he'd turned off my side of the comm unit, which meant I couldn't hear their side of the conversation. Kiernan wasn't telling me something. There was a cast of hidden shadows behind his features that told me he was holding back.

I was missing something. It felt like I was sitting before a puzzle, but none of the pieces fit together. Drew, who'd spotted Kiernan when he'd walked through the door, had stiffened, his arm tightening on my shoulder. He knew who he was.

Until the night I'd come home, I'd thought Drew was simply...Drew. I'd known him since I was sixteen. He was ambitious and headstrong, but never once had I seen the type of proclivities that would have him taking part in sex trafficking. That was his father's thing, not his.

Not that I had much to stand on. I'd been blind to his affair with my best friend, so it didn't come as much of a surprise that I'd ignored his other faults as well. Speaking of my trashy ex-bestie. She wasn't looking too pleased that I was hanging off his right arm. Her entire face was screwed up like she'd swallowed a lemon whole.

Hindsight was a bitch.

I'd known Brittany since college. We'd both been freshmen at UW. The one big difference being that I was seventeen, and she was two years older. I wasn't sure how I'd missed it. When I looked back on our friendship, there were things that didn't quite add up properly. I was a loner at college, mostly because no one seemed to want to interact with me. I'd chalked it up to being so young. Most people were a good year or two ahead of me. That and the fact that I had a bodyguard assigned to me at all hours of the day.

In the wake of the loneliness, I clung to my relationships with Brittany and Drew more, becoming emotionally dependent on the two. Which was why it had been such a low blow to see them in bed together.

It really shouldn't have been.

Now I could see it for what it really was. Manipulation. I

had a sneaking suspicion they'd been together long before we'd met. Not that it mattered now that I knew the truth.

A truth that would soon come to light.

Once Kiernan got me the hell out of here.

What I wanted to know was why Drew had a sellers pin on his lapel. I couldn't see him putting Brittany up on the chopping block. The backstabbing Judas may have been dressed as if she were a prostitute, but honestly, that was just who she was. She'd always had the body of a stripper, and she'd never been afraid to flaunt it. I was a fan of oversized T-shirts and sweatpants myself.

Her bleach-blond hair hung in loose waves around her face, drawing attention to the layers of makeup she'd drowned herself in. She wore a glitter bodycon dress that exposed her oversized plastic breasts and ass.

Brittany's focus steered to Kiernan as he strode past us and out of the room. Her eyes widened, and I could see the fear etched in her irises. She knew exactly who Kiernan was. Most people we'd seen tonight knew him as the business mogul, but she knew him as the heir to the Irish mafia. He was feared. Ruthless.

I wasn't blind to that side of him or Seamus.

"I've got to run to the ladies' room," I whispered to Drew as demurely as I could. Drew glanced down at me before nodding his head.

"Remember what happens if you run," he reminded me before turning back to greet another one of the men he was acquainted with. I didn't bother to reply. Instead, I slowly made my way toward the corridor that led to the bathroom.

The hall was nearly empty; only a few of the waitstaff remained, lingering around on their breaks. They paid me no attention as I ducked into the blue room. I closed the door softly behind me.

"Took you long enough." I jumped at the sudden disturbance of silence. Kiernan stood in the middle of the small room, his hand resting lazily in one pocket as he scrolled through his phone with the other.

The sight of him in a suit took my breath away. His red hair was pulled neatly into a bun, making his face appear even sharper. The black suit ensemble cut his body perfectly, making my mouth water and images of him fucking me with his suit on drift through my brain.

"I'm not exactly free to come and go," I reminded him. "I had to be sure no one was following me."

Nodding, he still didn't look up from his phone.

"Do you have it?" He turned his attention to me, one brow raised expectantly. Something was off about him. Kiernan had always been somewhat standoffish, especially compared to his brother, but this was different. My stomach churned with unease, but I ignored it. This was Kiernan. I could trust him...right?

I plucked the drive from my bra and held it out for him. He snatched it from my hand and shoved it in his jacket pocket.

"You did so well, *mo fraochÚn beag*." He smiled down at me, but it was tight, his lips pursed, eyes hard.

"Look, there's something you need to—" The door to the room burst open, interrupting the secret I'd been about to spill. Turning, my eyes widened as my father strode through the door, a look of fury painted across his face. He was flanked by his guards on either side.

"I'm sorry about this, Bailey," Kiernan whispered in my ear. "I really am."

What was going on?

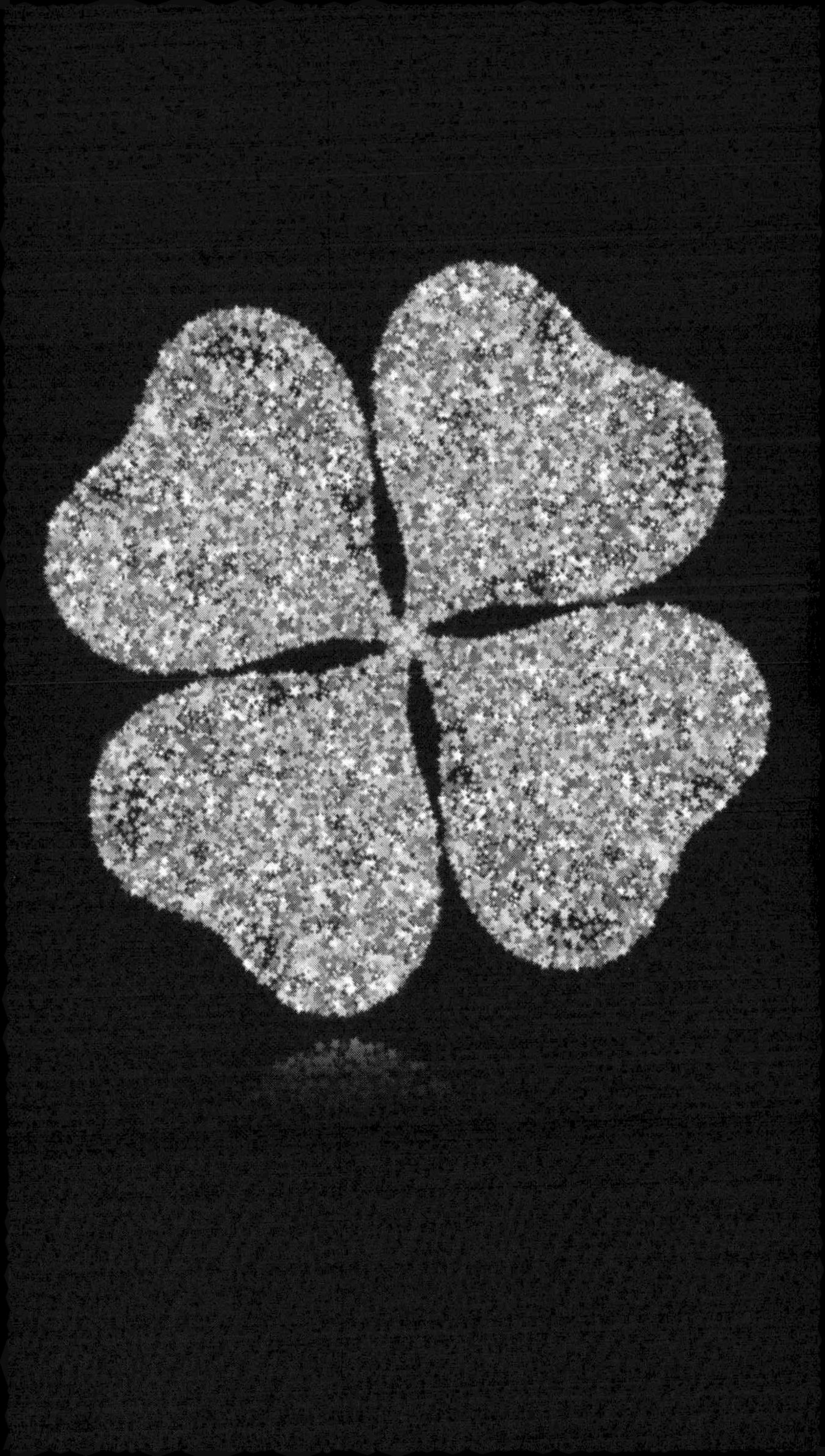

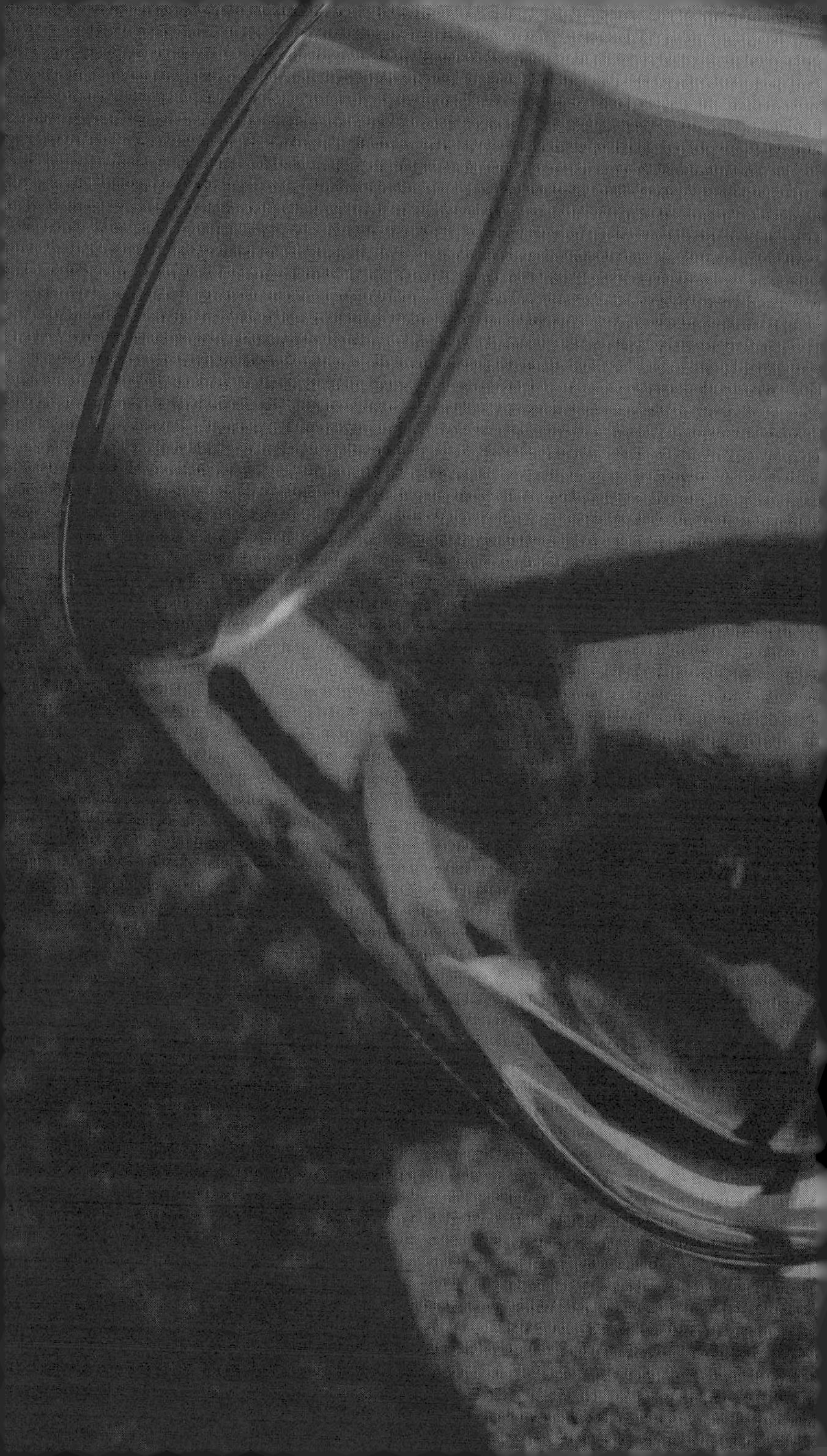

29

Kiernan

The utter look of betrayal on Bailey's face drove a knife deep into my chest. It lodged deeper than I was expecting, and suddenly, all I wanted to do was take it all back. My father and Seamus had wanted to alter the plan, but we couldn't. We needed the information on the senator, and taking Bailey with us after we'd obtained it would lead to suspicion.

This way, Crowe believed we were on his side.

But now—now I wanted nothing more than to hold her in my arms and tell her exactly how I felt. He'd no doubt discipline her, but she was his daughter. He'd see her as misled and try to point her back in the right direction. But it wouldn't matter, because once everything was out about him, we'd come back for her. When it was all over, she'd be ours.

Bailey was going to hate me for this, but I'd make her see it was for her own good.

"Kavanaugh," the senator greeted me coldly.

"Senator." Bailey's hand gripped my wrist tightly, her gaze wide-eyed and frantic as she looked up at me.

"It seems you have a few things of mine." His gaze turned

to Bailey, who shrank into my side as if I'd save her. But I wasn't her savior.

"Here." I reached into the inner pocket of my jacket and tossed him a drive that was nearly identical to the one Bailey had given me. The only difference was the information on it had nothing to do with what Bailey had managed to steal from the laptop. There was still incriminating evidence on it, but nothing compared to what I was sure Bailey had dug up.

"On it is everything she has managed to dig up on you over the last year or so," I told him casually.

"And how is it that my daughter came to you?" he wondered.

I smirked. "She thought we would have a vested interest in seeing you in prison," I lied. "Bailey approached us this last week, stating that she had information that would lead to a conviction no dirty judge would be able to look past."

"No, they—" Bailey started, but I kept going.

"You can even check her car's GPS logs," I added. "She was with us up until the time she returned to your doorstep. We wanted to make sure she was serious about turning over the information before contacting you about it."

"And what do you have to gain, Kavanaugh?" Crowe spat. "This is some sudden comradery you're showing when all your family has ever expressed is distaste."

My eyes darkened. We were about to see how good my acting skills truly were.

"My brother and I are set to take over my father's empire in less than a year," I told him. That was the truth. My father was set to retire soon, and Seamus and I would take his place. "For years, we've turned down deals that could have projected our family into better and more lucrative means, but every time, we're forced to turn them down due to our father's... moral compass."

"And you think I can help you with that?" he asked. "I'm a senator and—"

"Yes, we're all well aware of your title," I scoffed. "We're also aware of the underground flesh trade you have going with the late Elias Ward, and we want in."

"Your father will have objections to this."

"My father will no longer be a problem soon," I assured him, ignoring Bailey's mild gasp from next to me. "As soon as he hands over the reins, he's taking a nice long trip to Ireland. He won't be a problem."

The senator nodded his head once, seemingly appeased.

"I'm sure we can work something out, then," he glanced at my lapel. "I see you'll be bidding at the auction."

I nodded. "My brother and I are looking for something to share."

Crowe chuckled. "Then we can discuss business there," he assured me. "Hammer out all the details." He glanced at Bailey, and the hairs on the back of my neck stood on end. "I won't be bidding, but I have a nice piece I'm putting up on the auction block."

"I'll be sure to keep my eyes open."

Crowe smirked.

"You do that."

"Wait—" Bailey tugged at my sleeve, tears welling in her eyes. "Please don't—"

I brushed her off before she could finish. She stumbled back, her heel catching on the hem of her dress. With a small cry, she landed on the tiled floor in a heap, tears streaming down her face. I had to keep myself from flinching when her father's men tugged her up from the floor and proceeded to drag toward the door.

"Wait, Kiernan. You don't understand!" she cried as they dragged her from the room, her father following closely behind. "Kiernan, please. Let me go! Kiernan, don't let him take me away. He isn't who he—"

Silence fell as the doors slammed shut behind them.

The room suddenly felt cavernous and lonely. My chest stung, a sharp ache spreading through me as I struggled to maintain the little composure I had left. I took a cleansing breath, my head tilting toward the ceiling, eyes closed as I tensed and relaxed my muscles.

My phone vibrated in my pocket, and for a moment, I considered not answering it. Until I remembered that it could be important.

"Yeah?" I answered without bothering to look at the caller ID.

"Kiernan." Bridgett's voice was urgent. "Please tell me you haven't done the trade yet."

"They just took her away," I told her. "Why?"

"I've been doing all the digging I could on Toph Eriksen's missing daughter," she rushed. "And you're not going to believe what I stumbled on to."

My hand clenched around the phone.

"What?"

"Bailey Jameson is Toph Eriksen's missing daughter," Bridgett told me. "Richard Crowe kidnapped her when she was only three years old."

No. That couldn't be true.

"I'm running a DNA analysis just to be sure, but everything I've gathered points to her."

Motherfucker.

What had I done?

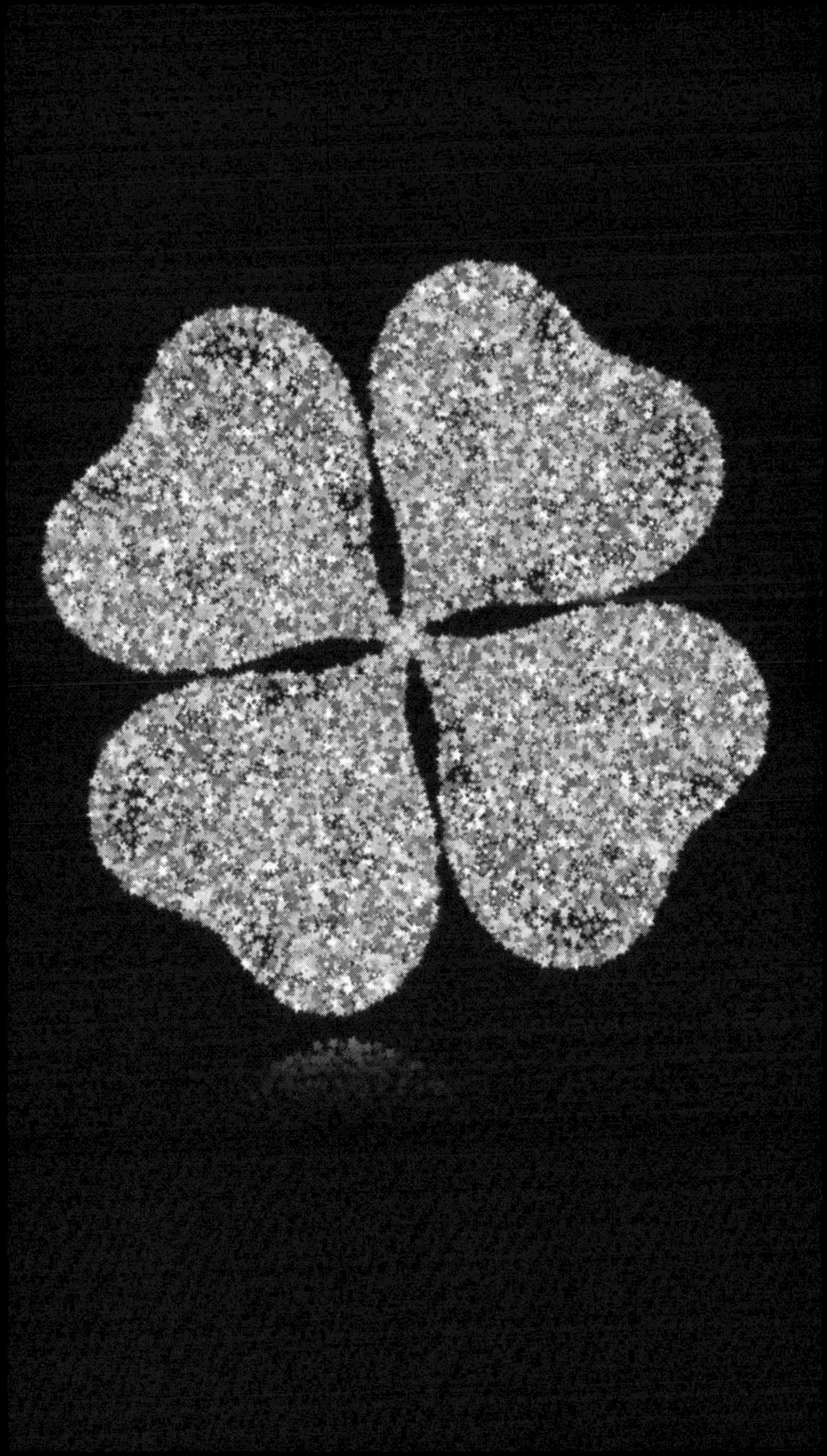

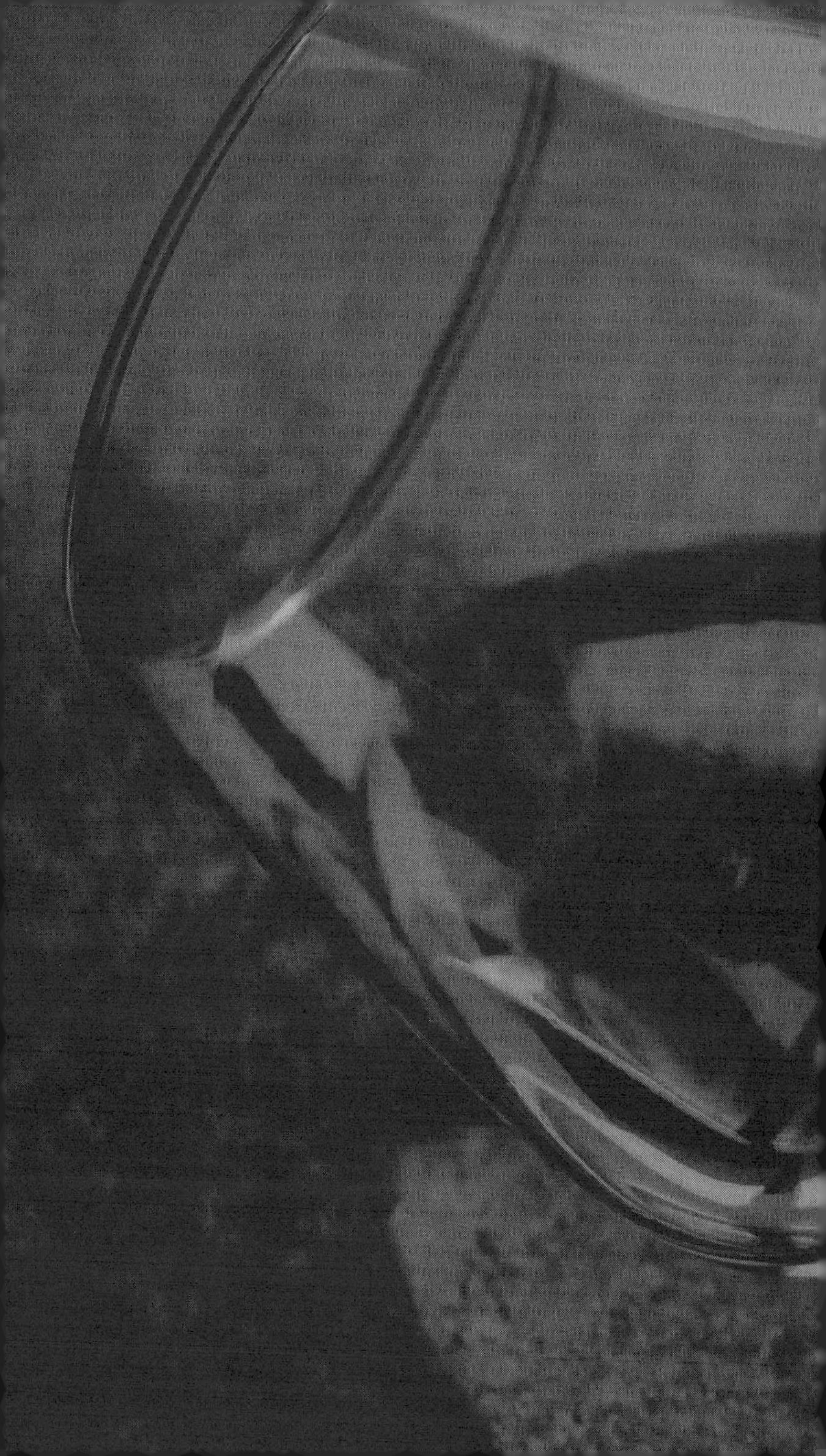

30

Bailey

"Kiernan?" My voice cracked as I said his name into the darkness that surrounded me. My throat was dry, my head heavy, and a weird metallic taste invaded my senses. "Kiernan!"

Jesus, did I get run over by a semi-truck?

What happened? The last thing I remember was slipping the USB drive to Kiernan, and then my father—

My stomach churned, bilious and sour. Groaning, I clutched it, unable to hold back the bile rising in my throat. *What had they done to me?* I heaved into a small bucket until my stomach was empty. There hadn't been much in there to start with. I'd been too nervous to eat earlier.

The cobwebs in my mind were starting to fade, and I shook my head a little to clear it. Pushing myself up off the floor, I looked around. Hushed voices and the sound of clinking glasses and moving chairs filtered through the walls. There weren't any windows in the small room, and I had to take several deliberate breaths to control the fear that threatened to swallow me whole.

I didn't do well in small spaces.

"Hello?"

Nothing. Fucking shit. *Where the hell was I?*

That was a stupid question. I was obviously in a basement of some kind, waiting for the auction to start. My father had planned this all along.

No.

Not my father.

The man who had stolen me from my father. The man who had used me as a pawn to control my actual father. The files in his office safe had been more than eye-opening. My entire life since I was three years old had been in those folders.

Now I knew everything.

Mostly everything.

Now that I looked back on everything, it was all coming together in my mind. I couldn't believe I had been so blind. The woman I'd remembered as my mother had been nothing more than a jealous woman. She'd stolen me and bartered me away, thinking she could fill the empty space in my biological father's life.

She'd been wrong.

God, was I pathetic. The number of people who had used me for their own gain before throwing me to the wolves was growing more every day. The junkie woman, Richard, the Kavanaughs.

Kiernan...

That bastard had handed me over to my father without a second thought.

Why? Had that been part of the plan the entire time? Use me and then throw me to my father when they'd had their fill?

God, why had I been so stupid? Of course this had been the plan. They'd used me. Gotten what they wanted, then they had gotten rid of me like yesterday's trash. I couldn't believe they'd done this. All of them. They'd never made me feel like a captive, and maybe that was the red flag I should have been paying attention to.

Instead, I let myself believe the lie they sold me. That they wanted me. Cherished. *Loved me.*

They'd been honest about the man who called himself my father. Richard Crowe was a despicable man. Wretched as they come. There had to be a reason they had done it, right? They were going to rescue me. That had to be the plan.

Didn't it?

Before I could be swallowed by the pity that threatened to overwhelm me, the silence was broken by the sound of several abrupt cries. Heavy footsteps thudded outside my prison, stopping directly in front of my door. The lock twisted and disengaged, and the door swung open on its rusty hinges. My heart raced, and I prepared myself to use whatever tactic necessary to get out of this hellhole. I wouldn't allow myself to be sold. There was a reason I'd caught on to Seamus's training so well. The style of fighting was different, specialized, but my father's men had taken me under their wing growing up. They'd taught me how to defend myself. How to fight dirty.

The heavy wooden door swung open, the light from the hallway outlining the broad frame that filled the doorway. He stepped into the cell, and I didn't waste any time launching myself at him, hoping to catch him off guard.

I'd managed to catch him by surprise, since he probably hadn't expected a docile submissive to fight back, and landed a blow to his face, knocking him backward.

"Little bitch," he sneered. His accent was thick, but I couldn't place its origin. It wasn't Russian, that I knew, and it sure as hell wasn't Italian. I didn't bother to stay and ask before I darted out the cell door and took off down the hallway without bothering to look back.

Except that it was full.

I ran smack dab into the hard chest of another mountain of a man, and he didn't look particularly pleased at my escape attempt.

Then my body lit up like the fourth of July.

I hit the floor hard, my body convulsing as shock after shock of electricity coursed through me like hot magma. My muscles were locked tight, and my teeth were clenched together so hard I thought they might shatter. The current pulsed through me again and again until I was begging him to stop.

The man whose nose I had broken cursed at me in another language as he bent down, a cattle prod swinging loosely between his legs. His hand came down across my face. I groaned in pain as he dragged me to my feet by my hair before tossing me to another guard.

"Get her in line with the others."

The brawny man I'd run into took my upper arm in his grasp, shoving me toward the line of girls who stood primly, one right next to the other, their heads bowed but their shoulders erect.

"Stand here," he barked, shoving me next to a young girl with strawberry blond hair who was wearing nothing more than a sheer slip. "You move and you get punished, understood?"

Recognizing this was not a battle I should fight, I nodded my head meekly.

"Good," he sneered. "Eyes on the floor."

I obeyed, but inside, I was going over all the ways I could carve him up. Him and the fucker with the cattle prod.

We stood in line for what felt like hours. My legs were beginning to burn, knees growing tired and threatening to give out. I was on the brink of tipping over like the little teapot when the door to the hallway burst open.

"Kneel." The harsh command had the girls scrambling to kneel. I followed, cursing him under my breath. At least I wasn't at risk of falling over any longer.

"As you can see, we have an amazing lineup this year." A nasally voice drifted through the room anxiously. "Some of the top women from our donors."

"Yes." A woman's voice joined his, her voice a smooth rumble that reminded me of dark chocolate. Her heels clacked along the stone floor, joined by the tapping of what sounded like a cane. "Ward does seem to have luck when it comes to finding the perfect candidates for our program."

Program?

Keeping my head down, I let my gaze wander slightly beneath my lashes. Red heels and a black cane entered my vision briefly before passing on down the line.

"I hate to resort to finding women this way," she continued, her voice tinted with disgust. "But with two of our assets having gone rogue, I'm in need of immediate replacements."

"Of course," the man acquiesced. "We are at the Doll-house's humble service, Madam Therese."

Dollhouse. I'd run across that name before while searching for Lina. One of her contacts had tipped her off to it, but none of her notes went into detail. There was an obvious connection to the trafficking ring, but until this moment, I hadn't known what it was.

Was it a brothel? Or some kind of secondary ring? The woman's voice held the same accent as the guards but softer.

I swallowed hard when the cold tip of the woman's cane rested beneath my chin, forcing my head up. She stood above me, clothed in a black wrap dress that was accessorized by a dead rodent's fur wrapped around her shoulders. Her silver hair was swept back into an elegant bun. She had a long, angular face with pinched red lips and narrow eyes.

This was what I expected a brothel manager to look like.

"This one has potential," she purred. The nasally man, who I now recognized as Tatem Jones from the pictures I'd seen, shook his head.

"I'm sorry, Madam Therese." He bowed slightly. "This one is not up for grabs. I didn't realize our men had cleared her from her cell. She is already slotted to go to someone else. I apologize for the inconvenience."

"Pity," the woman drawled. "I'd hoped to be the one to break that spirit in her eyes."

I'd like to break your nose and those coffee-stained teeth. Maybe feed you to a shark.

Her cane whipped out, hitting my side with fierce precision, causing me to shriek at the sudden pain.

Oops. Had I said that out loud?

Tatem shook his head at me before barking at the girls to stand.

"I'll take four and eight." She signaled to her men, who hauled the two girls away. Not that they put up a fight. And here I thought I had Stockholm syndrome. "Let me know if this one ever becomes available. I do love a challenge."

Tatem smirked. "I don't think there will be much left by the time her new owner is done with her, but I will pass along the message."

New owner. Like I'd had a previous one.

Then again, I had. Drew. My receipt of sale had also been among the folders I'd uncovered. Drew's father had bought me for his son for three million dollars. He'd wanted a strong link between him and Crowe, as well as something to lord over my biological father. I would have been expected to give him a child, since his woman of choice couldn't bear any.

Stolen Obsession

Tatem growled something in Italian, his words too fast for me to translate, and a few more guards appeared. They weren't as bulky as their predecessors and were distinctly Italian. They led us remaining women down a short corridor and up a small flight of stairs before guiding us to the back of a stage. The voices I'd heard through my cell were louder now. The clinking of glasses and cheerful conversation more distinguishable.

They were laughing. Having a good time while we were to be sold like livestock at the county fair. I staggered slightly when the guard behind me pushed me to move, but I managed to catch myself before I face-planted. The guard roughly grabbed my upper arm and pushed me onto the stage. The other women kneeled on the wooden floors, their heads bowed in submission, knees parted so obscenely that it gave the audience a full view of what they were offering.

Of what they were here to buy.

I kneeled, refusing to spread my knees apart. The guard growled at me in Italian, but I ignored him, choosing instead to search the crowd. I could see Drew in the back with Brittany on his arm, her ice-cold gaze on me, a cruel smile stretched across her Botoxed lips. The auctioneer, a man in his early forties, began to speak, acknowledging the generous donations given tonight.

The light of the room was dim compared to the stage, making it slightly harder to see out into the crowd. I just needed to find an escape. All attention was on the auctioneer as he described the "submissions" that were to be auctioned, so no one was watching me case the place. There were two doors in and out of the room, both marked by two armed guards. The trick would be determining which one led to freedom and which one led to a dead end that could end up getting me killed.

Drawing my eyes away from the doors, I pulled my attention to inspecting the other inhabitants, sweeping my gaze across the room until something caught my eye.

No, not something.

Someone.

Lina.

In a room filled mainly with men, she stood out like a sore thumb. She'd donned a swanky evening dress and low heels, and her head was bowed in conversation with someone who looked awfully familiar.

All at once, my heart shattered into a million pieces.

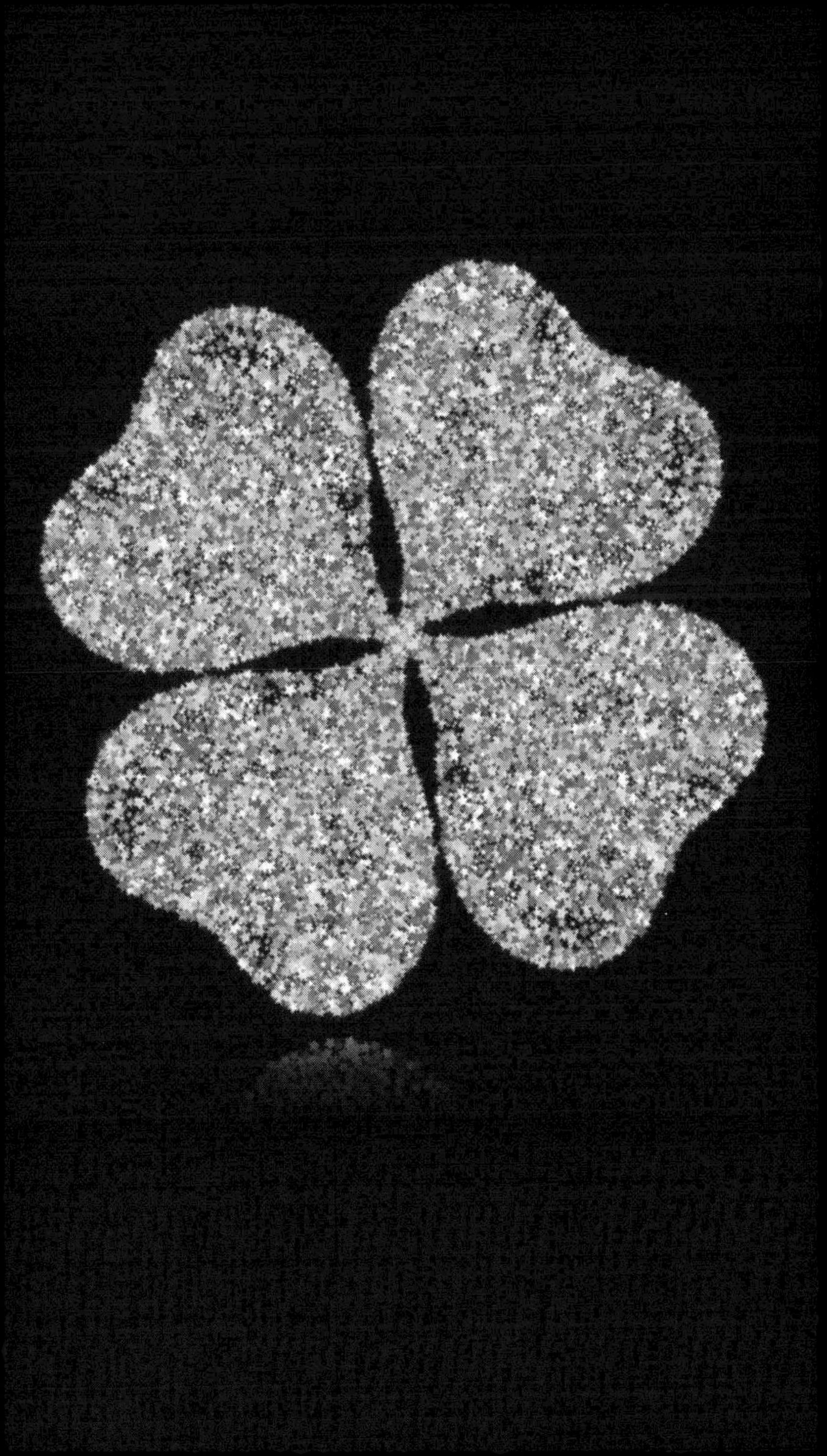

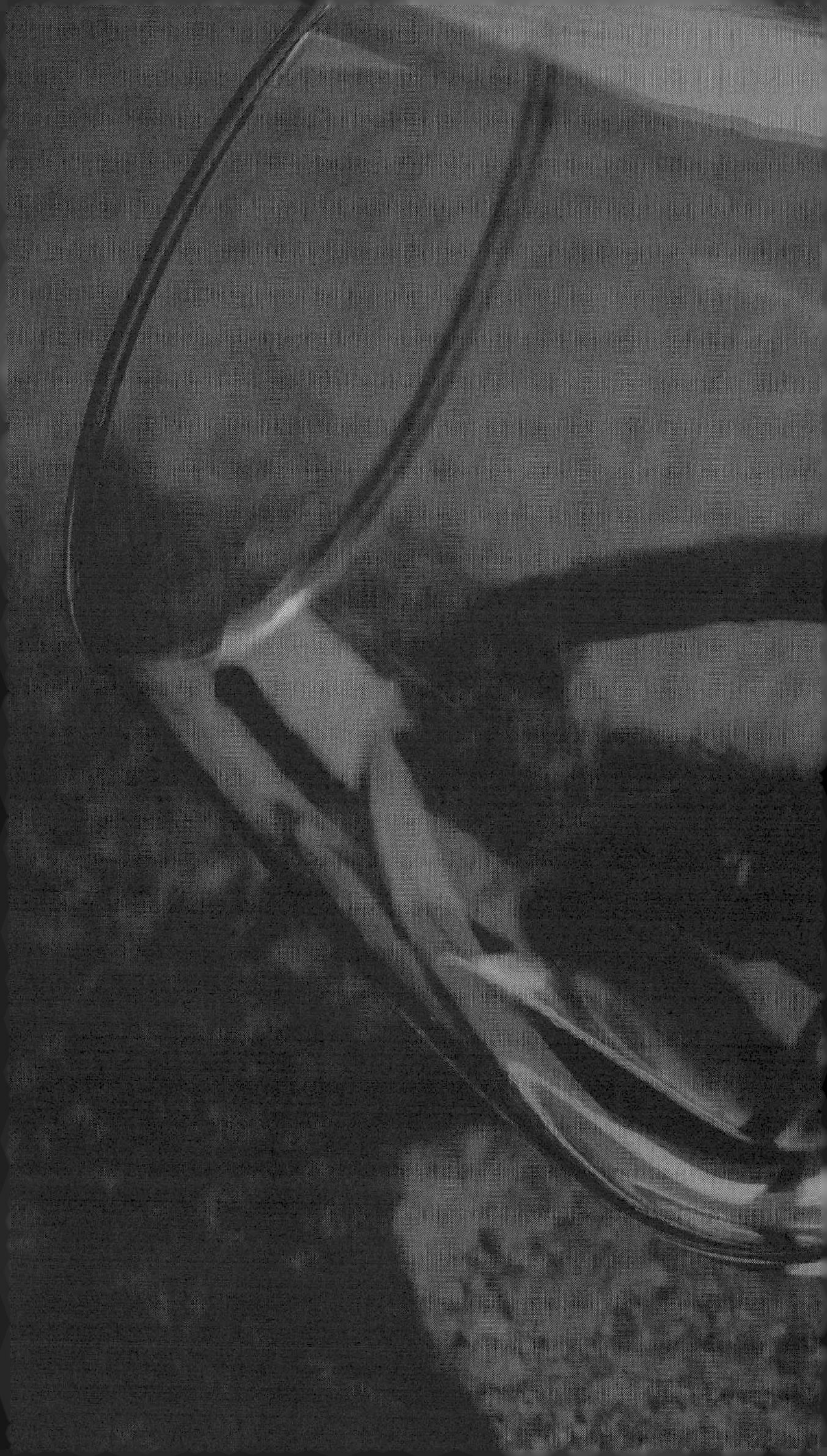

31

Bailey

I screamed his name, the heartbreaking sound of my anguish echoing across the room as tears streamed down my face. The room fell silent, and all eyes were on me. He'd come for me. He was here. I looked around the room. Where was Seamus? Had he not come?

My feet moved to go to him, forgetting for a moment we were in the middle of one of the most secure places in the city, and it was filled to the brim with guns and mafiosos. Growling, the guard behind me grabbed a fistful of my hair, pulling me back in line.

"Kiernan!" My heart clenched painfully when his emerald eyes met mine. The warmth I'd seen in them over the past week was gone, replaced by a cool indifference I saw the night of the gala. I brought my hands up to grasp at the one in my hair, pivoting on my heels so my shoulder knocked into his arm. This gave me the chance to stomp my foot down on his and plant one of my elbows in his gut. The goon released my hair when he stumbled back.

My freedom was short-lived. As I dove forward, a strong arm wrapped around my waist, hauling me back into a chest.

"Let me go!" I screeched. "Please. Kiernan."

I clawed at the arms of the one holding me, unaware of my surroundings. In my panicked state, I'd missed someone coming up on my side with a syringe. I winced at the sudden prick in my arm, and within moments, my body had begun to relax without my permission. The guard loosened his hold on me before stepping back.

A desperate sob caught in my throat as I sank back to my knees, hands clutching at my chest as the man I'd given my heart to approached the stage. He whispered something to Tatem, who nodded before taking a step back.

"Hello, *mo fraochÚn beag*." His smile was twisted and cruel. I stared up at him, casting him a scathing look and spat at his feet.

"Fuck you, Kavanaugh," I hissed. Kiernan's jaw clenched. "I trusted you."

The laugh he gave me was mirthless, void of any emotion, just like I would soon be. "It was too easy to get you to trust us," he whispered darkly. "Naïve little girl who just wanted to be loved for the first time in her life. So desperate for affection that she took it from anywhere she could. Including the two men who kidnapped her."

Through the haze of cigar smoke and the sound of cruel laughter, his words echoed in my head like a bad Cardi B song stuck on repeat. *So desperate for affection...*He wasn't wrong. I just couldn't believe he'd said it. Any hope I'd held on to that this was all part of the plan died with those words. He'd taken my darkest secret and thrown it back at me like it meant nothing. I'd shared that with them in confidence, thinking I could trust them.

He was right. I was naïve.

And now I'd pay the price.

"Don't worry," he chuckled, "Crowe has got a nice buyer

all lined up for Eriksen's whore of a daughter. I heard he's really into sharing too, and you were so good at taking us both. Weren't you?" He ran a finger down my wet cheek. "If I would have known we had Toph Eriksen's daughter under our roof, your stay might've been a little less cozy."

Callous laughter surrounded me, filling my ears until I felt like they'd bleed.

He'd let my father sell me.

The stone in my stomach plummeted, and I couldn't draw a full breath in. They'd done it. They'd actually let me be sold.

But to whom?

"She's all yours now." Kiernan took a step back to reveal the last person I thought I'd see.

"Lina," I breathed. But she didn't look like Lina. Not anymore. The soft glow of her face was hardened and narrowed. She stood taller, her shoulders back, head held high. A far cry from the meek but headstrong woman who'd mentored me through my career.

"You just couldn't leave well enough alone, could you?" she sneered at me, her lips curling up into an angry snarl. "Had to go poking your nose where it doesn't belong."

I blinked up at her. The drug Tatem had given me was starting to hit me harder. "I've been trying to find you." Disbelief was no doubt my current facial expression. At least I thought it was. I was having a hard time controlling my facial muscles. Whatever they'd given me was trippy. "I thought..." *What had I thought?*

Lina laughed heartlessly. "You really are naïve, little princess." She shook her head. "I didn't need saving. If anyone needed saving, it was you. You couldn't leave well enough alone. Had to stir up a whole bunch of shit."

What? I hadn't stirred anything up...had I? Maybe I had.

Wait...what were we talking about?

"Looks like your drug is finally starting to work, Jones." Lina cocked her head, studying me. Huh, why did I feel so warm and fuzzy inside? Medications had always been touch and go with me. My body usually took a while to absorb most sedatives and pain medication, meaning that it took longer for them to kick in, and when they did, it was never all that pleasant.

"Victor," she barked, the sound floating in the air before my eyes. I snorted. You couldn't see sound...could you? "Get her loaded up in the car and don't let her escape."

I wondered if it could be felt.

Maybe. Maybe not.

A sliver of laughter slipped through me, and then a hysterical giggle. The burly mountain man named Victor slung me over his shoulder and I giggled again, smiling at the lights that danced across my vision in rhythm with the music that vibrated through the floor.

My gaze caught Kiernan's, and suddenly, the lights darkened and the tune grew sad. He looked sad. His brow was furrowed, and his hands were clenching and unclenching at his sides. It was one of his tells when he wanted to punch someone. Lina stood by his side, facing away from me, whispering in his ear.

If only I could shoot daggers into her back.

Fucking Judas.

Traitors.

Assholes.

Betrayers.

I let out a heart-wrenching sob as the bitter dagger of betrayal twisted deeper into my heart, and then I knew nothing at all.

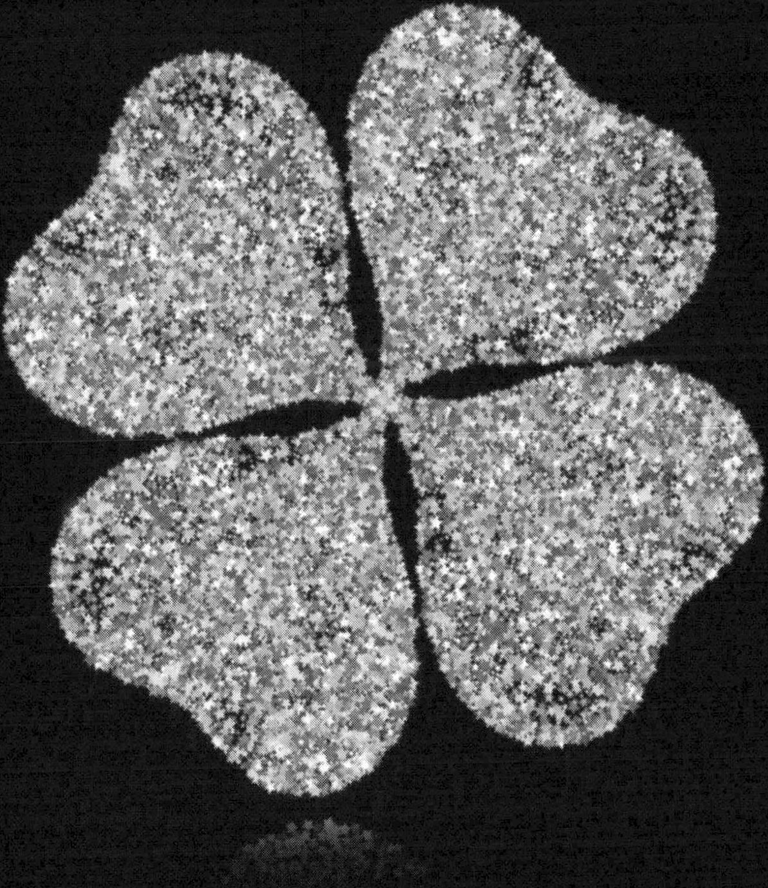

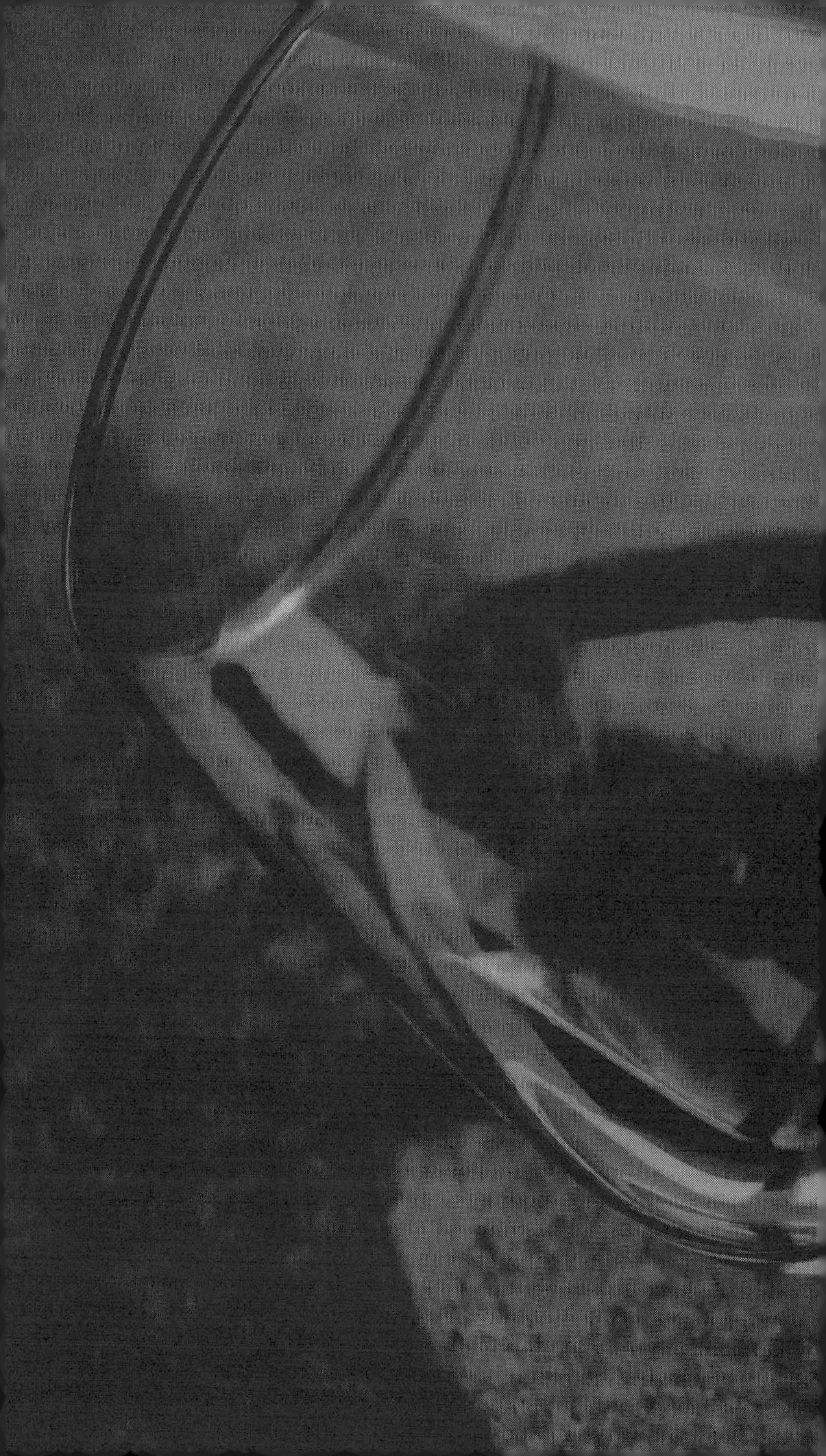

32

Bailey

The room was dark and small, holding nothing more than a thin, dirty mattress that reeked of sex and urine. I'd gagged when I'd woken up, facedown in the filth, barely managing not to wretch up the last vestiges of food that remained in my stomach.

I sat, my head buried in my hands, for what seemed like hours before the door finally opened to reveal the man who'd been nothing but a lie my entire life. He tilted his head, studying me, his cold eyes assessing in a way they never had before.

My body was still clothed in the sheer red dress I'd worn at the auction. A symbol of my non-virginity, apparently. The hairs on the back of my arms stood on end when the man I'd known as father stepped into the room with Drew on his heel, shutting the door firmly behind them.

"Hello, *daughter*." He drew out the former familial title. Drew licked his lips, his eyes lighting up as they roamed my nearly naked form. I kept silent, not wanting to engage them further, my eyes locked on the far wall. "I'm sorry it had to come to this. Although this is where the path would have eventually led." He shrugged nonchalantly. My life meant that little to him. "You just ended up here slightly sooner than either of us would have liked."

My jaw tightened to the point of pain. It wouldn't surprise me if I cracked some teeth with how hard it was clenched. There were so many things I could say. Sewage I could spill about his life, but I wouldn't. Even if Kiernan and the rest of the Kavanaughs deserved to be put in their place. I could easily tell Crowe about the information they truly had. I'd seen flashes of what had been uploaded and none of it was good. Every corrupt judge, politician, and police captain would go down for what they'd taken part in.

That was my hope.

Kiernan may have sold me out, but I didn't believe for one second the lie he'd told Crowe about their shared interests. The drive he'd handed over hadn't been the one I'd given him, which meant they still had a plan to take him out.

It just didn't involve me.

Crowe kneeled in front of me, his eyes burning a hole in my face, but still, I refused to acknowledge him.

"Let me tell you a little story." From my periphery, I could see a slow smile spread across his face. "Once upon a time there was a man who was building himself an empire."

Cue eye roll. My inner bitch was sitting in the corner, ready to pounce, but fear kept her contained.

"He went off to college with his friends, ready to conquer the world. But one night, a mistake was made. A drunken one, and from there, everything began to slide. The college was ready to expel them; internships were being rescinded...so he made his first dirty deal in order to keep everything from falling apart.

"Now, he wasn't able to do that for everyone." He shrugged. "Some of his friends wound up in jail, and others had their career opportunities disappear as if they'd never been offered. He managed to get away unscathed, along with a few others who he eventually went into business with, and the mistake of the past was buried."

There were only three people he could be talking about. Ward and Ford. Both of whom were now dead, and Knight, who still clung to this world like a bad sex tape.

"Soon, his career grew and grew. But he learned that not all dead things stay buried."

"Is there a point to this fucking story?" I growled, finally breaking. "Or do you just like to hear the sound of your own voice?"

A hand wrapped around my throat, stifling my scream. Not that it would have mattered in this place. No one would come running. He lifted me from the floor, pushing me down on the bed, his weight bearing down on me. Nails dug into flesh as I flailed beneath him. The smell of iron tinged the air. I'd managed to rake my nails down his face before Drew seized my wrists above my head, leaving me helpless beneath the man I'd once called father.

There was nothing fatherly about the bulge I felt pressing against my stomach.

The urge to wretch was high, and I had to fight against the need to vomit everywhere. The only thing holding me back was the thought that I wouldn't have anything to change into and I'd end up sleeping in vomit-covered clothes and mattress.

"Enough," he roared. The back of his hand against my cheek effectively stilled me. My chest heaved as I fought to take in air. It was like breathing through a straw. "Do you know what I've had to do to get where I am? To build this legacy? I own this city, and soon, I'll be on top of the world. The most powerful man in history. When your slut of a mother came back to Seattle after leaving to find herself, she sought me out. Told me she would ruin me. I couldn't let that happen. I *wouldn't* let that happen."

"So...you...killed her..." I wheezed. Crowe smirked.

"I didn't have to." He chuckled. "Lina did all of that for me. I just," he paused, "set things in motion. I knew Eriksen was set to be engaged to Lina. Back then, she was Marilina Brandt. I also knew that if he met your mother, he would call everything off. The two were fated to be together. So alike. And it worked.

"I knew Lina would be looking for revenge, so I did everything I could to help her get right under your mother's nose without her ever knowing. A few nips and tucks later and she easily became Lina Davenport. It was supposed to look like an accident, yours and your mother's deaths. Something Eriksen would never suspect was foul play. But your mother was sharper than I anticipated. Not surprising. Lina and your mother had been friends for years before college.

"Appearances are easily changed. Mannerisms are not." His eyes gleamed darkly. "Hence the sudden bloodshed. Elizabeth and her entire squad of Vixens were cut down like the dogs they were. But somehow you escaped. Imagine my luck when I get a call from one of your father's club whores. She saved you from the massacre just to broker a deal with me. Drug money for you."

"You killed her," I rasped.

He smirked. "Made it look like a dirty accident. Overdose. Some forged paperwork later, and you were reborn Bailey Jameson. You were only three, so I wasn't worried too much about you remembering much. As you grew, there were a few things that snuck through, but that was what therapy was for."

Tears escaped. "You...buried my...memories?" Dots were beginning to dance across my vision. If he kept this up, I'd pass out from lack of oxygen. My lungs were working overtime trying to keep air flowing through my body and to my brain.

"I needed to make sure you never remembered anything that I hadn't put there."

"Fuck..." I struggled against him, "you."

"If only there was time for that." He let go of my throat. I gasped as air surged into my lungs. The room spun slightly, but the dots in my vision receded. Standing, Crowe straightened himself. "You'll be going to a nice little place Lina has set aside for you. Somewhere we can keep an eye on you and make sure your father stays in line. I've lost count of how many times he's tried to rescue you over the years. Until he saw what I was willing to do if he didn't obey."

The beating.

The starvation.

All things my brain had been conditioned to accept as punishment for something I had done wrong. The very therapist I had gone to in order to keep my traumatic past at bay had, in fact, been conditioning me over the years to accept the abuse.

That fucker was definitely going on my kill list.

Right after these two fuckers.

And Lina.

And Sarah.

Shit, that list was getting long.

Inner psycho was sharpening her teeth in one corner and saying *fuck it*.

"Well, I'm so glad you came to read me a bullshit bedtime story," I sneered. "It's cute how you try to make yourself out as the martyr, when you're nothing but a coward who couldn't make it to the top without greasing a few wheels."

No reaction.

Shit. That wasn't good.

"I didn't just come here to tell you my story, Bailey," he assured me darkly. "I came to show you exactly what happens to those who double-cross me."

He reached into his pocket and pulled out a small cattle prod.

Well, shit.

"So," he smirked, his eyes lighting up, "let's begin."

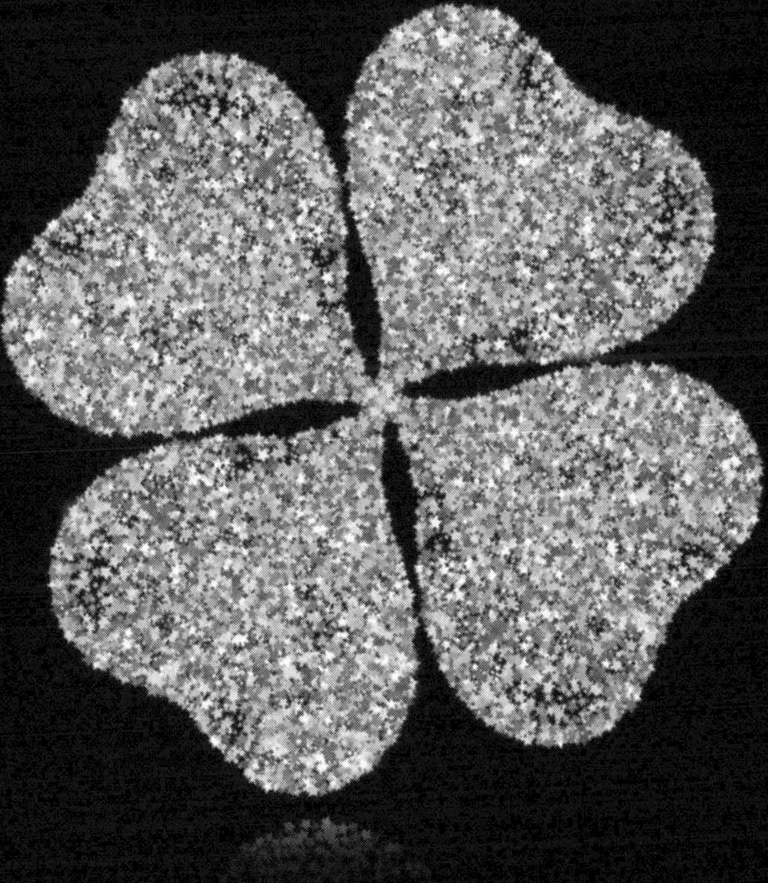

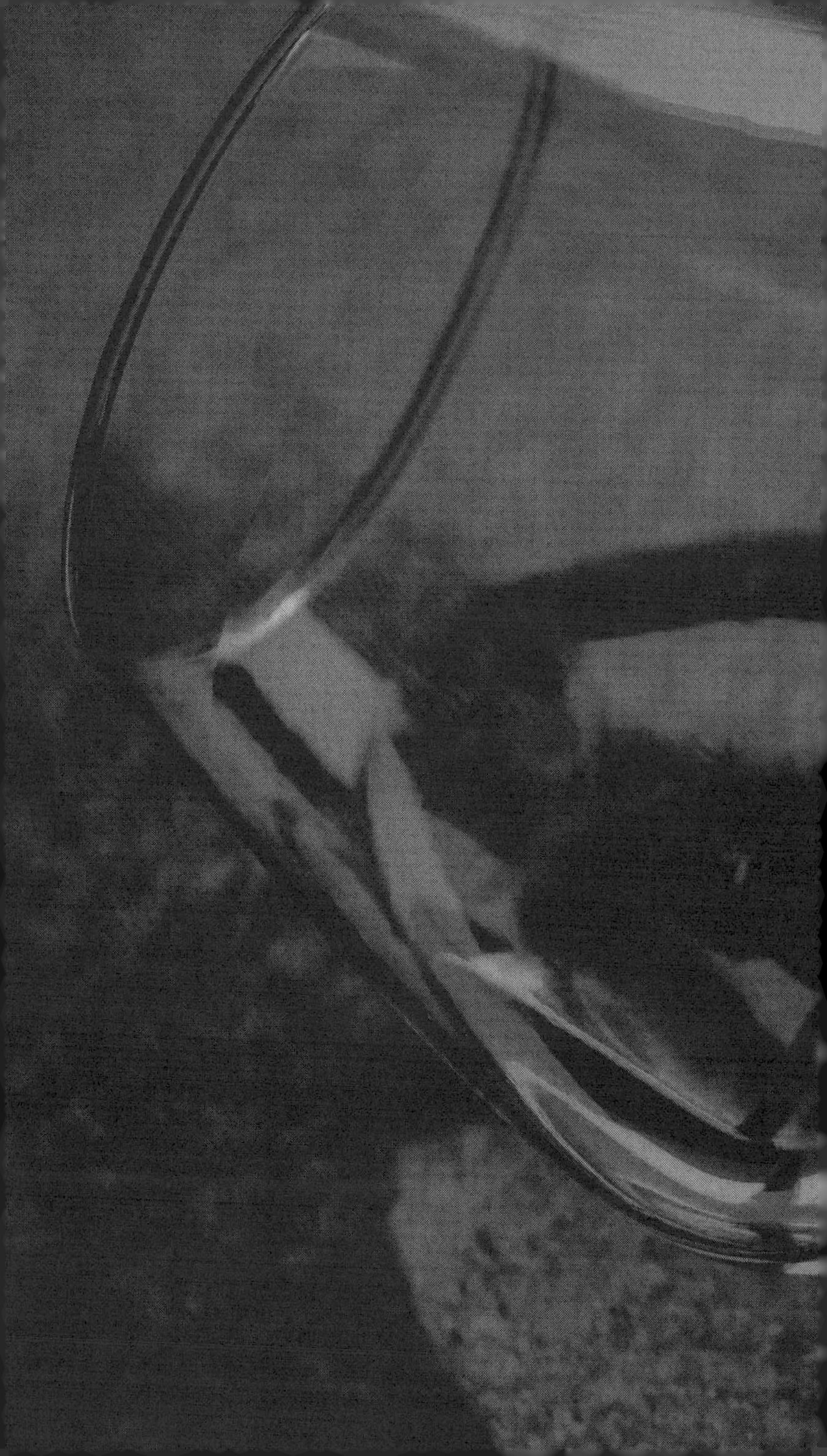

33

Seamus

It wasn't meant to be this way. She was supposed to be a means to an end. Nothing else. We'd have our fun with her and hand her over. That had been the plan we discussed without Father the night we found out she was a Crowe.

Then she took our hearts.

All of them.

Even our father had developed a softness for her. But still, the plan never changed. Then we learned who she truly was. Kiernan had lost his shit when he'd found out she was the daughter of Toph Eriksen. Enemy number one. The senator's puppet. We'd wondered how Crowe had managed to get the Iron Horsemen to do his bidding, and now we knew how.

Bailey.

How it had all come around was still a mystery. Bridgett didn't have all the pieces of the story. How had Crowe gotten his hands on her? Did Eriksen know Bailey was his daughter, or did Crowe have something else on him?

None of us could have known that Crowe wasn't her real father or that he already had plans in motion to sell her. His original plan had been to hand her over to be groomed before being put on the auction block. Us involving her in our scheme and then outing her had moved up his timeline. Something that hadn't made her ex-fiancé, Drew, too happy.

No, he hadn't really been her fiancé. She'd been sold to him.

"Goddamn it!"

We'd been lucky that Crowe had believed us when we'd informed him that we were looking at backing his presidential bid. He'd been skeptical at first, especially since getting in bed with him meant putting our hands into the skin trade. Something we'd always been fiercely against. However, Kiernan had managed to sell him on the fact that we were looking at expanding the business once our father handed over the reins to the kingdom next year.

And the greedy sucker bought it.

"Calm down, brother," Kiernan huffed from across the room.

"Don't tell me to calm the fuck down," I roared at him from my seat. "It's your fault she's in this position in the first place. If you hadn't insisted we go through with the fucking plan, she would be here and not god knows where."

Kiernan looked thoroughly chastised. "We'll find her," he assured me with a confidence I didn't have.

Because we hadn't found her yet. Everything was coming up empty.

I scoffed. "And if we don't?" I asked. "Crowe is watching us closely. Too closely. If he thinks we're going after Bailey, it's over. We need to take him down, or else he could easily give the order to Lina before we can get to Bailey."

"Matthias has men on both Crowe and Lina," Kiernan assured me. "We just need one of them to slip up enough to get the information we need. Bridgett is putting together everything we need to ruin Crowe at the speech he's giving next week announcing his presidential bid."

"Are we sure it's going to work? He's got a lot of powerful people backing him. Including this mysterious financier and whoever is running the flesh trade through the city. I'm starting to wonder if they're one and the same."

My brother shrugged. "We always assumed it was Ward who had been running the trafficking ring because he ran the stables. None of us bothered to think that there was someone higher up."

"If we had, shit might have gone down better."

"Yeah." Kiernan sighed. He'd been depressed since his confrontation with Bailey at the auction. He's said some hurtful shit, and it was weighing on him. Kiernan hadn't meant a word, but our girl didn't know that. She didn't know any of this because we'd been the ones to turn her over to her father in the first place. The look of hope she'd worn when she'd seen Kiernan's face in the crowd of lustful men and women ready to buy her flesh had nearly broken me. She'd believed we had come to save her, even after everything that had happened.

Her screams still haunted my sleep.

"All right." My father strode into the room with three tankards of beer in his hands. "Let's get this all sorted out."

Kiernan and I exchanged a look. Why was he wanting to help? Bailey's father was his enemy. He'd been more upset with the fact that Toph Eriksen was her true father than when he thought Crowe was. Then again, it hadn't been Crowe pulling the trigger on our men, filling the streets with their blood.

"Don't start with the twin ESP shit," he scolded, setting the tankards down on the table in the middle of the room. "Look"—he ran a hand through his graying hair—"with everything that's going on with Ava, I've come to realize some things. You can't choose who you love. I also know that I would do anything for my family. Eriksen hasn't been killing our men because he enjoys it, or even because he wants to." *Hopefully.* "He is no doubt doing it because it was the only way to keep Bailey safe. I realize that we could have rescued her earlier, and if maybe I hadn't been so stubborn and distracted, she might not be in the predicament she is in now."

Wasn't that the truth.

All hell had broken loose at the gala just after Kiernan had handed over Bailey to Crowe. A sniper had taken a shot at our sister from one of the balconies concealed by heavy curtains that were only used during performances.

We'd been so caught up in the aftermath of the gala that we'd completely missed every red flag regarding Crowe and his involvement with the information we'd found on Bailey.

For days now, I'd been going over the audio from Kiernan's comm device dozens of times. Trying to pick up anything I could, but all I could hear were her screams and the sound of her heart breaking. It took several times before I could get through the audio without the urge to vomit.

"I've been going over things." My father tilted his chin toward the board we'd set up with all the new information we had. "We didn't know all the players before, and now we do. I noticed something about Lina at the gala that had me wondering a bit."

"What was that?" I asked.

"While Bailey was here, she mentioned that she recognized the tattoo on one of Crowe's guards," he said. I remembered that. She'd mentioned it idly, but I'd seen her gaze drawn to the photo several times when she was going over the evidence we gave her. "Then I found this."

He pinned a photo of Lina wearing a black leather jacket with a logo on the back to the board.

An Iron Horsemen logo.

"Up until twenty-five years ago, Eriksen was never seeking any kind of expansion," my father continued. "We'd never had an issue with one another. Then, out of nowhere, he started killing our men in the streets."

"We know that is most likely because Crowe was directing him to." Kiernan pointed out what we already knew. "Using Bailey as a tool to get him to do his dirty work."

"Except that Crowe would never have wanted the Iron Horsemen to expand."

I traded a look with my brother.

"You know..." I bit my lower lip. "That Horsemen we roughed up a few nights before the gala, he was adamant that Eriksen wasn't expanding and that there was no way in hell they'd even try."

"Look here." Kiernan pointed to the board we set the map up on. "Every red dot is a hit that we believed was done by the Iron Horsemen."

"They're all concentrated in the lower district." My father stepped up to the map, surveying what we'd laid out so far. "Near the shipping ports."

"Why would Eriksen need the shipping ports?" Kiernan asked. "He does all his shipments by ground. The only things done by sea are drugs and humans."

"And we know that Eriksen doesn't ship drugs by sea, either."

"So why would he be trying to run us out of the port?"

"He wouldn't," my father noted. He turned his attention to another board. I'd strung up every picture Mark, Ava's hacker friend, could pull off their network from that night. "This was everyone that was there?"

I nodded. "There are only a few people we couldn't identify."

"This one of them?" my father asked, pointing to a tall woman seen talking with Kiernan. My brother nodded. "You can't tell much because of how grainy the footage is, but that's Sarah Crowe."

"That's Bailey's 'stepmother'?" Kiernan asked in disbelief.

"The old witch herself," my father muttered darkly. "Quite the social climber, that one." He pointed to another woman whose back was turned toward the camera. "That is Lina."

I squinted at the photo.

"How can you tell?" I asked. "You can't see her face."

"The jacket." He pointed to the other photo. "It's the same as the one Lina is wearing in this photo. Look at the patch."

Peering closer, I was able to just make out the patch of the Iron Horsemen. Underneath the main symbol was something I hadn't expected.

"She's Eriksen's old lady?"

My father nodded. "You can't see it as easily in the other photo because the back of her jacket is more obscured, but you can see that both jackets have matching symbols that have the president's moniker on it."

Well, fuck.

"All this time, she's been pretending to be Bailey's best friend," I hissed darkly. "Her mentor. But really, she was just keeping an eye on her investment."

"So who works for who?" Kiernan asked, puzzled. "I thought it was Lina who worked for Sarah, but now I'm beginning to think Sarah works for Lina."

"She does." Ava's quiet voice snuck up behind us. She was stealthy that way. Years of being invisible and having to sneak around gave her some pretty neat ninja skills. "So does her ex-fiancé, Drew."

"And you know this because…?" Kiernan let the question hang in the air. Ava smiled, but it didn't reach her eyes. "Well, we know Drew works for Christian. His logo was on the side of the containers he was using to ship his cargo. Bailey confirmed that."

"All right, that was a gimme," I joked. Ava chuckled, the sound full of sorrow. She'd be hurting for a while. Two weeks was just a drop in a pond when you compared it to an eternity of grieving. But she'd never be alone. We'd always be right beside her. We were family.

"That woman," Ava pointed at the picture of Lina, "is the one Elias placed in charge of the strip clubs and brothels." She moved her finger to point it at the photo of Sarah Crowe. "She was an investor. One of his top investors, in fact. They were the only two women he let in on his business dealings."

"How progressive of him," Kiernan drawled sarcastically.

"Elias believed that he'd have less trouble with a woman in charge than a man," Ava elaborated. "Said that men think with their dicks, but a woman thinks with her bank account."

Our father laughed. "I'm putting that on a T-shirt."

"But why Bailey?" I wondered. "We know she wasn't supposed to be in that alley, but everything points to the fact that she was meant to see Drew cheating on her, and she was meant to break down. They wanted to grab her."

"I have a theory about that," our father said. "I've gone over everything Bridgett compiled on Bailey. She had to do some further digging, but once she caught a thread, she followed it." He sat in one of the chairs at the table and took a gulp of his beer.

"Let's start with what we do know, or at least what Bailey knew and told us," he continued. "She was born to a crack addict who died of an overdose. Crowe somehow found her, but no one is sure how. He took her in and pretended that they'd adopted her but told Bailey she was his illegitimate daughter."

"Yeah," Kiernan sneered as we took seats across from him. Ava slid in next to our father, her head resting against his shoulder. "That about sums it up. But I doubt that crack whore was her real mother."

"That's right," our father confirmed. "The woman Bailey thought to be her mother was, in fact, nothing more than a jealous biker bunny who had at some point most likely kidnapped Bailey. When I suspected this, I had Declan down at the crime lab run Bailey's hair through CODIS, and it popped up with a match for a woman named Elizabeth Winters."

Kiernan and I glanced at one another. "That's Bailey's mother, right? Bridgett mentioned her name when I had her searching for Eriksen's daughter. Before we knew who it was."

"Elizabeth Winters was the president of the Vixens MC. Her father was the president of the Iron Horsemen out in San Diego."

I gave a low whistle. That was a piece of information I hadn't expected. The Vixens Motorcycle Club was well known for their sudden and gruesome deaths nearly—

"Well, fuck," Kiernan and I breathed at the same time.

"Their deaths are still an open case," my father told us. "But knowing that Lina is most likely the one pulling the strings from behind the curtains, it makes me wonder if she had a hand in their deaths."

"Did we ever get a name for the woman Bailey knows as her mother?" I questioned. "I can't remember her ever mentioning it."

"Fuck, I wonder if she actually ever knew the bitch's

name," Kiernan spat. "It always seemed to me like she just blocked it out."

"Or forgot," Ava chimed in. "If the woman wasn't Bailey's real mother, she'd have no distinct, memories of her. There wouldn't have been a bond strong enough for her to remember."

"What did the birth certificate say?" I asked. "The one that Crowe submitted to the adoption agency." Kiernan shuffled through a small stack of papers we'd kept on Bailey.

"Riley Jameson," Kiernan read out. My fingers flew across the keyboard. Bingo. "Riley Jameson, twenty-one, died of an overdose in her apartment in First Hill on May 2, 2000. Police were seen carrying a crying toddler from the scene."

"Sounds like who we were looking for."

"Jesus, her LiveJournal is still active." I clicked on the link. "Fuck, this is old." Riley Jameson's page popped up on my screen, and I scrolled through the old posts and photos. It was a mess. LiveJournal had been around since 1999 and predated sites such as MySpace and Friendster.

"There." My father pointed to one of the photos. "That looks like Lina hanging off Eriksen's arm and that," his finger shifted to another woman I didn't recognize, "must be Riley Jameson."

"They were club girls."

"Look at how he holds them at a distance," Ava interjected. "See how his arm isn't actually touching them, but they're curled toward him? He's trying to keep his distance."

"That would make sense," father agreed. "He married Elizabeth not long before this photo was taken." It had been dated in the corner as having been taken in 1997. The year Bailey was born.

"I'm assuming Eriksen doesn't know his new wife was the one who undoubtedly killed his late wife."

My father shook his head.

"But why were they all killed?" Ava questioned, her brow furrowed as she scrolled through the news release on the Vixen massacre. "If it was a personal vendetta, why kill the rest of them? That takes time and planning."

"No one has a clue about why they were suddenly massacred," Father admitted. "But they didn't have all the information we have. Bridgett managed to gather some information from one of the disgruntled bikers from Eriksen's crew. Apparently, he'd been branded and removed for raping one of the biker bunnies who said no."

Kiernan grunted in disgust. "That term gives me hives."

I chuckled. "Kind of gives me furry vibes."

Ava groaned at the image. "Gross."

Ignoring our antics, our father continued. "At nineteen, Eriksen was engaged to marry a Marilina Brandt, the daughter of another biker president. Then he met Elizabeth and fell in love. According to the biker, the marriage was called off. It shouldn't have been that big of a deal. Eriksen hadn't met the girl, and he managed to salvage the relationship with the other club and make an even better deal. Eriksen married Elizabeth in a private courthouse ceremony. Only for her to end up dead three years later. Bridgett managed to dig up a new marriage certificate. Lina Davenport married Toph Eriksen two years after Elizabeth's death."

"I'm betting Toph doesn't know Lina Davenport is actually Marilina Brandt."

Father sighed. "From what I was able to get out of the new president of Brandt's chapter, she was thrown out after she killed one of their club girls in a jealous rage. Word was she was also selling flesh with some of the local traffickers for extra cash and drugs."

Stolen Obsession

"Why did she end up fixating on Elizabeth and Toph?" Ava wondered.

"Greed," I presumed. "And jealousy. Every picture I bring up that has Lina in it. She's staring right at Toph as if he's her sun. It's never reciprocated."

"I believe it started long before then." My father dragged out a photo from one of the folders he'd brought in. "When I was digging up information on Senator Crowe, I came across something I didn't think held any value. Not until that photo of a younger Lina popped up. These two ladies look familiar?"

It was a college sorority photo taken in front of the University of Washington. Underneath it, the words *bad bitches rule the world* were scrawled in sloppy loops. The same loops as Bailey's resignation letter.

"You probably recognize two of them." My father pointed to the two strawberry-blond girls who were posed on either side of their raven-haired friend. "The one on the left is Sarah Bradshaw, Crowe's wife. Marilina Brandt is the one on the right. The dark-haired one in the middle was Bailey's mother, Elizabeth. They met their freshman year of college in an economics class. All three of them were studying finance and business.

"Later that year, they joined Alpha Delta Pi, where they met Elias Ward and Richard Crowe, members of Sigma Nu. From what Bridgett has been able to piece together, the three girls had a falling out after a disastrous frat party one night where the police were called. Elizabeth alleged that Richard Crowe, Sarah's boyfriend, drugged and raped her that night with his fraternity brothers while her friends stood and watched."

"Jesus." I was going to be sick.

"The case was buried, of course." My father waved a hand dismissively. "The Crowe family was untouchable, even back then, and so was Ward. Everyone knew that Ward was connected to the Romano Don, and Dante's father wasn't to be messed with."

"What happened after that?" Ava asked curiously, sipping on the coffee she'd brought down with her.

"She unenrolled from college and started the Vixens. She met Eriksen somewhere along the way, seemingly mended bridges with Lina, and the rest is history." He shrugged. "But what's really important was what the Vixens MC fought again, because I believe that was part of the reason they *all* ended up dead."

"Human trafficking." Ava let out a breathy laugh. "She combated human trafficking, and if Sarah and Lina were working with Richard and Elias, they were all a hindrance."

"Not only that," Kiernan jumped in. "We've been wondering why Eriksen would need the port. He doesn't. Crowe and Lina do."

"And making sure she married Eriksen meant that she'd have not only status, but people she could control and manipulate. It also feeds into her obsession." It was all coming together. "I wonder how many of Eriksen's men even know that their boss isn't the one giving the orders anymore."

"I think it's time we go find out."

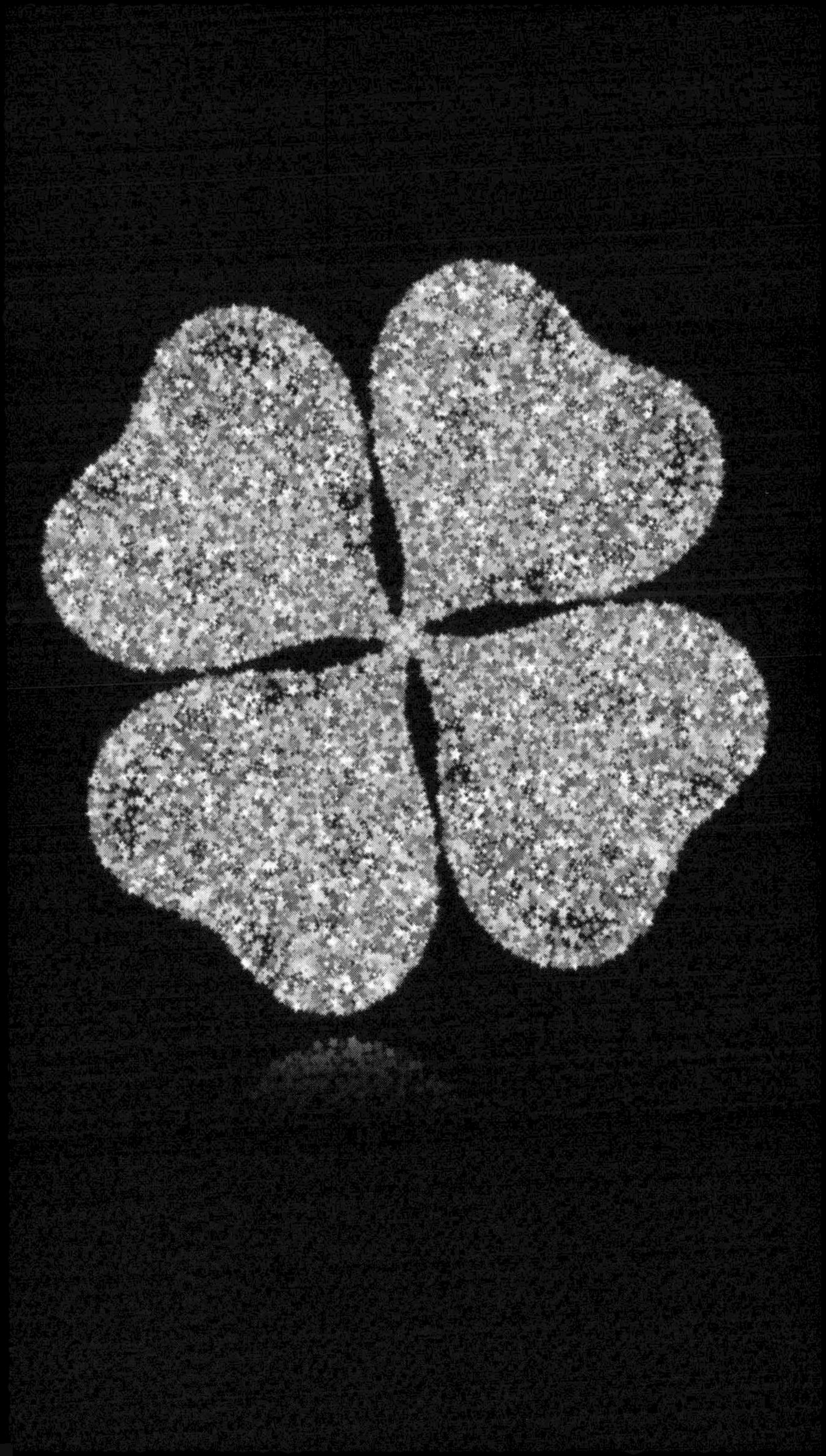

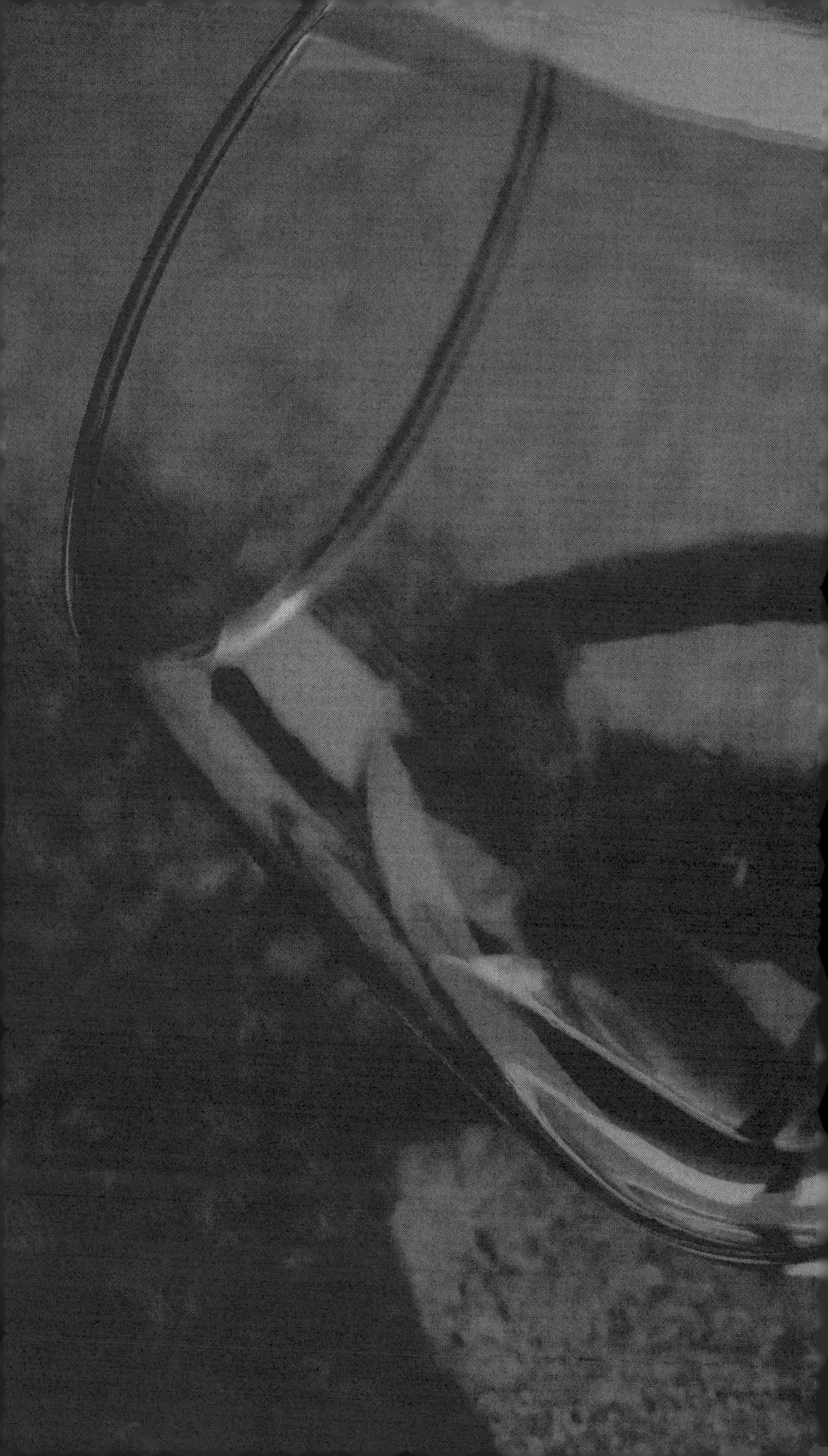

34

Liam

It was the last place I expected for him to want to meet.

Eriksen.

The warehouse was dilapidated, vines growing over and through leftover barrels, abandoned cars. Anything they could grow on, they took over without remorse, spreading across the graveled lot. We hadn't brought any men with us.

There was no need.

It hadn't been easy to reach him. We had to be sure that Lina didn't intercept any messages. If she did, we'd all be dead, and so would Bailey.

Fuck.

Bailey.

I could tell from Kiernan's downcast look that the guilt over what had happened to her was overwhelming him. Ava had reamed him, no doubt spurring the feeling of regret even further. I'd counseled him against handing her over, but he'd been sure that nothing would happen to her. That he and Seamus could easily get to her once Crowe's indiscretions were revealed.

He didn't know the man like I did.

Didn't know what he was capable of.

For once, I wished I hadn't let my son learn from the consequences of his own actions. I'd always allowed them to experience what it meant to fail. Unless it would harm them physically. And even then, I wasn't too worried about a few bruises or broken bones. They needed to learn that every action had a reaction. Sometimes it was good, but other times there were real consequences.

He was feeling that now.

Kiernan couldn't have known what would happen to her, but he should have thought about the worst-case scenario. He knew Crowe wasn't a good man. He was aware of what had happened to Bailey in the past. I'd explained to him what she'd told me the night she broke into the safe.

Still, he chose to move forward.

And I did nothing.

Now I stood with my sons in a warehouse that time had frozen. Nothing had changed since the night of the massacre. Nothing was out of place. You could still see the bloodstains clinging to what was left of the rotted wood floors. Bullet holes riddled the metal walls, allowing the sun to sneak through and cast an ethereal light over the darkened room.

And there he stood, in the middle of it all, the one man I'd grown to hate more than any other. I'd been so blinded by rage and hatred that I never bothered to dig up the truth behind the hits. Even after all these years, I still made mistakes. Ava's mother once said I was ruled by my emotion. My men were family to me. Not just pawns to be manipulated and used as cannon fodder.

"You came." I stopped a few feet from him. He'd come alone as requested, but I wasn't stupid enough to believe that he didn't have some kind of backup.

"You sent me a photo of my daughter," he rumbled. "Said

you had a plan to take down Crowe. I'd be stupid to ignore that."

"Thank you for listening." Seamus spoke up. "We need all the help we can get, and so do you."

The corners of Eriksen's lips turned up in a sneer. "I've been trying to get my daughter out from beneath Crowe's thumb since she was three," he spat. "What makes you think you can? And why would you care?"

"Bailey was under our care for some time," I admitted to him. "We didn't know she was your daughter. She doesn't even know she's your daughter. We used her to gain access to some confidential information that was on Crowe's laptop."

"Was she caught?" he growled, taking a threatening step forward. "Did he find out?"

Kiernan cleared his throat awkwardly. "I handed her over to him," he admitted. "My plan was to get him to trust us by turning her in. I gave him a fake drive, thinking that he'd never truly hurt her. I didn't know—"

"Where is she?"

"We don't know," he admitted. "That's why we need your help."

Eriksen narrowed his eyes at my son, but I could see the gears in his head turning.

"My wife is good at tracking people down," he admitted.

"You shouldn't—" I started, but Seamus beat me to it.

"There was a reason we asked you to come alone," he said. "And why we had to go through such crazy channels to contact you."

Eriksen's gaze flickered between us suspiciously.

"You might want to brace yourself for this," I told him. "It's not pretty."

"Your so-called wife works for Crowe," Kiernan informed him. "And she isn't the only one."

"And you know this how?"

Kiernan flicked his gaze to me, and I nodded.

I truly felt sorry for Eriksen.

His whole world was about to be shifted out from under him.

The scream of pain he released as Kiernan showed him our proof left my soul aching. I knew exactly how it felt to lose everything. I'd always suspected that Katherine was dead, but to hear it from the mouth of the daughter I never knew I had shattered my world. Even further when she'd told me that Katherine hadn't left me of her own free will.

I'd never get the love of my life back, but I had Ava and a drive for revenge. One I would never let go of, and the other... well, revenge was a dish best served cold.

"There's a brothel," he began, his voice thick with sadness. His jaw clenched. "I have a few spies there that help me get intel. They also get some of the women out from time to time if they can."

"You think she's at that brothel?" Seamus asked.

Eriksen nodded. "I got word a few days that security had suddenly increased. Crowe himself came down to pay a visit. That's never happened before."

"Have you heard from them since?"

He shook his head. "No." He sighed. "But I can guarantee you that's where they are. Crowe doesn't visit his brothels. Ever. They're run under a subsidiary company. His name isn't anywhere under it so that nothing ties him back to them if they go down."

"How do you know it's his, then?"

Eriksen smirked. "Because the company it's listed under is owned by Derik Cole."

Dead men can't own companies. Derik Cole was one of Elizabeth's first victims. Hung himself from the rafters with pictures of his victims spread out beneath him. It had made national headlines. If the brothel was ever discovered, all anyone would find was a dead man's name.

"Can your spies get her out?"

"Not with the extra security," he admitted sadly. "All the girls are under lock and key under the main house. The only time they're let out is if they're needed upstairs for premier clients. That's how I get my intel. One of the clients is a friend of mine. I wouldn't be able to get new intel through him either. He only comes once a month, and if we break his pattern, they might suspect something."

I nodded, understanding.

"Then I think it's time we set our plan in motion."

I glanced over at the boys. They nodded.

"And what is this plan?" Eriksen asked.

Smirking, I handed over a large manila envelope I'd brought with me.

"I think you're going to enjoy this."

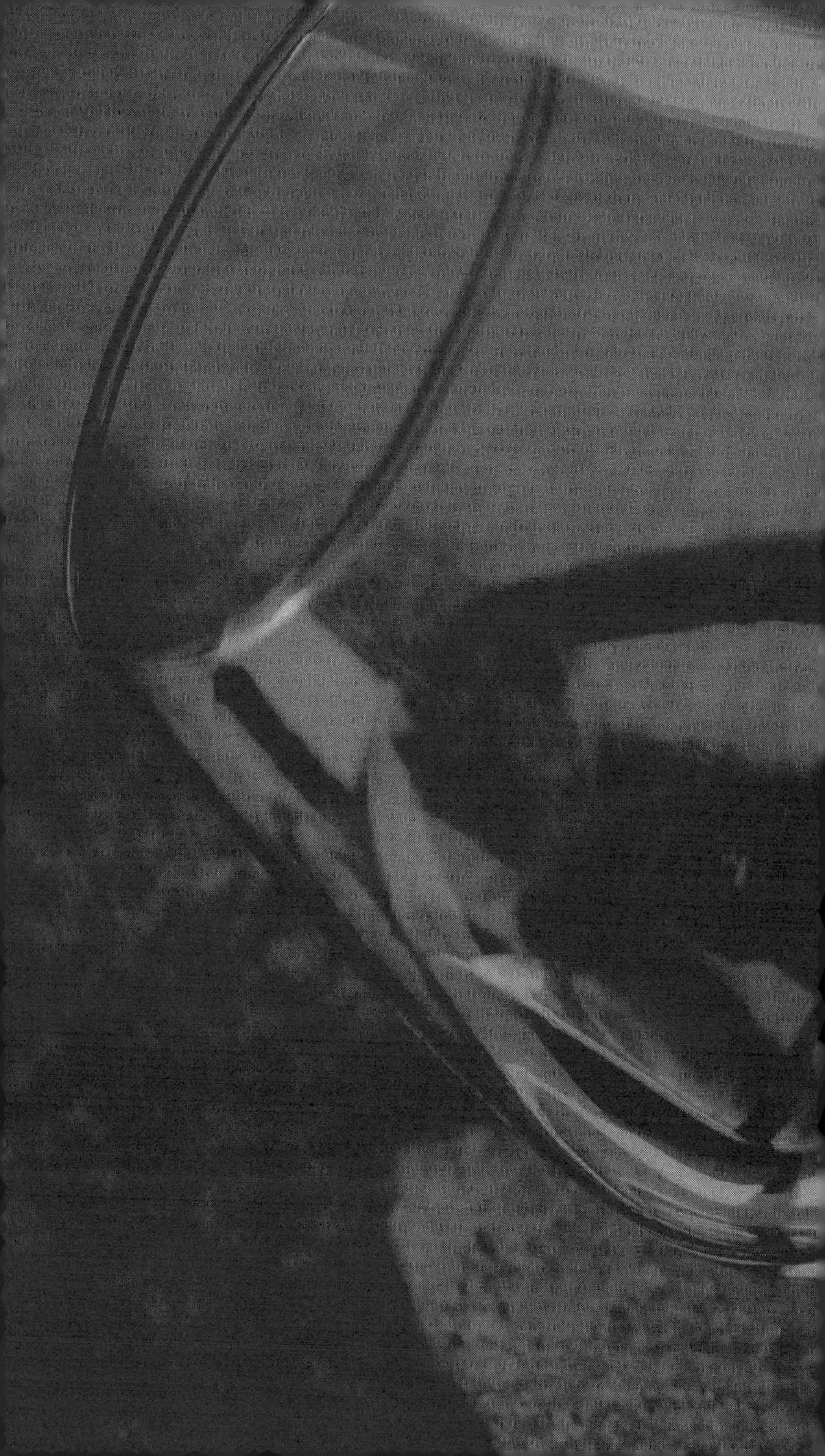

35

Bailey

"Make sure you do a good job this time, *puttana*," Giuseppe spat at me as he exited the kitchen. "I'm tired of that burned shit you keep fixing every night."

Keeping my eyes cast down to the floor, I muttered a weak *yes, sir* to appease him as I scuttled past his hulking frame. Clean. Get hit. Maybe get to eat. Sleep. Then rinse and repeat. That had been my life for the last few days. I hadn't seen hide nor hair of the man I once called father, but Lina was around. Too much, in my opinion.

For example, here she was, sitting at the wobbly square piece of wood they thought they could call a table, scrolling through her tablet like it was just another day.

"Come sit down, Bailey," she commanded haughtily. Bitch didn't even look up from her screen.

"I'm supposed to be—"

"Did I ask you what you were supposed to be doing?" She snarled at me, her gaze lifting from her tablet to glare at me.

"No," I whispered as I took a seat on the rickety stool across from her. It put me at a height disadvantage, but I figured that was the point whenever she had me sit here. To make me feel small and insignificant.

"You remind me so much of your mother." She tilted her head to study me, eyes softening for a moment as if she was lost in thought. Or a memory. Then it was gone. Replaced by the cold-hearted bitch I'd come to realize lurked beneath the surface. Our entire friendship had been nothing but fake. Just like everything else in my life. "It's almost sad you never got to know your real mother. The only memories you have are probably of that junkie whore who whisked you away in the middle of the massacre. Otherwise, you'd be dead. Just like her."

"Does Eriksen know what you did?" I asked her. "Does he know who you really are?"

"Of course not," she sneered. "Why do you think your mother and her little whore of a motorcycle club had to die? She'd recognized me. It took her a few years, but she managed to uncoil who I was." Then she laughed. A dark cackle that made my skin crawl. Like the evil queen from *Snow White*.

I would have liked nothing more than to shove an apple up her ass right then.

"Here's the thing, little pathetic Bailey." She smirked. "I wanted to kill you. So did Sarah. God, that woman hated your mother after she ruined her job prospects after college."

Jesus, this woman was high on something.

"I think you have the wrong—"

"I'm talking," she roared, her hand whipping across my face, that careful façade she'd always had around me breaking. I gritted my teeth against the pain. After three days, I'd begun to grow used to expecting blows. Pain was nothing new. I'd been on the receiving end of it for as long as I could remember. Not because I had done anything wrong, but because Crowe had wanted to keep my biological father in line.

Stolen Obsession

Fixing herself, she leaned back in the chair. "Where was I? Oh, yes. Your mother ruined my chances at happiness. You see, I'd been promised to him. We were supposed to be married. He was my chance to get out of the hell I'd been born into. But *no*. Instead, he met your mother. My old college bestie. Worked out a better deal with my father, and I was right back to where I started.

"Sarah wanted to just let you rot right next to your mother in your own little grave for everything she did to her, but I thought of a better idea."

There it was. The Cheshire grin that never boded well for me. It was the same grin Sarah used to give me before locking me in the cellar without food for days at a time.

"I convinced her to have you work in the brothel instead. Crowe can still control your father while I implement my plans for expansion, and you get to earn us some good money. God knows how many of your father's enemies out there would be willing to pay top dollar to fuck his long-lost daughter. Plus, I doubt you'll last all that long anyway."

"Fuck you," I hissed as I stood. "You put me in one of those rooms, and your clients will come out with their dicks stapled to their foreheads."

Lina laughed like this was fun for her. Maybe it was. There was no mistaking that the woman clearly belonged in a mental institution, with the word *psychopath* tattooed on her broad, Botoxed forehead. "If you do anything more than lie down and spread your legs like the whore you are, I'll make sure every single one of the Kavanaughs winds up with a bullet in their heads."

"They're the ones who put me here," I scoffed. "Do you honestly think I care what happens to them?" There was that grin again.

"Oh," she handed me the tablet she'd been scrolling on, "but I think you do."

I wish I could say she was wrong.

I stood beneath the showerhead, letting the warm water cascade down the length of my body. It had been nearly two weeks since I'd been shoved into hell. Tears rolled down my cheeks as I hugged myself, taking my time to gather what was left of the little hope I had left. I hated myself for crying, for showing that weakness, even if no one was around to witness it.

Lina warned me this day would come, but I'd clung to the small sliver of hope that they'd come rescue me. Every turn of the lock had my heart racing in anticipation that it was them. That it was the day I was free again. They'd come. I knew they would.

I'd been so utterly naïve.

This was my fate now.

A whore.

A dead one if Lina got her way.

"Bailey?" Yelena called from beyond the partition. The shower room was gym style. There was no privacy in hell, but the girls tried to put up boundaries since everyone here was determined to strip them away. "Are you—are you ready?"

My heart broke for the sweet girl who was a few years younger than me. Barely past her eighteenth birthday. She'd been the first to befriend me, helping me where she could when she saw how Giuseppe was nearly starving me on Lina's orders. She'd sneak me food in the middle of the night, and we'd just sit and talk.

"I'll be right there." I tried to keep my voice from cracking, but I knew she heard it. The vulnerability, the sorrow. I couldn't step into the shower without thinking of the first night with Kiernan or any of the nights afterward when he and his brother would take turns washing me. Caring for me.

The betrayal still stung like a bitch.

I was stalling. Refusing to leave the false sense of security the shower provided. Once I got out, there was no going back to who I was before. I'd be raped. Forced to take one client after another until I was nothing more than a shell of the person I was before.

Yelena's shriek had me scrambling from the shower to see what had happened. "Get out, *puttana*," he snarled at her, pushing her toward the door before he stalked toward me. Oh god, was this how my night was going to start? With him?

Giuseppe reached past me to shut off the water and grab my towel. "Arms out," he commanded roughly. When I didn't obey, he slapped me and then repeated his order. This time, I did as he asked, my skin crawling as he started to dry me. The contents of my meager lunch were beginning to make a reappearance as his hands skated over my body, lingering on my pussy and breasts.

Taking a deep breath, I tried to block it out. Yelena said that was how she managed to get through each night. She picked a spot on the wall or the ceiling and let her imagination take over. That was sure as fuck what I was going to do. Right now, I was imagining all the ways I could bludgeon this man to death with his own severed arm.

When he finished, he turned me away from him and then proceeded to drag me against his body, my back to his chest.

"Maybe I'll take a night with you, little raven," he purred in my ear as his hands gripped my breasts to the point of pain. I squealed when his fingers twisted my nipples. I bucked against him, trying to dislodge his hold, but that only seemed to egg him on. "Fight me, *puttana*. I love it when they fight back. Makes me hard for your cunt."

I stilled in his grasp. After a few more minutes, he seemed to grow bored with my sudden compliance. Pushing me away, he tossed a small negligée at me, barking at me to put it on.

"Let's go," he barked. Like an obedient puppy, I followed him from the room. Yelena stood quietly behind the door to the shared bedroom, a large metal pipe in her hand. She put her finger to her mouth and winked at me before slamming the object down on Giuseppe's head with more force than a woman her size should have.

With a grunt, Giuseppe fell to the floor, unmoving.

"Yelena," I gasped. "What did you do? They're going to kill you."

The slip of a woman laughed. "Oh, honey." She smiled at me as she hit Giuseppe in the head again. "Many men have tried, and none have succeeded."

"Now," she straightened her shoulders, "let's get you out of here."

"What?"

I was dreaming or drugged. Maybe both. But somehow, I'd warped into a different reality, because I couldn't for the life of me understand what the hell had just happened.

"Yelena, you just killed Lina's right-hand man." I stared at her in disbelief. "There is no way in hell we're getting out of here by ourselves."

Yelena laughed as if I'd just told her a joke. "Who said we're by ourselves?"

That's when the alarms went off.

Cue the lights going out.

I expected screams from the women. There were a few, but otherwise, it was quiet. Too quiet. It took a few moments, but soon, the emergency generator kicked in, and the sub lights flashed on. It wasn't much, but having some light was better than traversing the brothel in the dark.

"Come." Yelena took my hand and led me down the corridor of rooms. One by one, the doors opened. I braced myself for an attack. There were more than a few girls here who had drunk too much of Kool-Aid. No such attack came. From each room came one of the working girls, a weapon in her hand. Some of them were covered in blood, but all of them looked fierce and determined.

"You see, Bailey, your mother believed in ending the sex trade in Seattle. She fought tooth and nail with her family to make it so."

"I don't know anything about her," I admitted sadly. "My entire life, I was told I was raised by a junkie."

"Fucking Crowe." One of the women behind me spat his name like a curse. Samala was her name. She was tall, at least six feet without heels, and her ebony skin glowed beneath the emergency lights. Her hair was dreaded down her back like an Amazonian warrior.

"Your mother was a warrior." Another woman spoke up from the back of our little processional. "I was sixteen when she rescued me from a shipping container where I'd been left to die with several other girls who were deemed too tainted to be sold because the men who had brought us over from Russia had carved their names into our skin for fighting back."

"And you still ended up in a brothel," I scoffed.

"Because we chose to be here."

I looked back at the women who were at my back, bewildered. "Why would you choose to be a whore?"

"Whore is a word used by weak men to make themselves feel powerful," another woman spat. "We chose to be here to honor your mother as she honored us."

"Did you know her?" I whispered. We were coming to the end of the hall, and none of us knew what lay beyond.

"I did not," she admitted sadly. "She was murdered before I was born. But my mother did. She was part of your mother's motorcycle club. They called themselves the Vixens. My mother was one of only three women to survive the massacre. Your father kept them hidden and safe until they recovered. Then he helped them start over."

"What do you know about my father?" I asked. "Why did he never come for me? He knew I was alive but..."

The woman smiled softly at me. "Everything he has done has been to keep you safe," she assured me. "He tried so hard to get you back, but there was one fault in all his plans. He never suspected his wife to be a traitor."

"Lina," I breathed. "He married that bitch?"

The woman let out a small chuckle.

"Your mother never trusted her," she admitted. "So neither did we. We continued in secret. We have kept your mother's legacy alive, the legacy of the Vixens, in the hope that one day you would get to witness what she built. For you."

Gunshots startled me from asking more questions. The women didn't seem bothered. Just prepared. Screams of pain seeped through the locked door. More gunshots. Someone was yelling orders.

"What's going on?"

Yelena looked back at me, a smile on her face.

"Time for you to go home, little vixen. There are some people here who have worked very hard to rescue you."

"Who?"

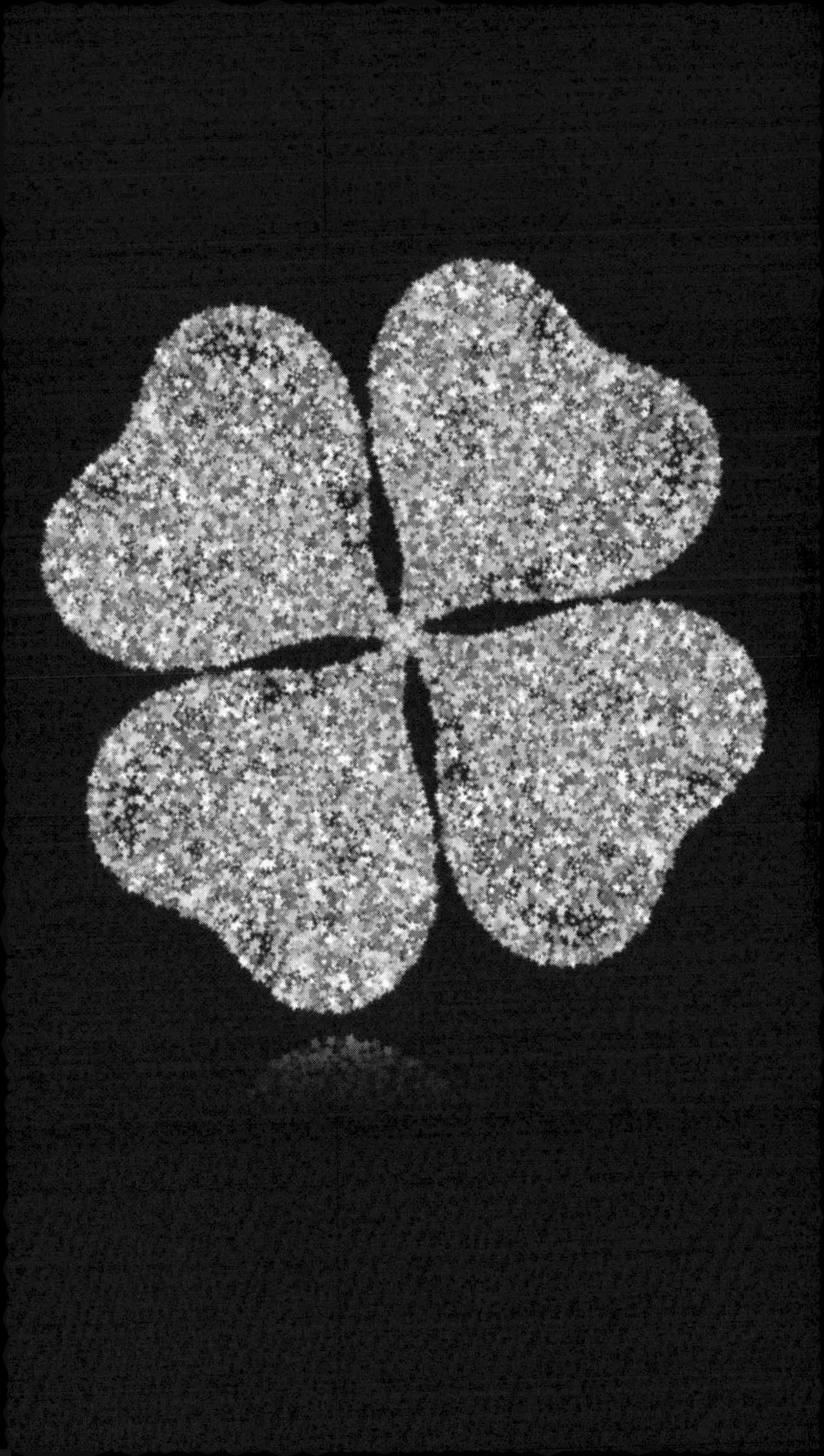

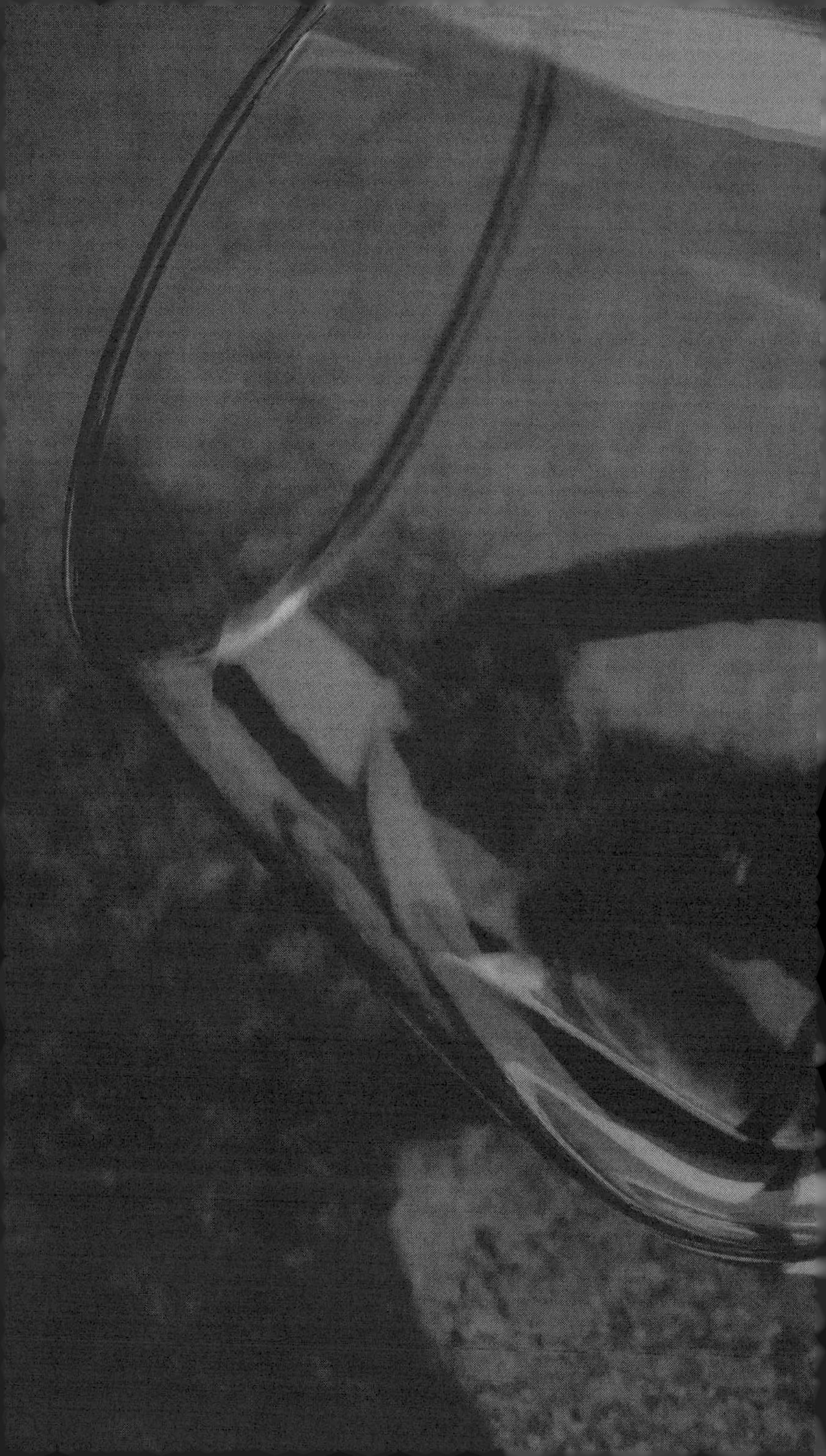

36

Kiernan

"We need to breach soon."

Seamus fidgeted with his gun, a sign that he was anxious. We all were. None of us knew how this was going to play out, but we did know one thing. We'd get Bailey back or die trying.

"How is it that you have people on the inside?" my father asked Eriksen as he strapped on his Kevlar.

"Not me," the large Nordic man boomed. "Vixens."

"I thought they all died the night of the massacre."

"There were a few who survived. They were barely alive when we got to them," he admitted with a shrug. "It took nearly two years for them to fully recover and be able to leave my compound safely."

"And now they what? Go undercover as whores to take down trafficking rings?" I asked.

The bearded man nodded. "Well, not them. They could never pass as workers. Not with their injuries," he pointed out. "Most are the children of the original vixens or women Elizabeth and her people saved. After her death, they wanted to honor her. They've slowly been dismantling the underground brothels for all these years."

"How long have they been undercover here?"

Eriksen scrunched his nose. "Too long."

"Did you know?" Seamus asked from beside me. "About Lina and Sarah?"

He shook his head sadly. "I'd known that Lina was up to something. She'd always been a social climber, even in the club. She was always clinging to me. Making snide comments about Elizabeth. I should have suspected something back then. Elizabeth had voiced her concerns about her but...well...she was a club favorite. I can't believe I was so blind."

"They had it planned all along," my father told him. "Crowe put everything into motion a long time ago. From the looks of it, he spent a pretty penny to make sure no one recognized Lina as Marilina."

Eriksen's throat bobbed. "I never once thought Lina would betray me."

"That isn't an excuse," I bit out. "You knew she was a social climber. You were so focused on doing everything Crowe ordered that you didn't bother to look around and see what was right under your nose."

"And there is nothing I regret more than that," he promised. "Trust me. And I'll spend a lifetime making up for my mistakes. As will you."

"You can count on that," Seamus and I vowed.

Eriksen smiled. "I'm glad she found you two. Even if it is a little—unconventional."

"Should be our new family motto," my father muttered beneath his breath, and we laughed.

"Everyone in position?" Vas, my sister's right-hand man and former Sovietnik to her husband, asked over the comms.

In the wake of her husband's death, she'd taken on the mantle of *Pahkan*.

"All set," I responded. "Make sure my sister stays safe."

Vas snorted. "I think you should be more worried about the people who crossed her by hurting her new friend."

"Send pictures," my father joked. "We breach on two."

"One," Seamus started.

"Two," I snarled. The wood around the doorknob splintered as the bullet from my gun shattered the lock. Seamus kicked the door open, stepping aside to let our father and Eriksen take the lead. Just as we stepped inside, the power alarms blared and the power cut out.

Right on time.

We pulled down our night-vision goggles and advanced. Shots rang out as our backup made progress through the rear door. I fired two shots into the chest of one of the guards. He fell, and two more took his place.

Shit.

I ducked behind a ratty sofa as shots rained down on me. Keeping crouched, I peeked up from behind the sofa, ducking down again when they spotted me and fired. But now I had their position. Taking a deep breath, I steadied myself and pointed my gun through the back of the couch. Failure wasn't an option. I had to get to Bailey. There was so much I needed to say. I'd spend the rest of my life apologizing.

Two shots through the dilapidated piece of shit furniture, and they were down.

One man screamed as Eriksen dove from his hiding spot and stuck his knife directly through his throat.

"Fucking traitor," he hissed. That was one rat down in his organization. How many more were there?

"Clear!" my father hollered from another room.

"Clear!" Eriksen echoed.

Cautiously, I stood, peering at the wreckage around me. There had been fewer guards than I thought.

"Clear," Seamus and I hollered at the same time.

"This way." Eriksen pointed to a large wooden door that looked like it led to a basement. I disengaged the outside lock and knocked three times in a row. Our code to let the girls know it was all clear. That we were friendly.

Then we waited with bated breath, hoping that everything went as planned. There had been no way for us to breach the fortified basement, and even if we could, it was too easy for the men down there to take them hostage. This way, we had the element of surprise.

One of Eriksen's men moved toward the door, a pair of heavy iron mechanical claws in his grasp. He placed them between the heavy metal door and the wall, and a few moments later, the lock on the door busted open.

My heart stopped as the door swung open and Bailey appeared. Her hair was a wet, tangled mess; her face and body were bruised, but she was beautiful.

"Fucking hell," I growled, removing the jacket I'd worn over my Kevlar and placing it around her shoulders. "Whoever saw you in that better be fucking dead."

"Oh, he's dead." One of the women cackled behind Bailey, her Russian accent thick. "Very, very dead."

"Good," I whispered as I cupped her face in my hand and pressed my lips to her forehead. I breathed in her scent. She always smelled like freshly cut flowers. "I am so sorry, *a stóre*," I murmured.

"We're sorry, wildcat." Seamus came to stand beside me. "None of this was ever supposed to happen."

Her throat bobbed as she stared at us, and her crystalline gaze clouded with tears.

"Are you hurt?" I asked.

Bailey shook her head. "Just some bruises," she whispered. "I'm okay."

"Good." I breathed a sigh of relief as I hugged her to my chest. She stiffened in my arms at first before slowly relaxing into my hold. "We have so much to talk about."

We'd never let her go again.

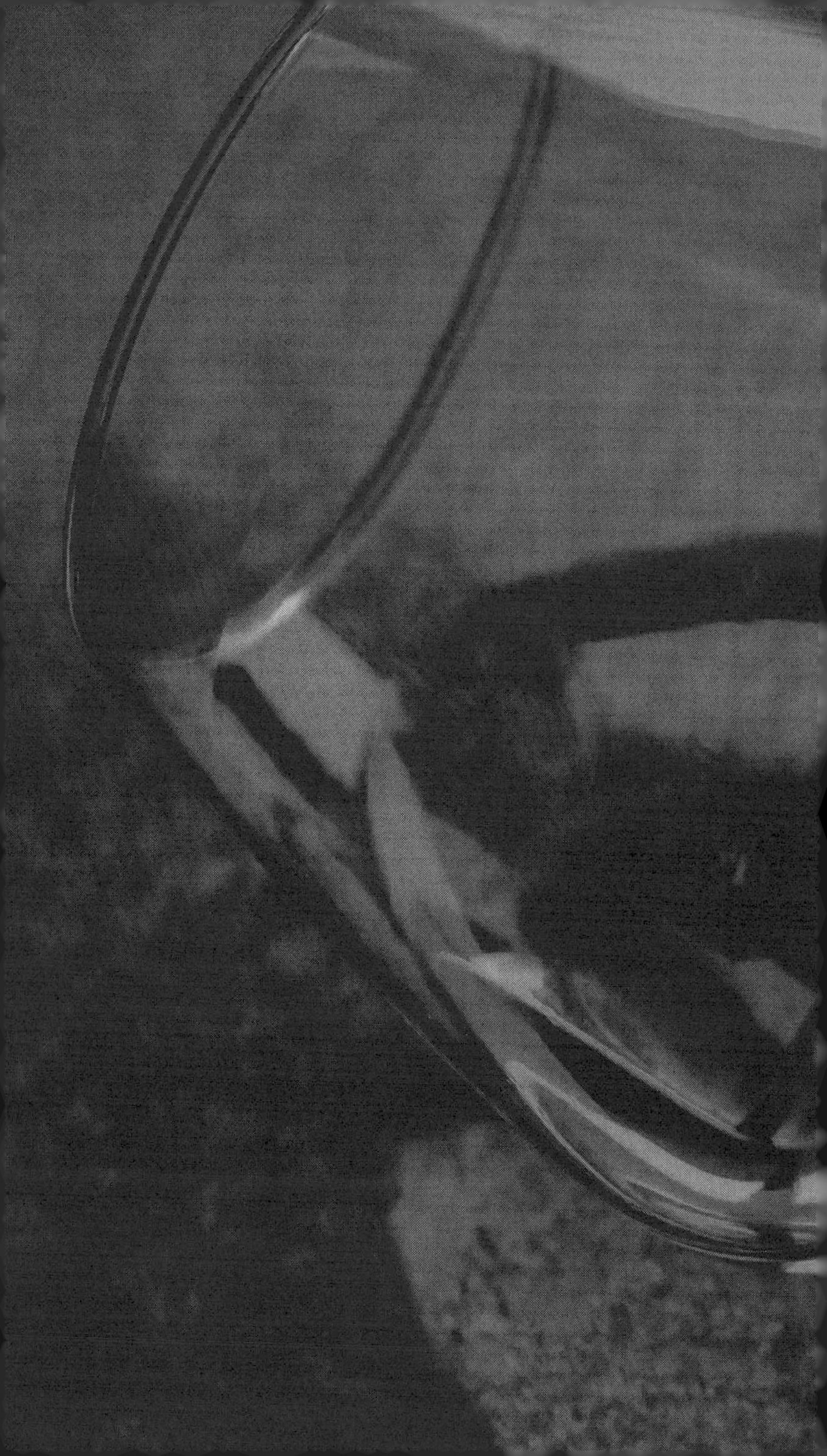

37

Bailey

It felt as if I was walking through a dream. My body moved and obeyed, but my mind was far away. Kiernan hadn't let go of me since the brothel. He'd hauled me into his arms and refused to set me down.

I was scared of how safe I felt in his arms, even after his stinging betrayal. But I'd come to find that when I looked back at it, he'd never truly betrayed me, even if it had felt like it. The twins had taken me up to shower the moment we arrived at the bar. They'd whisked me away with the promise that once I'd rested, we'd go down to talk with my father.

My father.

That word held a different meaning now. I didn't know if I'd ever be able to call him that. Not when the word was so tainted.

"He's not going anywhere, *a stóre*," Seamus assured me as he carefully washed my sore and battered body.

"What does that mean?" I asked curiously. They'd been calling me that just as long as they'd been calling me their whore. It was probably something along that line. Like slut or something equally derogatory. The only difference was they never referred to me as their whore outside of the bedroom. They'd used the other phrase no matter where we were.

"It means treasure."

That was not what I was expecting. Nor was I expecting the redness that crept up both twins' cheeks. They were embarrassed.

"I like it," I whispered softly, kissing his shoulder and then Kiernan's, since that was all I could reach without having to stretch on my tiptoes. Slowly, I ran my hands down their chests, toward their obvious arousals.

"Not now, wildcat." They both let out pained groans when I stroked their lengths. "This isn't the time for that. You've been through something traumatic."

I was mad as hell at them. But I was also cracked and hanging on by a thin thread. I needed something to ground me. Even if it was sex with the two men who'd betrayed me. They'd broken my heart, shattered it, but now, within their presence, those pieces lit up and trembled with delight.

Even after everything that had happened, it still wanted them.

Needed them.

Loved them.

Even if my brain refused to accept that.

But I didn't need to love them to experience freedom. I needed them to shut off my mind, otherwise I would begin to spiral.

I'd begin to break even further.

"No one touched me," I assured them, my voice soft but strong. "But all I could think about, even after I thought you'd betrayed me, was every time we were in this shower together. The three of us, and how good you made me feel. How much pleasure I got from touching you and giving you both your own pleasure."

Kiernan chuckled, his gaze on his brother as he pulled me against his chest. He snaked his hand down my chest, tweaking my nipples as he went before he cupped my pussy.

"Have you been a good girl?" Kiernan whispered in my ear, his gaze still holding Seamus's. Seamus looked torn between taking what he wanted and being a gentleman.

"Have you been a good boy?" I snarked, then gasped as he slapped my pussy. God, that felt so good.

"We're the ones in charge here, *mo fraochÚn beag*."

It didn't bother me like I thought it would, the degradation, because when it slipped from his lips, there was nothing but love and safety behind it.

"Understand?"

I nodded my head, unable to get the words out as he sank two digits into my tight heat.

He groaned. "So fucking tight and ready for us."

Seamus, who had been standing back, watching his brother finger me while he stroked his cock, grinned.

"Let's see if we can stretch her out a bit."

"The mouths on you two." I moaned in ecstasy when Seamus's mouth latched on to one of my rigid nipples.

"Speak fer yerself, lass," Seamus smirked. "You've got the mouth of a drunken sailor."

"And your mouth, lad," I teased, "should be busy giving me orgasms."

"Aye, aye captain." He winked at me before kneeling. Then his mouth was on my clit, licking and sucking while his brother fingered me.

"Oh, fuck," I moaned. "Please..."

Kiernan removed his fingers from my pussy, and I felt the loss, but Seamus was immediately there to fill it, his tongue lapping at my entrance before he speared me with it.

"Holy—" I shrieked as Kiernan unexpectedly inserted a finger into my ass.

"What do you think, Bailey?" His heated breath brushed against my cooling skin, causing my entire body to shiver with delight. "Think you can take both of us again?"

"And again," Seamus piped up.

I didn't get the chance to answer before Kiernan spun me around and hauled me into his arms. "Better hold on."

His name fell from my lips as he thrust himself inside me to the hilt. They didn't give me time to adjust before Seamus was notched at my back entrance. "Remember, Bailey. If this gets too much, just say whiskey."

"Okay."

That was the last coherent word I would get out the rest of the night; I was lost between them. My beautiful Irish gods.

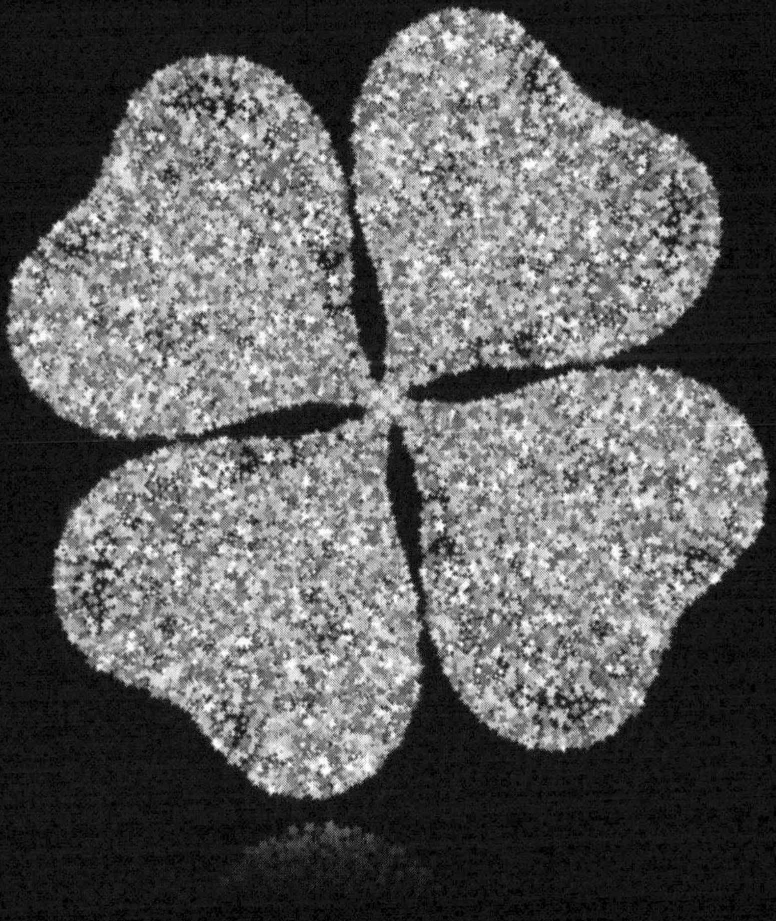

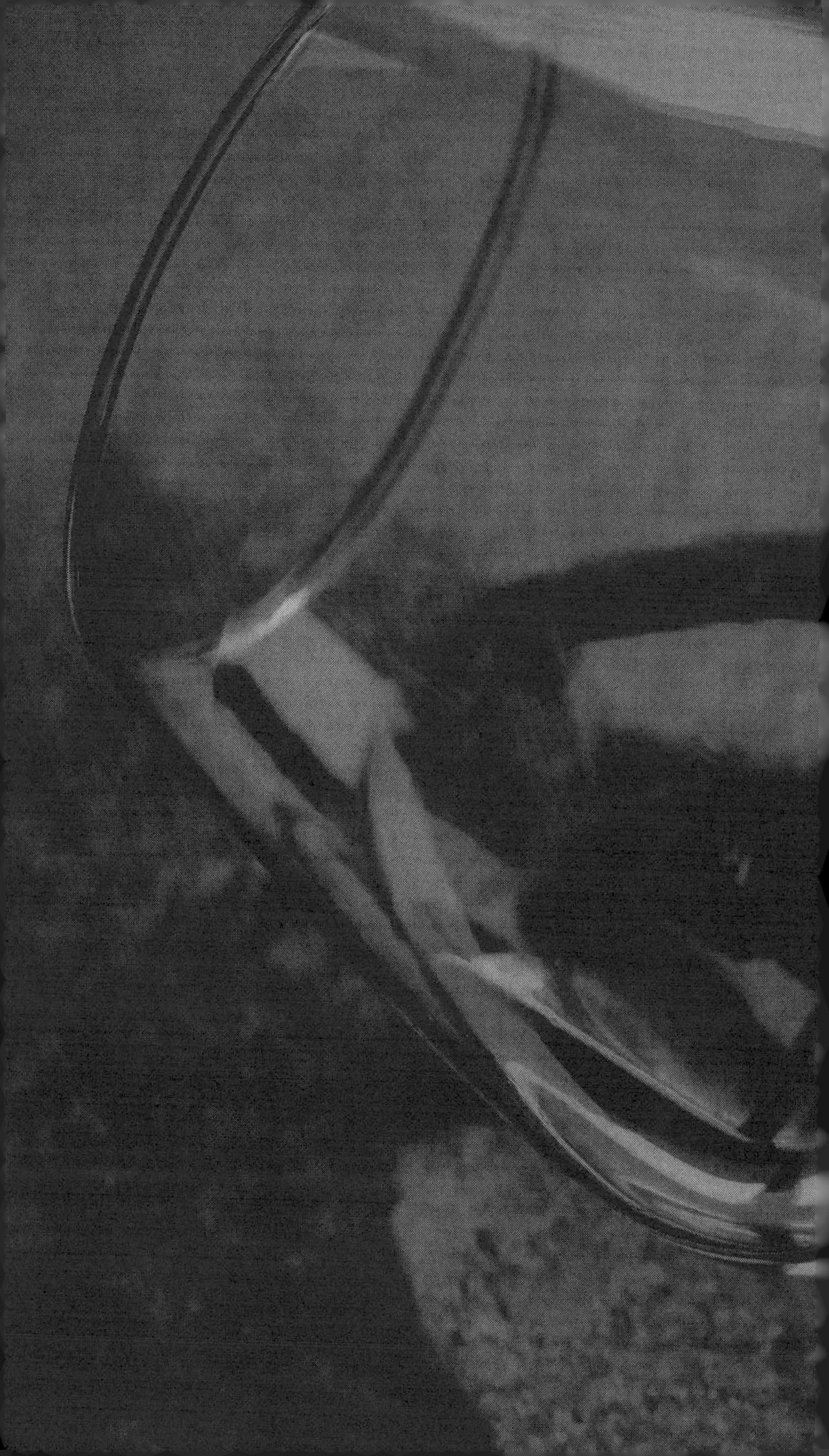

38

Bailey

You can do this.
You can do this.

I'd been standing outside the door to his suite for a little over ten minutes, pacing frantically. I wrung my hands, slid them through my hair, buried my face in them, and kept muttering those words to myself repeatedly until it all began to meld together.

"Okay," I breathed, stepping up to the door, fist raised to knock. "You can—"

It swung open before I had a chance to finish.

I wasn't sure what I imagined my biological father to look like, but this sure as hell wasn't it. He was a mountain of a man, standing just a bit taller than the twins, with beefy tatted muscles that were easily seen beneath the tight, painted-on black T-shirt. His graying black hair was cropped short, but he had a bushy salt and pepper beard. He looked like a mountain man. His eyes were the same crystal blue, with deepened edges hidden beneath bushy brows.

Jesus, I was related to the brawny paper towel man.

"Hello, Bailey." His voice held a deep, thunderous timbre that sank into my bones.

"Hu—hi," I stuttered out.

Kill me now.

The big man grinned, the simple action lighting up his face.

"My name is Toph Eriksen."

I swallowed against the lump in my throat. "I'm Bailey."

"I know."

Insert facepalm here.

"Right..."

He chuckled warmly. "I see you got your mother's awkwardness. She could stampede right through a sea of half-drunk bikers without a second thought, but introduce her to someone new, and she was all thumbs."

"Can you tell me about her?" I asked. "And...you?"

A sadness crept into his features. Longing and regret. He opened the door wider and motioned for me to enter. I stepped inside, my footsteps tentative. I'd been shocked when Seamus had informed me that his father had set Toph up in one of the rooms on the guest floor. I hadn't expected the hatchet to be buried so easily.

The television in the den was going. The footage of Richard Crowe's failed announcement for his bid for presidency had been running on repeat for the last twenty-four hours. I learned that a few things had taken place yesterday; not just my rescue. While they'd been breaching their way into the brothel, Ava and her right-hand man Vas had gone after Drew and Brittany.

Both of whom were now dead.

I could breathe easier on that front.

At the same time all of this was going on, Crowe had been in the middle of giving his speech on doing what was right for the country and how if the people elected him as president...blah, blah, bullshit. Unbeknownst to him, the screen behind him began to play every depraved home video he'd made with the underage girls he'd trafficked into the city.

Shocker.

So much for family values.

He'd been arrested on the spot. A lump grew in my throat as I watched the footage replay. Reporters hammered down the door at the house, and cameras flashed as Sarah was led away in handcuffs for her part. Complicity was a bitch. She'd gotten what she deserved.

"Dalia. Dalia." The reporter on the screen hounded my former "half sister."

"What do you have to say about the actions of your parents? Were you involved? Did you know what they were doing?"

She pressed by them, her gaze hidden by a pair of dark sunglasses. Were they red rimmed from crying, or was she as stone cold as her mother? The twins hadn't been able to find anything that linked Dalia to her parents proclivities. But that didn't mean she never knew.

The screen flashed to show Crowe's face, and I flinched. It was the same look he'd had back in that room. It was full of anger, but there was a knowing twist to the corner of his lips. What did he know that would give him such confidence? Did he believe that the charges wouldn't stick? The entire city—no —the entire nation, had seen what a despicable, corrupted individual he was.

"He won't be a problem anymore, Bailey," Toph whispered next to me. His assurance felt confident, and it warmed me.

"He's got nearly every judge and politician in his pocket,"

I murmured, unable to tear my eyes away from the screen. Toph grunted.

"He won't live long enough to even get bail. Trust me." He flipped off the television just as my name and photo filled the screen. The Crowes weren't the only ones to have their lives blasted on television. My entire life story had been laid out for the world to see.

They heralded me as a victim.

But I was much more than that.

I was a survivor.

Toph waved for me to take a seat. I sank into the warm leather chair across from him, gratefully accepting the tumbler of whiskey he offered me.

"You were three when I last saw you," he told me, taking his own seat. He leaned forward, elbows on his knees, fixing me with his full attention. No one except the twins had ever done that before, and it stirred something in me. "I've seen..." he hesitated, "photos, but they were..."

"After I was beaten," I finished for him. His hand clenched tightly around his own glass. He gave a terse nod.

"They never told me about you," I told him. "I was raised as an outcast. Told lies and manipulated to believe that each of those beating was something I deserved. They had a therapist who repressed my younger memories until all I knew was what I was told. He made it seem as if I deserved and needed to accept whatever I was given. I was raised to believe that the beatings were for my own good. I never questioned them...I just accepted it. I was weak."

"You are not weak. Not then and not now." He growled the words so fiercely it startled me. "You were manipulated and groomed. None of that is your fault. The only weak one here is me. I should have—I should have listened to your mother, but I chose my club over her."

He took a swig of his whiskey. There were tears in his eyes, the crystalline blue shining under the lights of the room.

"Your mother was the center of my world." He smiled fondly. "The first time we met was fate. She'd been chasing down the same scumbag we had. He'd stolen from us, but your mother never cared about that. She cared about what he'd been doing to his teenage daughter. She and her ragtag group of biker women swooped in and took him right from under our noses."

He laughed.

"Then she delivered him to our door a day later with our missing money and a note stapled to his forehead that he was ours now." He shook his head, smiling. "She'd castrated him and used it to..." He coughed. "Let's just leave it at that."

I couldn't help but chuckle at his reticence.

"After that," he smirked, "I was a goner. She was everything. Took me forever to get her to agree to a date. Made a fool of myself trying to take her to some upscale restaurant. I'd dressed up and everything. She'd laughed in my face and made me drive back to the compound to change. Ended up having hot dogs and beer at the pier. It was one of the best days of my life."

I smiled at him warmly as I took a sip of my whiskey.

"What was the second-best day?" I'd asked the question expecting him to say the day that he married her or describe some other memory of my mother.

His gaze held mine and he smiled. "The day you were born."

Shit. My inner child was openly crying while holding on to her stuffed unicorn. Not small cries either. These were big gulping sobs that could probably start a tidal wave.

"I used to play you AC/DC while you were growing in

your mother's stomach," he snorted. "She told me that if you were born with a mullet, she'd never forgive me."

I let out a watery laugh, tears welling in my own eyes.

"You weren't." He sighed dramatically. "But you were still beautiful all the same. I remember the first time I held you; you wouldn't stop crying, and then the nurse placed you in my arms. The world shifted beneath me, and I swore I would do everything to make sure you always felt loved and cherished. I swore I'd protect you and your mother with my life but..." He hung his head.

"What was she like?"

Another fond smile. "You look so much like her," he said. "You've got my eyes and hair, but everything else is her. Lizzie was all fire, but where I was brash, she was calculating. Her world had been tainted in college, but still, she managed to see the good in it. Her smiles could light up a room, and her laugh —her laugh was infectious. She'd give you the shirt off her back and never ask for anything in return. She'd built a community around her. A community of people she loved and respected. One she trusted."

I beamed. "The Vixens." Yelena had given me her number after the rescue and ordered me to call her when I was settled.

"The Vixens were her family. Victims of sexual assault or trafficking. Some were family members of those who fell into those categories. They wanted justice any way they could get it. They ran an underground network of vigilantism. People reached out to them to exact the justice the courts refused to give. It was her life's work."

He rubbed a hand down his tired face.

"Your mother was supposed to meet a potential *client* at the warehouse her club operated out of. She'd taken you with her, set you up in your playpen in your room there. She often brought you along to the club because she hated being separated from you. There was no way of knowing it was a trap. One of the club girls I'd banned for doing drugs had somehow managed to gain access to the warehouse. She sold the information to one of your mother's old friends."

"Sarah Crowe," I breathed.

Toph nodded. "Sarah had been after your mother since college. She'd set her up to be drugged and raped by her boyfriend and his friends. What I hadn't known was Lina had been in on it too."

"There was no way for you to know who she was," I assured him. "Crowe admitted that he'd paid good money to have her nipped and tucked enough so that no one would recognize her as Marilina Brandt."

"Your mother knew," he pointed out with a deep sigh. "She might not have known exactly who she was, but she knew something was off, and I—I didn't listen. Lina was a club favorite, and I chose my men over her. It's still my greatest shame."

"If there is one thing I've learned, it's that you can't linger on the mistakes of the past." My teeth sank into my lower lip. "You can't move forward if you're stuck there, and I'd like very much to move forward with you." I paused, heat spreading across my cheeks as a sudden bout of shyness crept over me. "If you would like that too, I mean."

His answering grin settled any nerves that had crept into my mind.

"I would love that." He leaned back in his chair, shooting me a devilish smile. One full of mischief. "Have you ever ridden a motorcycle before?

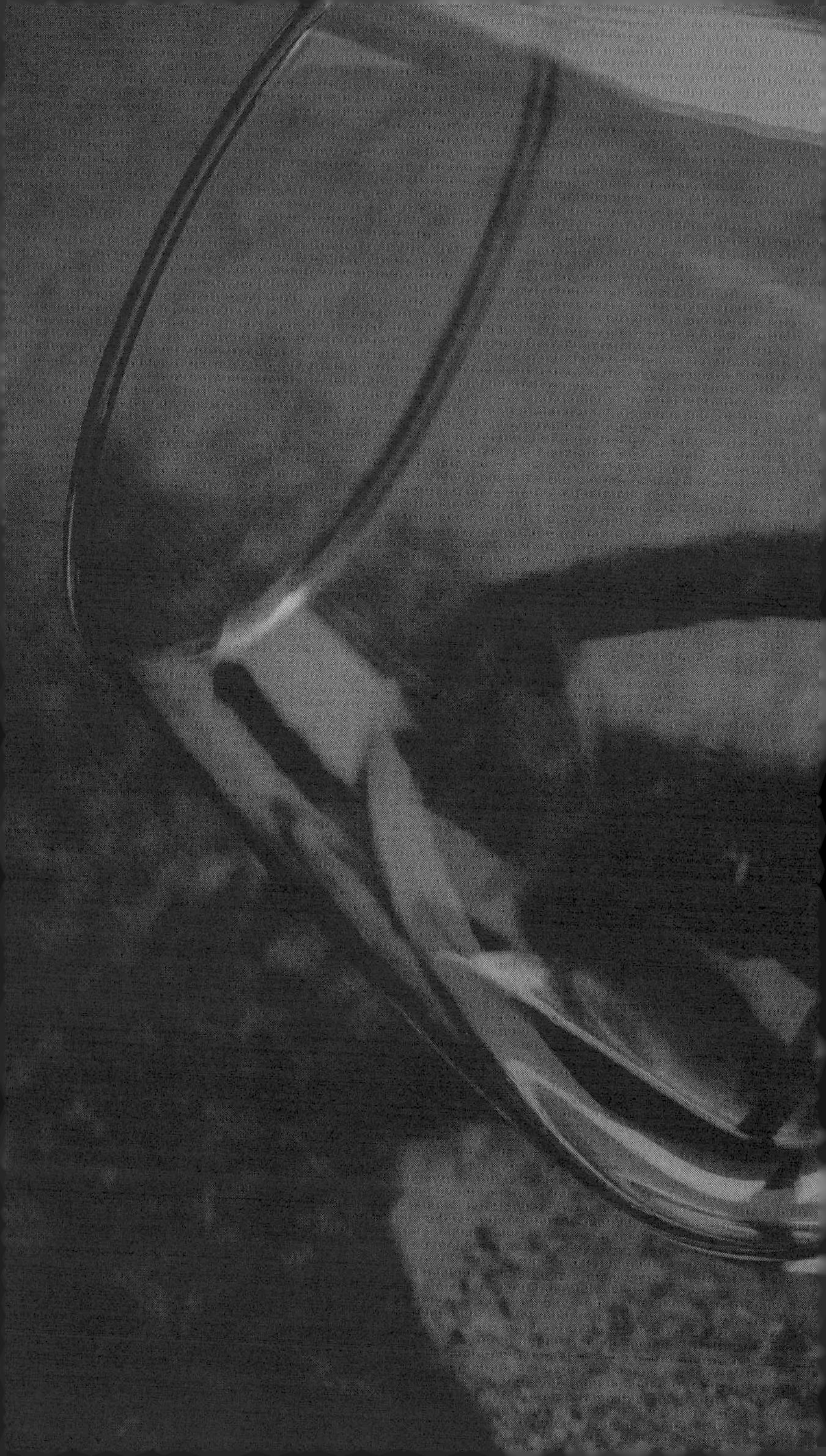

39

Kiernan

I watched her like an obsessed fucking lunatic. Every move she made had my eyes tracking to her and my body on high alert. Jaysus, I needed fucking therapy. I snorted. That wouldn't fix the sudden need I had to be with her, near her—inside her.

We'd begun to mend the broken trust, but it wasn't easy. Shit, the wall she'd built between us was proving harder to take down than the Berlin Wall. Sure, we'd come together the night we'd brought her back, but that didn't mean shit in the long run.

Bailey was waiting for something. Waiting for us. I knew deep down in my gut that the next few days would either bring the three of us closer together or break us apart completely. She wouldn't choose just one of us, and we wouldn't let her.

I'd been the one to betray her. To utter those cruel words. I'd had to. It was the only way to keep her safe, but that didn't matter to her. She might not have believed me when I'd handed her over to her father, but on the day of the auction, I could see that my words had shattered any hope she'd clung to.

Bailey's rich laughter reached my ears, echoing across the near empty bar. It was late, and last call had been ordered a while ago. A few people still lingered, mostly staff and a couple of my father's men, but otherwise, it was a ghost town. I turned my gaze from where I'd been busing tables with Seamus to find our girl huddled at the bar with Ava. The two were smiling, and it was good to see that.

Ava had been a little off since the raid on Drew and Brittany's a few days ago, and I could sense there was something she wasn't saying. I wasn't about to pry, though. Our relationship was still new, and Ava was hurting. So much had gone down that night, and the responsibility that had been placed on her shoulders was enough to cripple most.

But Ava wasn't most people, and she had the backing of some of the most powerful men on the West Coast.

"I'm out of here." Ava sighed as she stood from the barstool. "Let me know what you think about my offer. I could use a woman with your talents." She reached out to Bailey and gave her a small hug.

"Will do." Bailey smiled at her. "Let's meet for lunch next week."

Ava grinned. "Sounds good." She turned toward Seamus and me. The two of us quickly turned away so neither of them would know we'd been spying. "Bye boys," she hollered back to us and gave a small wave.

We turned toward her and smiled, giving slight waves of our own as she slid out the door with Leon, her bodyguard, right behind her. Sighing, I heaved the tub full of dirty dishes behind the bar and slid it back to the kitchen for the washers to take care of. Seamus did the same.

"So," Seamus coughed nervously as he undid the apron

about his neck and chucked his dirty rag. I followed suit. "What was all that about?"

Bailey raised a brow at my brother, her bright eyes narrowing slightly. "What was what about?"

Seamus cleared his throat. "The whole, umm, you know...offer."

Bailey pursed her lips. "Eavesdropping now, are we?"

Seamus shrugged unapologetically.

"She offered me a job," Bailey exhaled. "The Dashkov corporation needs a PR manager, and she'd thought it would be something I'd enjoy since I'm not going back to my old job."

I cocked my head. "You aren't?" That came as a surprise to me. She'd loved being an investigative reporter. Bailey had worked hard to get where she was, and whenever she would talk about her job, her eyes would light up.

"No." She shrugged a shoulder nonchalantly. "Honestly, with everything with Lina, it made me wonder how much of my work was what got me my position and how much of it was Lina pulling the strings to put me there. Investigative reporting was nice but..." She trailed off, her eyes searching ours as she bit her lower lip subconsciously. "Kind of hard to be an unbiased investigative reporter when your *boyfriends* are the heirs to the biggest Irish Mafia boss on the West Coast."

Bailey had whispered the word *boyfriends*, her voice unsure as it rolled over the word.

"Well, we certainly aren't your boyfriends, wildcat," Seamus snorted. Bailey's face fell, and it made me want to punch the fucker, despite knowing what he was going to say next. "I'd say we're well past that."

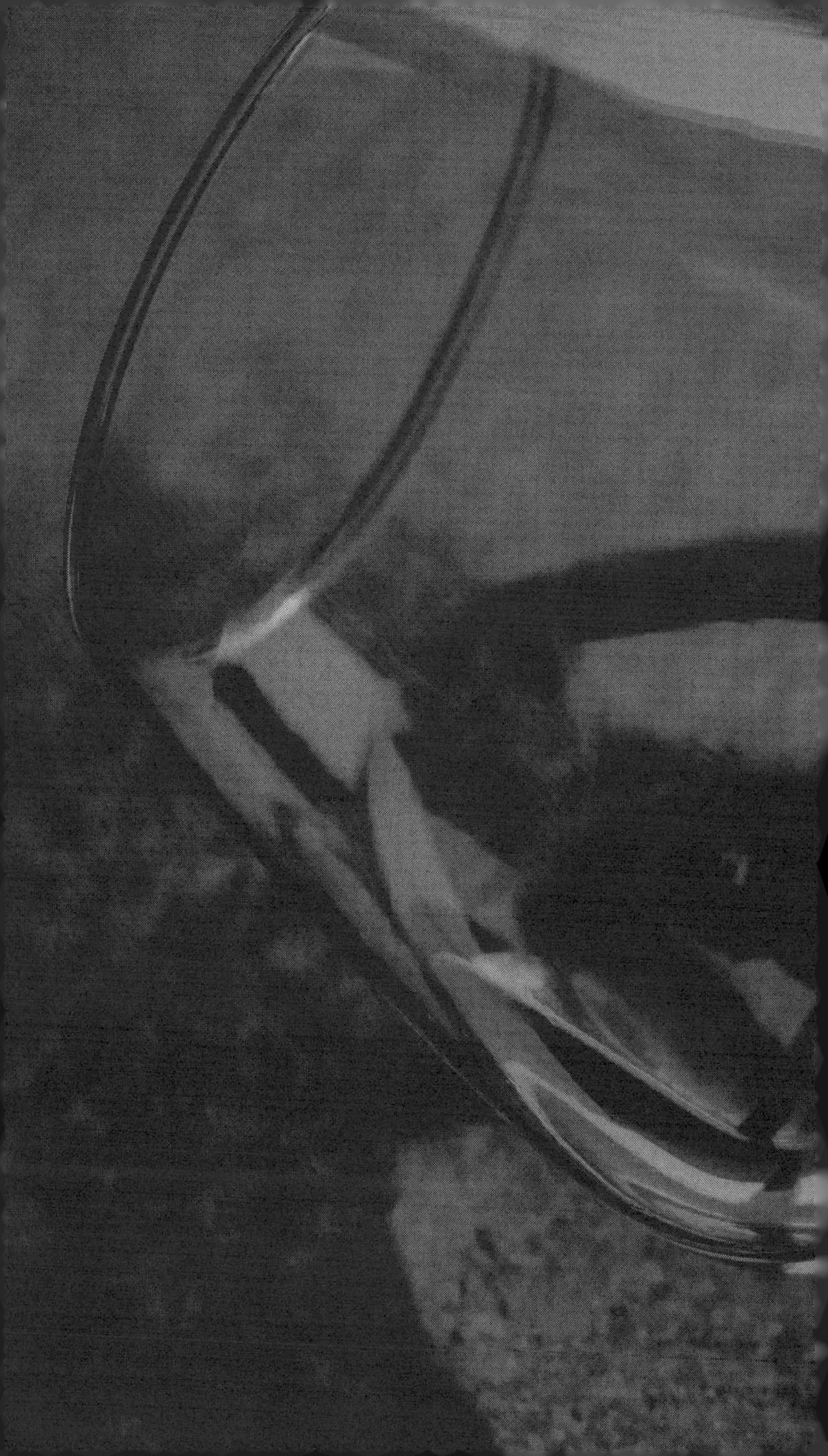

40

Seamus

We sure as fuck were well past being "boyfriends."
I didn't give two flying hillbillies if she thought differently. That was the way it was. I'd spent the last two weeks going out of my mind trying to find her and fix the shit we'd landed ourselves in. I hadn't slept, I'd barely eaten, and I'd nearly lost my mind with worry that we might not get her back.

Boyfriends. I snorted. No fucking way.

"Really?" She eyed us both skeptically, and that was enough for me to lose my shit. "Seamus." She squealed my name when I picked her up and threw her over my shoulder like a goddamn caveman.

"You coming, bro?" I looked back at Kiernan, who was caught somewhere between wanting to laugh and trying to figure out what the fuck I was doing. When he saw the clear determination in my face, he smirked and nodded his head, trailing after me as I took the stairs two at a time up to our apartment.

"What the hell do you think you're doing, Seamus?"

Bailey's hands slapped at my back. "Put me down, you neanderthal."

I chuckled, letting Kiernan open the door before I slid in and marched us back to the bedroom. Setting her down on her feet, I slowly began peeling her layers of clothing off, starting with her shirt. She didn't try to stop me.

"You listen to me, and you listen well, Bailey Eriksen," I growled out her new last name, my gaze never leaving hers as I continued to divest her of her garments. Everything but her underwear. "I went through hell looking for you. Wondering what had happened to you. Every time I closed my eyes, all I could hear were your screams. Every night, I conjured up the worst things they could have done to you. I searched and searched without sleep, without food, because I care for you. Because I love you."

I let that last statement hang in the air for a moment.

"You can't love me," she whispered almost brokenly. "We haven't known each other that long. Four weeks isn't enough to fall in love. Hell, it's more like a week and a half if you count the fact that I was held captive for two of those, and the other days were spent spying for you."

I slapped my hand against her ass, causing her to jolt.

"You don't get to tell me if I'm in love or not," I hissed at her. "There isn't a timeline for this sort of shit, wildcat. Call it love at first sight if you want to, but I know how I fucking feel."

"He's right, *a stóre*." Kiernan spoke up from behind me. "You can't tell us how to feel about you, and we understand if you don't feel the same way. But you need to know this isn't some fleeting emotion. I love you, and I'm not saying that lightly, Bailey. We've never once uttered those words to anyone outside of our family."

I nodded my head in agreement. "When I first saw you, I

knew I never wanted to let you go," I told her. There was no doubt it would take some convincing on our part to show her we meant what we said. Bailey didn't believe words; she believed the actions that came along with them. We could tell her we loved her all we wanted, but if we didn't show her how we felt, we might as well have been blowing hot air, in her opinion.

"You gave me away," she muttered sadly. "You set me up and let him take me."

"That was the biggest mistake of our fucking lives, Bailey," he choked. "Neither of us suspected what he would do. We'd planned to come for you after we ruined him. I never suspected..." He swallowed audibly. "I—" I nudged him.

"We will spend the rest of our lives showing you how much we love you," Kiernan promised her. "We're hard men, Bailey. We plan and plot and kill. We sell drugs and weapons. We're not good men, but that doesn't mean we aren't capable of loving you."

"You can't expect us to change what we do," I continued. "Or who we are. But we're willing to make concessions for you. We'll open up. For you. But out there, in the world, we have to be what we are."

Bailey needed to hear this. She needed to know that we would always be who we were raised to be. Leaders. Killers. We wouldn't change that, but there were things we would change. No more women. No more extreme partying. She would be it for us. We'd open up for her in ways we never could with other women.

Our family was different from most when it came to women. They weren't just figures to be brought out for social events and then put on a shelf to get dusty until they were needed again. The women in our family were integral parts of our business and our community. Bailey knew this. We just needed to be sure she understood it.

"I don't want you to change," she whispered after a beat of silence. "I never want you to change."

And that was all we needed to hear.

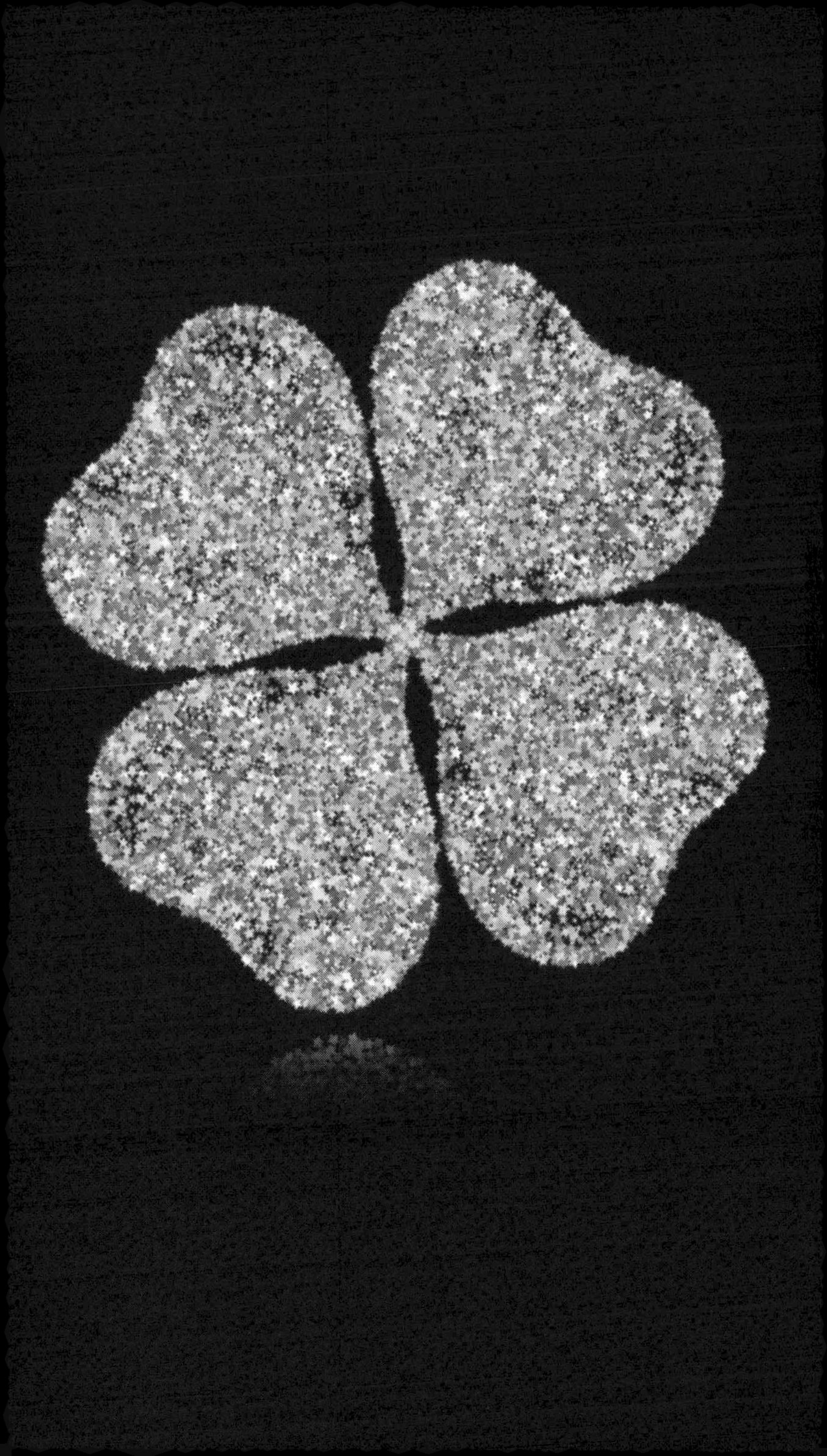

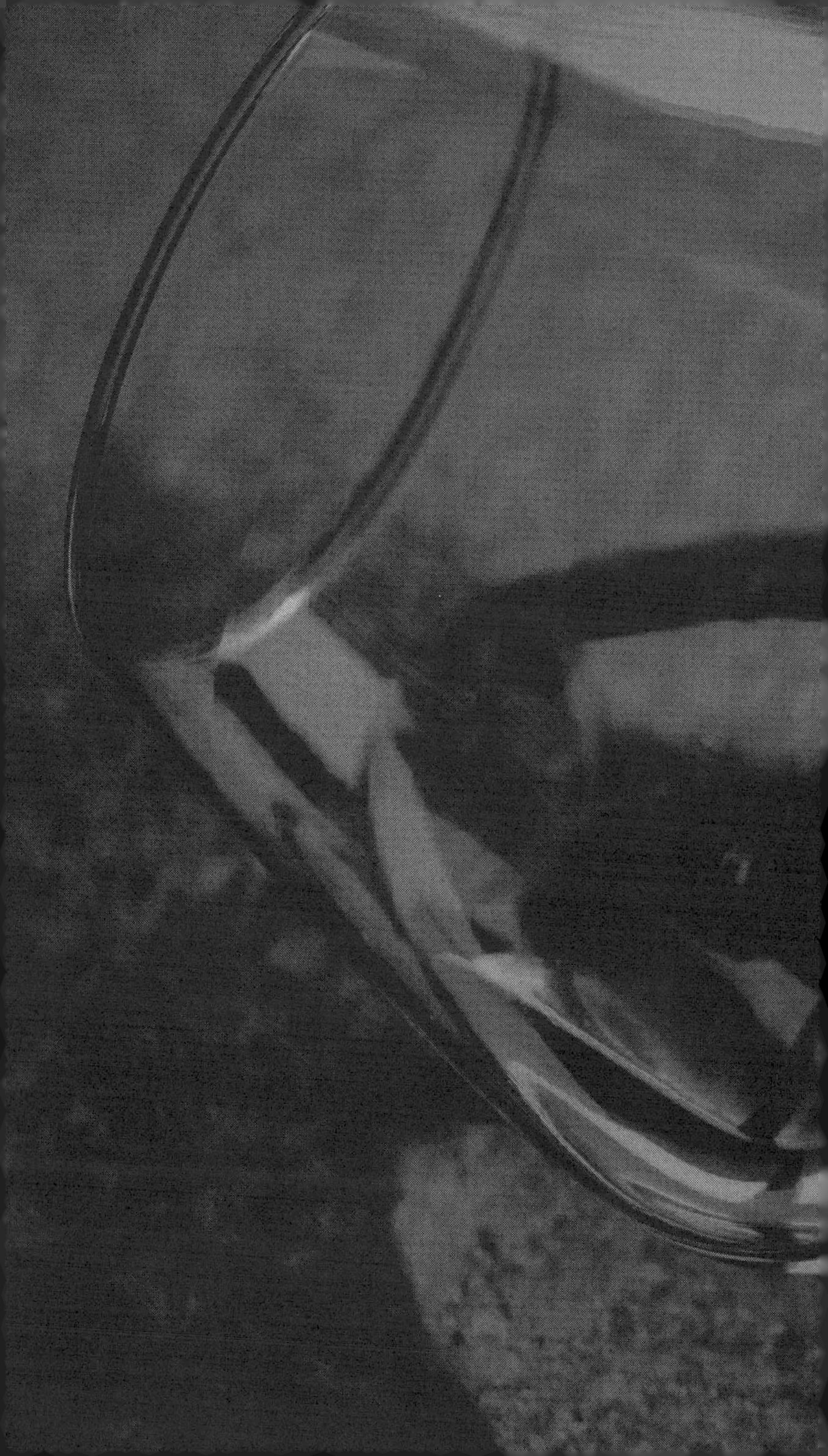

41

Bailey

Love.

They loved me. My eyes widened slightly as I stared at the two of them, searching their faces for any sign of deception. I didn't find any.

"We love you," Seamus reiterated. He was making sure I understood how deep his words were. They weren't superficial. They were bone deep and cutting. "We're not sure when it happened, just that the minute we realized you were gone, we wanted nothing more than to get you back."

"You're everywhere," Kiernan whispered, stepping toward me, his hand threading through my hair. "An itch we can't scratch. An obsession we never intend to get over. Every moment of every day, you're our first thought when we wake and the last when we go to sleep."

Well, shit, a girl could get used to this. Hussy was cartwheeling herself around in my mind, and even my inner cynic had taken up pom-poms and was waving them around like a cheerleader at the Super Bowl.

Since the night I returned, they hadn't touched me. Hadn't pushed or prodded for more. They knew I needed healing and to wrap my head around the convoluted mess that had become my life. The woman I thought to be my best friend had betrayed me. My belief about my mother being some crack addict had been nothing more than a fabricated lie. My whole life had been a lie.

Then there were these two dumb fucks.

I'd trusted them to protect me, and they'd given me away like a party favor. Kiernan had uttered cruel words that had pierced the very heart I'd given him without knowing it. It hadn't been love at first sight, but I'd steadily grown to trust them. With every kiss, every touch, every whisper, they'd endeared themselves to me.

Then fucked it all up.

These men wouldn't grovel or plead for me to forgive them. It wasn't who they were, and I wouldn't want them to. But the primal, lust-filled looks in their eyes told me they had ways to make me forgive them, and I wasn't about to stop them from doing exactly that.

"I love you both too." My teeth bit into my lower lip shyly. I'd never uttered those words to anyone before. "But if you think saying that is going to make me forgive you, then you are way off base. I want something more."

Seamus and Kiernan smirked, mischievous glints lighting up the gold flecks in their emerald eyes. "And what is that you were thinking, wildcat?"

Licking my lips, I dragged my hungry gaze down their bodies, eyeing them like a wolf eyed its prey.

"Orgasms."

There was a mild pause between them, just long enough for my words to sink in, and then Kiernan acted. Throwing restraint out the window, he surged forward, drawing me into his body, and kissed me with more passion than I'd ever dreamed of knowing.

Stolen Obsession

His lips on mine caused my head to spin. Kiernan had always been the reserved one. The brother who calculated risk before reward. But there were bolts of intensity lingering beneath the surface that sent shock waves racing through my body. My desire surged to dizzying heights as he plundered my mouth, pouring every single ounce of his apology into his kiss.

A soft moan escaped me, and his tongue stopped exploring to graze across my lips before he delved deeper, hungry and desperate and searching for more. Kiernan lifted his hands to run his fingers through my hair, and I clung tight to him when my knees shook beneath me. I really was screwed. He'd always held back when he kissed me, but this, this was something more, and I loved every bit of the reeling, quivering blob of hormonal jelly I had become in his arms.

Kiernan's kisses moved from my mouth to my neck, and I moaned at the delicious sensation, my hands weaving in his soft ginger hair to pull him closer. My eyes were open, peering at Seamus, who watched the two of us in silence for a few beats before he began to slowly undress. My gaze tracked his panther-like movements as he discarded piece after piece until he was bare before me, the hard evidence of his arousal on display.

Stalking forward, he tapped his brother's shoulder, his gaze holding mine, sending a sizzle of excitement through me as he took his brother's place. He pulled me close with one hand on my hip, the other cupping my cheek gently. Desire flamed in his gaze as he held me, pausing for an instant before he brought his lips to mine.

The kiss was featherlight and coaxing enough to provoke a shiver before I melted into him, opening up and following exactly where he wanted to lead me. If Kiernan's kiss made my head spin, then Seamus's took my breath away.

In this, as much as everything else, there was a balance to be found between them. The raw passion of one brother that started a wildfire that seared me with its power, and the smooth sensuality of the other, tempering the inferno into a blaze that would burn through the night.

They had broken me apart the night of the auction, and those parts were kept jagged and in pieces every night I was stuck in that brothel, but slowly, they were putting me back together again, stronger than I'd been before.

Seamus drew back sooner than I wanted, and I leaned in to close the distance before I was aware of it. Judging by the satisfied gleam in his eyes, that was what he'd intended.

Bastard.

"Who's going first?" Kiernan licked his lips seductively, his tatted, callused hands skirting down the buttons of his shirt, revealing the tattooed expanse of his chest inch by inch. Seamus smirked as his own hands divested me of my bra and panties.

"Why don't we let her choose?"

"No way." I shook my head. "You two always have this weird ESP shit going on. I'm not choosing. I will never choose."

There was more weight behind those words than just simply choosing which one of them would get to dominate me first. I would never choose between the twins because I loved each of them equally. They needed to know I wouldn't be the tie breaker or the referee. It was important for them to know that if we were going to have a healthy...whatever the fuck this was. Ava warned me the two of them were competitive, and fuck it all if I was going to be some kind of trophy.

Not gonna happen.

The twins shot each other a look, the wheels in their heads turning.

"Flip a coin?" Seamus suggested, his hand running soothingly up and down my arm.

"You've got to be fucking kidding me," I mumbled so they couldn't hear me. This was how they were going to decide? The toss of a coin?

Inner bitch was giving me a smarmy smile like she knew this would happen.

"Rock, paper, scissors?" Kiernan offered. Seamus considered it, then gave a short nod and held out his fist. I cursed under my breath. Fucking children. "Count on three," Kiernan told him, his own fist at the ready. "One. Two. Three."

Two rocks.

"Fuck," Seamus swore. "You know we never solved anything like this." He chuckled.

My eyes were rolling so far in the back of my head I thought I saw brain matter.

"One," Kiernan persisted, his competitive nature coming out to play. "Two. Three."

Two scissors.

"Jaysus, Kier," Seamus groaned. "Just grab a fucking penny or some shit."

"One more go, brother."

I'd had enough of this. Ignoring the pissing match going on before me, I quietly backed myself up against the bed, lying my naked body out on the mattress. I brought my knees up till my feet were flat against the bed, my eyes still watching the brothers go through another match.

My fingers plucked at my nipples until they began to harden like diamonds beneath my ministrations. I let one hand wander down the length of my body, gently caressing my skin along the way.

My eyes fell closed as I gathered my arousal and circled

my clit. Once. Twice. Before I plunged two fingers into my tight, wet heat. Fuck, how had I never done this before I'd met them? Nights with Drew might have ended better if I had.

The bickering had stopped, and I opened my eyes to find their gazes fixated on the hand playing between my legs, mesmerized as I purred and hummed with pleasure. I moaned softly as the pressure gathered in my core, the coil tightening, and they echoed the sound.

"Jaysus—" the two muttered in unison, their voices hoarse, laden with desire.

The moans grew into small cries as I edged closer to my release. Kiernan and Seamus wouldn't be outdone by my hand, however, and the pair eagerly joined me on the bed. I was sandwiched between them, my hand suddenly torn from my eager pussy, and I heaved a dramatic sigh. "You couldn't give me another thirty seconds?"

"Shoulda, coulda, and all that shit." Seamus reached for me and pulled me to my knees, drawing my body flush against his before he kissed me. Kiernan's heat was at my back, his hand running across my thigh and tracing along my back before he snaked an arm around my waist and nuzzled into my neck, breathing deeply.

He grasped the hand that I'd had between my thighs and lifted it to his lips, licking softly at the wet arousal that still lingered there before drawing them into his mouth and sucking them clean.

"I think I just came," I whispered, my eyes on his mouth where he suckled at my fingers.

"Not yet, you haven't," Seamus whispered in my ear. I drew in a shuddering breath as his lips descended the side of my neck. He reached between our bodies to slip his fingers inside me. My hips bucked forward into his hand as he stroked my clit, murmuring against my skin. "Fuck, Kier, she's soaked..."

"Aye," Kiernan agreed and lowered my hand from his mouth before proceeding to cup my breasts. "And she tastes fucking amazing too. Like sunshine."

"Holy shit," I gasped, their words driving my need even higher. No matter how many times they had tasted me or fucked me, they always made me feel special. Like it was the first time all over again and not like I was some cheap, used whore.

Kiernan rolled my nipple between his fingers as Seamus continued to circle my clit. I bit my lip to contain a shrill yelp, and he chuckled. "You know the rules, wildcat," he reminded me. I yelped for real when Kiernan's hand came down hard on my ass. "Don't keep those to yourself. We want to hear everything we do to you."

"Then earn it." The breathiness of my voice dialed back the snark I'd meant to put in that sentence.

Kiernan grinned against my neck, squeezing my breast harder, and I moaned louder than ever. "Earn it, you say? I think we can do that, *mo fraochÚn beag*. Seamus."

Seamus smirked, taking his cue, and with another deft flick of his fingertips, I came undone. Throwing my head back, I pulled him closer, calling out his name in an exhilarated shout. Seamus swore under his breath as my body rocked harder against his.

"Fuck, wildcat," he hissed like he was in pain. "I want nothing more than to be inside you right now."

Everything felt hazy after my orgasm, but I was alert the instant Kiernan's heat disappeared from behind me, my skin still warm and tingling where his had been. I blinked lazily, bringing everything into focus, and my gaze met Seamus's. His eyes were alive and wild as he sat on his knees before me, and I smirked as I lowered myself back on the bed, pulling him along with me, closing the distance between our bodies.

I twisted my head to look at Kiernan. He was watching us with the same rapt fascination he always did when we were together. If I was ever worried that he'd be jealous of me fucking his brother, I'd just remember the look of hunger that hung on his lips.

"Taste her, Seamus," he urged, and I let out a shiver at the low, intense growl.

Seamus sucked the fingers he had stroked me with, and I felt another rush of heat barrel through my body at his groan of pleasure. I ran my hands up and down his back, feeling the smooth contours of muscles that rippled with strength before pausing with a hand on his ass.

"Fuck me, Seamus," I whispered, yanking his hips to mine.

Seamus didn't waste any time pulling my legs apart and taking himself in hand. My fingers glided over his as I guided him to my entrance. Then he thrust himself inside me. Something between a moan and a sigh escaped my lips as I reveled in the sudden fullness of having him inside me. I rocked my pelvis against his, the friction our bodies created driving me higher and higher.

It wasn't the fast fuck I was used to. His rhythm was slow and deliberate, nearly pulling himself out before burying himself to the hilt again.

My hands gripped at his back again, my nails digging into the rippling muscles beneath them as he set a pace that was both delicious and agonizing. With every stroke, my body tingled and my blood sang, my breath catching in my lungs as ecstasy began to climb again, higher and higher with every movement. I could feel the heat of his skin, smell the whiskey on his breath. Reaching up, I grasped a handful of his tousled hair as I leaned into his rhythm, eager for all he had to give me.

Seamus kept his emerald eyes on me, studying every nuance and expression, reading my responses carefully. I could tell he wanted to push forward with reckless abandon like he normally would, but this wasn't about just fucking. This was about forgiveness, and he was showing me how much I meant to him with every controlled movement. He kept his strokes long and slow, letting satisfaction build to its climax. I bucked against him, thrusting upward in my impatience to finish, but he wasn't going to give me that satisfaction.

This might have been about the two of them groveling, but there was one thing that would never change, especially in the bedroom.

Their need for control.

"Calm down, wildcat." His gaze held mine as he slowed his thrusts even more. He glided his hand up my body, exploring every inch of skin along the way. "We have all fucking night."

I squeezed my eyes shut as he kept me on the edge, dangling at his whim. "Should have known you wouldn't be able to let go of control."

A smile tugged at his lips as he leaned down to trail a path of kisses from my shoulder along my neck. "It'll be well worth the trouble, *a stóre*," he promised, and I let out a groan of frustration.

Seamus clutched at my thigh, guiding my leg around his waist while grabbing my ass and shifting my body beneath his to change the angle. My arms wound tighter around his shoulders as I cried out at the jolt inside me, deeper than ever and enough to drive me crazy, but not enough to grant me release.

Somewhere in the dense recesses of my mind, outside the

melding flesh that was Seamus and me, I heard Kiernan groan and curse. I turned to look at him. He was shaking, his entire body thrumming desperately, his eyes darkened with lust, boring into mine even as Seamus continued to fuck me into insanity.

The thought pushed me even further, and I leaned up to Seamus, kissing the base of his neck to the stubble along his jaw, unable to keep from rocking my hips against his in my race toward euphoria. My fingers curled reflexively, my nails digging even deeper into his skin.

Seamus's current pattern of fucking was borderline sadistic, driving me crazy with sheer desire, and yet I was ready to beg for more. Kiernan's fervent stare watched me as if I was the most beautiful creature alive and he would go crazy if he looked away. My mind was beginning to fracture, and my heart skipped erratically; it felt like that millisecond at the top of the roller coaster right before the rush of the drop.

"God, Seamus," I moaned urgently. "Seamus, please. I'm so fucking close."

"Aye," he agreed breathlessly. I doubted he could take much more himself. He leaned forward onto his arms, hands splayed on the mattress at either side of my head, and changed his thrust from long and slow to hard and fast. My body tightened around him almost instantly. The muscles of my pussy clamping down on his cock caused him to give in at last, losing control as both of our pleasures came in a rush of electricity.

Blood pounded in my ears as I moaned and cried his name over and over in a fevered litany. Everything stilled. Seamus touched my face with one quivering hand as he gazed down at me, eyes shining with unrestrained passion.

My body relaxed as he slowly pulled out of me, lowering himself to the bed beside me. Kiernan flashed me a devious grin as he shifted forward. A pleasant, effervescent feeling bubbled in my veins, tingling through my body like the calm after a storm. A blank peace had fallen over me, a hazy dream shutting out the ugly reality that had been surrounding me. I couldn't tell whether I was floating on air or sinking into oblivion. I reached out a languid hand and brushed my fingertips along Seamus's arm, trailing down to his hand and across his knuckles.

I'd fallen for them in that first week leading up to the gala. Probably dick drunk, but fuck, I'd be dick drunk for the rest of my life if it meant days and nights like this.

The dream haze was cast aside with a stirring movement to my other side, and I recalled Kiernan, eyes dark and hungry as he watched and waited for me. The wildfire sparked to life again the moment he touched me, pulling me close.

"C'mere, *mo fraochÚn beag*," he murmured heatedly. "I know you've got something left for me—"

I let out a breathy sigh of affirmation. "Kier..." He bowed his head to mine for another deep kiss, then he took hold of my hips and guided me onto my side, fitting his body around mine.

He rocked forward when I wiggled my hips against him, his rock-hard cock grinding against my ass, my skin warm and soft where it met his. He drew my hair back over my shoulder. His lips brushed at my throat, his tongue lapping at the sensitive skin behind my ear. I shivered and whimpered as he slipped his hand between my thighs and moved my legs to make room for himself, and holy god, even the slightest graze of his fingers lit me on fire. I was wound up tighter than a spinning top.

One hand clasped firmly at my hip as he aligned our bodies and thrust deep.

A gasp tore through me at the impact, pulsing out from head to toe, and for a moment I could swear I saw stars.

Leaning forward, he stilled inside me long enough to whisper, "Remind me of your safe word."

"Whiskey," I breathed.

"Remember to use that," he reminded me. "If you want me to stop."

"Don't stop."

Kiernan chuckled, his breath hot on my skin, sending a wave of goose bumps down my body. Then he began to move. Sending me spiraling into delirium. He was nothing like Seamus, whose slow and steady manner had all but unhinged me long before he gave me any relief. Kiernan held nothing back from the start. He was a wildfire compared to Seamus's slow burn. His thrusts were hard and swift, pushing me forward even as I arched back into him. My body had scarcely recovered from Seamus's lovemaking, and Kiernan's assault on my senses was all the more intense for it.

The combination of our positioning and his pierced cock had him reaching depths and flicking on nerves I'd never known existed before now. These two Irish mobsters had torn me out of the vanilla sex I'd always known and thrust me into their kinky, hot fucking, and I loved it. Each time with them was something new and exciting. Kiernan's aggressive rhythm set every nerve on fire, jarring me all the way down to my bones.

I reached out with desperate hands for something to hold on to. My fingers latched around Seamus's wrist, the nails biting into his skin as my free hand twisted the bed sheets in my fist.

The restraint Kiernan seemed to always have while his brother fucked me had snapped, leaving something far more animalistic behind. His kink had always been watching, I'd seen as much when he watched me get myself off, and I briefly wondered if it was because it added fuel to the fire he already had burning him alive.

He bowed close to me again, kissing the nape of my neck, his fingers tightening at my hip. He reached to lock his hand in the one that I had still clutching at the bed sheets as he pounded into me.

I let my eyes fall shut, my bottom lip caught between my teeth, biting down hard before my mouth fell open. I gasped and panted, my breathing becoming short and ragged. Seamus leaned forward, his lips pressing to mine, the taste of him familiar and safe.

He was hard again; I could feel the length of him pressing my leg. He didn't break my grip on his wrist, simply moved his hand to his cock while I held on. There was nothing slow or deliberate about it now, pumping from base to tip and tightening his fist urgently, the motion traveling up my arm. I opened my eyes to find his locked on mine. His hand moved faster as he hurried to finish with us—me and his twin.

I was about to lose my fucking mind. Seamus was beating off while Kiernan fucked me senseless from behind. This was them groveling. Asking for forgiveness. Words were one thing, but the way they caressed me. Looked at me. Their actions meant more than any pretty prose they could spit my way.

We were breaking down a barrier together. A wall of distrust that had been built between the three of us. One I knew would take time to fully pull down. I loved them; there was no doubt about that. I thought maybe I knew it that first week they pretty much held me captive. Again, I was pretty sure I was dick drunk.

Even with my freedom, though, that feeling never ceased. It was still there, buried among the hurt and pain the gala auction had caused.

Now we were healing in the one way we all knew how to.

Kiernan's lips brushed against my ear, his voice harsh and gravelly, his accent just a bit thicker as he whispered, "Scream, Bailey."

"Scream our names, wildcat," his twin agreed, the words forceful and demanding.

As if my body had been waiting for their command, it surrendered. I buried my face in the mattress to muffle the sounds. Kiernan growled in discontent and seized a handful of my hair, forcing my head back as ecstasy exploded again in a chain fire, breaking anew with every breath and motion. It was more than I could contain. And I couldn't help but obey, releasing the screams they wanted from me, the sound echoing wildly throughout the room.

Kiernan clutched me tighter, pinning me down as he drove harder to ride out his own climax. I moved with him, his thrusts rough and relentless as he came with a groan and a curse. He released his grip on my hip and rolled onto his back.

I lay on my side, the two men on either side of me, our chests rising and falling rapidly as we struggled to catch our breath. My stomach was wet with Seamus's cum. He'd come at the same time Kiernan had, with my hand on his wrist the entire time.

"Keep that up, boys, and you'll be forgiven in no time," I teased. The twins chuckled, slightly breathless.

"We are sorry, wildcat." Seamus sighed, his voice raw and desperate. "We never meant for any of that to happen."

"And you have to know," Kiernan pulled me into him, fitting his body around mine, "you have to know that nothing I said was true."

My throat bobbed, tears clinging to the corners of my eyes. "I know that now," I assured him. It was a struggle to keep from crying. "But nothing happened like you said it would. I thought you'd both lied to me. Used me. Can't blame a girl." I shrugged a shoulder.

"They already knew, wildcat," Seamus explained as he ran a hand up and down my arm soothingly. "We didn't have all the information like we thought we did. We might not have known each other long before that night, but we cared about you. Our plan had been to ransom you back to your father, but we would never have put you in a situation like that, even if we hadn't fallen for you."

"We love you." Kiernan kissed my neck.

"Pretty sure he's loved you since the moment you broke his nose," Seamus joked. "I know I fell in love with you for that."

Laughter spilled from my lips.

"I love you both too."

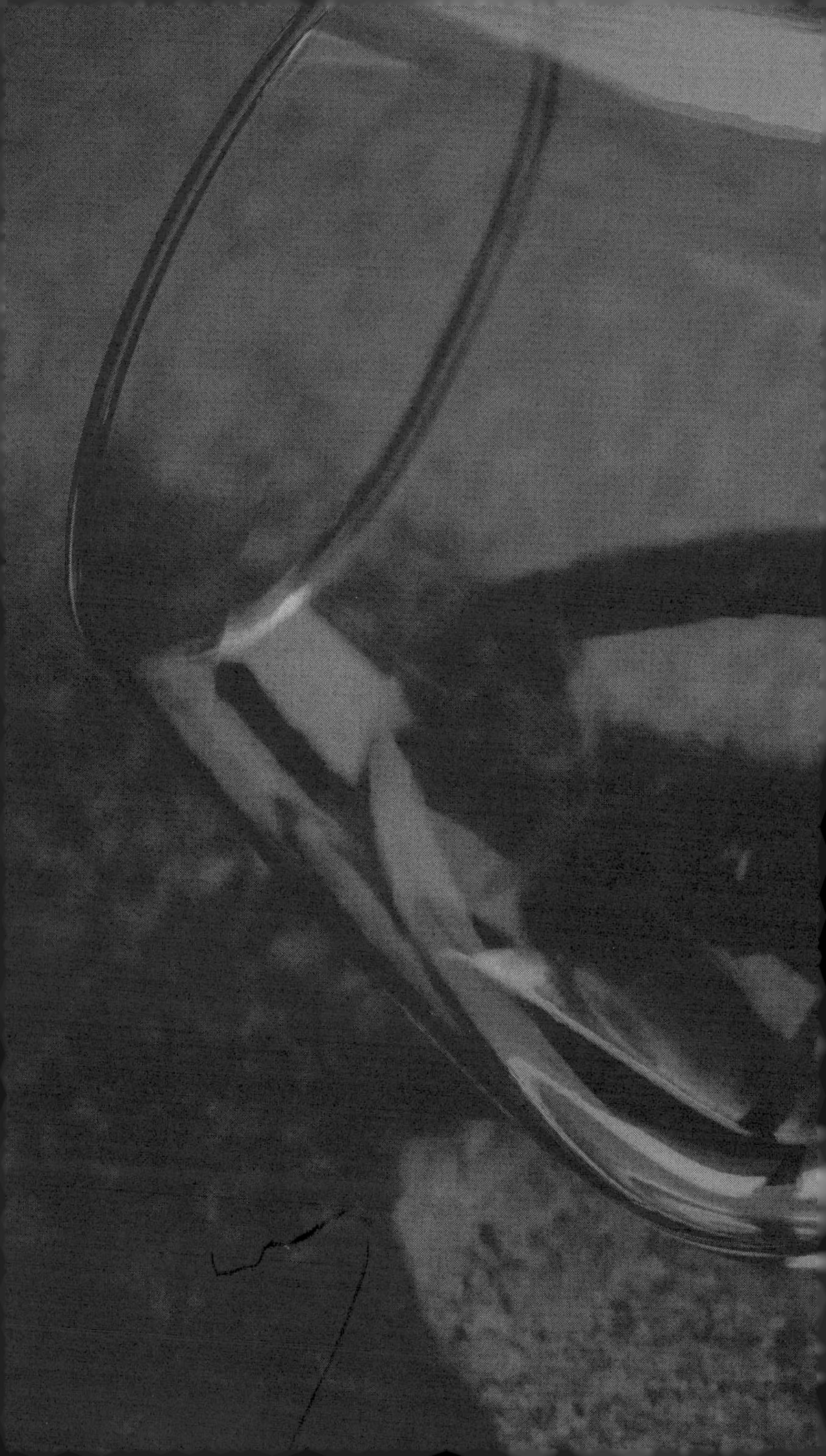

42

Bailey

It was fitting that she would face justice in the same place my mother met her end. Toph—no, my father—had been keeping her strung up by her wrists with very little food or water since they'd caught her a few nights ago.

The very men she'd come to rely on, the ones who'd betrayed my father, had turned on her the moment they were offered a deal. Bought loyalty wasn't loyalty at all. It was an illusion that was easily shattered by the next highest bidder.

Kiernan had cleared the room. Leaving just him, me, and the woman who ruined my life.

"You think this is over, little girl?" Lina spat at me, blood dribbling down her chin. My hand had begun to ache from how many times I'd sunk my fist into her face. "This goes so far beyond what you can even comprehend."

"Why don't you tell me, then? And I promise to make your death less painful."

She screamed, the sound lighting up the deepest part of my soul. Kiernan groaned in satisfaction from where he stood in the corner of the room, watching, his eyes lit with a dark flame of desire as I drug the blade of the knife across her skin.

"Or you can just stay quiet." Kiernan shrugged.

My knees shook at the dark, naked lust of his voice. His eyes were molten pools. He was speaking to her but looking at me.

"I've found that the Iron Princess here has a thing for knives. Who knew my treasure had such a dark side." He kept going, eyes still on me. "She loves the feel of it sliding across the skin. How it just gives beneath her with ease."

"Fuck you," she hissed at him. "I'm not telling you a damn fucking thing."

"This is going to be fun." I cackled as I circled her like a shark circling its prey. The tip of my knife followed me, running around the delicate skin of her neck. I made sure it was light enough not to make her bleed, but she'd feel the pressure and know that all it would take was one wrong move, and she'd bleed out like an animal. "Taking revenge for all the women you sold. For the children you enslaved. They might not be here for your execution, but I'll damn well make sure everyone knows about it."

Once I'd come back around, I moved the knife lower and cut several shallow grooves into her chest. She grimaced but didn't cry out. I thought about everything she'd done to me. What she'd planned to do to me. Besides Brittany, I'd only ever had one friend—her—and it had all been a lie. My entire life had been a lie. Drew. Brittany. Lina. It had all been one big lie.

The grip on my tenuous control slipped as I carved into her skin. Anywhere and everywhere the blade would reach, I cut and then watched as her blood spilled onto the concrete floor beneath her.

Lina hung limply, fat tears streaming down her blood-stained cheeks. The darkness inside me stirred at seeing her so vulnerable, so broken. Exactly what she'd tried to do to me.

Stolen Obsession

I leaned into her ear and whispered, "You will never take advantage of another person, ever again."

"You're just as self-righteous as your mother was," she hissed at me, the venom in her tone dampened by her hiccups. "All she had to do was keep her fucking mouth shut about the rape and everything would have been fine. But she had to go and be a fucking—"

She didn't get to finish that sentence, and I got a sick kind of satisfaction at having slid the new blade Kiernan had given me through her skull.

Definitely giving it a five-star rating on Amazon.

"Such a good girl," Kiernan purred in my ear, sending tingles straight to my sopping wet cunt. Spinning around, I launched myself at him, kissing him with every ounce of passion I could muster. He'd been there every step of the way, relishing in my darkness. Just like Seamus, he sought my obedience in the bedroom, but stood at my side as an equal in the streets. "So perfect."

He chuckled as I ripped at his shirt, the buttons flying, revealing his heavily muscled and tattooed chest. The shirt fell to the bloodstained floor as he unzipped his pants, freeing his hard, pierced cock.

Then he pounced, ripping the top of my dress down so that it pooled at my middle.

His arms wrapped around my waist as he lifted me off the floor. My back hit the wall, leaving me breathless as he caged me in, biting and licking at my neck.

"So fucking hot," he breathed in my ear, his fingers sliding beneath my dress. When he didn't meet any resistance, he paused and tilted his head to the side with a smirk. "Is my little whore not wearing any panties?"

I arched my back, moaning when his mouth covered my hard, aching nipple.

"No," I breathed. Kiernan's cock notched at my entrance, pausing for less than a second, our eyes meeting, before he buried himself to the hilt. The blood on my body from torturing Lina transferred onto his skin. I should have been repulsed, but the only thing I felt was aroused.

Kiernan drove into me over and over, thrusting me against the concrete wall of the cell so hard that I knew there would be bruises by morning. My nipples were stiff and ached, begging for his mouth.

"I'm going to get you some nipple clamps," he groaned in my ear. "Make Seamus pull on them while I fuck your ass. Maybe attach a chain to my piercing so that every time I thrust out, it pulls at your nipples."

"Jesus," I moaned, every sensation heightening as adrenaline coursed through my body as his piercings dragged along my inner walls. "Kiernan."

His name was a screamed prayer on my lips as I struggled to breathe through the vast desire coursing through my body as I writhed in his arms, my orgasm crashing over me.

"Fuck, Bailey," he roared. "I can feel your cunt milking my cock, baby."

He roared as he came, his hips jerking erratically before he flooded me with his seed. Kiernan slumped forward, his head resting against the cool concrete behind me as he held me in his arms despite his exhaustion. My entire life, I'd been lost in an unending circle of loneliness. Until they'd come crashing into my life, pulling me from the wretched darkness that surrounded me.

Now there was no looking back.

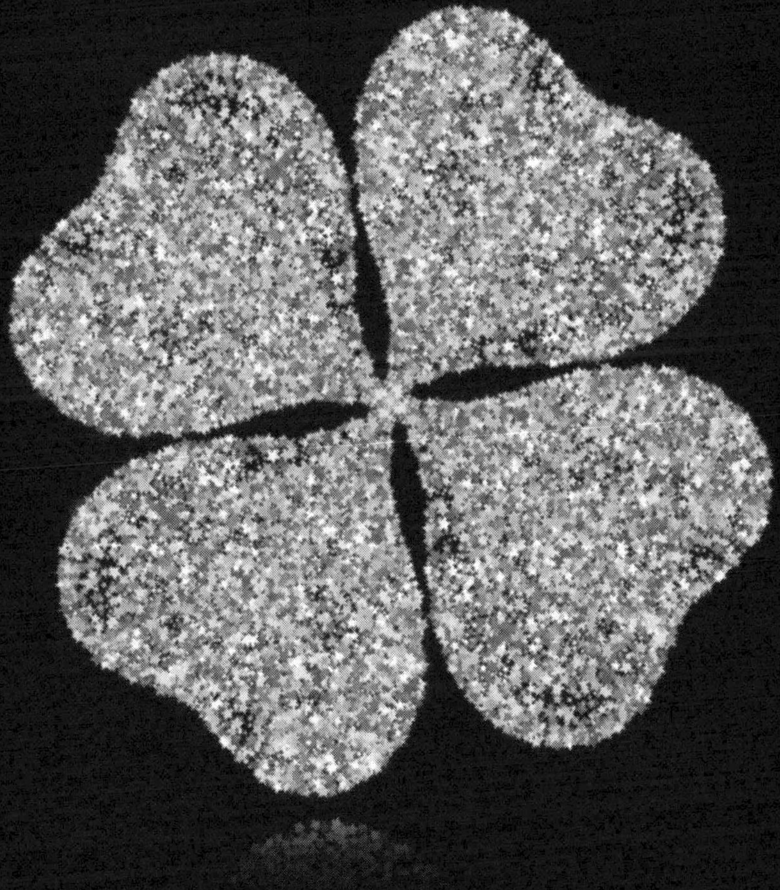

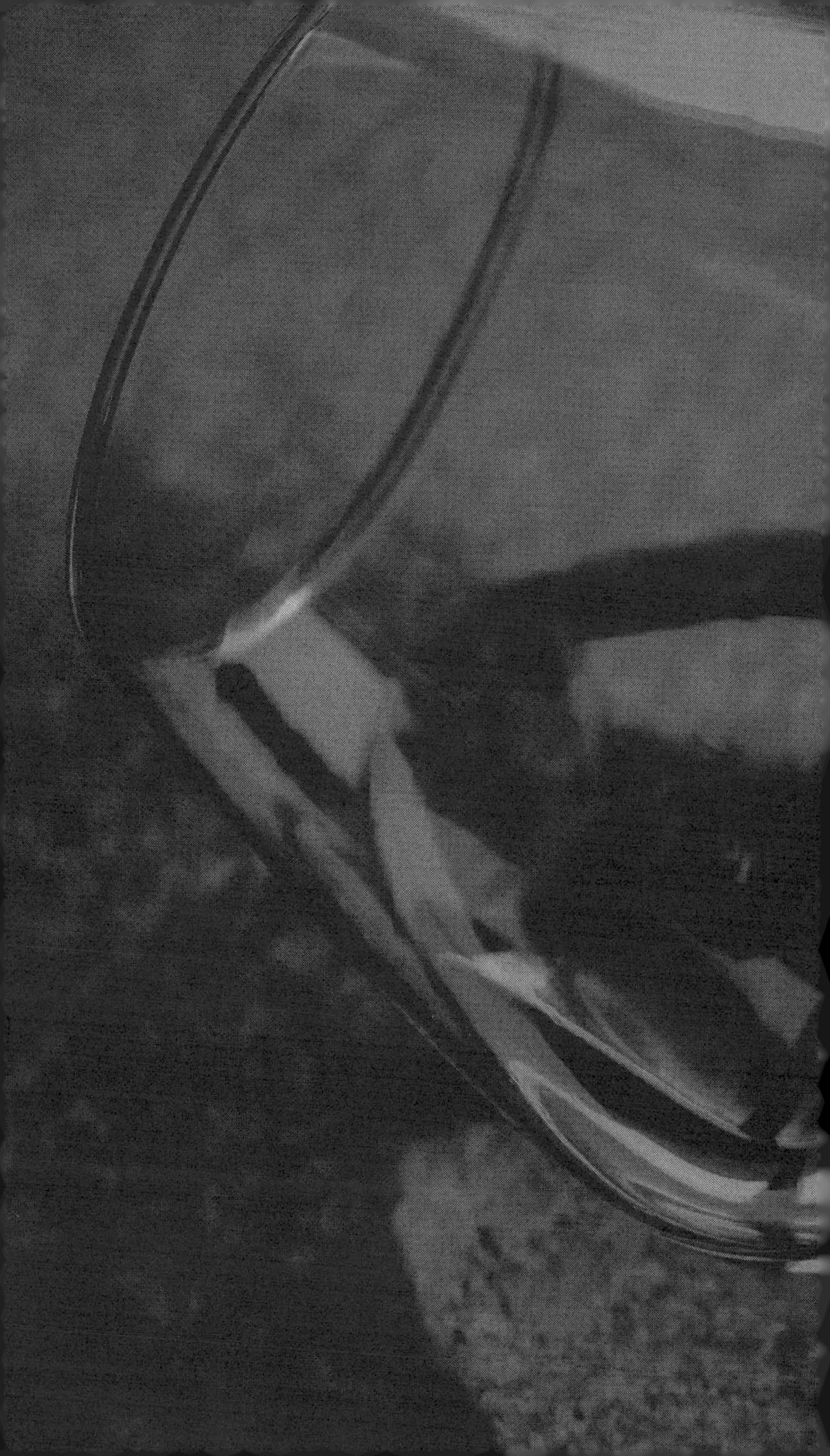

Epilogue

Bailey

Six months later...

After that night, the pieces of my life had begun to fit together. For the first time in years, I was happy. Loved. Cherished. Surrounded by family and friends. Things weren't always going to be easy. There was a war brewing on the horizon and too many unanswered questions.

Nothing in the future was certain.

The trust between the twins and me hadn't been an easy fix, but they were quickly making up for it with the number of orgasms they were giving me each day. Sex wasn't our answer for everything, but when we'd run out of words to say, it was where we went to get back on track.

Drew and Brittany were dead.

Good riddance.

"It happened by accident." Vas shrugged unapologetically. "He was reaching for something under the covers. Thought it was a .45. Turned out to be his little .22, if you know what I mean." He winked at me.

"I really wish I didn't," I deadpanned. That sent him

laughing. The guy was a hoot. I also knew he was lying. Drew had been shot more than once and in a few strategic places. Ava didn't seem bothered by his death, but whenever Brittany's name was brought up in the following weeks, she'd flinch. Was she regretting shooting her?

Richard Crowe had been stabbed in his jail cell. There were no leads on who did it, but I could see the glint of satisfaction in my father's face whenever the news ran the story. I know he'd done that for revenge. He'd been the one who started it all, but when he looked at me, his eyes full of love and pride, I knew he'd also done it for me.

To give me peace.

As Crowe's daughter, I had never once felt protected and safe.

My new therapist said it was his way of making up for all the things that he'd been unable to protect me from before. That I would need to be patient with him because it would be likely that he would start displaying an overprotectiveness and possessiveness I'd never experienced before.

I was surprisingly okay with that.

It felt good to know that someone cared enough about me to display those emotions.

Shaking off the thoughts, I gazed out at the city that had given me more things than I could have ever imagined, even if the seas had been stormy. It was time I gave back in a way that mattered. Being an investigative reporter had been my life, but there was only so much the written word could do.

Now it was time to take up the mantle of the legacy I'd been destined to inherit.

"You ready?" Yelena called to me. She looked so cute in her leather getup, complete with a helmet she'd glued cat ears to.

"More than ready." I smiled over at her as I donned my

own helmet before circling my finger in the air. The roar of the engines behind me set my blood on fire. Beneath me, my own motorcycle roared to life.

A brand-new 2021 Indian Scout Bobber Sixty in matte black.

A gift from my father.

"We ready?" I asked into the comms system. A chorus of *hell yeah* rose behind me. This was my family. Or at least part of it. Women who were hurt, damaged, and in need of repair, just like me. Ones my mother had risked her life to save and who'd returned the favor many years later by saving me. They were all given the chance at freedom again because of one woman's selflessness.

Many of them had been rescued by my mother as children. Raised by affiliates of the club. Some of them, like Samala, were descendants of those who survived. Or Yelena, whose mother had been killed in the initial attack.

The warehouse where the old Vixens club was held had been torn down. A new compound replaced the old. The design was similar, but with one difference. In the center of the new club, stretching up toward the skylight above, a memorial stone had been erected with the names of those who had been massacred that fateful day. At the top, with angel wings sprouting from her back, was a statue of my mother, her arms hugging the stone.

The top read *Hoc Defendam*.

"This I will defend."

The world was a dark and dangerous place. Deception and violence lurked in every corner. But that didn't mean it wasn't worth defending. It just meant that more light was needed in the darkness.

Hope was a powerful motivator for the weak and damaged. Prey could easily become the predator under the right circumstances. Taming animals into submission at the end of a whip only taught them to submit until the time came to strike.

We were a pack of wild animals, waiting for a moment to show the predator just how dangerous prey could be. I'd been beaten once. Bent but never broken. Two men had put me back together without even knowing it. Two men became the love and safety I'd never known.

And I'd make sure that other women who'd been victims would get the same chance as me.

I would give them hope.

I would give them vengeance.

"Vixens"—I revved my engine—"ride out."

Ready for more? Make a deal with the devil in Cruel Vows, following Vanya and Adrian. Unravel the mystery between them today on Kindle Unlimited.

STALK ME

Jomccallauthor.com

Acknowledgments

Thank you to everyone who put up with rewrite.

I wanted to make the twins better than they were before and you all gave me the grace to do that without any judgement.

Thank you to all of my Alpha Readers for your amazing help and rereading this shit time and time again until I had it just right.

To my amazing betas who are always ready to take everything I've got whenever I've got it.

To my amazing ARC team! You all put up with so much! Thank you for sharing your thoughts to the world!

My amazing editor Beth who is so patient and kind and calls me out when I make words up.

AND TO ALL MY READERS. You keep my going!

Also by Jo McCall

SHATTERED WORLD

Shattered Pieces

Shattered Remnants

Shattered Empire

Shattered Revelations

Shattered World: Ava and Matthias Complete Story

SHATTERED WORLD STANDALONES

Shattered Revenge

KAVANAUGH CRIME FAMILY

Stolen Obsession

Twisted Crown

Crooked Fate

SOVEREIGN BROTHERHOOD

Cruel Vows

Click here to read Cruel Vows on Kindle Vella

Wicked Vows

Brutal Vows

SAVAGE KINGS DUET

Savage

Click here to read Savage on Kindle Vella

Click here to read Savage on Patreon

Kings

Jo Savage PNR Books

FAIRY TALES WITH A TWIST

Hunted by Them:

Menage MC Shifter Little Red Riding Hood Retelling

Bad Wolf MC (Hunted By Them Spin-Off)

Bad Wolf MC (2024)

Made in the USA
Columbia, SC
23 April 2024